5/17/11

A Touchstone Book
Published by Simon & Schuster
New York London Toronto Sydney

5|11
$15

HOLLYWOOD
Car
Wash

A NOVEL

Lori Culwell

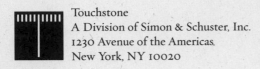

Touchstone
A Division of Simon & Schuster, Inc.
1230 Avenue of the Americas
New York, NY 10020

Copyright © 2007, 2009 by Lori Culwell

First Touchstone trade paperback edition April 2009

TOUCHSTONE and colophon are registered trademarks of Simon & Schuster, Inc.

For information about special discounts for bulk purchases, please contact Simon & Schuster Special Sales at 1-800-456-6798 or business@simonandschuster.com

Designed by Jamie Kerner

Manufactured in the United States of America

10 9 8 7 6 5 4 3 2 1

Library of Congress Cataloging-in-Publication Data
Culwell, Lori.
   Hollywood car wash : a novel / Lori Culwell.
      p. cm.
   1. Women college students—Fiction. 2. Television actors and actresses—Fiction. 3. Fame—Fiction. 4. Hollywood (Los Angeles, Calif.)—Fiction. 5. Motion picture industry—Fiction. I. Title.
   PS3603.U638H66 2009
   813'.6—dc22
                              2008041137

ISBN-13: 978-1-4165-8778-1
ISBN-10:   1-4165-8778-0

For Stephan and The Rose

HOLLYWOOD Car Wash

SEASON
ONE

1

REALLY, IF IT HADN'T been for my perky college roommate and her obsession with spinning class, none of this would have happened in the first place. In fact, I wouldn't have found out about the audition if it hadn't been for Carrie Ann and her annoying habit of getting up so early, which had led her to wake me up at 11:30 A.M. on a Monday in February. I'd been up all night and was really hoping she'd be gone all day so I could catch up on sleep.

No such luck. The door of our room closed with a loud thud and she flipped on the light, perhaps to spite me.

"Amy! Wake up! You're going to be late!" she said perkily.

I groaned. How one could at once be an early riser and a theater person was beyond me. I could tell she'd already been out in the world doing productive things while I was still sleeping off an all-night student film shoot that had gone on well past four A.M., and I resisted the urge to smack her in her already showered and made-up glory. *People should not be allowed to be chipper before noon,* I thought. *At least not people who live in the fine arts dorm.*

She redeemed herself by producing coffee and a huge muffin from a bag. I decided to speak to her again.

"What are you talking about?" I said, glancing over at the clock. "It's Monday, right? I don't have to be anywhere until three thirty. I have voice class, then English."

"I know that," she said. She was breathless with excitement. "There's an audition on the bulletin board for a TV show! You have to go right now . . . I signed you up for one of the first slots."

I laughed. "You signed me up for that bogus TV show thing? When I actually wake up, you are so dead." I attempted to cover up my head with a pillow to block the fluorescent dorm room light. A "modeling and acting school" had been posting the same fake TV show audition for months. I thought everyone in the department knew this.

She rolled her eyes. "It's not that one," she said insistently. "You have to go! You would be so perfect!" Carrie Ann perched herself on the edge of my bed. She and I had been roommates since freshman year—a situation that worked out, in part, because we were so different we had never competed for a role. At five foot one with a head of curly red ringlets, Carrie Ann never met a musical she didn't like. I, on the other hand, was tall, had dark hair and pale skin, and fancied myself a cross between Parker Posey and Hope Davis in terms of being a serious indie film actress. We were the drama department's version of the Odd Couple.

I sat up. "It's probably an audition for some Stuckey's commercial. Now seriously—go away."

Undeterred, she kept bouncing on my bed. "You *say* that, but if you really want to be in indie films, you have to be willing to do anything! I would take *any* part on Broadway, just to get myself there. I would sweep floors! Remember what Mark Twain said about being willing to be lucky. You have to be willing! Plenty of well-known indie actors have been on TV! Michelle Williams was in *Dawson's Creek,*

Parker Posey was on *Boston Legal,* and even your beloved Philip Seymour Hoffman was once on *Law & Order,* if you'll recall." She seemed prepared to go on this way forever.

"OK, stop!" I said. "It was E. B. White who said that thing about being 'willing to be lucky,' not Mark Twain." I huffed myself out of bed and pulled on a sweatshirt from the floor.

"I am not putting on makeup," I said, tying my hair in a knot and putting on my glasses. "If I get the job it's going to be on the basis of my talent, not my skills with mascara."

She rolled her eyes. "It wouldn't kill you to look your best!" she called as I passed her on my way out the door, hoping maybe she'd be gone when I got back. I knew she was right; I was just tired and cranky from shooting all night.

I shivered in the still-cold winter air as I sprinted to the drama department from the dorm, stopping to check the bulletin board. Hanging from the middle of the board was a typewritten sign.

Audition
Autumn Leaves
Women age 18–20
Fresh-faced, Midwest types
Monday (yes, today!)
Auditions start at 12:00 pm SHARP
Bring any photos
Sides provided

The audition notice had already attracted a lot of attention. Serious-looking drama types had begun to crowd around the bulletin board.

"Is it a lead?"

"I don't know . . . it doesn't say."

"It's probably extra work . . . my cousin was an extra in *War of the*

Worlds, and he had to stand in the freezing rain for hours and hours. He said it sucked."

"Are you going to do it?"

"No, man . . . I'm staying true to my craft. Besides, they're not going to cast a real-looking person from Michigan for a Hollywood TV show. Never gonna happen."

I pushed through the crowd and into the main theater, where I'd starred in a production of *Miss Julie* the semester before, hoping to get in and out before anyone I knew spotted me there and mocked me. I arrived just in time to see the big exit of Rebecca Hartford, my drama department archrival. Apparently, she'd had the slot right before me. *Great,* I thought. She was beautiful, blonde, and had questionably large boobs. Rebecca had been beating me out for parts since we were both freshmen. She was the only girl in the department with headshots, courtesy of an overzealous stage mother who got her into pageants when she was a little kid. Crap! Double crap! Why did I think she wouldn't be all over this audition (and willing to do whatever it took to get out to Hollywood)? Just seeing her brought out the competitive side of me. I had only one shred of hope: In the back of my mind, I silently reasoned that there are even better-looking girls than Rebecca out in Hollywood and that if they'd wanted her type, they could have gotten it out there. Still, she was working her audition slot like she usually did when there was a man in the room.

"Thank you *so much!*" she called back, lingering in the doorway. "I'm really looking forward to hearing back!" More lingering, a slight toss of the golden blonde hair, and a throaty giggle followed. *Someday,* I thought, *I will kill her.*

As I walked down to the stage, I saw Jody Barker, one of my acting teachers, who was running the audition, and Eliot Jones, the cochair of the department. "Hi, Amy," Jody said, smiling and handing me a bunch of stapled-together papers. "Glad you're here. We're just going to ask you to do this scene . . . I'll read along with you. Some brief background—this character's parents have been killed, she's just found out, and she's now going to have to go live with her gay uncle, whom she's never met before. This scene is at her parents' funeral."

I drew in a sharp breath at the description of the scene. This was definitely not something I wanted to start thinking about. *I just woke up,* I thought. *I am not ready for this.* The truth was, I hadn't even told that many people at school that my dad had died at Christmas my senior year of high school, something I was still grieving. That was hard enough, but having everyone in my high school give me that sympathy face every time they saw me made it that much worse. I'd made it through freshman year of college without telling that many people, and I was trying to keep it that way.

For a moment, though, I was frozen. Theater was usually where I stopped thinking about my dad. Besides, I wasn't at all sure I wanted to get out these emotions and use them for a TV show audition. Weren't some things supposed to be off-limits?

"Amy, are you OK?" said Jody. "We need you to start. The tape is rolling."

Her voice snapped me back to reality. Maggie Gyllenhaal would never let something like this get to her. She'd use the emotion in her performance. I took a deep breath and looked down at the script.

As I read over the lines, I decided that instead of giving the typical "hysterical crying" audition they were probably expecting, I would go for the most realistic portrayal possible, even though a totally real performance was unlikely to even get me a callback. I fumed inside— if TV people who wrote some melodramatic show wanted to see what it was like to get news like that, I thought, I would show them. Tragedy of that magnitude doesn't make you hysterical, in fact—it just crushes you and ends up making you feel like there's a wall between you and the rest of the world. Time stands still, and all of a sudden, all you can think about are all the things you're never going to do with that person, or that you haven't done, or that you didn't know you should've done. The more I thought about this, the more I felt like crying.

All at once, I was right back to when we got the phone call about my dad. Who knew a ringing phone could sound so ominous, but it's true; I knew something was wrong the minute it started ringing. I replayed the events in my head: my mom making a gargled little cry that caught in her throat, her telling us that we had to go to the hospital right away, and then, after a blur of days in the hospital—the last day of his life.

Right before they took him off the respirator, we were supposed to say good-bye—only I didn't know what to say. It seemed so final, like I would never get a chance to tell him anything again. He would never see me get married, or have kids, or even graduate from high school. His life was about to come to an end, and I was supposed to think of something to say.

I told a joke.

It was one of my dad's favorites—"This grasshopper walks into a bar, and the bartender says, 'Hey! We have a drink named after you!' The grasshopper says, 'Really? You have a drink named Steve?'"

Dad was in a coma, so he probably didn't hear, or if he did, he didn't laugh. After I finished, I told him I loved him, and I laid my head on his chest, to hear his heart beating for the last time. Then we left, and shortly after that they came out and told us he was gone.

I thought of the grasshopper joke, read my lines, and before I knew it, it was over and I was on the way to lunch. While I was eating, I actually laughed about how stupid it was to make a show with that premise and how wrong they were going to get the portrayal of the character. *I would never watch that show,* I thought. *Not in a million years.*

A FEW DAYS LATER, I was sitting in abnormal psych class, willing myself to stay awake through a lecture on "pica, a mental disorder that causes sufferers to eat dirt and cigarette butts," when I heard my cell phone ring in my backpack. I lunged for it, scolding myself for leaving it on. Because it was faster to just answer the phone than try to turn it off, I tried to answer with my head inside my backpack.

"Hello?" I whispered frantically. "Hold on one second." My abnormal psych professor had promised an instant F to anyone who talked on a cell phone during his lectures; rumor had it that even the buzzing of a phone on vibrate would set him off. I ran up the stairs and out of the lecture hall.

"This is Shannon from the drama department," said the voice in the phone as I made it outside and closed the door. "Can you come into the office right now to meet with Dr. Simon?"

"Of course," I said, intrigued. This was definitely preferable to the horrors of abnormal psych. Dr. Ellie Simon, dean of the drama department, was one of the coolest professors on campus. If the University of Michigan had a "rock star" equivalent, she'd be it. A renegade actress/punk/writer/performance artist from New York, she was supposed to be a personal friend of David Mamet. She was one of the most popular professors in the drama department and, in my estimation, a one-woman antidote to my mother's theory that "no one can make a living in the arts." Her production of *Miss Julie* the semester before had made history in the drama department by selling out every night and getting a rave review from the local paper, which praised my "haunting ability to capture grief onstage." This performance had led to my being cast in the cool student film I'd just finished. I felt like I was on my way, and I owed it all to her.

Twenty minutes later, I walked into the drama department office. "Hi, Dr. Simon," I said, poking my head in the door. "You called?"

She looked up, taking off her funky black glasses to reveal kohl-rimmed eyes. Maybe she was older than my mom, but you could never tell. "Amy—come in. Sit down."

"Is this about the honors program?" I said. "I'm almost done with my application." In reality, the application was sitting under a pile of laundry in my closet and was on my to-do list, right under "Do laundry."

She smiled. "Actually, this is about your audition on Monday. Last week, I got a phone call from Kim Wilson, one of my old friends from New York. She's a casting director in L.A. now. She's been working on a pilot, and the actress playing the lead has just been fired, so she's in a panic. Kim couldn't find anybody else to replace her, so she called me to see if I could audition some students. I sent the tapes yesterday, and she called this morning. They loved your audition, Amy. They want to fly you out to Los Angeles to meet with the producers of the show. You've made it to the last part of the audition process."

For once, I was actually speechless. "Is there some mistake?" I said in disbelief. "I don't even . . . I mean, I don't . . . sorry, what are you talking about?" I stammered. My mind flashed back to the "dead parents" audition. *Great,* I thought. *Just what I need. The thing I don't want gets me a callback.* It didn't even occur to me to ask why the last person got fired.

She smiled excitedly, getting up from her desk and hugging me. "Congratulations! I know, you have a lot of questions, and this is all happening really fast." She opened up her desk and pulled out a thick manila envelope. "All of the information is in here."

"Is anyone else from the department going?" I said, mostly because I couldn't think of a better response. My mind was still racing. Did they seriously want to portray real people feeling real emotions about death on a network TV show? Maybe it had been too long since I'd watched TV.

Ellie looked up. "Nope, just you. This is great news! You should be happy!"

"OK, great . . . thanks!" I said, gathering up my stuff and trying not to have a panic attack. "I'll call you if anything exciting happens."

Maybe she could tell what I was thinking. I was almost down the stairs of the drama department building when she called back to me from the door. "Oh . . . Amy? I'd recommend not mentioning the fact that you don't watch TV while you're in L.A." She smiled. "These are good people, they have good writers, and from what I've read, it's going to be a show that even *you* might watch. What I'm saying is . . . this is a really good opportunity, Amy. Don't blow it."

I laughed. "You know me too well," I said, giving her the thumbs-up. "I promise to behave myself and to not mouth off about stupid TV *or* get a boob job while I'm in Los Angeles. I will make you proud."

I took the long way back to the dorm to try to sort through my thoughts . . . was it creepy to be doing well at an audition based on the fact that my dad *actually* died? Was I exploiting the situation? *Should* I have been exploiting the situation? Wouldn't repeatedly revisiting those emotions put me in a permanently depressed state? Was it wrong to sell my emotions to a TV show? Was I getting ahead of myself? I finally decided that an all-expenses-paid trip to L.A. couldn't be bad; the odds against getting the part were probably huge anyway, so it couldn't hurt to take the free ticket. Maybe I could meet Richard Linklater or Cameron Crowe in a coffeehouse, and they could give me my big indie film break.

I more than anyone recognized the irony of the situation. I was not "L.A." in any sense of the word. I dressed in black. I loved indie films. I delighted in my pale skin. Because I'd promised to suspend my hatred of the Hollywood bullshit machine for forty-eight hours, I found myself with absolutely nothing to wear.

Two hours later, I was standing in front of my closet in a panic, attempting to pack for L.A. The floor of my tiny dorm room was covered with every piece of clothing I'd ever owned, and I was still not confident about my look. What, exactly, does one wear to a big Hollywood TV show audition?

I knew what I had to do. I took out my cell phone and called in reinforcements.

★ ★ ★

"AIM, GO WITH A little skirt and a tank top. You don't want to look overdone."

My best friend, Vincent Ferrillo, an aspiring stylist, had been at work on my wardrobe since getting my emergency call. He'd shown up with a toolbox full of makeup, a set of hot rollers, and a stack of old *Vogue* magazines under his arm.

"Vince, she said they wanted someone who looks like they live *here* . . . Don't you think I'm going to look ridiculous if I try to look like I'm from California? Then again, what if they said 'Midwest,' but they really meant 'Hollywood Midwest'? Who even knows what they're thinking?" I lay down on a pile of clothes, flummoxed. For the first time in years, I wished that I was more in touch with what people on TV were wearing.

"Definitely the Hollywood Midwest," said Vince emphatically. "Who would do a series about real people who live here? I mean . . . look around you, Amy. My God," he whispered in a hushed stage voice. "Did you *see* the photos of the spring formal in the campus paper this week? Tragic! We are leaving here as soon as possible, lady! Get going and blaze the trail to the promised land! Now, decide on an outfit so I can give you a crash course in Hollywood gossip. Finally, this wealth of information will come in handy!"

I laughed. Vince always knew how to make me feel better. I even let him tell me about who Paris Hilton and Nicole Richie were, and why he had a mad crush on a blogger who'd named himself after one of them.

"Maybe you'll actually meet a guy you like there," said Vince, splaying out across my bed. "That would be the best."

"Why do I need a boyfriend? I have you, darling!" I laughed. Vince was always encouraging me to have a relationship with a guy, but after what happened with my dad, I guess I was still afraid to get emotionally involved. Even since I'd been at UM, my dating history had basically consisted of hooking up with a few guys while working on plays or films, and even then, I still preferred the company of my friends. Truthfully, since my dad died I'd felt a little like my feelings were on autopilot, and I certainly wasn't interested in forming any new attachments. Of course, this usually meant I attracted the guys who wanted to get married, and then I ended up dumping them. One thing I'd learned: Emotionally distant girls drive guys crazy.

"Promise you'll send for me when you get established," Vince said.

"What am I, your husband in a nineteen-fifties movie? Who sends for people anymore?"

"Promise, or I am getting out Carrie Ann's *Les Mis* box set and singing along to every word."

"I promise! Now get out—I have to leave in, like, five hours!"

2

M Y CELL PHONE RANG at five thirty the next morning. I was barely asleep and answered it right away. "Hello? Are you downstairs?" I whispered frantically. It was so early my eyes were squinting and I could barely think straight.

"Car service arriving for Amy Spencer in fifteen minutes," said the woman on the line.

Even early riser Carrie Ann was still asleep, her hair fanned out on the pillow like a big red flower. I couldn't believe a driver was waiting to pick me up, and Little Miss Excitement wasn't even awake to see it.

I threw the remaining clothes still strewn on the bed into my suitcase, zipped up my backpack, and headed for the door, trying to make as little noise as possible. Carrie Ann raised her head sleepily at the click of the doorknob. "Break a leg," she said, her head falling back onto the pillow heavily. I really wished she could go with me. I needed the moral support on my trip to Plastic Land.

Out in front of the dorm, it was so dark the streetlights were still on, and the buildings looked like sleeping giants. The car pulled up slowly, looking for me. *This is crazy,* I thought. *Is this really my life?* I took a deep breath as I slid into the back of the car, determined to be as Zen as possible.

I wanted to not like first class so much, but it made me feel like Cinderella. My parents had always been frugal types, so they would never have dreamed of flying first class, even if they could have afforded it. As I walked onto the plane and sat down, I thought of our annual Florida family vacation—my mom, my dad, and my younger brothers all crammed together in coach, too much carry-on luggage, too many wriggly kids. Then I thought about my mom and brothers, sleeping in our house in Bay City—I hadn't even called to tell them what was going on.

THAT AFTERNOON, I OPENED the door of the casting office and walked into a crowd of the most beautiful girls I'd ever seen in person. Each and every one of them was over five foot ten, had long hair and perfect skin, and looked about fifteen years old. Tall, giraffe-like girls languished against the walls, in the doorway, and in every corner, like I'd landed on a planet inhabited solely by beautiful mutant aliens and I was the sole colonizer from the Land of Normal People. I stopped myself from laughing out loud.

If this is my competition, I thought, *I am leaving right now.* I wanted to tell someone in casting that I had never seen a girl who looked like any of these girls in Bay City, except for one tall, thin girl named Natasha who supposedly moved to Japan to model and was never heard from again. One thing was clear: if any of these girls were what they were really looking for, this was going to be a very short trip.

"Amy Spencer?" said a voice from within the sea of gorgeousness. I turned around to see a short white girl with black and purple dreadlocks, chunky bracelets, and an underbite sitting at a desk with a clipboard. Her arms were covered in tattoos, and she had a pierced eyebrow. I moved toward her with relief. Perhaps she would be able to lead me to safety.

She smiled. "I'm Lisha," she said.

"Is this my audition?" I said, still mortified. "Is there some mistake?" She seemed like a normal person, so I considered telling her that the mere presence of so many beautiful girls was not only statistically abnormal, but was kind of freaking me out.

She looked around and laughed. "No, this is a different casting call . . . they're trying to find the one model in all of Hollywood that actually has rhythm. It's not going well, as you might imagine. Your audition is next door, in the main office. Don't worry; I'll make sure you don't get lost in the beautiful girl forest." She smiled.

I followed Lisha out of model land and down the hall. "Bizarre, isn't it?" she said. "But I guess if you're abnormally tall with wide-set eyes and perfect skin, what else are you going to do but become a model? You can't play basketball, and people stare at you all the time, so you might as well try to pimp yourself out while you're still young enough."

"Right," I said, laughing. "Did they tell you any of their model trade secrets?"

"Well, I did just learn the disturbing fact that if you eat toilet paper, it makes you full and it just comes right out in your poop," she said.

"What? Are you serious? That is . . . sick and somehow fascinating," I said, taking mental notes for my upcoming abnormal psych paper. An interesting mixture of pica and anorexia, for sure. Picarexia, maybe?

Lisha knocked on one of the doors in a non-model-inhabited office. "Kim?" she said. "Amy's here. Are you ready for her?" She motioned me into the room.

"OK . . . good-bye! Nice to meet you," I said, fearful that my new friend was leaving me.

"Oh, don't worry," she said. "You'll be seeing me a lot over the next few days."

Kim Wilson was a gorgeous African-American woman with skin the color of caramel, shoulder-length brown hair, and a gigantic diamond wedding ring. She was immaculately dressed and smelled like expensive perfume, and she had a motherly vibe that put me at ease. She took me into her office and closed the door. "I'm so glad to meet you!" she said enthusiastically. "We really liked your tape."

I sat down in her office. "At this stage," she explained, "we have what's called a working session, which is with the creator of the show and the director who's going to be working on the pilot. They'll want to see how well you can think on your feet. So . . . do you think you're ready to meet the producer and the director?" she said, leading me into a room even smaller than the studio theater at my drama department.

In the corner of the room sat two men, who stood up when I came in. One was maybe forty, tall, with dark hair graying at the temples and kind blue eyes. The other was shorter, with a shock of white curly hair and a beard. "This is Amy Spencer," Kim said. "Amy, this is Josh Stein, the creator of *Autumn Leaves*." The dark-haired man smiled and shook my hand.

"Nice to meet you, Amy—we loved your tape," he said.

"I'm Paul Jones," said the white-haired man. "I'm going to be directing the pilot. We're just going to do a working session today, to see how you deal with the script, take direction, that kind of stuff. If all goes well, we'll take you to studio, then to network to test."

I couldn't begin to think of the right thing to say, so I shrugged.

"Overwhelmed yet?" said Josh, laughing. His smile reminded me of my dad's.

"A little . . . it's been sort of a whirlwind," I said.

"This is the same scene you did on the tape, only it's more of the script; you've just found out your parents were killed in a plane crash, you go to the funeral, and in the next scene, you have to decide where you're going to live. This next part is when you find out about your gay uncle and how he and his partner want to adopt you." He smiled. "You really captured the emotion that we're looking for in your audition tape." He looked over at Paul. "Everyone else was too . . . hysterical. You know what I mean?"

"Yes . . . I do," I said quietly. "I'm glad you liked it."

We read the scenes, then Paul asked if I could improv.

"Like, comedy?" I said. "I can try . . . but where does improv comedy fit into this show . . . ?" I trailed off. I could feel them both looking at me, and my face turned red. *I am so not getting this part,* I thought.

Paul smiled warmly. "We'd just like to see you improvise a dramatic scene, without words, with these chairs as your parents' coffins. Think of whatever you want . . . just try to convince us of the feeling. A lot of the effect of this show is going to be communicated through close-ups on Autumn's face, and we just want to see how you do in the quiet moments, when there's no dialogue."

I couldn't tell if he could see the horror on my face as he described this improvised scene. Before I could chicken out, I sat down in a chair and took myself back to that day, and my dad, and the very same thoughts and emotions came flooding back. When I was in the middle of the grasshopper joke, I thought, *This is crazy,* and looked over at them. There were four of them sitting side by side, and all of them were staring at me. Two of them had their mouths open.

And just like that, the working session was over, and Kim was walking me toward the door. "Good job," she said, putting her hand on my arm. "You're really good."

I didn't know, though, if she was telling me that because that's what she really thought, or because I'd just really freaked her out with how totally wrong my audition was. Once again, I walked out having no idea how the process was even going, or if what I was doing was working, or really, if I was doing anything at all.

* * *

LATER THAT SAME DAY, I was in a beautiful hotel room (also paid for by the studio) at a hotel that Vince was always saying was "the new Hollywood destination," when my phone rang. It was Kim, with good news. "Listen," she said. "You're going on to the next level—to the studio to test, then to network if they like you. You're getting really close, Amy—this is great! Now, do you have an agent? You need someone to negotiate the terms of your contract on your behalf."

I gripped the phone so as not to drop it from sheer surprise. "I . . . don't have an agent," I said slowly, resigning myself to the reality that this meant I would have to go back to Michigan immediately. "Can I not go to the next audition if I don't?" I heard myself say. I was disturbed that I suddenly cared so much about this.

She laughed a hearty laugh. "Now that's a problem I can actually solve—any agent would want a piece of this contract if you get the job. Just leave your phone on, and I'll have my friend Todd call you. He's an agent at International Artists Unlimited."

What seemed like a minute went by, then the phone rang again. "Hello?" I said.

"Amy Spencer?" said a chipper voice. "This is Todd Whitley. Kim told me you need representation, and I'm happy to step in on your behalf."

Then he started talking. There was no time to ask questions or even to get a word in edgewise. "Listen, Kim faxed me over the preliminary contract, and I'm glad I came in when I did, because the numbers were really looking a little thin."

"There's . . . a contract?" I croaked, not quite believing what I was hearing.

"Yes. Yes! This network loves to! screw new actors who don't have any credits. They've got you on a fifteen-thirty deal with a two-banger. If you were my client, which for right now you are, I'd say no to this. Can I say no to this?"

I didn't want to ask too many questions, even though I had no idea what he was talking about. "Um . . . yes?" I said nervously, trying not to sound like I just got off the plane from Michigan. Which, of course, I did.

"OK, great," he said. "I'll call you back if we hit any snags, but there shouldn't be any problems. I've worked with these guys before, and I'm pretty sure I can get them up to twenty-forty at least, with a three-banger and a suite guaranteed. Talk to you tomorrow! Break a leg, Amy Spencer!"

He hung up, and I stared at my cell phone for a second in disbelief. What just happened? Was I supposed to know any of those terms? I wanted to call someone, to tell them everything, but what would I tell them? Should I do a little dance of joy around my hotel room? What, exactly, would I be celebrating? I didn't know the answers to any of these questions, so I ended up ordering a hamburger and some champagne from room service and toasting myself. *Tomorrow,* I thought—*if there's any good news tomorrow, then I will call everyone and tell them. Right now, I'm not even sure myself.*

BY 9:00 THE NEXT morning, I was walking through the lobby of the most beautiful building I had ever seen, following a Gucci-clad assistant in stiletto heels to the boardroom for the next audition. She led me to the lobby, where I got nervous all over again.

Other people in the waiting area included an impossibly thin, tan girl with tiny hips, perfectly straight long blonde hair, and sparkling blue eyes (possibly a model, definitely successful at something); a similarly beautiful brunette with giant green eyes and curly hair that went halfway down her waist; a very tall girl with stripey brownish blonde hair who looked vaguely familiar; a dark-haired girl with big pouty lips. They all seemed to know each other.

"Hey, Alicia," said the thin, tan blonde girl to the dark-haired girl with pouty lips. "I haven't seen you since producer auditions for . . . *Gossip Girl,* right?"

Alicia laughed. "Totally. I've been so swamped this pilot season, too—I shot another one for the CW, but then my agent called about this. Seems kind of last-minute. Like, do they not know the upfronts are in eight weeks?"

"I know," said the blonde. "And—like, how many different types are they trying out for this role? It's so random that we would *all* be up for the part that Sara had, right?"

The tall, stripey-haired girl looked up. "I know—I got called from a modeling gig in Costa Rica. My agent said they were casting a wide net," she said, glancing over at me. "I guess he was right."

I didn't know what I could add, and I felt my ears growing red. Yes, I was the only one who got her shoes at Ross and considered makeup optional. It was painfully obvious that I was only there on a fluke and that there was no way in a million years I was getting this part. I didn't even know what a two-banger was. I wanted to get up and run out of there, but a brunette in her midthirties with a blunt-cut bob haircut and a square jaw emerged from behind a closed conference room door. She was wearing a beautiful black suit, had perfect red lipstick and tiny round glasses, and was carrying a stack of thick manila envelopes.

"Hello, everyone," she said as she found each person and gave her her respective envelope. "Thank you all for coming. First thing, we'll need you to sign the contracts your agents approved. In case you're not familiar with how it works, this is your offer for employment. If you get the role, it becomes a binding contract and you go to work. If you don't this contract is null and void, and you are released from further obligation. We will ask you to stay through the length of everyone's audition, in case the producers want to see one of you again. Your agents will let you know later in the day if you'll be advancing to the network."

I opened my manila envelope and pulled out the contract, which was legal size and covered in red and blue SIGN HERE stickers, along with an expensive-looking black pen, which I made a mental note to steal whether or not I advanced to the next audition. *What's the difference?* I thought. *It's probably all just a fluke anyway. Who cares?* I unscrewed the black pen and folded the bottom half of the contract over, preparing to sign.

My nonchalance went out the window a moment later when I got to the bottom of the first page, where the salary was detailed next to a yellow and red SIGN HERE arrow. Because I didn't know what to look for, my eyes went straight to the numbers. I read the passage three times, remembered my phone call with Todd from the day before, and finally put it all together.

$40,000 for the pilot . . . $20,000 for each episode thereafter, for a total of twenty-two episodes . . . increase contingent upon sale of show . . . increase contingent upon success and renewal of show . . . increase contingent upon syndication . . .

My heart began to beat so loud, I was sure the perfect blonde next to me could hear it. I looked around at all the other actresses as they looked at their contracts. Why did they all look so calm? Were they seeing what I was seeing? I tried to add all the numbers together . . . $40,000 for the pilot, $20,000 per episode . . . twenty-two episodes. That sounded like almost $500,000, just for the first year. *This* was the "twenty-forty" deal Todd was talking about the night before? Was this some kind of joke?

My eyes filled with tears and my lip started to tremble as I thought of the pressure that much money could take off my mom. My parents were both twenty-two when they had me, then a few years later my brother Adam came along, then Ian. No one had expected Dad to die so young, least of all my mom, and after he was gone I sort of became the second parent in the house. Dad had had some life insurance, but on a software engineer's salary there wasn't a lot to put away, so his death had left her with three kids and a mortgage. Plus, Dad's insurance had only covered half of his medical bills. Mom tried to act like it wasn't too much pressure for her, but I worried about the bags under her eyes and her increasingly thin face. The last part of my senior year was really hard on all of us, and I'd gone off to college at her urging, but I knew the bills were piling up. Even with a part-time job at the campus coffee shop and a zillion student loans, I was still having trouble making ends meet, and yet, on weekend trips home I felt too guilty to ask her for money that I knew she didn't have. The silence between us had been growing while we all just tried to keep it together; I knew it was too much for her, and I'd been trying to think of a way to help her. Maybe this was it. Maybe now we could just be a family again, without having to worry about how much everything costs and if we were going to lose the house or how we were going to pay for Ian's science summer camp. It would be really nice to just breathe again and for my mom and I to get back to being close . . .

Dammit! I thought, trying to focus. *I got this far in the audition process because I didn't even care . . . now that I need it, am I going to push it away? How can you tell if you're doing that? This job could actually save my family,* I thought.

Just then the best-looking guy I'd ever seen in person walked up and started talking to the receptionist. I looked up just in time to see him looking at me, and as subtly as I could, I wiped the tears from my eyes and tried to get my cool indie chick vibe back. He smiled.

AFTER THE AUDITION, I stood outside the studio for a good twenty minutes, just wondering what to do. Everything up to that point had happened so fast, and now it seemed that time had ground to a halt while I waited for them to make up their minds about whether I was going on to the next audition or going back to Michigan to finish my abnormal psych paper. And though I was dying to call everyone back home and give them the blow-by-blow update, I didn't feel like I had enough of a handle on what was going on to adequately describe it. Vince and Carrie Ann would be waiting in our room for me to call and give them an update, which I didn't really have. To top it off, I didn't even tell my family I'd gone to California for fear of getting their hopes up.

Fifteen minutes into my self-imposed stupor of indecision, the cute guy from the studio waiting room walked up behind me, startling me back to reality.

"Don't know what to do or where to go?" he said, laughing. "Welcome to Actor Purgatory!"

The quizzical look on my face must have belied my underlying sense of confusion and indecision. "Yeah . . . I . . . um . . . what do you . . . ?" I stammered, then immediately felt embarrassed at my total inability to even form a coherent thought.

He laughed. "This is the worst. It's like, the longest day of your entire life, waiting to hear about your fate from total strangers who could care less about you." He stuck out his hand. "I'm Matt Pierce. I play Zach in the pilot—the next-door neighbor/boyfriend."

"I'm . . . Amy," I said. "So, what's the secret for surviving Actor Purgatory?"

"Try to keep your mind occupied," he said. "And don't call anyone until you know something either way. The more people get excited for you, the worse you feel if you don't end up getting it. Silence is golden."

Maybe it was the fatigue or the adrenaline rush of being in Hollywood at an audition, but I couldn't stop thinking about how good-looking Matt was. He looked like he belonged on TV or in films, whereas I felt like a total fluke, someone who just walked in off the street, or maybe a tourist on vacation.

"Hey, do you want to get some coffee? It might help kill the time." Matt's blue eyes looked deeply into mine, and he smiled.

"Oh—no, I should probably just go back to the hotel. They'll probably be cutting me loose soon anyway, and I have to go back to the airport." Matt shrugged, and for a moment I stared at his firm biceps and wondered what his abs must look like.

"OK, but don't go far—if they call you back, they're going to want to see you again *right away*! One of the other rules of Actor Purgatory is that you are on call, all day, without regard to your feelings or how this makes each minute seem like hours." He laughed again. "I hope I see you again, mysterious Amy Spencer," he said, strolling away and leaving me in the wake of his handsomeness.

Finally, I got into a cab in front of the studio, mostly because I couldn't think of anything else to do. I felt like telling the driver "just drive," like Holden Caulfield did in *Catcher in the Rye*. But . . . do people really do that? Where would we go? Doesn't everyone need a destination, and not just existentially? I couldn't even take a spontaneous cab ride without questioning the very nature of existence.

Eventually, I put the cab driver (and myself) out of our collective ennui and had him take me to the closest Starbucks, figuring maybe a double latte would create the Ritalin effect, pushing me past the point of excited agitation and back into the calm zone. Two hours later, though, I was still obsessing when my cell phone started to buzz. One more latte and I could've answered the phone with the power of my mind.

This could be it . . . don't sound too eager . . . is it wrong to want this?

"Hello?" I said, trying not to sound too overcaffeinated and desperate.

"Amy Spencer! This is Todd. Good job, girl! You made the cut, and the network wants to see you in an hour. Do you need the address?"

The truth is, I wanted to hate L.A. With every audition and every new person I met, I looked for evidence to validate my theory that Los Angeles was the den of iniquity and bad acting that I'd railed against since becoming an indie film snob in high school. Somehow, though, I didn't see it. Everyone was so nice, the weather was beautiful, and the show seemed like it was going to be really good. Plus, there was the money. Maybe I'd been too quick to judge Los Angeles without getting to know it first. Was I rationalizing, was I seeing the real L.A., or had it taken me one day to lose my edge?

Everything was moving so fast, I didn't even have time to make up my mind.

EVERY PLACE I WENT to was nicer than the last. The waiting area at the network was nicer than any nice house I'd ever seen, in Bay City or on TV.

"Um, excuse me," I said to the woman at the front desk. "Is everyone here who is going to be here? I mean . . . is there anyone else coming?"

She looked at her list. "Nope, just the three of you. Good luck!"

So that was it; Pouty Big Lips, Alicia, and I were the only ones left sitting there in the lobby, waiting to audition for the part. We were joined by a girl who looked just like Dakota Fanning, as well as my new friend Matt Pierce. I looked from one of my co-auditioners to the other, and each of them gave me the now-too-familiar Hollywood Once-over, starting with the not-fashionable "fancy shoes" my mom got from Ross and ending with my hair, which was becoming more unruly with every passing hour.

A clone of the well-dressed blonde executive from the studio came out to greet us. "Hello, thanks for coming," she said. "As you probably know, this is the last step—you're going to be meeting some of the executives as well as the president of the network. We're just going to ask you to read some more scenes from the pilot. Please stay until everyone is done, and you'll be hearing from your agents later today, whichever way we decide to go. OK, thanks!"

The two other girls went before me—Josh came out of the conference room to get them, and I was relieved to see that he was there.

He was the one person I'd met who seemed like he might actually live in my town or go to my school. When he came out for me, he smiled.

"You ready?" he said, motioning for me to follow him into the room. "There's a lot of them in there, but don't let it distract you. You're doing great."

The conference room itself was big, but so was the conference table inside it, and every seat was filled by a person in a suit. At the head of the table sat an older, gray-haired man, and to his right was a large woman with curly brown hair. Paul, the director, was also there, and Josh sat down beside him. I glanced around and tried to smile, hoping I wouldn't have to make small talk with all of them.

"Amy, this is Robert Washer, the president of the network," said Josh. The older man at the head of the table looked up and nodded, as did the rest of the group.

"So—Amy, I'll just read with you," Josh said. "We watched your tapes already from the other auditions, and now we'd like to see you read in person, and then with some of the other actors from the show." He motioned over toward a large TV/DVD player on a rolling cart. Unlike the room at the studio, there was just a tiny space for me to stand, right next to the TV. I almost laughed—I was supposed to blow them away with a final audition conducted in an eighteen-inch space?

"No big movements or anything, of course," he said. "We just want to get a feel for your performance in person." He smiled, handing me the pages of the script. It was the funeral scene from the pilot, scripted. I took a deep breath. The grief was now becoming so easy for me, I could call it up like my father's death was yesterday. The scene went by quickly, and I tried not to look at all of the executives staring at me.

When we'd finished the first scene, they brought in the Dakota Fanning lookalike, who Josh introduced as Emily Dean, and then Matt Pierce so they could see us together. Emily came in first, and I

was immediately intimidated by how professional she was. She nodded hello to some of the network executives, then pulled a script out
of a leather messenger bag.

"Are we still using the script from the pilot?" she said to Josh,
completely calm. She looked about twelve or thirteen, which was
younger than my youngest brother, Ian, and yet I still felt like she was
a professional woman in a young person's body. Matt was a little more
casual, but still he looked like he knew what he was doing.

Josh nodded. "This is the scene where Zach comes over to your
uncles' house to introduce himself, and Jessie asks him where he goes
to church. Uncomfortable—you know, take it from there."

And with that, we started right in. I was surprised at how good
they both were, and how fast the audition went by. Were they more
confident, knowing they already had the parts? We managed to make
each other and some of the executives laugh during the scene, which
I thought was a good sign. Still, it was all going by so fast that I still
didn't have the slightest idea how I was doing or if I would be told to
go home at any moment.

When we were finished, I looked down at my watch to see the
only promising sign of the day—my audition had actually taken
thirty minutes, which was more than the other two girls' combined. I
headed back to the hotel with a glimmer of hope.

THREE HOURS AFTER THE audition, I was back at the hotel, waiting for the Big Phone Call. I had, during that time period, made sure
my phone was charged exactly forty-two times, packed and unpacked
my suitcase twice, and seriously attempted some "mind over matter"
meditation in order to will the phone to ring. I so badly wanted to
call my mom to tell her about all this, but I didn't want to get her
hopes up, just in case this all went away as quickly as it had come. She
had enough to worry about.

Why oh why do they show you those big numbers? I thought helplessly. Monday I had been happy in my life as a broke college student with a crappy part-time job. Now it was Friday, I'd been seduced by the possibility of fame and money, and I was going berserk in a famous Hollywood hotel, waiting for a call from a guy named Todd.

What had I become?

I paced around the room, making a mental list of things I couldn't do as I waited.

- Couldn't go pee, because what if Todd called with news?
- Couldn't take a walk around the hotel, because what if Todd called with news and I was in an unfavorable cell phone area, causing me to miss the call and possibility causing the part to go to someone else?
- Couldn't go for a drive, because I had no car, and besides, I'd probably get into one of those unbelievable traffic jams and never be able to find my way back.
- Couldn't eat, because I was too nervous, and besides, based on the size of my competition, I shouldn't be eating anyway.
- Couldn't call friends, because, being unsure how to work my call waiting, I usually hung up when I tried to switch over, and also because I didn't want to cause Todd's call to go to voice mail.
- Couldn't take a nap—too much caffeine.
- Couldn't call Todd.
- Couldn't call casting people.
- Couldn't get hopes up.
- Couldn't not get hopes up.
- Couldn't kill myself.

After another hour of mental wrangling, I compromised by lying ramrod straight on the bed, cell phone resting securely on my stomach for maximum reception as well as access, willing myself to breathe in and out and flipping through an assortment of TV shows that could surely only be on during the daytime. *Who is Judge Hatchett?* I wondered. *Did she name herself that?*

At 5:55 P.M. the phone finally rang. I grabbed for it, staring at the screen. It was definitely Todd.

Ring. Don't want to pick it up too fast . . . that will make me look desperate.

Ring. Now I didn't want to answer it. Did I really want this news? If I let it go to voice mail at least I'd delay the inevitable.

Ring. *Don't do it,* I told myself. *If you answer, then you'll have to go back to Michigan to write your psych paper.*

I answered right before the call went to voice mail. "Hello?" I said, trying to keep my voice at a reasonable volume.

"Amy Spencer!" said Todd from what sounded like the inside of a coffee can. "How are you? I have you on speakerphone."

The sound of a cowbell ringing snapped me out of my momentary downward crazy spiral. Then I heard people cheering.

What the . . . ?

Todd came back on. "Congratulations! You got it! You're Autumn! You start shooting on Monday! We knew you could do it!"

Once I had pinched myself enough times to ensure that I was awake and that the Big Phone Call had really happened, I composed myself, scrolled through my cell phone's address book, and hit a number.

"Mom?"

"Amy! Oh my gosh! I miss you . . . how's school going?" She sounded tired.

"Mom, are you sitting down? I have something amazing to tell you guys!"

I told her, starting from the beginning, about the audition, and the trip, and the job, and the salary, and everything. At first, she thought I was making it up, and I had to convince her that I was telling the truth. When I was done, I heard her crying.

"Mom, are you there? What do you think? This is great, right?"

"Amy—this is . . . I don't believe it. This is a miracle. Your dad is looking out for us."

A little sob caught in my throat. "Do you think he knows? Do you think he's proud of me?"

She was silent for a long moment. "Amy, he's always with us, don't forget that. Even if you didn't get the part he would've been proud of you. But—yes. Your dad always said you were a star."

When we hung up, I called Vince, who screamed so loud I thought someone in the dorm would call the fire department.

"Call me every five minutes. I want to know everything!" he said. "So—are you finally happy?"

"You know what? I think I am."

I was, though I also had the feeling that I had just gone onto a roller coaster, and was about to start the uphill climb.

3

BY NINE THE NEXT morning, there were no less than *four* congratulatory baskets outside my room at the hotel (two fruit, one chocolate, and one assorted, containing caviar and fancy water crackers).

An hour after eating Godiva chocolate for breakfast, I was at the studio office building once again, where a lovely red-haired woman named Julie who had been charged with "facilitating my transition" had gotten me into the Screen Actors Guild and arranged a leave of absence from college with work credit for being on the show, behaving all the while like the normal rules of life didn't apply, which I suppose they really didn't anymore. Since the publicity shots had already been taken, Julie mentioned that those would need to be redone "as soon as possible."

Telling me I was about to be late to the very first "table read" rehearsal, Julie handed me off to Valerie, a studio intern, who filled me in on the latest studio and network scoop as she led me from one office to the next, opening doors with a keycard attached to her pants with a long chain. Valerie was a serious girl with long black hair, frayed jeans, and white Converse, and she walked fast.

"They're so lucky they found you—this show was about to go right into never-never land if they didn't start reshooting first thing Monday. We were all surprised that the network executives agreed, especially Mindy Steinman. She is truly frightening." She laughed, and my mind flashed back to the conference table full of network executives, trying to figure out which one might be Mindy. I had a vague idea, but I couldn't be sure.

"Now we're going to the table read, which is basically where you guys all read through the script for the first time. Only, I guess it would only be the first time for you, since all of them have already shot the script. I'm supposed to tell you a little about the cast members on the way to rehearsal so it's not so overwhelming for you, I guess."

I wanted to stop her, or at least slow her down for a second so I could get my bearings, but she kept going at top speed.

"Why'd the last girl get fired?" I asked praying the answer wasn't something like "She was too fat," because if that was the case, I was completely screwed.

Valerie paused. "Oh—she . . . didn't test well with the network execs, and she didn't really seem like she was on board with some of the changes they wanted her to make, you know what I mean? You have to, like, really be a team player to do this job, you know?"

I nodded; I didn't really know, but I didn't want to press the issue further since I didn't even know Valerie. For all I knew, she could have been the one who got the other actress fired. I felt like I was doing an OK job keeping my cool as we walked down the long hallway toward the rehearsal room, during which time Valerie barraged me with a nonstop summary of my fellow cast members "to get me up to speed."

"OK, I'm just going to warn you, the cast was pretty tight with Sara, who was Autumn before you. They were mad that she got fired, and they're not that thrilled to be shooting the pilot again. But Josh told them to be nice to you, and the network is backing him up, at least for now, so you should be fine."

We were still walking as she said all this, so I couldn't stop and stare at her like I wanted to. "Um—OK," I muttered. Actually, I wanted to turn and run away. My stomach gave a little lurch; the butterflies I'd felt all morning had intensified to a dull ache. *Don't think about it,* I willed myself. *They don't even know you. You'll meet them, they'll like you. Or they won't, but either way you're here.*

Oblivious to my churning gut and racing internal dialogue, Valerie continued to give me the rundown on all the people in the cast. "Greg Forster, who plays your Uncle Michael—this is supposed to be his breakout show," she said, pulling out a headshot of a guy I'd definitely seen on the cover of one of my mom's *TV Guides*. "He really made his name on soaps, so it's a huge deal for him to be doing a gay role." I couldn't tell whether this meant he was actually gay or not. Before I could ask she pulled out another photo and put it on top of his, all while we were still walking.

"Ross Wong is playing your uncle's partner. He's been on TV for a zillion years too. He's a really great actor." Again, no mention of his being gay or not. Was this important? I tried to take notes in my head.

She whipped another photo to the top of the pile. "OK—Michele McCann is playing your best friend, Amanda." I glanced down at the shot and made more mental notes: Michele was a beautiful girl with shiny brown hair, blue eyes, and flawless skin. "Her father is Robert McCann, one of the producers, but she swears she auditioned under an alias," Valerie said, rolling her eyes. "She's not so much in the acting department, but they're doing what they can with her. There's also a rumor going around that she's having an affair with Greg, but he's married, so we're all trying to ignore it."

She switched the photo again. "Then there's Emily Dean, who plays your little sister Jessie," she said, flashing me a picture of Emily, who I'd met at the final audition. "Oh, and Matt Pierce, who plays the 'boy next door' Zach, who will be your love interest in upcoming shows. You met him during the audition too, right?"

I nodded, briefly picturing super-hot Matt Pierce talking to me outside the studio and remembering how I had to tell myself not to stare at him, because he looked like Brad Pitt. "That's it for the regular cast. For one-hour dramas, they usually stick to six characters to form the ensemble . . . like, look at *One Tree Hill* or *The O.C.* Six people gives you the most stuff to play off of and still retain the brand recognition of the main characters. Plus it gives you the most permutations of the traditional dramatic formula."

We stopped, and all at once I realized we were outside the door of the very same conference room where I had auditioned for the studio executives the day before.

"OK, are you ready?" said Valerie. "First impression's the hardest, right?"

I took a deep breath. "Right." I could only hope that they liked me, or at least tried to accept me. We stood in the back for a second, and I frantically tried to match the faces in front of me with the photos.

"Amy!" said Josh excitedly. "Everyone—Amy's here!"

I watched as several of the actors' faces switched from not knowing who I was to being excited (or at least acting that way). Greg Forster got up from the table and extended a large hand. "Nice to meet you, Amy—looking forward to working together," he said, his voice deep and booming.

"Thanks," I said, looking at him for a moment. "I mean—me too. Thanks!" I was pretty sure he was on a show my mom used to watch. One person down; many, many more to go.

Next, Matt Pierce came over and hugged me. "Out of Actor Purgatory!" he laughed. "Now you have to let me take you out for coffee to celebrate!" He winked at me, and over his shoulder I could feel Michele McCann's eyes giving me the once-over.

"Hi," she said, looking over at Josh and the remaining executives.

"Nice to meet you." I looked at her for a second. Just like her photo, she had flawless skin, blue eyes, and dark hair. She was taller than me and had perfect arm muscles and abs that suggested an incredible amount of self-discipline. Something about her seemed totally disingenuous, like the girls in the drama department at UM who would sleep with the director to get a part. But since I was the new kid, I decided to give her the benefit of the doubt.

"Nice to meet you," I said, shaking her hand. I thought I saw her smile fade as soon as Josh walked away to the back table to get a cup of coffee.

Two well-dressed female executives came up to me next. "We wanted you the whole time," they said. "You are what the Midwest really looks like, you know? It's so great!"

I nodded, and kept nodding while several more executive types came up and said the same thing. "Thanks, thanks!" I kept saying while I was eyeing the cast, trying to figure out what they were thinking about me. Would they like me? Did it matter?

"OK, everyone, we're just doing the table read again today, so Amy can get used to the script," said Josh to the cast. "There have been some modifications, so everyone gets new pages." He smiled at me, handing me a thick script, a highlighter, and a pen and motioning for me to sit down at the table.

"Thanks," I said, looking him in the eye. "Really—thanks." I wanted to tell him how much I appreciated his believing in me and how committed I was to being good at this job, but I was a little embarrassed to say anything with everyone from the cast standing right there. They'd all obviously had jobs like these before and didn't think it was that big a deal. But to me—it was a big deal. The biggest deal, in fact.

Josh took my hand like he was going to shake it but squeezed it instead. "You're what I was waiting for," he said, winking at me. "You're going to be great, don't worry."

Practically as soon as we were all seated, a woman who I thought must've been the stage manager started reading the stage directions ("Camera pans in on Autumn, in high school class, walking along with her friends"), and then we were off and running, going line by line, reading through the whole script. I tried to concentrate and keep up, since I didn't want the cast to think I was an amateur.

At one point, when I was sure I didn't have any lines for a few pages, I looked around the table at everyone. I was at once fascinated and intimidated by how totally comfortable they all seemed—even Emily Dean, who I'd found out was eleven years old. I looked at her for a long moment, then over at Ross, who caught my eye. Ever so subtly, he gave me a thumbs-up and smiled.

By the end of the table read, I thought I might have earned their respect as an actress, though I had entered a level of exhaustion not previously known to man. At 3:00 that afternoon, I moved on to a wardrobe fitting, during which I was informed by the costume designer that I had "four inches and a good thirty-five pounds" on Sara McClellan, for whom all of the costumes had been made. Costume Designer Lady (Lola), who was about fifty years old with a bad smoker's hack, informed me that some of the costumes for the still photo shoot of the cast for publicity and marketing purposes would have to be cut up the back and *taped to my body*. She sighed. "I didn't know they were going to go in such a different direction," she said, eyeing my thighs. "I guess we'll just have to make it work." Then she joked, "Unless you think you can lose twenty-five pounds by tomorrow!" At that point, I began to seriously regret the club sandwich and cookies I'd consumed during rehearsal.

To recap: photos of me as the lead in a television show for a major network were going to appear in magazines, on billboards, and even on buses around the country. By 4:00 P.M., I had resumed the smoking habit I'd given up the previous summer, after Lola took a smoke break in the middle of the fitting and casually mentioned that "cigarettes might help with your appetite."

One hour later I found myself in the office of Sondra Mitchell, the publicity person for the studio, who was apparently having some kind of meltdown about the fact that the pilot had been recast this late in the season. According to Valerie, I was supposed to do whatever Sondra wanted in order to keep things on track for the show to launch.

"Ms. Mitchell?" I said timidly, poking my head into her office. "I'm Amy Spencer? Here for our marketing meeting?" Sondra was a power woman in her midforties with alabaster skin, spiky red hair, and a ton of makeup that looked like it took hours to apply. She even looked intimidating sitting down, which was why I was compelled to end every sentence as a question.

"Yes, hello, nice to see you," she said, sounding less than enthused. "Have a seat. We have a lot of work to do."

I plopped myself in the giant leather chair next to her desk. She looked at me for a long moment, sighed, and began.

"Listen," she said. "I don't want to make you uncomfortable, but you're going to need to tell me anything and everything about yourself, so I can design an appropriate outreach strategy to the media. Once the show launches, we're basically going to make you into a brand. We want to put you in the position to be the next Hilary Duff or Lindsay Lohan, you know? They both got their start in television."

With that, she reached into a sleek black leather portfolio, pulling out a pad of white paper and a typed list. "We're just going to go over a few basics about your life so I can decide which angle is best for you. Do you have anything major in your past that we should know about? Siblings in trouble with the law? A father in jail in Tijuana?" She attempted to lighten the mood with a short laugh, but it came out a little like a grunt.

I drew in a sharp breath. Even though some time had passed, I still hated saying it out loud.

"My dad . . . died," I said slowly, drawing in a breath. This was the point where people would always look at me sympathetically or pat my hand and ask what happened.

Sondra made a mark on her pad without looking up. "Of what?" she said, then quickly, "I'm so sorry." Then again, "Of what?"

"He . . . had a heart attack," I said. "It was two years ago."

Sondra's face remained expressionless, and she barely looked up. "Were there drugs involved or any other kinds of issues? Is there anything else that's going to come up later about this?" She grimaced, scribbling feverishly on her pad.

Anything else that's going to come up about this? Did she mean my feelings? "No . . . it was a heart defect," I said. Why were we still talking about this? Did she also want to know about the coma, and the ICU, and the mountain of hospital bills that didn't stop coming even after he died? I felt my face getting hot.

"He was forty, and he had a heart attack." I willed myself not to cry. She pretended not to notice.

"I'm not trying to sound harsh, but I don't want the *Enquirer* going to your hometown, digging up some dirt about how your dad was really a crazy drug addict who had just been released from prison and was doing speedballs in front of your local strip bar, and that's what caused his death . . . do you know what I mean?"

I resisted the urge to jump across the desk and strangle her. "He had a heart attack on the way home from work," I said. Then, more assertively: "That was it. Can we talk about something else?" My face ached from fighting back tears. "Let's move on."

She paused for a moment, and I wondered if she was going to push it even further. "What about you? Do you have any medical issues?" she said. "Anything that we might have to spin later, like Marcia Cross with her migraines, or Camryn Manheim with her rheumatoid arthritis, or Linda Hamilton with her bipolar disorder?"

I let out the breath I'd been holding, thankful that she'd moved on from the subject of my dad while at the same time impressed with her near-encyclopedic knowledge of celebrity issues. "No, none of that stuff. I'm fine, but I'll let you know if I start to feel sick," I joked.

Nothing. No reaction. Maybe she was frozen by Botox and was laughing inside. She looked down at her list.

"OK, what about sex?"

"What about sex?" I said, mentally gearing up for another mini-drama.

"I mean, have you had it?" she said, looking up across the desk. "I'm just trying to suss out whether or not to work the whole Jessica Simpson/Britney Spears/cast of *Seventh Heaven* I'm-a-virgin angle, since your character on the show is supposed to be sixteen. It's a stance some of the girls want to take. We can try it, but it's a little hard to back down off of if someone comes out of the woodwork and says you had some wild spring break weekend with them, or anything like that."

I made a mental list. Virginity: lost to high school boyfriend during prom of junior year. Subsequent experiences: Charlie, costar in freshman year of college production of *Hamlet* at UM; Henry, summer hookup between freshman and sophomore years; then one during a student film I just finished. Basically, one per project. So, a few. Not bad, not terribly slutty, but definitely nowhere near virgin territory.

"Yes, I've had it. Probably not with anyone who would talk to the *Enquirer*," I said finally, attempting to answer the question while giving her as little information as possible. Why was this her business?

"OK then . . . what about videotapes? Don't want those coming back later to haunt us."

"Oh my God!" I squealed. "I'm from Bay City, Michigan. We don't videotape ourselves having sex in Michigan, OK? These questions are crazy." Was this some kind of test?

"OK, OK . . . ," she said. "Listen, it's better for everyone if we're just open about everything from the beginning. Then we have a strategic plan ready to go for when it comes out. The one thing we cannot tolerate is being blindsided because you've kept something from us. The more information you give us, the more we can help you." She finished up with a little nod, as if to signify the end of this tender moment.

"What about beliefs?" she continued. "Are you a strict vegetarian, or a vegan like Alicia Silverstone, or macrobiotic like Gwyneth Paltrow? Do you not wear shoes made of leather, like Moby? This is something we need to tell the stylist, who you'll definitely need to see sooner rather than later. Also, we might be able to work that angle in the media, like in the *Vegetarian Times*. Chris Martin was voted World's Sexiest Vegetarian by PETA, for instance. Just make sure if you're going to claim you're a vegan, you don't get photographed eating a hamburger. Those people are militant when you betray them."

"Nope . . . I love steak," I said.

She didn't look up from her list. "Religion? Are you a militant Baptist or something? Were you raised in a commune, are you a Christian Scientist, or do you have any relatives that are Jehovah's Witnesses? Religion itself is not necessarily a bad thing, but those groups are very likely to pop up out of nowhere at critical times in your career and 'claim' you." She seemed serious.

"It's fine," I said. "I was baptized Lutheran, but I haven't been to church in a while."

Finally, she was done with her questions list and seemed satisfied that I had no major skeletons in my closet.

"We'll need to meet again before the show premieres, but I think we're going to try to market you as an overnight success Cinderella story, like Kimberly Williams when she was cast in *Father of the Bride* in the early nineties," she said. "Everybody loves a rags-to-riches story . . . one minute you're shucking corn in some field in Iowa and the next you're the star of a Hollywood TV show!"

I didn't bother mentioning that, in fact, I was from Michigan and I had never even been in a cornfield. Somehow, the real details of my life seemed less important by the moment.

That night we had an informal "meet and greet" gathering at the studio, where I decided to skip dessert and stick to salad in the interest of fitting into my costumes. I tried not to act excited that they were actually serving me alcohol, even though I was nineteen and my character on the show was supposed to be sixteen. Since everyone knew each other already, I sort of hung out in the back of the room talking to Josh, who (as it turned out) was from Milwaukee.

"So—how did your parents take the news?" he said.

"Oh—I, I mean . . . my mom freaked out. I still don't think she believes it's a real job." He laughed. "My dad—he passed away, so . . ."

"Oh, I'm sorry," he said. "This must be hard for you. My mom died when I was your age, and it took me a long time to learn to live with it. One good thing, I guess, is that you can keep your mind busy with learning the new job."

"Yeah, it helps to have something to do."

"Amy, I'm sure you're going to hear a lot of rumors from the cast, but I want you to know that you are the best person for the role of Autumn, and I'm glad that the network finally got it. You look like real people in my hometown." He smiled.

"Um—thanks?" I was dying to know why they got rid of the other girl, but I didn't want to press the issue. Still, I looked around at the other people in the cast, mentally comparing myself to them. "It seems like everyone here is just gorgeous. I mean—even the people who work in Starbucks are beautiful."

"I know—sometimes it's too much. Don't let it get you down. Trust me. I've seen too many models try to break into acting. What you have is real. Just remember that, and don't get too sucked in to the Hollywood game."

"OK," I said. "I mean, I don't think I have much of a choice. It's not like I can magically change myself into a hundred-pound blonde girl."

He laughed. "You'd be surprised what people are willing to do to make it here."

After another hour of meeting what seemed like everyone in the entire studio, network, and crew, Lisha came over and told me it was time for me to go.

"There's a car waiting outside for you," she said, handing me a file folder. "And here are some new pages. Oh, and . . . I just got a memo from the network about your costumes. You have another fitting at nine o'clock tomorrow so they can adjust all the sizes."

I guess I could've been offended that at every turn I seemed to be too big and too "normal-looking" to fit into the world of Hollywood, but at that point I was too excited to care.

I arrived back at the the hotel to find that my room had been upgraded to a suite, which Todd had gotten the network to pay for as my residence as a condition of my deal. More congratulatory baskets and flower arrangements had arrived, and the staff had kindly arranged them in the foyer. Of my suite. Where I now lived. Having never met Todd in person, I silently thanked him while lying in my posh accommodations, attempting unsuccessfully to decompress from what was at once the most exciting and most terrifying day of my life, and trying to go to sleep so I could start it all over again tomorrow. By 3:00 A.M., I decided I would try to survive on coffee, cigarettes, and adrenaline.

THE NEXT MORNING, I faced Lola again for costume fitting number two. "We found some more material, and we're going to try reconstructing the clothes we've already made to fit you. It's the only thing that's going to work by the photo shoot this afternoon." After hearing this news, I skipped breakfast in favor of coffee and more cigarettes.

One hour later, I was scheduled for a visit to hair and makeup, where I studied myself in the giant mirror, trying to take a "before" snapshot in my mind before they whipped makeup department mojo on me. My dark brown hair, usually attractively wavy, had settled into a curious bed-head dreadlock formation overnight. With the proper time and a flatiron, I could blow it out to look cool, but that morning it was being unruly and had taken on a Bride of Frankenstein theme. Because approaching it with a comb just seemed to make it angry, I had tied it into a knot and hoped for the best. I leaned closer to the mirror, looked at the dark circles under my eyes, and sighed. I hadn't slept much, and I looked a little disheveled and puffy.

First, I experienced the incredible pain of waxing body parts I did not usually wax ("Did you know you have a peach fuzz moustache?"), had an eyebrow plucking that would've put Vince to shame, and got a haircut/and blonde highlights that I'm sure would have been $800 in a salon. I almost felt like Cinderella, surrounded by those sparkly mice during her transformation scene, only I was starting to become paranoid that they were going to declare me too ugly for TV and send me packing. After two hours, though, I looked in the mirror, barely recognized myself, and determined that this, officially, was the best I'd ever looked in my life.

My elation at looking like a model was short lived, as I was soon reminded that while my face might look amazing, my body still had a ways to go. By noon, I was back in the wardrobe department a third time, having been fetched by Valerie and informed by Lola once again that "there just wasn't enough time or enough fabric to make all these changes to the wardrobe." I had tried on every piece of clothing made for an apparently elfin-sized actress, finding one skirt and a blouse that didn't make me look like a sausage. To every clothing change, Lola responded with a sigh, and she kept pressing on the meaty space between her thumb and forefinger. "Headache acupressure point," she said, and I wondered if it was my ass that was giving her the headache. When I put on the skirt that the other actress had previously worn in most of the publicity shots, it was so small that it wouldn't zip up all the way. Exasperated, Lola took out a pair of scissors, cut the skirt up the back, and taped the sides to the backs of my legs, exposing my underwear, a tattered pair of Old Navy bikini briefs that said ANGEL/ DEVIL on them. I turned around to survey the underwear/skirt/tape configuration, which from the back was just short of being a horror film. "Just don't make any sudden movements during the photo shoot," said Lola. "We'll make something better for the next round, but for now, we have to get you out there in front of the camera. The whole cast is waiting."

At this declaration, I think I had a stroke. *The cast was waiting?* The second time I was going to see these people, and I was wearing someone else's costumes that had been cut open and taped to my body because I was too fat to fit into them? Despite my incredible-looking eyebrows and beautiful hair, tears welled up in my eyes. "Is there nothing else I can wear?" I said desperately. "This is really . . . embarrassing." *Keep it together,* I thought.

"I know, honey, but stuff happens fast here . . . just make the best of it, and we'll bring some altered clothes out for the costume change at two o'clock." She threw a sweater around my waist. "Just wear this until it's time to take the shot, then take it off. No one will even notice."

Thirty minutes later, the repeat photo call for the cast was set to begin. I was escorted by Valerie (who did not comment on the sweater around my waist or the fact that I was walking like something was seriously wrong with me) through the labyrinthine halls of the studio from the costume department to a large room that had been converted to a photo studio with a backdrop and many bright lights. Everyone in the cast was gathered, costumed, and ready. My head was spinning, and the tape holding my costume was beginning to pull at my legs. I feared I would not survive the afternoon with my dignity intact.

"OK everyone," said Beth, the photographer. She seemed harried, her blonde hair pulled into a knot on the top of her head and her glasses slightly askew. "You remember photocall from before.

We just need you in the same positions—parents in the back, kids in the front—we'll just put Amy in the center of the group where Sara was before." She pointed to a blown-up *Autumn Leaves* poster hanging on the wall of the studio. I stared at it for a second and realized that I was actually wearing the exact same clothes as her. *What did this girl do to get fired from the show when so much of the process had already been done?* I wondered to myself. But there was no way I was asking anyone that question, lest the same thing happen to me.

The cast quickly got into position for the first photo—one of those super-serious nighttime-show shots with everyone looking straight into the camera. Michele was right next to me, and during one of the shots I was pretty sure I noticed Greg Forster's hand on the small of her back. That shot didn't last long, though, and then we were switching again so Matt Pierce would have his arm around me. After five hours of this, I was amazingly exhausted, my face ached from the smiling and posing, and I had to keep willing myself not to compare myself to the other girls in the cast, who were noticeably tinier than me.

Miraculously, no one mentioned the sweater, the tape, or the underpants, though I did feel quite certain I was going to die of shame right before the "unveiling" of my outfit and my almost-naked behind. Ross Wong was the only one who even mentioned it. "Don't worry about it," he said. "Things always go wrong. That kind of thing happens all the time. I once played Judas in a production of *The Joy of Christmas* where they had to stop the show because they used live animals, and one of the goats bit the head off the plastic baby Jesus doll and ran offstage." By the end of the story, the whole cast was laughing so hard, they had apparently forgotten all about my mortification.

After the photo shoot was over, Valerie gave me a ride back to the hotel. Just before I got out of the car, she handed me a thick script. "The writers just put in some revisions after the table read. You do know that you need to be completely off book for this script by tomorrow morning, right?"

I smiled through my aching face, trying to mask the panic that I felt inside. "Sure, no problem," I said. I couldn't risk showing fear to someone I'd just met, who on top of it worked for the network. What if I told her that it was going to take all night to memorize that script, and she told someone at the network, and then I got fired like Sara?

She raised an eyebrow. "OK, superstar." I couldn't tell if her tone was kidding or sarcastic, so I just laughed and hopped out of the car. The minute I got upstairs to my room, I called Vince for a pep talk.

"Tell me I can do this," I said. "This is hard, I don't know anyone, and the people are all totally competitive, even in pictures. Plus, I haven't slept, I'm afraid to talk to anyone, and—"

"Oh my God—stop!" he said. "Don't worry. Everything seems worse when you first start. Remember your first day at Coffee Union? They forced you to work a double, and you cried and wanted to quit. Who came down at two A.M. with *US Weekly*?"

"You did," I sniffed, laughing. Vince always knew how to take the edge off my obsessive worrying.

"You got through that, and you'll get through this—only for about a zillion times more money," he said. "No one can get to my girl. Now—take a nap, set your alarm, and learn those lines. You can do it!"

I stared at my still-made-up face in the mirror, slapping my cheeks a few times.

"You're right," I said finally. "I am strong. I can do this."

After we hung up, I took a deep breath, looking at myself in the mirror. It wasn't until then that I finally burst out crying—maybe from relief, or fear, or disbelief.

For better or worse, first thing in the morning I was starting a whole new life.

$\star \quad \star \quad \star$

"CUT! LET'S TAKE THAT again. Amy—wait a second before you start talking. OK, everybody back to one." Paul did not sound happy. I watched as everyone went back to their original places for the scene; I knew they were wondering why the producers went with a total amateur like me, and right then, so was I. I tried to remind myself that, underpants incident aside, I was good enough to get the part, I was the new star of the show, and technically, this was still my first day of work.

Two days into the shoot, I'd already worked a total of forty-eight hours and was surviving on less sleep than I ever thought possible. Was it the exhaustion that was making me mess up, or the fact that I was learning everything for the first time? Whatever the case, shooting kept getting held up because of my mistakes. Apparently my one student film hadn't quite prepared me for the rigors of shooting a one-hour drama, and so I was learning on the job.

To be fair, I *was* given a crash course in acting for television right before we rolled on the first scene. This consisted of Paul, looking over at me and saying, "Make sure you keep everything small, no big gestures. It all has to stay within the frame of the camera, but don't look into the camera unless we tell you to."

After another few hours of missed cues and frustrating takes, I was 99 percent sure I was about to be fired. Since the show was a combination of big-name writer/director/controversial script, the producers had all been on set every day, and I wanted to do the best job possible, but it was a little overwhelming with script changes, blocking changes, remembering when to speak, and getting back into character after they shifted the camera and the lights a million times. So far I'd managed not to lose it in front of anyone, but I was blinking back tears as Jo, the stage manager, came over.

"It's fine," she whispered, patting my arm. "Don't worry. This always happens. Just be patient with yourself, and you'll get the hang of it." I needed a supportive word so badly, I felt like hugging her. She squeezed my shoulder. "You'll see. Tomorrow will be better."

It was Emily Dean, who played my little sister Jessie, who helped me the most. Even though she was only eleven, this was her fifth pilot, and she'd done a bunch of movies. She was a showbiz veteran and my lifesaver, subtly teaching me how to hit my marks, how to tone down my acting for the camera, and how to convey more emotion with just my face. Ross was also great, and I learned just by watching him shoot the scenes that I wasn't in. That's where the lack of sleep came in—when I could have (should have) been napping, I was either learning my lines, watching other scenes, or lying on the couch in my trailer, feeling terrified that this was my last day on the set and that the next day I'd most likely be going back to Michigan to become an accountant.

We finished the scene on the fifth take, and I went back to the trailer, where I had learned to cry silently so as to avoid sparking rumors around the set that I couldn't hack it ("Did you hear Amy sobbing in her trailer?"), stopping for fruit and Diet Coke at the craft services table on my way.

I was only through the first Silent Tears Kleenex when Ross poked his head in my trailer. "That was better!" he said, smiling broadly.

Little choking sobs started to clutch my chest. "Ross, they're going to fire me for sure. I've missed my mark at least twelve times today."

He sat down on the couch. The "three-banger" that Todd negotiated as part of my deal turned out to be a really large trailer, and I ended up with a sofa bed as well as a dining area, TV/DVD player, and chair/mirror. Actually, on day two (in another "pinch myself" moment) I realized that the trailer was approximately the same size as my dorm room.

"Don't worry . . . if they see something in you, they'll teach you what you need to know. Nobody gets fired for trying too hard, Amy."

Ross was rapidly becoming my new mentor. "What do people get fired for, then?" I said, hoping he'd dish the Hollywood dirt and take my mind off my imminent unemployment. Perhaps exhaustion was making me shallow.

"Well," he said, "I saw someone get fired after the very first table read for going 'This is where I'm feeling emotion, this is where I'll be crying,' and stuff like that." He laughed. "She was gone the next day. It's better to just go for it, and if it's wrong someone will tell you. You're already doing better than her, and she's done many more TV shows than you!" He wouldn't give me the woman's name, but he said it was "someone I'd seen on TV before." "She did fine—she got another job," he said. "It all worked out. No one really goes away in Hollywood unless they give up on themselves, or get into drugs, or start taking the situation for granted and burning bridges. Remember that, no matter what happens."

Ross was by far the most stable of all the cast members, myself included. He did yoga in his trailer, followed a macrobiotic diet, and could usually be found reading books in between takes, rather than smoking and gossiping like the rest of the cast. Already I'd decided that if I ever needed to confide in someone, it would be him.

I'd also decided to try to get through the rest of the week with only one box of Kleenex.

I TOLD MYSELF THAT I probably shouldn't, but of course I hooked up with Matt Pierce after his second day of shooting on the pilot, midway through the first week. Maybe I needed to take my mind off the stress of the new job. Or maybe it was Matt's blue eyes, and the fact that he was so attentive and interested while at the same time being breathtakingly gorgeous. Vince warned me not to do the "hook up and run" with a coworker, but I didn't listen. Besides, Matt's character was only incidental, so he wouldn't be in every episode. I kind of thought this made him a little less off-limits.

I didn't mean to kiss him, but once he'd given me a ride home from the set for the second day in a row, I felt like it would be rude to not at least ask him to come up to my suite for a drink. I could tell that he liked me and I thought he was so hot—I didn't know if I should share my "emotional distance" problem with him, but what could be the harm in just making out with him?

"You're doing great," he said, drinking a beer on the couch. "Everyone is surprised at how fast you're picking things up."

"Thanks," I said.

"It's so great that they cast a real person from the Midwest," he said. "I'm totally sick of all these fake perfect girls. No one in Iowa looks like this, for sure."

"What's that supposed to mean?" I said, grinning and poking him with my foot. "Are you calling me fat?"

His eyes widened. "No—oh my God! I'm saying you're more perfect than all the girls who are trying too hard."

"I'm just giving you a hard time," I said. He had probably been the best-looking person in his whole town in Iowa, but he was just like the guys who went to my high school. He was so sweet, I felt terrible about the fact that I was probably going to end up hurting him.

"It's probably a very bad idea if we get involved with each other, right?" I said, as I finished my second glass of wine and he leaned over to rub my shoulders. I knew I was going to let it happen.

"I don't think anyone has to know," he said. "Besides, I don't think I'm going to survive if I don't kiss you right now." He chuckled.

I turned around. "OK, but promise we'll still be friends? You are the first person who was really nice to me when I got here, and I don't want this to interfere with our friendship."

"I promise," he said, taking my face in his hands. "We will always be friends." Then he kissed me, and we had more wine, and before I knew it, the whole night had slipped away.

By the end of the first week, I was hanging out with him all the time, *and* I had managed not to embarrass myself, get fired, or lose the network millions of dollars with my ineptitude. Jo was right; the process was actually getting easier the more I practiced. I had, however, gained three pounds due to stress eating—something I hardly needed, considering I was still feeling the "you're too fat" vibe from the costume department.

I blamed craft services. Having been only recently introduced to this concept, I was surprised at the startling amount of free things to eat that could be found on a set. I started keeping a mental list the second day, just so I would remember to tell Vince and Carrie Ann about it when I saw them again.

1. Omelet bar. That's right. A person making omelets, for a show in which my character's name was in the title.

2. Fruit. Not just the mealy, questionably ripe kind of fruit that I'd grown accustomed to eating in the dorm. This was good fruit, cut up at regular intervals throughout the day. Plus, on the first day, the chef asked me what kind of fruit I liked, and now he was making it in case I wanted any pineapple, red seedless grapes, strawberries, or even watermelon, balled especially for me.

3. Cheese. Not just the Kraft American Singles kind of cheese like my mom used to make sandwiches out of when I was in the fourth grade. I'm talking about Swiss cheese cut into fancy squares, a wheel of Brie that seemed to never get hard or run out, and a variety of other amazing assorted cheese.

4. Candy. Free candy. Free M&M's, free giant Snickers bars, free Skittles, free Sweet Tarts, free Dove dark chocolates, *free candy*.

5. Popcorn. The one "empty carbs" item that you're never supposed to eat while watching your weight was, much to my chagrin, available in huge buckets all over the set. Caramel corn, cheese corn, regular, light, kettle corn, and all the rest. It also did not help that every trailer was equipped with a microwave, ensuring that the smell of delicious popcorn was almost always wafting through the set from somewhere.

6. Soda. Like, every kind of soda known to man, in seemingly endless supplies. Unfortunately, this cast seemed to go through Diet Coke at an exceedingly fast rate, so unless you hoarded your stash, you were almost guaranteed to end up with a warm can. Full-sugar Coke and Dr Pepper, on the other hand, were always cold.

7. Sandwiches of every variety: turkey, roast beef, vegetable for the multiple vegetarians on set. Stacked high with your choice of bacon (for the nonvegetarians) and the aforementioned assortment of wonderful cheese choices. How do you say no to a free sandwich?

8. Dessert bar. As in, after lunch, a tray of tiny fancy desserts appeared, including many things I had never had before. Pie, chocolate cake, cheesecake, profiteroles, cupcakes, and tiny tart-looking things with gelatinized fruit on top. Why the cruel torture?

9. Muffins. Blueberry muffins, banana nut muffins, cranberry muffins, chocolate chip muffins, kinds of muffins I never even knew existed. I swear, there was a muffin wrangler just for all the muffins.

10. Bagels, hot bagels, of every variety under the sun. Toasted, untoasted, sliced, topped with your choice of seventeen kinds of cream cheese.

The first four days of shooting, all bets were off. Then slowly, insidiously, I began to notice that not only was I the only one who could consistently be found at the craft services table as they put out each "course," but that my costumes were beginning to be even tighter than before.

And so, the dilemma: while the "starving college student" side of me wanted to stuff most of these items into my coat and run from the set whooping like a child or someone recently released from a refugee camp, the "newly employed actress on a Hollywood television show bearing my name" side of me concluded that eating all of these things every day was producing even more weight, something that had already been mentioned as undesirable. Still, it was a cruel irony to put this amount of fancy free food in front of someone who, up until very recently, was poor and hungry, ate when confronted with stress, and could not, no, *would* not say no to free chocolate cake.

To compound the craft services dilemma, I couldn't shake the feeling that I should've been hoarding this food, in case I woke up from this dream and wasn't making outrageous money as the star of a cool TV show. Still, I didn't want to get a reputation as someone who was stealing food from the craft services table, so I willed myself to walk numerous times per day past three tables filled with food so bountiful and luscious looking, it might have actually been a psychological test.

WHILE I WAS TRYING to avoid the craft services table, I discovered that the many smokers on set had fashioned a makeshift smoker's lounge in back of the set for the main house. I started spending some quality time there, smoking cigarettes during the times I was not trying to frantically learn lines before scenes or watching the other actors to try to see what they were doing right. I only had to hang out there for two days before I started hearing the rumors about Sara, better known as the Girl Who Got Fired from the Pilot.

Auditions had been going on for several months for this lead character, with limited success, since everyone was deemed either "too Hollywood" or "too overdramatic" to convincingly play the role. Then Sara had been cast, the pilot was shot, and everyone thought things were fine until they all got calls from their agents about a sudden reshoot. Everyone had called Sara, but no one ever found out the real story of what happened, so it was still this big weird mystery and everyone was still talking about it, especially since the recasting had actually happened, and now we were redoing the pilot, which apparently is something they never do. What could be so bad that it would cause someone to actually get fired, thus costing the network hundreds of thousands of dollars to reshoot? No one knew for sure.

One person said she committed suicide, then someone else said they'd seen her the week before. Michele's theory was that Josh didn't like her. She was suddenly fired under circumstances that were unclear (rumors ranged from "she wasn't Midwestern enough" to "politics within the network" to "she and the girl playing her little sister Jessie didn't look enough alike"). Since the show had a preorder for at least nine episodes in addition to the pilot, the network started putting serious pressure on Josh to recast the lead in time for the pilot to start reshooting on Monday so the show could still be released in time for the fall lineup. That's where I came in.

During one of the many other cigarette breaks during the day, I learned that my "best friend" Michele McCann was also a show business veteran at age twenty-one. This was her fourth pilot. Also, she was frustratingly thin. She had, without a doubt, not an ounce of fat on her entire body. Finally I broke down. "How do you stay so . . . skinny?" I said, hoping that I wasn't insulting her.

"Well, you really just cut down on your carbs and reduce your total caloric intake until you've reached your desired weight—of course, it might be a little harder for you, because you've got a bigger frame. You could stand to lose about ten pounds, to start," she said, taking a drag off her skinny Virginia Slim. "If the show takes off, they're going to want us to look more . . . similar. Do you know what I'm saying? Similar? I mean, this isn't *Ugly Betty*."

Her shiny chestnut hair offset her sparkling brown eyes and clear white skin as she cast a knowing glance across my body.

"Right," I said, "I totally know what you mean."

"I do four or five spinning classes a week," she said seriously. "Then I do the elliptical, then weights. Figure at least two hours a day, or just stop eating and that might get you there, but you're not going to be toned if you just do it that way." She was at least as militant about the daily maintenance of her perfectly taut, muscular abs as she was about finding clothing small enough to show them off. "Your body is your instrument, and you have to have absolute discipline over it, or this business will eat you alive."

This was a lot for me to take in all at once. "When was the last time you had pizza?" I said, praying the answer was "last week." I already didn't like Michele at all—she wasn't even trying to hide her affair with Greg Forster, and the two of them were always talking to the writers, trying to get the size of her part increased. I found her "being nice to me" thing very transparent.

She crinkled her perfect nose. "Ugh—not for years. I'm completely organic. You really have to be if you want to take your career to the next level. Really, it comes down to this: do you want to eat that crap, or do you want to be successful? If you just want to eat junk food, there are like a million people I know who want your part in this show. In fact, my best friend auditioned for the reshoot, and we totally thought she got it until they brought you in at the last minute. Everyone in town was really surprised when the network went with an unknown from Iowa."

I started to say, "I'm from Michigan, and you have anorexia," but Josh walked up with one of the network executives. "How's it going, girls?" he said. "Just wanted to let you know—we added a new scene this morning. It's at the beach." Michele's eyes went immediately down to the bagel in my hand, and my heart sank. I tried to think of the last time I'd worn a swimsuit. So unfair! Technically it was still winter when I left Michigan.

Michele chimed in again. "Josh, I was just telling Amy how glad we are to have someone new and so talented in the cast. We're all really excited about the show."

Josh looked over at me. "Great, Michele," he said. Maybe he had some idea how fake she was, I thought hopefully. I tossed my bagel in the trash and went back to my trailer to learn the lines for the new scene while simultaneously vowing never to eat again. Michele was definitely a bitch, but she might have been right; I probably needed to lose weight to stay competitive in this world.

EVERY DAY WHEN I arrived on set, my costumes were already in my trailer. Having been told on the first day that it was customary to try on all the costumes when you arrive (thus giving the wardrobe department ample time to make needed adjustments), I optimistically tried on the first one, which was invariably too small, then moved on to others (also too small). After a few discouraging days of this, I surmised that the wardrobe department was still holding on to the hope that I might go from a size six to a size zero overnight, and they'd been neglecting to make the necessary alterations. This resulted in a never-ending trek between my trailer and the wardrobe department, holding my tiny costumes in my hand and praying that we wouldn't have a repeat of the underpants incident.

A few days into the second week of shooting, I faced Lola with a forced smile. "This one doesn't fit either," I joked. I was getting sort of fed up with the whole "we didn't have time to let out your costumes" thing, but I figured she had enough to deal with. I certainly didn't want to ruffle any feathers by pulling a diva move like complaining about my costumes during the shooting of my big break. Also, I really didn't know the hierarchy of anyone on the set, and I didn't want Lola narking me out to the network, claiming I wasn't a team player. My only consolation was that no one at the studio or the network had ever mentioned my weight, even though I was clearly larger than the rest of the actresses. Michele speculated that the probable reason for this was that they were going to "try out my angle" for the test audience, and then they'd let me know. "It happens all the time," she said. "My friend got called in for a pilot, and at the end they asked her to come back to test, but they said they wanted her to be 'more attractive' by the next day. I mean, isn't that weird? Like, aren't you your most attractive every time you go into an audition?"

One thing was for sure—if they expected me to be "similar" to Michele McCann by the time we started shooting season one, I was going to have to swear to never eat pizza again.

A WEEK AFTER SHOOTING WRAPPED on the pilot, I was still trying to sleep off the exhaustion when suddenly there was a furious knocking at the door of my suite. Since I was positive I'd put the DO NOT DISTURB sign on the door after dragging myself back to the hotel at four A.M. on the last Friday night of shooting, I could not imagine who could be knocking on the door, especially at 11:00 at night. In my experience (at least in the past three days, when I'd actually been there and not the studio), housekeeping came in the morning.

"Go away!" I groaned. "I'm sleeping!"

More knocking. Good Lord. I felt like a grumpy three-year-old on the verge of a tantrum. I pushed my sleep mask up onto my forehead, pulled on some pants, and flung open the door in a rage. "What do you—"

I stopped abruptly as I beheld Vince, complete with many bags, on my doorstep.

"Vince? What are you . . . ?"

I trailed off as he grabbed me up in a huge hug. "Hello, darling!" he said excitedly. "How's my TV star?"

"Oh my God!" I screamed. "What are you doing here? How long are you staying? Isn't this place amazing?" I wanted to cry from relief at seeing a familiar face, and to immediately tell him everything that had happened since I'd been gone.

I was screaming, and he was screaming, and after a minute, I thought maybe we'd woken up every guest at the hotel. I pulled Vince and his suitcases into the room and shut the door, in case the security guards came looking for the source of the noise. He was as excited as I was. "Aim—I turned in my final projects and I'm done with school. I . . . live here now!"

All at once I forgot all about the fatigue, we ordered room service, and he gave me the scoop. He'd been amassing credits for a double major, but then the guidance counselor for his department had told him he had taken enough to finish his degree. The dean of the business school had called Vince's father, a prestigious Michigan alumnus himself, to congratulate him on Vince's success, after which Vince's father had promptly called to inform him that he was to start the following Monday as a marketing manager in the family business. After which Vince had filed his graduation papers, taken the rest of the money from his college fund, and ridden a Greyhound bus to Los Angeles.

Carrie Ann and I had been friends with Vince since we all moved into the dorms freshman year, when he was dating our next-door neighbor, a beautiful dancer named Scott. After he and Scott broke up, Carrie Ann and I had gotten Vince in the friend divorce and had been living happily ever after. An aspiring stylist a year ahead of us in school, Vince was always on the verge of giving it all up and moving to San Francisco, Los Angeles, or New York to "be with sane people." Growing up gay in Michigan, the son of a wealthy businessman—not a cakewalk, to say the least. Only the allure of the free tuition and cigarette money promised to him by his father in exchange for a college degree in a "normal" subject like business had kept him in Michigan. And now he was free.

"What are you going to do for work?" I said. I knew his father had probably cut him off as soon as he mentioned he was opting not to work for the family business.

"You know what?" he said. "Something will work out. This has already been an amazing month—for both of us!" he said, still high on having broken free from the Midwest. "It's about time I started living my life for me. I'm totally going to find Perez Hilton and make him my boyfriend, and we are going to live happily ever after."

And with that, Vincent Ferrillo became a permanent resident of Los Angeles and I got 100 percent less lonely.

A FEW DAYS AFTER Vince's arrival, I came home to find my first paycheck from the network waiting for me at the front desk. Since I knew it was going to be more money than I had ever seen in one place in my life, I took the still-sealed envelope up to the suite so I could have my conniption fit in private.

Even after taxes and many other things were taken out, I was pretty sure this one paycheck accounted for more money than my mother made in a year. Mostly, I was excited to have the big paycheck so I could start helping her with the bills, get a car, and buy some new clothes. OK, so I wasn't totally altruistic in my intentions, but my heart was in the right place.

With Vince by my side, here's how I spent my first big paycheck:

1. Bought three pairs of fancy jeans (one Blue Cult, one Citizens of Humanity, and one Rock & Republic). Was surprised to discover that, despite my procrastinatory attitude toward dieting, I was already wearing a smaller size than when I left school. Maybe all of Lola's wishful thinking was actually working by osmosis.

2. Leased one brand-new BMW X5 SUV, white. Physically could not stop myself after Vince told me that this was the exact car driven by Maggie Gyllenhaal (though he may have been making this up just to make me get the car—not sure). Perhaps also attempting to make up for the fact that in high school, I had an old Chevy Cavalier that looked like a shoe—a car that didn't even make it to my freshman year of college. Yay for my fancy new car!

3. Shopped for celebratory outfits. Despite my newfound wealth, I declined to purchase a $2,500 jean jacket with mink at the collar and sleeves that Vince suggested. "Who am I, J. Lo?" I said. Vince just laughed. During this shopping excursion, I actually consented to visit several thrift stores on Melrose. Usually I was bored after five minutes of pawing through used, stinky clothes, but somehow Vince always unearthed some rare and valuable treasure to add to his amazing collection of vintage clothing. On this trip, it was a lovely Hermès scarf, discovered just as I was hitting my thrift store limit.

4. Paid off one of my dad's hospital bills.

5. Made one advance payment toward my mom's mortgage.

6. Upgraded cellphone which by now I was mostly using to avoid Matt Pierce's calls and texts.

At first, my mother sounded mortified that her teenage daughter was offering to pay for these things that a parent should pay for, but as soon as I'd made it clear I wasn't taking no for an answer, I could hear the relief in her voice. After the checks actually arrived, she called at a time she would usually have been asleep, and we both cried when we started talking about how well everything was working out, and how maybe Dad was taking care of us from wherever he was. "Amy," she said, "I just wanted to say thank you. Your dad would be so proud."

It made me feel so good to hear this, and to finally be making a difference in my family's lives, that suddenly the stress of the job and the weight loss and the constant thinking I was going to be fired was all worth it. Right then, my life started to have meaning.

5

A FTER ANOTHER FEW WEEKS enjoying my friend and my newfound wealth, I got a call from Sondra Mitchell.

"We need you to make an appearance at the network upfronts in New York next week; that's when the pilot is debuting, and we want to make one hundred percent sure we have the green light for season one," she said. "It's very important to impress the advertisers—the more they like you, the more likely the show is to get picked up. We're putting the cast on a private jet; we'll have a car pick you up on Tuesday morning. Oh, and Amy—when you come back, we'll need to have the first of several meetings about your media strategy."

Even after the extremely personal Sondra interview on the first day, the grueling hours shooting the pilot, and the snarky comments from Michele and Lola about my appearance, I was definitely still not at the "jaded" point with the job yet. In fact, if Sondra had told me I had to go to Alaska and carve the name of the show into a block of ice while dressed as an Eskimo, I would've gone willingly. The fact that I had to go do something for work *and* I got a free trip to New York out of it was just more icing on the already-delicious cake. Private jet? Chocolate sprinkles on the icing on the cake.

If I was excited about my first first-class flight on the way out to California for the audition, I was positively geeked out about the prospect of flying on a private jet for the first time. In fact, every time something like this happened, I tried to remind myself not to get used to it, that indie film people didn't need money for their art. Still, I had to admit—it did feel good to have money. I was in the middle of a chorus of "I hit the big time . . . I'm on a private jet! Whoop whoop!" when my phone rang and I saw Carrie Ann's number and re-alized there was something else that was going to make this trip even better—Carrie Ann was going to be in New York at the same time.

She had sailed through auditions for Broadway Bound, a program put on by the UM drama department every year to get theater kids "in touch" with the Broadway experience by sending them to New York during summer break. Since school was over, she was due to start Broadway Bound any minute.

"Hello? Carrie Ann?" I said. "Are you in New York right now?"

"Yes I am!" she said. "I was just calling to give you my New York address! I've been here for three days, and I love it already!"

"Well, guess what?" I said excitedly. "I'm coming there in two days, on a private jet, and my show is putting me up at a fancy hotel. Can you stay with me for three days? We can eat room service, catch up, and watch movies! It will be so fun! I can't wait to see you! Say yes!"

She shrieked. "Oh my God . . . yes yes yes! I'm so excited to see you and hear everything about the pilot, and Vince, and every-thing! I'll text you when I'm done with class. Amy, wow . . . this is going to be great! I can't wait to see you! We can explore the city together!"

Two days later, I felt cooler than ever when the network sent a limo to take me from the hotel to LAX. I was taken to a secret part of the airport I didn't even know existed, which I immediately dubbed

Airport Room of the Rich and Famous. This is the room where celebrities have their passports/IDs checked, go through security, and wait for their flights so the paparazzi won't get to them. After all, Catherine Zeta-Jones can't be seen doing things that common people do, like waiting in line at baggage claim.

The private jet was beyond everything I ever thought it would be—a whole plane of first class! Fancy leather seats, food that you requested before the flight, and a flight attendant to bring you things like freshly made skim cappuccinos and just released issues of *People* magazine and *US Weekly* for the flight. The air even seemed smoother when flying in a private jet. Is it possible that for more money, you can fly even higher, up to the really good air? I'd heard that Air Force One flies at 45,000 feet. Maybe that's where we were.

My lack of knowledge of the trappings of the rich and spoiled never ceased to amaze and amuse Michele McCann, who I wanted to kill 99 percent of the time. "Have you never done anything?" she laughed when I picked up the phone and stared at it. I gave her a "ha ha, you're so funny" look as I dialed my mom's number (from the plane!). I wondered what Michele was like in high school. Was she fat? Was she a cheerleader? Was there anything about her that would allow me to ever get the upper hand? I knew it was taking all of her available acting skill just to pretend like she liked me, and that she was longing to see me get fired so her friend could take my job. Still, I was determined to enjoy every moment of my newfound success, her snarky Hollywood attitude aside.

My mom was excited to hear from me, though she seemed appalled by the concept of the phone in the plane. "Isn't that expensive?" she kept saying. "Don't waste your money!" I cupped my hand over the phone and my mouth at the same time in a lame attempt at privacy, whispering "It's free, Mom—it's all free," to which she replied, "I still don't believe this job, Amy." Finally, she relented. "Send me a postcard from New York, and tell Carrie Ann I said hi!" she said. "I can't wait for your show to come out! I've told everyone to watch for it in the fall!"

Since the event was the very next day and we had so little time to prepare, during the flight we had a mandatory marketing meeting where Sondra whipped out another bullet-pointed list, explaining that the "upfront" is the chance for the advertisers to preview the shows, that it was really important, and that we all had to make an effort to talk to as many media people as possible. There was also something about us posing in an *Autumn Leaves* photo booth at the after-party at a restaurant called Cipriani. I tried to take it all in, even attempting a few notes, but I was still so excited about the private jet, seeing New York for the first time, and seeing Carrie Ann that already I was tired from smiling.

TWO HOURS AFTER WE landed, Carrie Ann and I had made a picnic of expensive room service food on one of the super-fancy hotel bedspreads.

"I can't believe they're paying for all of this, Aim," she said, her mouth full of $35 chopped chicken salad. "You are, like, the ultimate rags-to-riches girl."

I laughed, nodding my head. Apparently, my being cast in the show was still the talk of the school, even though the news had had a few months to cool off. Carrie Ann caught me up on drama department gossip as we dug into sweet potato fries lovingly laid out for us on a silver platter. I was thrilled to be eating again, since the wardrobe department had taken my real measurements and had time to make costumes in the right sizes before we started shooting season one.

If we started shooting season one, that is. Sondra had made it sound like our entire future was resting on how the advertisers reacted to the pilot screening and our appearance at the upfront. I was trying to put this out of my head as Carrie Ann told me everything about school.

"Throw me the key to the minibar," she said, climbing over the pile of rubble. "I want to see what kind of wine fifty dollars buys you in this place." She laughed, pulling out a half-sized bottle of merlot and holding it up for examination. "Did you see this list of prices? Good Lord! You know, we could go down to the corner deli and buy, like, seventeen bottles of Strawberry Hill for the price of this little guy."

"Yes," I said. "But then we'd be wasted, and we'd have to pay for it ourselves."

Carrie Ann laughed, attempting a piroutte on the bed. Even though she was only nineteen, everyone was convinced she was going to end up on Broadway in the next couple of years—her nickname in the department was Baby Bernadette. Hanging out with her was the one thing I missed about school.

"We should go out on Thursday—you can show me everything!" I said. "Empire State Building, Coney Island—I have always wanted to come here."

She laughed. "I haven't been here for long enough to find my apartment. But I think I can get us there—it's nice, especially if you like Dominican food." She was determined to replicate the life of a Broadway hopeful, right down to the noisy third-floor walkup apartment above a restaurant that smelled like empanadas. "It's the 'humble beginnings' part of my biography story on A&E," she said, jumping up and down on the bed. "Wait till you see the place I'm taking voice class—it's right down the street from where they do *Phantom of the Opera*!

"So tell me again about shooting the pilot!" she squealed. "How are things going with Matt? Did you get to meet any more famous actors? This is so totally exciting—it's all happening for us!"

That night, we stayed up way too late, talking about our dreams and watching movies on pay-per-view. "Naomi Watts," Carrie mumbled as she nodded off. "There's a girl who never gave up on her dreams."

★ ★ ★

"JUST FOLLOW ME AND Greg," said Ross, putting his arm around me. I must have looked nervous as we waited backstage to go out and introduce the show at the upfront. Perhaps this was due to the fact that somehow, in the list she'd distributed on the plane, Sondra had neglected to mention that our first-ever public appearance as a cast was to be held at 2:00 P.M., on a Wednesday, in Madison Square Garden.

We were to follow the cast of the network's most popular one-hour drama—an order strategically planned by the network to leave the audience as excited as possible by the time they saw us and our brand-new pilot. "What if they hate it?" I whispered, and Michele shushed me. She looked nervous too, but apparently it was easier to focus her energy on making me feel stupid. I craned my neck from the backstage area to see the audience members, trying to calm myself down. Suits as far as the eye could see. Oddly, the suits were being worn by people who looked to be my age or a little older. Why were all the advertisers twenty-two years old?

"Agency people," said Greg Forster, sneering. It was 2:00 P.M., but he already smelled like the Johnnie Walker Green Label he always seemed to have handy. "Like some fucking kid in a suit knows what constitutes good TV." I looked over at Michele incredulously, as if to say "I get shushed and he doesn't?" but I already knew she'd be avoiding my gaze. She wouldn't dare say anything to him, no matter how belligerent he got. In the Hollywood hierarchy, at least for that moment, Greg outranked her, and she was nothing if not aware of her place in the system (even though she was constantly trying to ascend to the top). "Shits in suits," he kept muttering, leaning against the wall, and I silently prayed he'd pull himself together for the speech so that I wouldn't have to call my mother and tell her the dream was over, and that I'd be moving back home.

The order was set: Greg and Ross first, then me (the newcomer), then the rest of the cast would walk onto the stage; we'd say a few words about how we were really excited about the new show, how it was great to be there, and how we were looking forward to meeting them in person at Cipriani. Standing next to Ross, I said a mental prayer that he'd be doing most of the talking. All we needed was for Greg to start shooting his mouth off about how much he hated network executives. I was no expert, but "shits in suits" sounded like something people would remember when it came time to make important decisions about advertising dollars.

The emcee for the afternoon was a comedian named Dave McGinnis, and I could hear his witty onstage banter wrapping up. "Get ready," said Ross. And just like that, we were walking onstage and introducing ourselves. Greg was even cordial and funny, which somehow made me respect his acting skill a little more.

The rest of the day was a blur of new faces, and chatty conversation, and people pulling me aside and telling me how good they thought the show was, but I really couldn't tell if it was real or if it was all a façade, like Michele's "best friends" act when other people were watching us. Even weirder, I was stationed for two hours outside the *Autumn Leaves* photo booth so that network executives could have their picture taken with me, but Sondra told me in no uncertain terms that I was not supposed to ask them about whether they'd support the show: "The talent has no business talking to the advertisers about the fate of the show." But by the end of my two hours, when I had smiled so many times my face ached once again, I had "Are you going to sponsor my show?" on the tip of my tongue and could barely contain it.

"Wow, are you antsy?" said Ross, walking up to relieve me. "You look a little like you've had too much coffee."

"That bad, huh?" I said, trying to laugh it off, but the obsessive thoughts were getting really out of control. I grabbed Ross's arm and pulled him behind the back of the booth, trying to keep myself to a loud whisper. "Let me get this straight—*all* of these people know if the show is going to get picked up, and yet they're casually eating crab puffs and drinking champagne like it's no big deal? Do they not know how important this is?" This last part came out louder than I intended it to, and Ross put his hand over my mouth. "Shh-hhh . . . they don't know. They have to vote, or at least reach a consensus, for something to get picked up. Besides—half of these people are just low-level assistants at the agencies who just want some free food and pictures with some famous people. You probably know more than they do."

He took his hand off my mouth cautiously, as if to see if I was going to start screeching again. Instead I took a deep breath and let it out slowly. "OK—I'm sorry. I'm just getting myself a little too excited. Aren't you dying to know?"

Ross laughed. "Careful—you can't get too attached to the outcome with this industry. Everything could go away in one minute. You have to just focus within, and try not to let the external details bother you too much."

I stared at him for a second. "You are totally serious about this," I said, still trying not to jump up and down. "You're not nervous at all?"

"Nope. If this falls through, then that's just the way of things. But what you're experiencing right now—that's what's right for you. I'm just saying you have to take things with a grain of salt, Amy. Everything's OK right now, you know what I mean?"

I tried to understand and really get what he was saying, but in truth I was dying for the future, dying to know if we got the full pickup, and dying to know if I was staying a working actress living in Hollywood, or going back to being a college student in Michigan. Maybe the be-Zen-about-everything mentality worked for him because he'd already experienced success and was speaking from the other side, but I wasn't feeling it. I wanted to know immediately if not sooner.

I'D BEEN BACK FROM New York for two days and was still trying to keep myself from obsessing 24/7 about whether the show was officially getting picked up when I came home to find Vince packing excitedly. "Aim—I found an apartment," he said. "It's a one-bedroom, it's in West Hollywood, and it's *mine mine mine*! There's totally room for both of us, in case you can't sleep and want to stay over. We could get a Chinese curtain thing and a fold-out couch. It will be just like *Three's Company*."

"Wasn't Jack *not* gay in that show?" I said, laughing. I was excited that he was having good luck in L.A. too, if a little shocked at the speed with which he'd found an apartment. "Where's the place?" I said, pulling a Perrier out of the minifridge and plunking down in one of the overstuffed chairs. I couldn't believe he was actually *choosing* to leave the hotel, after all that time in Michigan when he was telling me how cool it would be to live there.

"It's right down the street, at Fountain and Laurel," he said. "I already have a cute neighbor who was laying out by the pool when I went to sign the lease. I actually think he was on that show *Passions* . . . I love it already!"

I understood his desire for independence, but for some reason the knowledge that he was leaving made me want to start crying. I was barely keeping it together as it was, and without someone around all the time to bring me back down to planet Earth, I feared that I might never sleep ever again. As roommates, Vince and I had been a surprisingly good match, and I was sort of not encouraging him to get a new place, for selfish reasons. Having a roommate again, even for a short time, had somehow made the experience feel more real and more permanent, and Vince was the only person I really felt like I could be myself around.

"You're going *now*?" I said. "Don't we even get one last night together, my darling? How will I survive the shock of living alone again?"

"Call your boyfriend," Vince said, throwing the phone on the couch. "I'm sure he'd be thrilled to hear from you."

"Don't call him that," I said. Just as Vince had predicted, I was already tired of Matt Pierce.

"No time to lose," he said in a phony French accent. "I have furniture to buy, wall dressings to hang, fabric to drape! Plus, I have my first-ever private client meeting tonight." He stopped, lowering his voice and looking around. "It's one of the Desperate Housewives. I met her at the Coffee Bean while I was looking for Perez. Things happen fast here, baby!"

I laughed. "Congratulations!" I said. "I don't think you have to sign a stylist-client confidentiality agreement, though." He made a face and went back to his business.

I was in the middle of watching Vince pack up the (surprisingly large) amount of clothes that he'd amassed since arriving in L.A. when my cell phone started to buzz. "This is Elizabeth from Mindy Steinman's office at the network," said the serious voice. "Can you come down for a meeting at four o'clock today? Mindy just has a few things she wanted to discuss with you."

With that, I made Vince promise not to leave without writing down his new address and headed down to the posh network offices, where I got a secret thrill from being waved in at the golden gate.

I checked my watch as soon as I arrived, noting with surprise that it was 3:30 P.M. This meant that I had actually made it all the way to the west side, parked, and found the right office in under forty-five minutes, even in midday traffic on the 405, and that I was actually early for a meeting, an occasion rare enough to warrant a self-congratulatory pat on the back. I was sitting on the leather couch in an otherwise deserted-looking office, in the middle of a copy of *The New Yorker* I had in my purse for just such waiting occasions, when I heard a voice through the crack in the door.

"This just won't do, Elizabeth," it started. Then, more: "Did you go to college?"

A terrified voice replied meekly, "Yes, Ms. Steinman. Harvard."

"And . . . Harvard is still teaching English, I'm assuming?"

"Yes, Ms. Steinman." I cringed on Elizabeth's behalf.

"I'm just wondering then, Elizabeth, how it is that you have not yet mastered the basics of English required for you to write a simple memo. Please be aware of the fact that if you feel you're not up to handling this job, there are probably at least ten thousand film students out there who would do it for free."

"Of course, Ms. Steinman."

A disgusted sigh, then: "Elizabeth, Amy Spencer from *Autumn Leaves* is on her way in now. Please make sure she's brought directly to my office when she arrives, and let me know if she's late."

My watch said 3:45 P.M., and I was starting to get nervous. If I kept sitting outside the office and the door opened, Mindy Steinman would know that I was already there, and this poor Elizabeth girl would get in even more trouble. However, if I left and tried to come back, I might get in trouble. What was the right move?

The berating continued, and I couldn't bear to listen anymore. Finally, I made an escape to the hallway, where I stood outside the main office reading and rereading an article on the evolution of Wikipedia until exactly 3:55 P.M. As I opened the door to go back in, I felt a sense of relief when I saw that Elizabeth had made it out alive and was sitting at her desk.

"Hi there," she said flatly. "You must be Amy. Just have a seat, and Mindy will see you soon."

Four o'clock came and went, and I studied Elizabeth. She had longish blonde hair and was wearing a white cotton tailored shirt and black pants. Since she was typing what I was pretty sure was an "I hate my boss" e-mail, I surmised that she was not illiterate. She looked upset, but I wasn't even supposed to have heard the conversation, so I kept my nose in my magazine for what seemed like forever, checking my watch at five-minute intervals. What was she doing in there? Why did she want me there right at four P.M.? Was this some sort of psychological game? Was I waiting for a fate even worse than Elizabeth's?

At 4:42 P.M., Elizabeth's phone rang. She answered it and looked up at me. "Mindy will see you now," she said. As she hung up the phone, I thought I saw a look of dread on my behalf in her eyes, or maybe it was a "better you than me" look. Elizabeth had all the classic signs of an abused wife from my Psych 101 textbook, right down to being unsympathetic if she saw that someone else was going to get it.

"Amy, nice to see you. Shut the door and have a seat," said Mindy Steinman, executive producer. Maybe because I was so nervous at the final audition, I hadn't really noticed anything about her, but as I walked into her office, I came to realize all at once that Mindy Steinman was an impractically large and somewhat unkempt woman. With long, dishwater-brown hair curling around her round, pasty face and down her back, she was easily three hundred pounds. Because my parents trained me to think nice things about people of all sizes, I decided that she would have been great in a Boticelli painting, all fleshy curves and pale skin. Actually, she looked a little like Fran, the woman who owned the junk shop back in Bay City. Like Fran, she wheezed and lumbered like a freight train as she got up, poured herself a glass of water from a bar on the wall of her office, and settled herself back behind her large oak desk. As I watched her holding the water up to her fat lips, the thought of her eating made me a little nauseous. Suddenly, I felt trapped, and all at once I realized that Sondra Mitchell was, in fact, just the gargoyle at the gate of Mindy Steinman hell.

"Amy, the network just confirmed they're picking up *Autumn Leaves* for a preorder of thirteen episodes, which means we start shooting on July Fourth for season one."

"Oh my God—that's so great!" I said, trying to hide the relief in my voice. I then immediately doubted myself. I thought it was great.

Was it great? Did she want twenty episodes? Did things usually get picked up faster? Why did I let her make me so nervous?

She made a face. "Great? No, Amy, that's unheard of." She spat the words out like the unexpected and unwanted pits of grapes she'd thought were seedless. "Great," she repeated again, chuckling.

"Oh, I didn't know . . . I thought . . . I mean . . . that's fantastic! I'm really excited to be working on such a great show!" I stammered as I tried to dig myself out of the hole I'd gotten myself in. When did this meeting take a turn for the worse? I remembered the overheard Elizabeth conversation and vowed not to speak again until spoken to.

She'd already moved on to the next thought. "There are just a few . . . changes that the network has asked us to make, in order for the show to be as successful as possible. You want the show to be successful, right?" She leaned forward in her chair, scowling over thick black glasses, which had formed a dent in the fat on the side of her head.

I nodded. I wasn't sure I got whatever hidden meaning she was trying to convey. I started to squirm in my chair. What was she saying? Had *I* not mastered the English language?

"First off, we've decided to go a different direction with the writer of the show," she said. "So we won't be working with Josh anymore. The network thinks that the show has more potential as the next *Beverly Hills, 90210* or *The O.C.*, and Josh wasn't on board with that. So we've brought in a different team to retool." She paused momentarily, to see if I was getting all this. "This is going to mean we have to make you as commercially appealing as possible. Do you get what I'm saying?"

A sinking feeling began to grow in the pit of my stomach. Josh was gone? Why was this the first I was hearing about this? Could they just arbitrarily change everything like that? What did she mean by "commercially appealing"? I nodded, fighting the tears that were already starting to wet my eyes. Josh was so great—this show was his baby, and he'd fought to bring me in. I wanted to show solidarity with him, but there was no way I could quit, or even say anything about them getting rid of him. I had too much at stake, and my family was depending on me.

She leaned back in her chair, which groaned. "Listen, I'm not going to lie to you. I think your look is too 'regular folks' to work for the long term and the new direction. But Josh got his way with his 'authentic Midwestern girl,' and now it's too late to reshoot again.

"So," she continued, "if this is going to work, we're going to have to make some changes and make the best of it. We'll need to do some serious thinking about your weight."

As she lifted her arms in the air to gesture for emphasis, I watched in horror as the fat on her arms shook like pink wings and resisted the urge to stare. She paused for a moment.

"We focus-grouped the pilot, and I'm telling you, you barely squeaked by . . . I mean, this isn't an 'issues' show with one overweight character. Do you follow what I'm saying?" She stopped and leaned forward again, and I thought I saw a grin hidden somewhere in the fat rolls in her neck. "The other actress was let go because she didn't pass the focus group. It's too late for that now, but you seem like more of a team player. Is that right?"

I felt my heart drop into my stomach. Was it even legal for her to be saying these things to me? I felt like vomiting on her expensive desk. Somehow, I fought through the panicky feeling growing inside me long enough to smile weakly.

"Right," I said, summoning my courage. "Yes. Great."

She leaned forward again, propping herself up on chubby, trembling arms. "The first thing we'll need you to do is lose at least fifteen pounds. I don't believe you're really a size four . . . I had Lola in the wardrobe department send over your clothes, and they're all at least sixes."

My head started to spin. Yes, I had gained the freshman fifteen and not lost it, but isn't that what everyone does in college? Didn't they originally want a real Midwestern-looking girl? Was the show's new direction about a girl with an eating disorder?

She was dead serious. "We need you to be committed to the show, and that starts with your look. We start shooting season one in four weeks, and we need you to be *max* a hundred and fifteen pounds by then, or we really are going to have go another direction." With that, she opened up her desk drawer, pulled out a prescription bottle, and tossed it across the desk at me. "Here, try these. Once we get that weight down, we'll also need to develop a new persona for you, including your hair, your style, and your name."

Again, I nodded, steeling myself against the torrent of uncertain and scared tears I had inside. *It has to get better,* I kept telling myself. *At least the show's picked up. You can handle this. Just get through this meeting, and then you'll figure things out.*

"My . . . name?" I said weakly.

"Yes, we'll deal with that before the show comes out. 'Amy Spencer' is way too Michigan to capture the minds and hearts of teenagers across America. No little girls are going to want to be Amy Spencer. They want to be Mischa, or Lindsay, or . . . those girls from *The Hills.* You know what I mean. I'll have Sondra get in touch with you."

I could feel Elizabeth's eyes on me as I walked out of the office. I knew she'd heard everything, and I expected at least a sympathetic glance from her, since now I knew what she faced on a daily basis. Instead, she simply cast a disapproving glance at my thighs, then pursed her lips and sighed, as if she couldn't imagine how I could be thin enough in four weeks.

From that day on, Mindy Steinman was known to me only as Attila, and every time I thought of that first meeting, I felt the exact same feeling of dread.

6

"TURN THIS MUSIC OFF … MY God!" said Vince, hitting the pause button on my iPod with the toe of his boot. "Fifteen hundred songs, and all you can play is 'Agnus Dei' over and over again? This shit would make Richard Simmons want to commit suicide."

The day after my "we're going in a new direction and you're too fat" meeting with Attila, I was lying on my bed surrounded by diet books, listening to Rufus Wainwright, and trying to figure out the best way to lose fifteen pounds in thirty days *without* taking the mysterious black pills or ending up in the hospital. The meeting and her proclamation about how little she liked me had thrown me into a funk, which I was drowning in Diet Coke and frozen York Peppermint Patties I kept in my freezer, just for occasions such as this. I was mentally gearing up, preparing to never eat anything delicious ever again.

"I'm having a food funeral," I said grumpily. Clearly, the only way for me to keep my job was to lose the weight, and the only way to lose that much weight that fast was to stop eating entirely, or to eat only things that tasted like cardboard. "Go away, Mr. Six-Pack Abs Despite

Eating Taco Bell," I said, hitting play, then making a face at him and turning the music up even louder. I couldn't wait until he heard the "I'm Depressed" playlist I'd put together for that evening. "It's impossible!" I wailed. "I am trapped in a hell of my own making." I couldn't even imagine the thought of telling my family that the only good thing to happen to us in three years was gone because I couldn't suck it up and drop a few pounds. Besides, I was probably overreacting about the whole Mindy thing. Everybody has to sacrifice to get what they want, right? I mean, I didn't have to pay my dues with years and years of slogging around L.A. auditioning, so maybe this was just the inevitable price to be paid for something this good happening.

"Ugh—bite your tongue!" he said. "A million girls would kill for this job, and you have it. You'll figure it out. We're going out. And brush your hair, Sasquatch. If any celebrities happen to be there, I don't want you embarrassing me." I had to admit, having an overdramatic gay best friend was handy sometimes. He would never let me go outside until I was at least presentable, and somehow, he could tell me really offensive stuff without it sounding so bad. I'm pretty sure I would have killed Carrie Ann for that Sasquatch comment, but Vince could pull it off. I was in the middle of thinking how I wished *he'd* been the one to break the "you're too fat" news to me the day before when I remembered that I'd promised to go to some after-hours party with him at Maxfield, and instantly I began trying to strategize ways to get out of going.

He anticipated my every excuse. Before I knew it, he'd picked an outfit for me, I'd pulled a fashionable scarf over my still-unruly hair, and we were out the door, leaving the diet books strewn on the bed.

"ORDER SOMETHING GOOD, LIKE the fried portobello mushrooms," I said to him, gazing wistfully at the appetizers menu. So much delicious food, all of which was forbidden to me.

After three weeks on my Attila-mandated diet, I had lost exactly eight pounds (mostly from depression and stress) and gained a near-obsessive desire to eat vicariously through other people. I had accompanied Vince to Dolce, so we could both check out the restaurant for the first time and so I could watch him eat. Since I'd been on food restriction, I'd tried four different diets, one involving grapefruit and hotdogs, and had endured two ill-fated days on the Atkins diet, after which I decided that I'd rather get fired from the show than ever see another piece of steak. The Perricone Diet was out too, as I couldn't even stand the smell of salmon. Finally, I arrived at a modified South Beach–style diet that allowed me to eat enough to keep from going insane. This, of course, was all before I got used to just eating as little as possible, then just not eating at all. It is actually amazing how long the human body can survive on nothing but water and Diet Coke.

Vince ordered a cheeseburger, and I made do with a Chinese chicken salad, but without bread, dressing, or those good crunchy things. I was also looking forward to some black coffee for dessert, which had become one of the main parts of my new food pyramid, along with Diet Coke, water, and cigarettes.

Jon Voight walked by. "Do you think he'd introduce us to Angelina if we asked nicely?" I whispered to Vince, who laughed.

"Yeah, I bet he's never heard that before. Besides, aren't they estranged?" he said.

The people at the next table ordered fried calamari, and I watched with the intensity of a peeping tom as they dug in, dipping crusty fried bits into the cream sauce. This weight loss thing was hard; just when the pressure was on the most, it seemed like I was surrounded by delicious free food everywhere I turned—like when you learn a new word, then you hear it all the time. I knew that this was probably the previously unidentified price I'd have to pay for this good fortune falling my way, but somehow that concept wasn't making me any less hungry. I was 99 percent sure the only way to really lose that much weight was to stop eating altogether, and I was using that as a last resort.

"Did you try the pills?" said Vince, sipping a beautifully frothy full-fat latte. "I'll try them for you if you're scared." Vince had always been known for his fearless attitude toward the consumption of anything questionable, from food to drink to pharmaceuticals. He never got sick, went crazy, or lost his good attitude. In fact, Vince was the only person I'd ever known who had tried every kind of drug there was and was still not afraid to try the newest and latest.

I hadn't tried the pills Attila had given me, partially because I found the idea of taking drugs out of some unmarked bottle from an executive's desk creepy, and also because I was considering the weight loss a willpower thing I should be able to just do on my own. Still, if I didn't start losing more weight fast (like seven more pounds in the next seven days, to be exact), I was totally screwed. I finished the last of my salad and took a sip of Vince's latte, vowing that if I didn't lose two more pounds by the very next day, I was biting the bullet and trying the pills.

BY THE NEXT MORNING, I'd *gained* a pound and was starting to panic. I knew Attila (or at least one of her evil emissaries) would be there on the first day of shooting, if for nothing else then just to check on my weight loss progress. Now I *had* to take the pills.

I got out the bottle, which I'd been carrying around in my purse since the World's Most Awful Meeting, trying to work up the nerve to take one, or to call the police and report Attila as a drug dealer. As I rolled the unmarked bottle back and forth in my hands, I wondered what sort of clandestine transaction had to go on behind the scenes to end up with her having pills in her desk drawer, all handy like that. She was obviously not taking them herself, so maybe she just had them on hand for all the people she considered "overweight." But—where did they even come from? Did the network have its own doctor on staff, just for this sort of problem? Did she have a meeting with him or her first, to discuss how fat she thought I was? Moreover, if I needed medical marijuana to combat the stress of having her as an executive producer, would they be able to prescribe that? The curiosity was killing me. Still, despite the "new direction," I didn't even want to entertain the fact that they might give the job to someone else. I had bills to pay. This thing was bigger than me.

After twenty minutes of trying to work up the nerve, I finally opened up the bottle, shook out one of the pills, and swallowed it with water, hoping it didn't make me go nuts or have any other bad side effects. I then went up to the roof of the hotel to smoke cigarettes and watch the cars go by. Where were all those people going? Were they all taking pills too?

After an hour or so, the gnawing hunger in the pit of my stomach had started to subside. *This could work,* I thought, noting that I'd gone at least fifteen minutes without thinking about how much I wanted a Cinnabon. I did feel a little like I'd had too much caffeine, but that wasn't an unfamiliar feeling for me—in fact, I kind of liked it.

After a few days, I struck a balance with the pills—one in the morning, one in the afternoon, and one if I was going out at night (to keep me from drinking too many cosmos). The steady stream of pharmaceutical goodness successfully calmed my food obsessions. I kept the black pills with me in case I got hungry and some white pills (Xanax, I think) I got from Vince in case I got too jumpy, and beside my bed I kept some leftover blue pills prescribed by the student health doctor at UM for insomnia for when I really needed to sleep. I wasn't proud, but by July fourth I was a triumphant 114 pounds, a weight I couldn't remember being since the seventh grade.

★ ★ ★

WHEN WE SHOWED UP on set to start shooting season one, the first thing I noticed was that the living room looked different. "What happened to the nice furniture?" I said to Ross as we gathered around the main house set for a kickoff meeting with one of the producers.

"New direction," he said, sighing. "Focus groups thought that Peter and Michael were too rich . . . apparently having too much money is even worse than being gay. They toned it down during the break," he said. I laughed, relieved that he wasn't thrilled about the changes either and that my weight wasn't the only thing the focus group people didn't like. "Won't people be confused when they see the pilot, then your house looks different in the very next episode?" I said, trying not to sound naïve, bitter, and hungry all at the same time.

He laughed again. "Pilots are the most rarely shown of any of the episodes—they're where the studio and the network decide what works and what needs to be changed. Did you ever see the pilot of *Sex and the City*? Sarah Jessica Parker had a bob haircut, she talked straight into the camera, and one of the scenes had the four women eating Chinese food while sitting on the floor of Carrie's apartment. Most of that was changed by the first episode, but by the second season, it was all gone."

"What else did they change? Do I still have a sister? Do we still live in Malibu?" I said, half-kidding.

"Oh yeah, changes like that would require that they reshoot the pilot again, which they couldn't do. But . . . things like people's professions, or sets, or people's appearances . . ." He trailed off, sounding embarrassed. He'd obviously noticed my weight loss and was trying to avoid drawing attention to it. I loved him for that.

Michele McCann walked up beside us, and I could feel her eyes surveying my body. "Hi, guys," she said enthusiastically. "The new set looks great, right?" Ross excused himself immediately; privately he'd told me that he found Michele "chaotic" and that he tried to stay away from her. I had vowed to do the same if possible, though I was in most of her scenes. I noted with disappointment that she looked exactly the same—apparently the elusive focus group had approved of her, which was sure to only make her attitude worse. "Wow, you've really made a lot of progress toward your weight loss goals, Amy," she said coyly.

I waited for the other shoe to drop. "Only ten more pounds to go!" she said. *Wham!* I couldn't tell if she was being cruel and sarcastic, or if this was just her version of cheerful encouragement. Maybe I was too weak from lack of food to come up with an appropriately biting retort.

WE'D BEEN SHOOTING SEASON one for about three weeks, and despite the fact that the writing team was all different and we were on our third director since the pilot, I felt like things were falling into place and the cast was starting to gel. I was excited to go to work every day, and the scripts were actually getting pretty interesting— after the pilot where Autumn and Jessie's parents are killed and they go to live with their uncle and his partner in Malibu, we did the "new kid in high school" episode, then started on a new story arc where the two uncles get married and adopt the kids. Not only did I feel like I was getting a great education in acting for the camera, but from the buzz around the set, this show was actually going to be making a difference in the world.

The show's fall premiere was rapidly approaching when I got the call from Sondra Mitchell. "We'll need you in the office at eight A.M. sharp on Saturday, Amy. We've got a team assembled to focus on marketing and branding your persona," she said. "We've got a lot of work to do on you before the show premieres!" I noted with irritation that she knew Saturday mornings were the worst time to schedule meetings because of the long Friday-night shoots, and that I had never received so much as a "good job" for the not easy task of losing weight before shooting resumed, and now I was being reconstructed like the Bionic Woman.

While I'd been learning to subsist on amounts of food heretofore only tolerated by prisoners in POW camps, Attila had assembled a team of people to make me "marketable" enough to carry a major network show when it launched. Apparently making a brand out of me was going to require the services of more than a few professionals.

I ARRIVED AT THE network early on Saturday morning, delirious from shooting all night, and was immediately surrounded by the entire marketing team and handed a thick, spiral-bound report. I was shocked to find my own name on the cover. The office was packed with well-dressed, ambitious marketing types—all of whom were holding the report. As I read over the agenda for the day (page one in the "Amy Spencer report"), I was surprised to find that not only was the entire day dedicated to me, but that I had meetings scheduled approximately every ninety minutes until 7:00 that night. *What is going on here?* I thought. *Am I joining some kind of cult?*

"Um, what is all this?" I said to Kristen, the one girl in the marketing department I found remotely friendly. "Can this really all be for me?"

"Oh, yeah," she said, looking serious. "There have been so many meetings about you, making your strategy, crafting a new look, the whole thing. This is Super Saturday! The day when it all comes together!" She smiled excitedly, and I tried to smile back. I so wished someone had warned me about "Super Saturday!"

The kickoff meeting for Super Saturday started promptly at 9:00 A.M. Sondra Mitchell was the captain of this ship, and Attila was nowhere to be found. I imagined that, in typical Jabba the Hut style, she existed only in her office at the network, her tentacles of influence and evil reaching far and wide. Young, attractive marketing executives packed the conference room, filling all the chairs and leaning against the walls. I couldn't help but notice that most of them were staring at me.

Sondra opened up the "Amy Spencer" book, which made a cracking sound as she turned the pages. "As you are all aware from yesterday's informational briefing, the success of this show rides on our branding of Amy." She looked pleased with herself for the strategies she'd come up with, as well as completely uninterested in hearing what I thought. In fact, as she looked around the table at the no less than fifteen men and women assembled in the conference room, she made very little if any eye contact with me, as if she'd really prefer I not be there at all. I turned the pages of the Super Saturday book, stopping on a page called "Life History." It contained, in bullet-point form, everything I'd told Sondra at our first meeting, from my dad's death to who I'd had sex with to what high school I had attended. Super Saturday indeed!

"I'm just going to jump right in with one of the big line items to accomplish for today—the name change. Now, as we've discussed, we as a team feel that 'Amy Spencer' is not a powerful enough name for the girl who has the lead in this groundbreaking network show. While we thought 'Spencer' could work with anything, we agreed that 'Amy' is just too bland, so we've decided to change just the first name. I've asked you each to come up with a list of alternatives, and I wanted to jump right in with some brainstorming."

I watched in horror as each executive produced a list. They'd thought about alternate names for me? Didn't anyone want my opinion on this?

A pale, blond-haired man of about forty threw out the first shot. "I was thinking 'Carmen,'" he said seriously. " 'Carmen' has power and a little bit of Latina mystery."

"Hmmm . . . ," said Sondra. "Might be tough to sell to the Latina market. She doesn't have any Latin relatives, nor does she speak Spanish."

"Well, Christina Aguilera doesn't speak Spanish either, and she enjoys that market share," said Blond Guy. Still, no one looked at me.

"I was thinking more 'old Hollywood glamour'" said Sondra. "Who has something along those lines?" I sat back in disbelief, waiting to hear the next suggestion. "What about 'Lana'?" said Kristen. "Like Lana Turner. Lana Spencer could be our new Hollywood starlet." I tried to shoot Kristen an "et tu Brute?" look, but she carefully avoided my eyes. She'd obviously known about this for a while and hadn't said anything.

"Interesting, but sounds a little too much like a porn star . . . any others?" said Sondra. I sat back, relieved at least for the moment, since I hated the name "Lana."

"What about something unconventional, like 'Guinevere'?" said another of the young executives, this one a young-looking brunette in a suit. "Strange names are really big these days. At least that would get her name in the papers. I've got 'Guinevere,' 'Pixie,' and 'Fabergé.'"

I laughed out loud at the prospect of introducing myself as "Pixie Spencer" and was met with several uncomfortable glances. Was I not on board? Was I not being a team player?

"Simpler," said Sondra. "Too complex, and then she seems inaccessible, like Samaire Armstrong. She's cute, but her team should have changed that name. Also, 'Fabergé' might be too 'urban,'" she said, being careful to make the politically correct air quotes with her fingers.

"What about 'Star'?" said another nondescript executive. " 'Star Spencer' is the perfect combination of Hollywood and real folks." A hush fell over the room as everyone nodded their heads.

"Hmmm," said Sondra. "Still a little porn-ish, but we can spin it as a childhood nickname, like Miley Cyrus's team did with her," she said, continuing to not look at me. "We'll go with that for now."

My mind was racing. Could they just change my name like that? Weren't there court papers involved? What about my driver's license?

Did I have to start calling myself Star from now on? What was I going to tell my mom? Amy was her mother's name . . . she was not going to like this. Shouldn't I even get a vote? Is this how it went for Portia de Rossi (Amanda Lee Rogers), Carmen Electra (Tara Patrick), or even Bob Dylan (Robert Zimmerman)? Did I even have a choice in this matter? Had I even lost control of my name?

I was just about to raise my hand to ask a few of these questions when Sondra started again, already using the new name like they hadn't just decided on it the moment before. "Another objective of this meeting is to introduce Star to the individual members of her team, her points of contact for things like appearances, endorsements, and things like that. Kristen, you've been assigned to media—magazine requests, promotional appearances for the show, and requests for interviews. Offers for other types of work can be referred directly to Todd Whitley at International Artists Unlimited. You know Todd, right?" Kristen nodded, looking over at me guiltily.

"Now," Sondra continued. "Many of you will recognize Brynn Harper, a great stylist who has worked with everyone from Brittany Murphy to Mandy Moore. Brynn is just great at finding the swan in the ugly duckling!" she said cheerfully, casting a glance in my direction. "Brynn will be working with Star this afternoon, just getting the hair, skin, and makeup choices up to speed for casual appearances and off hours, and also working on poses for candid photography."

I looked around at everyone taking notes. What, exactly, was the definition of "casual appearances and off hours"? Did they mean the grocery store? Did I have to adhere to some sort of standard outside of the eighteen hours a day I was on the set? Was I contractually obligated to wear makeup at all times? I started to sweat.

She continued. "Gina from wardrobe will be coordinating with Brynn on an ongoing basis regarding designers' requests for placement on the show; fashions they'd like to see worn off set, exclusively and nonexclusively; and appropriate fashions for casual use. Gina works with Lola, so she'll be making a weekly report of Star's weight and measurements."

I wanted to crawl under the table. If I had a personal version of hell, I'm pretty sure it would include a brand-new name and a weekly report of "weight and measurements."

"Tim here is going to be working with Star on media training. As we all know, this is a controversial show for the network with some challenging content, and we want to make sure all of the cast members, especially Star, are on the same page so the press doesn't misinterpret any of our messages based on offhand comments. Tim's team also coordinates the placement of promotional items like *Autumn Leaves* merchandise, so if you need an 'I Love My Two Gay Dads' sweatshirt, go to him."

Everyone at the table chuckled, and I realized that I had just seen Sondra Mitchell make a joke.

"I'll be handling Star's etiquette, on the set, during appearances, and after hours. That will be the last meeting of the day. On Monday morning, we'll reconvene here with individual reports on progress and next steps, and coordinate this into a full-scale presentation to Mindy on the status of this situation by the close of business. Are there any questions?"

I left the first meeting with the creepy feeling I'd first experienced with Mindy confirmed and growing. I felt like I was on the ascent part of a really scary roller coaster, and at any minute I was going to look down and see just how bad it was going to get. Maybe I was finally seeing the reality of the Hollywood life, but it was definitely too late to do anything about it. There really was no turning back.

FOUR HOURS LATER, BRYNN Harper and I sat at a table strewn with Polaroid shots of my face. "Listen, I'm not going to lie," she said, pointing at one of the photos. "When you smile with your mouth open like that, you look like someone's retarded cousin. Your tooth-to-gum ratio is all wrong, and your smile creates three folds in your neck. We really have a lot of work to do to get you ready."

My first session with stylist to the stars Brynn Harper had not begun well. After what must have been a hundred Polaroids taken in an attempt to capture and refine my best "angles" for future photographic and publicity purposes, I was told that the smile I had used in every school photo since I was five made me look like I was both mentally challenged and fat. She also hated my hair and informed me that my "personal style is absolutely tragic, and not in a Kelly Clarkson–'before'-picture kind of way."

"You need to go home and practice your good faces every day in the mirror, so when you do personal appearances, the magazines have a number of good shots to choose from," she said earnestly. "If you keep making that face, you are going straight into the 'star bloopers' edition of the *Enquirer*. Have you noticed how much more press Keira Knightley is getting now than when she first started? Somebody obviously told her that she looks much better when she keeps her mouth closed. Have you seen her giant teeth?"

I was trying not to be offended—Brynn knew everything about the construction of a celebrity image, and the network was paying her big bucks to "streamline" me before the show premiered. However, she was acting like I was her biggest-ever challenge. In fact, I thought the hair and makeup department was doing a pretty good job on my hair, and I knew I didn't have anything glaringly wrong with me, like a big bump in my nose. I was thinking about telling her to get over herself when she started in again, taking out a magnifying glass and holding it up to my face.

"Your skin is bad . . . not Cameron Diaz bad, but broken out and blotchy nonetheless. What do you use to wash it, a washcloth and Dial soap?" She laughed. At me.

"Um . . . yeah, that's exactly what I use," I said, laughing. "Actually, I'm not kidding. It's always worked for me."

"Oh, you're killing me," she said. "I can't believe the makeup department on your show hasn't told the producers about your skin problems. We need to get you to a dermatologist to get some of those pimples injected right away. Here's the number of the guy Leo DiCaprio uses," she said, scribbling the name at the top of a pad of pink Post-its that had previously been used to stick the words "Don't Make This Face!" on the Polaroids.

"Also, you need to get on a regimen of products, so when the magazines ask you, you can tell them what you're using. I'll have La Mer send some things over, and you'll probably like Dr. Hauschka as well. If nothing else, you could just start using Proactiv like Jessica Simpson—maybe they'll use you in their infomercials!"

I started to internally panic at the list of products and services that seemed to grow longer by the minute. The big paychecks *had* started to come in regularly, but I had vowed to help my mom and my brothers and bank a lot of the rest for the future, and I wasn't sure if I would have to pay for this stuff myself. How to ask without incurring her wrath?

"Do I have to pay . . . I mean, how much is all of this stuff?" I said, attempting to choose words with the least potential for mockery.

She laughed again. "Oh, that is so cute. Honey, don't worry—it's all covered. If your show gets big, you're not going to be paying for much of anything. You'll see."

Brynn had also brought a huge collection of designer clothes in an attempt to construct some kind of personal style for me before the show launched and I embarrassed the entire network with my collection of colorful vintage T-shirts, which now included I'M A PEPPER, SILLY RABBIT . . . TRIX ARE FOR KIDS! and MY LITTLE PONY. "Ugh—so last year," she said, picking up the shirt I'd worn to the office that day. "You should really never go out in public wearing the same thing twice anyway."

For the record, it's not that I didn't care about fashion. I cared enough. It's just that when you're a college student in Michigan, a

$700 pair of shoes doesn't even *exist in your universe,* and so fashion was like a spectator sport for me—a sport that I wasn't even remotely rich enough to participate in. Anyhow, I got the feeling from Brynn that even if I *had* made an effort up to this point, I still would have fallen short of this new world's standards.

"Next, your hair. I'm getting Ken Paves to come over to do blonde highlights on you. He's Jessica Simpson's best friend, you know . . . we want to make you blonde, but not too blonde . . . you still have to be believable as the all-American girl. Look at Sarah Michelle Gellar. When *Buffy* first started, she had dark hair, and by the end, that show was a huge hit and she was practically a platinum blonde. It just goes to show—blondes make for good television." She stood behind me, picking up individual sections of my hair and then tossing them down again, making clucking noises with her tongue. "Your hair is dry and frizzy. It's got no shape at all!"

As she circled me, I silently thanked God that I'd started with the getting of the part, then the shooting of the pilot, *then* the weight loss and the makeover, because I'm pretty sure I would have killed myself if Attila and Brynn were the first people I saw when I got to L.A.

Just when I thought she'd lost hope and was going to recommend to the network that they have me killed so they could focus the show on someone less monstrous, she said: "You have really expressive eyes. Let's focus on those and really play those up for now."

I walked out of the conference room, which now looked like a level-five disaster area, carrying a giant pile of clothes and noting bitterly that the one thing she liked about me was something over which I had absolutely no control.

THE STYLE MEETING WAS followed by media training ("Try not to say 'gay' if you can help it—the proper term is 'homosexual'"), product placement ("If there's a Coke in the scene, be sure to hold it so

the logo is facing the camera"), magazine photo shoot/interview requests ("Stick to bullet points, and don't let them put you in anything
too revealing that would compromise your brand equity"), and several
other meetings. By the end of the day, my main focus was willing myself to stay awake, since I already knew I was going to forget most of
what they were telling me. My last meeting of the day was etiquette
and standards, with Sondra herself. Though I arrived in her office
fifteen minutes early for the meeting, she was already a few hours into
her "I hate everyone" face. She handed me another list.

"OK, now I'm going to go over some basic rules—just try to keep
these in mind when you go out, talk to people, or give any interviews.
At first, we're going to try to just limit your exposure, to make sure
we start positioning you in a way that's appropriate to your target
market."

Since I felt a little like I was still in school, and since I understood one third of what she was saying, I got out my black and white
composition notebook, wrote the headline RULES FOR CELEBRITY, and
started taking notes.

1. No smoking: "You can smoke in private, but it's better
overall if you don't let anyone take photos of you smoking," she
said. "You'll end up on websites and in materials of those anti-
smoking organizations, and you just don't need that, especially
since Autumn is supposed to be this wholesome Midwestern
girl, and that's what we're billing you as. It's not that big a deal—
just something you want to watch out for because it does you
more harm than good." I wondered if she knew that without
a constant stream of nicotine, I'd be getting a lecture from another department on my "weight issue."

2. No trash-talking: "You're going to be updated by the marketing department if you're doing interviews about the show;

this is more for in your regular life. The media loves to create feuds between hot young stars (Nicole Richie vs. Paris Hilton, Lindsay Lohan vs. Jessica Simpson, etc.). So, if a reporter asks you, even casually, if you like someone, always just say yes, don't comment, or change the subject to something fun, like clothes, music, or a movie you just saw or a book you just read. Actually . . . we'll make a monthly list of music, movies, and books you can mention in the media. That's a good idea," she said, making a little note for herself in her portfolio.

If you give them one tiny comment, there's going to be a whole spread in the center of *Life & Style* magazine the very next week. Trust me. Even though there's no such thing as bad publicity, it's better if they focus on something good. This also applies to working on film sets; even if you hate everyone you're working with, don't *ever ever ever* go on record saying that you don't like a director, or your fellow actor has bad breath, or anything like that. You'll see."

3. Don't be a drunk: "There will be a lot of opportunities for you to drink, even though you're not twenty-one yet, and that's fine—just don't be photographed drinking, or you'll end up in some big exposé. I mean, look what happened to Tara Reid and she was that cute little virgin girl from *American Pie.* So sad." She paused for a moment, as if in reverie. As she talked I considered my brief and unsuccessful attempt at becoming a Michigan drama department party girl, which ended with Vince and Carrie Ann carrying me home and two days in bed. "OK," I said, nodding.

4. Don't talk about your plastic surgery: "Have it; everybody does—in fact, you might need some," she said, making another note. "But definitely don't admit to it. And don't 'out' anybody else or speculate publicly on who has had it. Stuff like that will come back to haunt you. In this area, it's best to just *deny deny deny!*" At this, I wondered what surgery she thought I needed, but I just kept nodding and taking notes.

5. Don't get caught doing drugs: "If Kate Moss taught us anything, it's that it's a bad idea to snort cocaine if there's anybody watching. Matthew McConaughey is another good example of this—yes, he's hot, but somewhere in the back of people's minds, he's always going to be Stoned Naked Guy with Bongos. I don't even need to mention Farrah Fawcett or Courtney Love. Some directors will not work with you if they think you're just going to be high all the time or bring drugs onto their sets, because it will make their insurance go up, and if they think you're just going to freak out and hold up their shooting schedule, producers are not going to back a film that you're in. Just be aware of what you're doing at all times when you're out in public and someone might have a camera. It's much easier to deny if there's no proof, or if it's just some nobody's word against yours. That we can spin." I kept nodding. Some of these theories Vince had speculated about during late nights in the dorm with his *US Weekly* and *People,* but it was like having an all-access backstage pass to actually be hearing them from an industry person's mouth. I wanted to call Vince and scream, *"You were right!"* Instead, I just kept nodding and writing, trying to keep accurate notes.

6. Always be thinking: "In other words, every time you're not alone, you're working. Things can change in a heartbeat: your show could go off the air, you could get cast in an action movie and become as big as J. Lo overnight. Make sure you make as many friends as possible when you're starting out, because you never know when you're going to need help."

7. Don't be a weirdo: "It's really simple—being weird to a certain extent can be your strategy (think Drew Barrymore), but if you do it too many times, you get a reputation as a loose cannon. Remember Sean Young? No? That's because she supposedly went crazy and stalked one of her costars. Look—Joaquin Phoenix gave this weird red-carpet interview about a frog eating through his skull, and then he didn't win the Academy Award for *Walk the Line*. Philip Seymour Hoffman might be totally weird in private, but you'd never know it—thus, he won for *playing* a weirdo, Truman Capote. Get it?"

I stopped nodding for a moment. This particular item was so multifaceted, I felt like I needed the Cliff Notes. I made a mental note to Google "Sean Young" when I got home.

After quizzing me on different made-up situations ("What do you do if Lindsay Lohan comes up to you in a club and slaps you in the face?"), Sondra was satisfied that when the show premiered, I could be counted on not to go crazy and embarrass the network. "OK, we'll call you in again if we feel like we need to do any follow-up with you," she said. I noticed it was already dark outside, and I longed for my sweet bed. I was totally exhausted, and all I wanted to do was go back to the hotel where it was safe, smoke cigarettes, drink some vodka, and process all of this new information. Hopefully, I wouldn't be in any of these situations anytime soon. Maybe the first few times I could just bring my notebook with me, for reference.

AN HOUR AFTER THE conclusion of Super Saturday, Vince was listening wide-eyed at rapt attention as I told him about the day of meetings and the truth about everything. "They changed your *name*?" he said in disbelief, grabbing a Camel Light out of his messenger bag and lighting it. "Can they just do that?"

"Well," I said, "it went by so fast . . . I don't know. I didn't feel comfortable objecting. Besides, 'Star' is kind of a cool name. Maybe they're right . . . Amy Spencer *does* sound like the name of a girl who milks cows."

He laughed. "Cows? Whatever. You will always be my little Aim." He paused. "They're right about your hair, though . . . it still needs work. And for the record, that thing about Lindsay Lohan is a trick question. She would throw a drink in your face, not slap you!" he said, blowing smoke rings and laughing.

"Vince—I'm being serious. Would you tell me if this whole thing went too far? Do you think I should have not taken the job?" I didn't want to bring this up with him because he seemed to love L.A. so much, but I was still fighting this undercurrent of homesickness and loneliness that crept back in practically every time I wasn't shooting something or sleeping. I kept expecting it to go away or hoping that I was going to catch some of Vince's ever-present enthusiasm.

He stopped and really looked at me for a minute. "You are doing that thing, and you should stop. Just because something is good doesn't mean it's automatically going to go away. Your dad would not want you to think that, and it's OK for you to let yourself be happy."

"Really?" Sometimes he said these things and I wanted to believe him, but I was really afraid I would never trust anything again. It did seem like everything good came with a catch, and the more good things happened, the harder I expected the fall to be.

THE PREMIERE OF THE show was officially the first time I'd ever been on TV, and I was beside myself with excitement. Carrie Ann had taken a few days off school and flown out for the party, which she, Vince, and I (and the rest of the cast) attended at Greg Forster's fabulous house in the Hollywood Hills, right up the street from the hotel. The house was three levels, built into the side of a mountain, with sweeping views of the city below.

"This is the nicest house I've ever seen," Carrie Ann whispered. She, Vince, and I were wandering around Greg's house before the show started, eyeing a wall filled with expensive art. "By the way, what's the deal with Matt? He is so hot, and he looks like he really likes you."

"Shhh—I'm avoiding him," I whispered. I'd seen him a few times since the pilot, but he was starting to get on my nerves with all the calling and texting.

Vince poked Carrie Ann. "Mr. Iowa totally loves her, but already she's annoyed. I feel bad for him."

Carrie Ann rolled her eyes. "Oh my God, cry me a river—perfect job, money, and now a super-hot guy is into you." I couldn't tell if she was kidding or not. "You should get over that thing where you can't commit. He seems really cool."

Right before the show was about to start, we all gathered in Greg's huge media/screening room.

"I got you guys some drinks," said Matt, smiling as he put his arm around me. Carrie Ann smiled at him, then shot me a look like "How do you not like this guy?"

We sat down, and the music for the opening credits started. My stomach flip-flopped. Would people like the show? Would they like me? Would we be a hit, or would I be on my way back to UM? *Whatever happens is fine,* I told myself. *We're good for thirteen episodes, and after that at least you'll have a good story of your life in Hollywood.*

My face appeared on the screen, which was very hard for my brain to process. All of a sudden, I wondered what my dad would think of all this, then I tried to put that out of my mind before I started crying.

I held my breath for what seemed like the whole hour. I was good. In fact, everyone was good. At the end, I had to admit, this was totally a show I would watch. It was edgier looking than most nighttime soaps, the writing was great, and I felt good that we were doing a show that might actually get people engaged in a real dialogue about same-sex couples. The feeling was totally universal; we all left Greg's that night on a high, optimistic about the future of the show.

THE DAY AFTER THE premiere, we were sitting at King's Road Café near Vince's new apartment, having brunch, when two teenage girls ran up. "Oh my God . . . Star Spencer . . . it's you! We totally loved your show! Matt Pierce is so hot! You look so much smaller in person! Can we have your autograph?"

I glanced over at Vince, who was putting serious effort into not laughing as I signed my name on the girl's math homework. Since I had never really gotten around to practicing the signature of my new name, it ended up looking like a combination of my old signature and that of a fourth grader. "Omigod . . . thanks!" squealed the girls as they skitted off down Beverly.

The girls' presence drew scattered glances from the other people in the restaurant, some of whom began a game of "Where have I seen that girl before?" Quickly, they all decided that I must be some B-level star at best and went back to their frittatas. I reminded myself that two weeks ago, Vince and I had seen Famke Janssen there and debated asking for *her* autograph. But now, apparently, I was the famous one.

"That was weird," said Carrie Ann, stabbing her salad a little too vehemently.

I started to obsess about what those young girls were saying about me as they walked away. Why had they said I was smaller in person? Did they think I was fat? The makeup person had to work on me for two hours just to cover my acne for the pilot. I made a mental note to eat better and work out more, and to try to integrate more of Brynn Harper's style tips into my daily going-out preparations. This bothered me, though—how come I couldn't just focus on the good? Was the Hollywood game getting to me already?

After lunch, we walked down to the nail salon for manicures. Carrie Ann seemed a little quiet. "What's wrong?" I said.

"I don't know," she started. "It's just . . . those girls . . . I just think the show is going to be really huge. The magazines are all giving it really good reviews, and I'm sure you're going to get good ratings. On the one hand, I'm really happy for you, but . . . I just have a feeling that you're never coming back now, and I'm just kind of freaking out for you. It all just seems so random, you know?"

"I know, it's totally weird," I said, just to fill the silence.

Vince made a face. "No, it's not," he said. "It's fucking great!

Hello . . . Amy is living the American dream right now, Carrie . . . of *course* she's never coming back," he said. "She's famous, she's rich, and she belongs here. Come on! You know it's what you want too!" he said, poking her in the ribs. I laughed, happy that he was trying to break the obvious tension, but Carrie Ann seemed determined to be serious. Was she jealous?

In truth, the whole roller-coaster aspect of it was freaking me out a little bit too, but there was no going back. I mean, wasn't this the reason we majored in drama in the first place? How could she be mad at me for being successful? The problem was, I actually didn't know what I *did* to get the lucky break, and I wasn't exactly sure what I could do to keep the luck going. From the first audition, it had all seemed somehow beyond my control, and I really felt like it could all end at any minute. Every time I tried to tell someone this, they'd just tell me to "enjoy the ride" and that I should feel lucky, because 90 percent of Screen Actors Guild members were unemployed. It's not that I wasn't happy and excited. In fact, I was *beyond* happy and excited. But . . . how do you enjoy a ride when you have no concept of its turns, when it will come to an end, or where you're going? Was Carrie Ann just pessimistic, was she jealous, or was she right?

TWO WEEKS AFTER THE show's premiere, Michele decided she wanted to be my friend, taking me to Robertson Boulevard on a Saturday afternoon for some celebratory shopping. "I can't believe you've never been here," she said, leading me into Lisa Kline. "You have so much to learn." I noted with little surprise that her "I'm being nice" voice was hardly different from her "I don't like you" voice. Maybe I needed to lighten up about her. With Vince always out and busy developing his client base and Carrie Ann not returning any of my calls or e-mails since she went back to school, I was feeling lonely, and I wasn't even at the top.

One of the reasons I'd never been to Robertson was the money. Even though I'd started receiving regular paychecks that exceeded most peoples' annual salaries, I still cringed when I saw flimsy T-shirts adorned with glitter that had $200 price tags dangling off them. Something about it just seemed wrong to me. Besides, I was still getting the "you're too fat" vibe from everyone at the network, so I felt bad buying anything in my real size. Still, I was curious about the "West Hollywood shopping" that everyone on set talked about, so I finally gave in and went with Michele.

We stepped out of Lisa Kline on the way to Ghost when I noticed them—two guys with cameras, trying to be subtle while they followed us down the street. "Do you see them?" I whispered to Michele. "Are they following us?" We tried slowing down, and the guys slowed down too. Once they realized we knew they were following us, they got out a set of even larger cameras and started blatantly snapping our every move. All at once, I was totally self-conscious, trying to remember all of my good camera angles. I knew they were trying to capture us in our "normal life" moments, but the very act of having cameras trained on me rendered me totally self-conscious, as if having the camera there had changed the act of shopping into a miniperformance. Right then, I developed a whole new understanding of those weird people on *COPS* as I realized it actually *is* impossible to "act natural" when you know you're being observed.

"Omigod! It's our first stalkerazzi experience!" Michele said, taking out her cell phone and dialing furiously. "Rachel! You're never going to believe who's following me right now," she said into the phone. "Silvio Jackson! Yeah . . . that sleazy guy who used to sit outside the Miramar Hotel, waiting for Britney to come out? . . . Yeah! I know! Really good, I know! Yes, I will totally get you on the show! OK, bye!"

"Don't smile at them," said Michele. "Don't even look at them . . . pretend like you don't see them. That's what big stars do."

We kept walking, proceeding quickly into Ghost. The camera guys stayed outside, but they were photographing us through the window, trying to capture what we were looking at, what we were buying. It was weird and exhilarating and fun, all at the same time. "This is so great!" said Michele. "This means the show is a big hit; why else would they care what kind of shoes we're looking at?" We went in four more stores, and the crowd just got bigger.

She was right—four days later, photos of our shopping excursion appeared in a few of the magazines, alongside a giant headline that screamed "*Autumn Leaves* Stars Are Just Like Us!" The day after that, Michele and I each received a box full of shoes and bags. I tried to match each item with how much it was at the store, and I came up with $5,000 for one box.

"We should go shopping together more often," Michele laughed. "We made out like bandits! I wonder if this is what happens when those girls from *The Hills* go out together on the weekends?"

I laughed. If this was what being famous was going to be like, I loved it already. Let the photographers follow you a little, get free stuff? What was the big deal?

THE DAY AFTER THE shopping photos came out, my phone rang with a number I didn't recognize. It was Attila, calling from a cell phone. I tried to imagine a Bluetooth hiding within the folds of her fat face as I tried to think of the right things to say. Why did I let her get to me? I was the star of a hit show!

"Hello, Star? I'm looking at a photo of you and Michele in Lisa Kline, and I don't like what I see. Why are you wearing an I'M A PEP-PER T-shirt? Obviously, your work with Brynn wasn't enough, so we're going to try a different direction. We're going to need you to be a lit-tle more upscale, to reflect well on the show. We're building a brand, after all. I've booked you an appointment with Jennifer Carlyle for

Saturday at two P.M. She'll be pulling together some looks for you. She's in Santa Monica." I was determined never to make the mistake of making small talk with her ever again, so I didn't mention that I had only been to Santa Monica once and it had taken me four hours to get home. My car had a killer GPS system, and I would just have to figure out how to use it. I took the address and hoped for the best.

Vince was beyond excited to hear this news. Apparently, Jennifer Carlyle was the best stylist in town, with a list of celebrity clients a mile long. "You are so taking me with you!" he screamed. "Jennifer Carlyle is the *shit*! She makes, like, seven thousand dollars a day being a stylist. If I work with her, that would totally be *my* big break!"

Armed with GPS and strong coffee, we arrived only slightly late at Jennifer Carlyle's groovy Santa Monica townhouse, the entryway of which was packed to the rafters with designer clothes. She opened the door on the first ring. "Star!" she said excitedly. "I'm so glad you're here!"

She and Vince shook hands, and I said a little prayer that they would hit it off. I silently vowed to do whatever she said, just so I could get in good with her on his behalf.

"So, Mindy sent me over the photos, which I had already seen of course. Do you want a Diet Coke?"

"Sure," I said, trying not to read into the fact that she'd offered me a Diet Coke instead of regular. Despite the black pills, I had actually *gained* back four pounds since we started shooting again, and I was hungry all the time anyway—this woman looked like she hadn't eaten since the 1980s. I seriously doubted she would be able to relate to the fact that if I even *looked* at a cupcake, the next day I gained a pound. I started to get nervous. Were all the clothes in her jam-packed foyer the same size as her? Good Lord. Why is everyone in Hollywood so freakishly tiny? Did I have any hope of ever being this size?

We stood in front of a giant gilt-framed mirror that was set up in her living room. I wondered how many of her celebrity clients had stood in that same spot while she constructed a carefully crafted image for them.

"OK, we need to start with your hair. I know they worked on it a little bit for the show, and the cut looks all right, but I think you could safely go much blonder, and much longer. I like my girls to have long, blonde hair and tan skin. Also, when you go out, *please* don't pull your hair back in a messy ponytail or one of those buns, unless you've just been to the gym. We want your hair long, and blonde, and flowing down your back. That way it'll make your face look thinner. I've made you an appointment with Byron Williams for tomorrow for extensions and color, and I've cleared it with Mindy."

I nodded, hoping that my hair didn't fall out from all the bleaching. I was sure she'd say that baldness was definitely not starlike.

"The problem is, you don't have a cohesive sense of style," she said. "What are you going for, in terms of a look? Old Hollywood glamour like Catherine Zeta-Jones, boho chic like Kate Moss or Sienna Miller, or modern elegance, like Carolyn Bessette Kennedy? Do you even know? You need to have a goal for the style we're creating, you know? Right now, when you're not shooting, you just look like a regular civilian on the way to the mall or something." She laughed. "We just need to step you up a notch."

"I totally agree," Vince said, nodding. "No one's *E! True Hollywood Story* ever starts with the girl in a corduroy blazer and an I'M A PEPPER T-shirt, Aim." I was so glad the two of them were on the same page regarding my utter lack of style. I knew he meant well. Her I wasn't so sure about. I was rapidly growing not to trust stylists at all.

"I have no idea," I said meekly. In fact, I really didn't know. Was it really not okay to go out in sweatpants if I was just getting gas or buying milk at the store? Did I need Rock & Republic jeans and Alexander McQueen heels just to go to brunch?

Apparently I did. Next, she directed me to the first of about a hundred outfits I would try on that day. "Put this on, and we'll see what looks good on you." I changed into what looked to be a very expensive Balenciaga top, and she took a Polaroid. "That looks great, and it hides your stomach—you need some earrings though," she said, pulling out a drawer that was full to overflowing with jewelry of all shapes and sizes. "The network wants you to look more put together. There is big money behind that show, and you're the face of it, whether you like it or not. You should be committed to building your brand," she said as she draped gold necklaces over my head. "There you go . . . very Mary-Kate," she said, turning me around and plunking gray aviator glasses on my face.

"OK, what about your skin?" she said.

"Yes," I sighed. "I'm seeing a dermatologist about the acne, and I'm still looking for the perfect concealer for the eye bags." What more could she say? I felt like already, I'd heard it all before.

"What? No! That's not what I mean; that stuff you can cover," she said, laughing. "You're too pale, girl! You need to look like you go out in California sun! You're not in Michigan anymore!" She pulled out a small pot of powder that said GOLD COAST on the side, produced a puff out of thin air, and started brushing it onto my face. When I thought we must have been almost done, to further compound my horror, she pulled out a tape measure, which she wrapped around my hips, clicking her tongue. "What's your diet plan?" she said. "You really should be thinner. Like, I have all of my clients in size twenty-five jeans—are those twenty-sevens? Those have to go."

Once again, I felt like crying. Twenty-seven was the smallest size I'd worn in three years. There was no possible way, short of an actual miracle, that I would be able to fit my ass into a size 25. I knew she would tell Attila I was being difficult, so I looked at Vince and laughed. "OK," I said, sighing. Would I ever win this game?

In fact, most of the clothes sent by the designers were too small. "Sample sizes are a zero," she sighed. "That's what you should be in order to wear the most names and get the most press," she said. "You should work on that. They didn't tell me you still had weight issues." She stood back, taking a Polaroid of me wearing a too-small size zero skirt. "We can make this work for now, but you'd look really good if you lost another ten pounds. I'm sure you get that all the time."

I wanted to tell her that I'd *been* working on that—that, in fact, the "weight issue" was *all* I'd been working on, that I'd actually had to will myself not to eat cookie dough ice cream the night before, and that I was, in fact, so constantly hungry that I might be justified in killing her. Instead, I just said, "Yes, I understand . . . I'll work on that," and continued to sift through endless piles of clothes I knew wouldn't fit, hoping to find a nice jacket or scarf.

She looked at me quizzically. "Yes, thinness is an essential part of the Young Hollywood look. Let me know if you need more help."

I looked at Vince again. I was already taking the secret black pills from Attila. Did she know that? What did she mean? I wondered what magic trick *she* had—she certainly looked like she had mastered the art of thinness.

Curiosity got the best of me. "Hey, if you have a secret for getting into size-twenty-five jeans, you just let me know." I laughed.

She pulled out a small packet of white powder, pressing it into my hand. Her eyes lit up. "Just for emergencies," she said, "like size-twenty-five jeans." She looked at me expectantly, pursing her plump lips. "Works like a charm, I promise. Everyone does it, don't even worry about it."

Vince high-fived Jennifer—they were already getting along like they'd known each other forever, and I didn't want to be the one who rained on their parade. He seemed totally unfazed by this transaction.

I froze. Did she want me to do it right then? Considering how long it had taken me to start taking the black pills, I highly doubted I was going to start snorting coke right in this woman's living room. This seemed to be one of those things that was normal in her world but so totally abnormal in mine; I almost looked around to see if the police were going to come.

"Um . . . I . . . I'm good, actually," I stammered, shooting Vince a "save me" look, and he swooped over and grabbed the envelope out of my hand.

"Thanks, Jen—we'll save this for tonight," he said, winking at me. In reality, he was probably going to take that cocaine right over to West Hollywood to do it with one of his club friends. I tried to act cool, but I was blown away by how natural it all was—Vince put the little envelope in his messenger bag, and then I finished trying on clothes like it was no big deal. Vince was always telling me I needed to act a little less like a grown-up. Maybe I did need to lighten up.

We spent another four hours trying on outfits and taking Polaroids, working on a style for me. Finally, we settled somewhere between "Kate Moss boho chic" and "classic" style. Who knew that clothes could be so complicated?

The next day I spent four more hours in the salon of Byron Williams, who straightened, extensioned, and colored my hair into Hollywood Fabulous oblivion. I had to admit, I looked cooler than I ever had in my life. I barely recognized myself. I was famous and rich, and now I was *hot*.

Now there was just the matter of getting into those size 25s. At least now I knew how everyone else got there.

"OK, WE'RE BACK IN five . . ." Dr. Drew pointed at me, and I put my headphones back on. One good thing about doing *Loveline* is that it's on at night, which was much better than having to get up at four A.M. to do Ryan Seacrest's radio show. After only a few months, I was already a veteran at doing press.

"So—Star. What's it like to be on the show that everyone's talking about?"

"Great—I mean, we're so proud to be the show that opens up discussions, you know? I mean, love is love, right? Isn't it time for us to move past antiquated laws?"

Michele kicked me under the table, and I looked down at my bullet-pointed list. I already knew that I had gone too far down the "politics of gay rights" road. Frankly, I was trying to keep my mind off the fact that my mother was probably listening and that at any moment, someone could call in with a question about their herpes or the fact that they wanted to be a man. Michele was obsessive about all the press we were doing and was always rubbing in my face the fact that *she'd* never gotten a memo from Sondra about "staying on message." I'd finally figured her out—she was nice to me when there was something in it for her or if there was anyone watching, and the rest of the time, she peeled away the "nice girl" mask to let her dark, ugly soul show through.

"We're proud of the show, and what it stands for, *and* we have some great episodes coming up that deal with everything from adoption to gay rights to Autumn's first time at the gay pride parade!" said Michele, glaring at me. I rolled my eyes; I wondered if she knew how phony everyone thought she was, or how everything she said sounded like one big long sound bite.

"Let's take a call," said Stryker, the *Loveline* host.

"Yes, hi—Dr. Drew? My name is Paul, and I'm from Orlando? I have this sore, and I think it might be herpes . . ."

I laid my head down on the desk, headphones still on. My mom had been excited about the cast being on *Good Morning America.* I had a feeling she was going to be less than thrilled about this.

THE CRAZY PRESS WHIRLWIND continued as I was asked to appear on Leno. Michele didn't talk to me for a week when she heard this, and she certainly didn't come to the taping. She was very bitter about the fact that while she studied the bullet points more than I did, I always got more screen time, better scripts, and more press.

There was no time to be nervous as I prepared for my first-ever guest appearance on Leno. I stood in my dressing room, surrounded by people I barely knew who I guess could have been described as an "entourage"—*my* entourage. Jill (the makeup girl) was applying last-minute touch-ups to my face, the foundation of which was already thick enough not only to make me look like a drag queen, but to be sliding off my face from stress and the heat of the lights. "Seriously, stop sweating!" she said, her voice rising a little too high. "What girl sweats this much?" Already, I could tell it was not going well.

I tried to stand as still as possible while the hair guy put the finishing touches on a blowout of my newly blonde hair as Jennifer draped me in dangly necklaces. Sondra handed me a typewritten sheet of questions and bullet points, which I tried to read without smudging my freshly painted nails. "Read it!" she barked. "You're on in five!"

Autumn Leaves was one of the most popular shows of the fall season—thus, me on Leno. Sondra pushed the paper precariously close to my face, leaning in after it. "Listen, Star, I jotted down some likes and dislikes for you, along with an outline of your eating and workout plan in case he asks why you've lost weight since the show first started airing."

I didn't dare laugh out loud. I looked over the list. "Golf?" I said, looking up. "Sondra, I don't even play golf. I have never even been on a golf course."

"Hey, watch your eyelashes!" said Jill. "The mink ones take longer to dry. We want your eyes to pop on camera!" Her voice had risen even higher; perhaps Sondra made her as nervous as she was making me. She came at me with the bitey end of an eyelash curler. "Stay still! Stay still!"

"Right," Sondra interrupted. "We don't care if you don't actually *play* golf. We're building a 'public persona,'" she said, making the little quote marks in the air with her fingers. She was on a mission that would not be thwarted by mink eyelashes. "Your persona is named Star, and she plays golf. Golf expands your market and makes you attractive to all the dads of Middle America. We'll get you a golf coach, set up a photo op out in Palm Springs. You'll love it. Cami Diaz plays golf. Cathy Zeta-Jones plays golf—golf is the new cardio!"

For the record, "golf is the new cardio" is definitely a statement I would have furiously mocked, were the context at all different. But, since I was trying not to get any further on Sondra's bad side, I simply said, "OK, I'll try to fit golf in there somewhere. Anything else? I want to be sure to be prepared!" I tried to act interested and engaged. I needed at least one advocate on the network's marketing team.

She perked up. "Well, I've also prepared a fun story about moving into your first house, since we all know you lived in Michigan until six months ago."

"Sondra, what's the story about? I still live in a hotel," I said. Were they just making up everything now?

"Yes, I know, but people don't relate to that. This is just a little story about how you moved into this new place, and you didn't know how to work the alarm system, so you ended up calling the police on yourself. It makes you look lovably scatterbrained and accessible."

"OK," I said, giving up and taking the questions and answers into the bathroom, where I began trying to figure out how not to pee on the ruffles of my Chloe dress while I learned as much about my life as possible.

Somehow, I'd always thought being famous came with a certain amount of devil-may-care freedom, but I was slowly discovering the truth.

A bout of furious knocking interrupted my momentary bathroom respite. "Star—what are you doing in there?! You're on next!" Sondra was even more worried about her job security than I was; after all, *my* firing would require changing the entire story line of a major television show, but if she was found responsible for me screwing up on Leno, she might actually have to join the Witness Protection Program.

So maybe she had it worse than me. Still, I was the one about to make a fool of herself on Leno. I paced backstage, going over and over the bullet points. This was just like a pop quiz in college, only the subject was my life.

I heard Jay introduce me, and I felt a little like I was melting. Was this my life? I felt a little dizzy as I walked out and heard everyone clapping for me. I looked out at Vince, who I'd brought along for moral support and who was sitting in the front row of the audience. He was beaming and waved at me. The lights were blinding me, and I waved at Vince and at everyone in the audience. I was super excited to be on my first talk show, and I hoped that nothing I did made me look like a dork. My heart pounding, I greeted Jay, shook his hand, and the interview got rolling.

Somehow I managed to talk about the show, tell my cute alarm anecdote, and keep my legs crossed so no one could see my underwear, all while adhering to the bullet points. My only iffy moment came when Jay ad-libbed, which Sondra had guaranteed he wouldn't.

"So, Star, this is the most exciting time of your life right now, huh? What do you like to do when you're not shooting the show?" he said.

And just like that, my mind was blank.

I knew I was supposed to have a witty response—this *was* the most exciting time of my life, for sure. Was I allowed to say that though? I searched my brain for a good answer, vaguely remembering something about golf. Then I froze.

"I . . . um . . . I . . . ," I said, laughing a little. The little voice in my head was going, *Say something! You're on Jay Leno!*

"I like cheese," I said, and Jay laughed. Cheese? Where did that come from? I thought frantically. I then tried to backpedal my way out of the weirdness by explaining that since we started shooting, I'd had no free time, blah blah blah, but Jay took it and ran.

"And there's a lot of cheese backstage at *Autumn Leaves*?" he said jokingly. "You and your two dads are having cheese tastings?" I knew he wasn't trying to make me nervous, but I really wanted to crawl under the couch, and I could definitely feel Sondra's eyes boring a hole in the side of my head from the backstage area. "And golf," I said weakly. "Definitely golf."

WE COULD TELL THE show was a hit when the extras started asking us for autographs in between takes, even though the stage manager told them not to. The show had only been for a few months, we were shooting a party scene on a set built to look like a country club, and the extras were restless with excitement. There were about fifty of them, waiting to spring into action, pretending to eat the fake food and looking like they were having a good time.

Michele and I were sitting in the Smoker's Lounge, which was next to the set for the country club where all the extras were waiting, so to kill time we were eavesdropping on a conversation between a short, balding guy with glasses and a bleach-blonde woman with enormous fake breasts. They were standing in front of a middle-aged black woman, and all of them were there for a party. Never let it be said that the country club in *Autumn Leaves* didn't let in people of all races, creeds, and sexual preferences.

"Yeah, I've done extra work on *CSI, Desperate Housewives,* and *ER,* and now this. I'm going to casting workshops all the time, and I'm doing the mailings to try to get an agent, you know?" said Big-Breasted Blonde. I'd heard other actors talk about the so-called "casting workshop," which sounded to me like one marginally influential intern charging twenty actors to watch them read. Still, without a huge stroke of luck, I might be where they were, so who was I to judge?

"It's tough, but you've just got to keep going and eventually you'll get your big break. My acting teacher said I'm good enough to be auditioning regularly and to just keep doing the workshops." We also learned that the balding guy had been "working toward the Hollywood dream" for eleven years, and despite having never gotten even close to a speaking part, he was optimistic that his big break was "right around the corner."

Bleach Blonde replied with an even more disturbing tale. "I just got a chin implant and a brow lift, and now I feel like I'm really ready to take on the modeling industry," she said. I heard Michele stifle a snicker. "She's got to be forty," she whispered. "Shouldn't she have tried to take on the industry before now? I'm pretty sure it's too late for her." I smiled, praying that the extras couldn't hear her over the sound of the crew members talking and the giant fan that was turned on between takes to cool the set down. All of the extras had been instructed not to make casual conversation with the regular cast members, and in fact, once the scene was over, they'd be going to a holding area where they would not even be able to use the same bathroom as the regular cast. So much for living the dream.

I wanted to stop listening, but I couldn't; their conversation was like a train wreck. In the absence of some positive affirmation, like a speaking role, I was sure that I would have packed it in long before they did. Every time I heard a story like this, in fact, it made me even more superstitious. Did these people "just know" they wanted to be actors, and if so, why weren't they more successful? I had wanted to be an actress since I was a kid too, and now I was one. Simple, right? Did some people "miss" their fate? Are some people just destined to be mediocre, and no matter what they try, they will never succeed? Why do some people (like me) get a "big break" with almost no effort at all, while Joe the Extra toils in obscurity for eleven years with nary a speaking part? If I said or did the wrong thing and got fired, thus losing the keys to Oz, would I ever be able to get back? This thought terrified me.

Finally, the stage manager indicated that the crew was finished with the lights and called the actors back, and the director came back to the set. Thankfully, this meant that we'd be able to start shooting the scene soon, and I wouldn't have to listen to the extras talk about their careers anymore. I would have been embarrassed to tell any of them just how easy it was for me or how I'd never paid any dues with the exception of not being allowed to exit. Somehow, being in the presence of desperation of that magnitude never failed to make me depressed and uncomfortable.

FOLLOWING THE AIRING OF my Leno appearance, I was surprised to find that no memo appeared to castigate me on my obvious lack of adherence to the bullet points. My fellow cast members actually complimented me on the good job I did. In fact, it appeared that my Jennifer Carlyle/Vince style plan had finally sunk in. I was thinner than ever, and two weeks later, I arrived on the set to find a memo from Sondra underneath my trailer door.

To: STAR SPENCER
FROM: SONDRA MITCHELL
CC: MINDY STEINMAN
RE: TEEN VOGUE

Teen Vogue has requested cover shoot for holiday issue. Photo shoot is Saturday the 14th, 8:00 am at Smashbox Studios, Culver City.

Please arrive early if possible, and stick to prepared, show-related bullet points (attached) and previous media training for interview. The reporter is a freelance writer, and the interview will be conducted during the shoot.

Have fun!

Sondra Mitchell

I held the paper in my hand. Me, on the cover of a magazine!? Who made these decisions? Who should I call first? I wondered if the *Teen Vogue* people were going to change their minds when I got to the studio and they saw my eye bags.

I pushed number two on my cell phone's speed dial. "Vince—you're never going to believe this. They want me to be on the cover of *Teen Vogue!*"

Vince screamed so loud, I had to hold the phone away from my ear. When he was done, he accepted my invitation to accompany me to the shoot—his first job as a solo stylist. He gasped, and I thought I heard him choke back a little sob. "Thank you thank you thank you, Amy! Your star is rising, baby! You won't be sorry!" he said, then hung up.

Sometimes you really need a friend to put things in perspective for you.

HAVING SLEPT EXACTLY TWO hours since shooting wrapped for the night (an epic no-turnaround Saturday), I picked up Vince at 7:00 A.M. for the highly anticipated *Teen Vogue* shoot.

He climbed into the BMW and handed me a very large cup of Starbucks coffee. "Is it wrong for me to say I love you right now?" I said.

He laughed and said, "I don't even want to see what's under those glasses, missy." In my first-ever "diva" move, I'd insisted that they hire Vince as my stylist for the shoot. He needed to build up his clientele and reputation, and I needed someone to keep me awake and sane all day. Plus, Vince had been styling me since UM, when I wore flannel shirts, took myself way too seriously, and (perish the thought) didn't pluck my eyebrows.

We sped down the 405, quickly leaving Mulholland Drive behind, passing the Getty, and racing toward the west side. Funky music was already pumping through the studio when we got there. In fact, this photo shoot felt so much like a party, I was rapidly overcoming my photo-shoot phobia (underpants incident, anyone?). There was the perfect amount of food, but not so much that I'd be grouchy from trying not to eat the Famous Amos cookies all day. Vince had outdone himself. He took the "keeping me happy" part of the stylist job very seriously and had been communicating nonstop with *Teen Vogue*.

My fear was almost conquered—that is, until it was time to try on potential outfits. After pulling on a cute skirt/sweater outfit, I noticed that each of the items was too small.

"Does this brand run small?" I said, a feeling of dread beginning to creep into the pit of my stomach. I had already wrestled my body down to a size 2/4. How much smaller did clothes get, anyway? "This doesn't fit," I said, peeling off the tiny, ill-fitting skirt and throwing it onto the chair in the makeshift wardrobe department. "What's next?"

Vince picked up the skirt. "This is a size zero," he said, sounding annoyed. "I said twos and fours, and I called yesterday to confirm the wardrobe. I even called with her measurements." He riffled through the different clothes hanging from silver clothing racks. "These are all size zeros."

Vince looked pissed—his first official solo stylist job was rapidly circling the drain, and I was precariously close to tears. "What's going on here?" he said, trying to get the situation under control.

"I'm so sorry," said the wardrobe assistant, a well-meaning but frazzled girl named Lisa. "After we pulled the wardrobe, a woman from an executive's office at your studio called. She said you'd been dieting a lot lately and you were actually a size zero now, so we got all new stuff." She looked like she was about to cry right along with me.

I felt the anger rising to the top of my head. Even in her absence, Attila was making her presence felt. I'd been hearing rumors that she'd started to audition other actresses to replace me. I knew Michele wanted me out too and that she was reporting on every line I flubbed and everything I put in my mouth. Even though things were good on the surface, I still felt like the bottom could drop out at any minute.

I was three seconds from total hysteria when Vince took charge. "OK, there's obviously been a misunderstanding," he said calmly. "We can use some of this stuff, but most of it has to go." He looked at me. "Go to hair and makeup and do the interview with the reporter while Lisa and I figure this out. Don't worry about it." He winked at me. "Be sure to stick to the bullet points."

Now I felt like crying from relief. "Really? No cutting the clothes?" I whispered as he walked me to the makeup area, his arm firmly around my waist.

"Honey, when have you ever known me to cut clothes?" He smiled.

Sure enough, my fairy godfather came through. By the time I had to change into my first outfit, Vince and Lisa had managed to pull together a complete new set of size-four outfits, including a beautiful geometric-print Diane von Furstenberg wrap dress. "How did you . . . ?" I looked at Vince.

"I worked stylist magic, baby. That's why they pay me the big bucks," he said. "I am a fashion superhero . . . able to make Diane von Furstenberg dresses appear out of thin air!"

I never did find out where he got the new clothes. Perhaps in some sort of karmic reward, he'd soon acquired two more clients just through word of mouth. By then I was on another diet, still trying achieve the Mindy-mandated size zero.

ONE WEEK LATER, VINCE and I were watching *Say Anything* for the millionth time when I got a call from the front desk at the hotel. "Ms. Spencer, you have packages waiting. Should we bring them up?"

The boxes turned out to be huge care packages from different companies wanting me to endorse their stuff. Jennifer told me she'd be contacting them on my behalf, but she didn't really say what would be in them or what I should do with them when they got there.

Once the boxes arrived in the room and the door was closed, we ripped into them one by one like hungry wolves with raw meat. Vince was in his element. He was taking notes, writing down what was in each box, what designer it came from, and who the contact was for the company in case we ever needed more. "This is unbelievable," he said, breathless. "There's fifty thousand dollars' worth of stuff here, at least."

The next thing I knew, he was assembling outfits for me out of what was in the boxes, making ensembles that showcased two or three designers at a time. There were eight boxes in all, sent from different designers and stores.

"This is, like, the greatest thing I have ever seen in my life. I am never, never leaving L.A.," sighed Vince. I agreed, secretly wishing I didn't love the trappings of celebrity quite this much. Did I lose some of my edge every time I accepted free clothes? I really hoped not.

"I DON'T UNDERSTAND WHY you don't want to meet my dad—he's only in town for a few days." Matt and I were "on again," and he'd been at my place for several days. As much as I liked him as a person, I was still resisting being called his girlfriend, though the tabloids practically already had us moving in together and getting engaged. It is amazing how much mileage they get out of a few photos of costars together after work.

"You saw the shooting schedule," I said. "I barely have time to sleep in the next week, much less go out."

Truthfully though, I was trying to avoid Matt's continued attempts to push our relationship forward.

"Right," he said, somewhat bitterly. Our relationship had become a little strained, due in part to the fact that he was getting a lot less screen time since one of the magazines broke the story that he was actually twenty-nine years old and audiences could no longer picture him as the boy next door. Word around the set was that his character was being phased out, and the weekly plotline was certainly backing that up. The last episode he'd been featured in had his character shoplifting, then getting sent to juvie. We were also on the outs because I insisted on seeing other people.

"I'm sorry," I said. "I have to get to the set. Stay as long as you want."

He sighed. "Fine. I knew this was going to happen."

I sighed. I never knew what to say when he got like this.

"OK—I mean, I'm sorry. Bring your dad to set on Wednesday and we'll have lunch and give him a tour."

He smiled and hugged me, and I made a mental note to listen to Vince and never get involved with a coworker in the future.

"HOW HARD CAN IT be? Just pick a charity from the list, and let's go. Mr. Chow's is waiting!" Vince waited impatiently in front of the door as I paced back and forth.

"Sondra wanted this done weeks ago . . . she's going to kill me," I said. Vince rolled his eyes.

The Charity List had been plaguing me since Sondra dropped it off in my trailer. I knew it had been weeks because the day she dropped it off, we were shooting the "Autumn's uncle catches her kissing a guy and has to give her the sex talk" scene, which might have been one of the most embarrassing days of my life. Not only was it my first on-screen kiss, with a guy I had just met (terrifically awkward), but I was also baffled by the multiple layers of the subject matter— getting a heterosexual sex talk (embarrassing) from Greg, a straight actor pretending to be embarrassed because he's gay and knows nothing about heterosexual sex (mortifying) . . . then my character asks about the differences between heterosexual and homosexual sex, and he tries to tell me (mind-bendingly uncomfortable). In my defense, I

didn't want to cry every five minutes like I did while we were shooting the pilot, but the day *had* required a number of takes, so by the
end we were all exhausted from doing multiple retakes and trying to
get the scene right. Since nothing like this show had ever been done
before, the executives were always on set trying to make sure that the
scripts didn't go too far for prime-time TV, that we were on the right
side of the political correctness line.

Apparently, "balancing" an episode like this one required an am-
plified PR strategy. That night when I got back to my trailer, Sondra
was waiting with the List, which had everything from a Mexican or-
phanage devastated by an earthquake to tsunami relief to a long list of
medical conditions. "What is this?" I asked.

"Here's the deal," she said. "We need a good story on you in the
press in about six weeks to distract from the Middle America backlash
we're going to get from this episode. We've got to put a photo shoot
together ASAP, so be sure you pick something sooner rather than
later."

"What's my cause?" I said. "Like, did I volunteer at my church or
something?" I couldn't believe anyone was really going to care about
my extracurricular activities. Was I applying to college again?

"God, no—religion is totally out. Disease is in these days," she
said, her face getting serious as she laid it out for me. "It's better if
it's personal to you, like if your mom had breast cancer like Brittany
Murphy's mom, or if you were in the tsunami like that model Petra
Nemcova, or you're from New Orleans and can talk about Hurricane
Katrina. It's also better if you pick something that has sick or starving kids, but not too sick, because no one wants to see photos of you
with kids that are too sick. It would be great if you had time to go to
Africa, because your skin would look amazing contrasted with the
little starving African kids, if you know what I mean." She winked,
and I tried not to roll my eyes. "Oh, and don't pick the ones that are
crossed off. Some of the other cast members are doing those, and we

can't have more than one of you on the same cause at a time—*that* looks contrived."

I stared blankly at the list. "Sondra, are you serious?" I said. "Can't I just pick something good, like raising money to fight poverty in inner cities? What about health insurance for the working poor?" I tried to remember some of the issues I'd heard my parents discussing at the dinner table when I was in high school. Sondra had already vetoed my dad's illness, calling it "too rare to get any press," which I thought was inconsiderate.

Sondra wrinkled her nose and let out a huge sigh. "Listen, I am *not* going to some filthy Boys and Girls Club with you in Hometown, America, just so you can be a do-gooder. It is my job to get photos of you out there that will give people warm feelings about you. We have to give people a reason to like you and to keep watching the show. I don't want to spend a lot of time on this though—find a ribbon to cut in Santa Monica, or go hug some babies in a pediatric oncology unit. Do not make me get dirty or put me in danger. Just stick to the list, and don't get carried away."

And so the list had been sitting in my trailer, gathering dust and making me tense as I wracked my brain for things that had an actual connection to my life. No one in my family had ever had cancer, my grandparents were still alive, and I'd never been in a natural disaster. The more I went through my family tree and decided I was totally boring and normal, the more I dreaded the inevitable Sondra phone call asking what charity I'd picked.

I scanned the list for the hundredth time. The Myasthenia Gravis Foundation? What *is* that? Africa was out, as I was unlikely to get a long enough break in shooting to allow me to go back to Bay City for the weekend, much less another continent. I'd never known anyone whose house was destroyed by a hurricane, and no one I knew had lupus, so I was out of luck. Some people get all the good diseases. Damn that Lance Armstrong! The heart defect my dad died of was so rare it barely had a name, much less a foundation. Also, I knew this wasn't really how it worked. Ross was on the board of several charities in L.A.; he did it because he loved it, and he helped a lot of people in the process.

And so I was lying on the bed, totally incapacitated, as I knew Sondra was coming by the set the next day and was going to want my choice. For a moment I considered writing "Eating Disorders of the Rich and Famous" on the list, but I knew this would get back to Attila, and I didn't need the headache. What I needed was a nice cousin with scoliosis or a paralyzed veteran uncle. What I had was nothing. Zilch. Zero.

"What about gay rights?" called Vince from the living room of my suite. "Gay rights are huge these days, your show is about gay issues, and you happen to have a gay best friend. We could get you some rainbow bracelets to pass out. Problem solved. Let's go." He put my purse next to my limp hand on the bed and tried to put my fingers around the handle.

I handed him the list. "Sorry . . . no gay rights causes on here." I didn't want to tell him that I'd already asked about this, and (even though the show's theme focused on two homosexual men adopting a teenage girl and her sister) Sondra had strictly forbidden me to speak out about gay and lesbian issues. "Are you kidding me?" she'd sneered. "The minute you attend the opening of some podunk gay, lesbian, and transgender rainbow queer center, I'm going to have to do *weeks'* worth of work to combat all the gay rumors that are going to start about you. You don't want to be on the cover of *The Advocate* your first year in Hollywood. I don't care if your dad is gay, which, by the way, Anne Heche's was, and that didn't even come out until she'd been with Ellen for two years. Don't even think about doing the gay thing, Star. Seriously. I'm going to have enough trouble keeping the gay media off Greg, who has played an action hero in every show he's been in up to now. Look at that poor Jennifer Beals in *The L Word*. She's married with a baby, and still there's all this speculation about her because that show is so popular. We can't have that with you right now . . . Please just pick something simple—I'm totally swamped trying to do individual PR for all of you guys as well as the show itself. Seriously, if the show gets much bigger, we're going to need you guys to hire your own publicists."

I surveyed the list again, determined to pick something immediately and get it over with. This shouldn't be so difficult. Dogs . . . I liked dogs. What about the Humane Society? Finally, I settled on a charity that rescued dogs, which seemed like the cause least likely to incur the wrath of my team. "Great, that's totally great. I'll arrange a photo shoot," said Sondra when I called to tell her. "Just don't go all Bob Barker on us."

THE FACT WAS, DESPITE how much I wanted to think of myself as an edgy indie girl, being a TV star was fun and got more so every day. Case in point: Vince and I were at a magazine stand on Hollywood Boulevard shopping for our weekly gossip fix when we spotted my *Teen Vogue* cover, already on the newsstands. "Oh my God . . . it's you!" he screamed, grabbing the magazine. We stood there, absorbing the shock and poring over every picture. "Wow," he whispered. "That doesn't even look like you." He paused. "But in a good way—you know what I mean. Is *that* what they do to Mariah Carey?"

"I know," I said. It wasn't just that I'd changed so much since Michigan—the weight loss, the new hair color, and the makeup alone made me look like a super-enhanced version of my former self. It was the retouching that we really marveled over—they'd completely gotten rid of my eye bags, shaved at least three inches off my waist, and even managed to make me look taller. I turned the pages slowly, staring at the photos inside . . . I *did* look totally hot, but I almost didn't recognize myself in the mass of hair, makeup, and airbrushing passing for me in the photos. The only place I could really see myself was the eyes, and even then I looked like myself wearing a "beautiful girl" Halloween costume. I shouldn't have liked the fake me so much, but I did.

"You were there, right? I slept for two hours the night before . . . I have never looked this good!" I said. I was completely amazed and impressed at the result. "I am so in love with this picture, I am carrying this around with me all the time," I exclaimed, putting one of the pages over my face. "This is my new look!" We started to read the short article that accompanied the photos. The reporter had also interviewed one of the makeup artists about working with me, and she'd said, "Star needs almost no makeup . . . her skin just glows." We laughed. Ah, if only that were true. I could hardly wait for *People* magazine to dig up old photos of me from high school to do the inevitable "then and now" comparison issue. Between the frizzy perm and the bad skin, I could just see an "ugly duckling turns into a swan" story on the horizon, like the ones they're always doing about Kelly Clarkson.

We marveled over the amazing photos until the newsstand guy gave us a dirty look. "It's her—in the magazine!" Vince said excitedly, pointing to me, then to the picture. We bought every copy at that newsstand, and we each walked toward my car holding a big stack. My mom was going to freak!

The crazier it got, the more I tried to remind myself that this whole life was fake and not to get too attached. Slowly, though, I could feel myself getting sucked in. I tried to stay cynical about the Hollywood scene, but I had to admit—I really, really loved it. Shooting the show was going great, I was getting along with my fellow cast members, and I was happy with the work we were all doing. Plus, every time I got a paycheck I still couldn't believe the money.

Added to the growing list of "amazing Hollywood moments," I noted that it was totally surreal to be driving down Hollywood Boulevard, in a BMW paid for by my huge paycheck from my starring role on a TV show, passing under a big billboard of that show, on the way to FedEx a bunch of magazines with my own face on the cover to my family in Michigan. I hated to admit it, but I was actually happy.

WE'D BARELY RECOVERED FROM the excitement of my first big magazine cover when the phone rang even earlier than usual one cold morning in December. "Have you seen the news?" I heard a perky voice say. It was Kristen from the marketing department.

I looked over at the clock, which said 8:30 A.M. "Ummmpp-nnnhhhh," I grunted from beneath my fortress of pillows. I wasn't called until 11:00 A.M. and had taken a time-release Ambien someone gave me in order to guarantee that I made the most of every resting moment available. "Star, wake up!" she shouted. "I have news!" I sat bolt upright in bed. She hadn't called me this early since before Super Saturday! and every time the marketing department said "news," it always meant I had to do something I wasn't going to enjoy. My stomach clenched. "Wha . . . what's going on?" I said, trying not to sound drugged. Could I get fired for sounding drugged?

"Omigod . . . they announced the Golden Globe nominations, and *Autumn Leaves* is up for four!" she shouted. "This is *huge,* Star! You should go in to the set early . . . the producers are going to be there, there's a party tonight, the whole thing." She was breathless with excitement, and I could hear shouts in the background as she hung up. My head was spinning. I wanted to call her back to ask if I was nominated . . . or did I? I picked up the remote from the nightstand, quickly turning on the TV and flipping to E! to see if their ticker had picked it up.

I held my breath as I watched the list of nominees go by, counting the nominations in my head as they came up: Best Drama, that was one . . . Best Actor, Greg Forster, two . . . Best Supporting Actor, Ross Wong, three . . . Best Actress . . . Star Spencer.

Oh my God! I thought, *I'm nominated for a Golden Globe Award!* I jumped

up on my bed, then started to run around the room. The phone rang
again. Vince. I answered the phone while at the same time yelling,
"Did you see it?"

"Oh my God!" he screamed. "How excited are you right now?
You're nominated for a Golden Globe Award! Call your mom! Call
your mom! Arrrgghhhhhhhhhhh so excited!"

I laughed. Finally, an event worthy of Vince's excitement. By the
time I got to the set, there was already a party going on. Since *Autumn
Leaves* was now bigger than *Desperate Housewives,* the cast had already
been asked to make an appearance at the Golden Globes and to present an award. Was this my life? Honestly, I thought I was doing a
good job on the show, and I was trying to learn as much as possible
and do the best I could, but . . . a Golden Globe? Weren't those re-
served for people who had been in the business for years? All at once
I felt legitimized and fradulent.

By the time I got to set, my trailer was filled with flowers, gift
baskets, and dresses. By noon Vince was packed in between the frothy
designer dresses, looking like a kid in a candy store. "Aim, *everyone* is
sending over samples," he said excitedly. "So far, Roberto Cavalli sent
over this amazing gold beaded gown, Elie Saab sent a seafoam-green
dress, and Roland Mouret sent a whole rack of stuff. We've just got
to get you into a couple of these so I can start working on a hair and
accessories strategy. We've only got a couple of weeks to plan, and
there's no way I'm letting you end up on the 'What Was She Thinking?' list for your first big awards show."

Vince had become the stylist for many other celebrities, and this
was his first event season too. He was sharing my feelings of extreme
excitement. We pinched each other at two-hour intervals as the designer clothes and gifts continued to pour in throughout the day.

"This . . . is . . . unbelievable," he said, paging through a million-
dollar jewelry catalog. "This necklace is worth five million dollars, *and*
they send this hot security guard to follow you around all night. We

both win! Omigod . . . and have you even considered the presenter gift bag? Epic! Mink-sleeping-bag epic! One of my other clients already got a presenter pre—gift bag, and she's not even nominated!"

During one of my breaks from shooting, I started trying them on, discovering that I was either officially small enough to fit into the sample sizes or officially important enough for people to know my real size. I couldn't tell, since most of them didn't have sizes in them anyway.

"Who cares?" said Vince, holding up a short black dress that had just arrived by messenger. "We are so not sending back the dresses you don't wear."

MORE EXCITING, PERHAPS, THAN the Golden Globe nomination, the fancy dresses, and the never-ending stream of gift baskets was the anticipation of reclaiming Christmas. Winter break from the show was about to start, and I was *counting down the minutes* until I could go home to Bay City, sleep in, and have Christmas dinner with my family. I had spent a ton of money on Christmas presents for everyone, and I was really excited to finally be able to give my mom and my brothers the great Christmas they deserved, to erase the bad memories surrounding the holiday.

Christmas in my family needed a lot of help. It was December 17 three years earlier when my dad had a heart attack on the way home from work. They'd taken him to the hospital, where he'd lain in a coma for a week, then died in the middle of the night on Christmas Eve. The rest of my senior year was a blur of sympathetic faces, awkward conversations ("I'm so sorry" or "He's in a better place now"), and practicalities. My mother had insisted I start college anyway, saying that it's "what my dad would have wanted." Adam was two years behind me in school, and Ian, the youngest, was just twelve. We were all shell-shocked. We'd skipped Christmas every year since then.

Really, this was a subject that my family never stopped thinking about, and I felt like I had to be the "strong one" to keep everything from falling apart. It was almost a relief to go away to college, away from the never-ending memories of my dad, people who knew him, and well-meaning neighbors who were forever asking us if we needed anything. But now, things were different. I was different. I was on a hit TV show, and I was determined to make this Christmas the best one ever.

The last day of shooting, my bags were packed, the presents were shipped, and I was ready to go when I was summoned to the network offices. I sped down there after shooting wrapped, praying that whatever they wanted me to do could wait until after the holiday.

"Shut the door, and sit down," said Attila. I wondered how long it would take her interns to notice if I bludgeoned her with the chunky wood paperweight on her desk, then left her body there. Actually, from the disgruntled look of her office staff, I was pretty sure they'd help me. Besides, I was leaving the next day for Christmas break, and nothing could spoil my mood.

By my third sit-down, I already knew that whenever she told me to shut the door, it was going to be nothing good. She did these meetings one-on-one so she could deny they ever happened. Despite the Golden Globe nomination, she was going to find a way to blame something on me. I braced myself and looked at my watch. Sixteen hours until my plane . . . what could be so bad? She'd yell, I'd cry a little on the way home, and then Christmas break would be under way. No problem!

She sighed methodically, her chubby hands riffling the weekly ratings reports. "I just don't understand it," she said. "People in your age group should really be relating to you more. I mean, those girls from *One Tree Hill* have popularity ratings that are twice yours. I guess you're just not as 'universal appeal' as we thought. Really, Star, it's just going to come down to numbers, and eventually we're just going to have to get rid of your character in favor of someone more appealing."

I wanted to ask her if she'd heard of a little thing called the Golden Globe Award, or if she'd picked up a magazine lately, or maybe mention that the paparazzi were following me like mad when I so much as went out for brunch, but I already knew this would have no impact and would most likely backfire. Talking common sense to Attila was the rough equivalent of trying to teach Swedish to a grizzly bear. In my mind, I knew that most of what she was saying was not true, but I also assumed, possibly erroneously, that she wasn't allowed to make up stuff like this just to torture me.

"What can I do to help?" I said, choosing my words carefully.

"Frankly, Star, I don't see anything that will raise your appeal, except maybe . . ." She trailed off.

"What? Mindy, I'll do anything!" With fifteen hours, forty-two minutes until my plane took off, I might actually have been serious.

She leaned forward as if to let me in on a trade secret and slowly opened her thin lips, which I noticed were a delicate shade of coral. She looked at me seriously. "Star, I'm glad you said that. It's about your teeth."

That was not at all what I thought she was going to say. My teeth? What could I possibly do about my teeth?

I was sorry I asked.

The next morning, instead of being on a plane back home, I was in the office of cosmetic dentist Dr. Ryan Tan. "OK, open your mouth and let me take a look," he said. "Your producer said your teeth were too 'real people' to work for television."

I lay back in the chair with my mouth open, wondering what he could do about my teeth that would still allow to me to get on the plane that afternoon. I'd had a few cavities, like every other kid in the U.S., and I had some fillings. I brushed twice a day and sometimes even remembered to floss. What else was there? Whitening? Filling replacement? Braces? I kept my mouth open while the dentist poked at my teeth with a little pick, hoping it wouldn't hurt too much.

"Your teeth are a little bit yellow for camera . . . you've never had braces, right?"

"No," I said hesitantly. I didn't know what he wanted to do, and I wasn't sure I had the power to say no. Would they have to write the braces into the show?

"You'd definitely look a lot better with veneers. Your producer wants you to get a whole new set over the break."

My eyes started to glaze over as he described the process of getting a complete set of veneers—a series of procedures that did not sound easy. He took a mold of my teeth as "before and after" slides of formerly snaggle-toothed people flashed on the computer screen in front of the dental chair. In my mind, I could hear my mom telling me that my teeth were one of my nicest features. I wondered if she always said this because we didn't have the money for expensive dental work. Did my teeth look that bad?

I tuned back in to what he was saying just as he got to " . . . then we file down your teeth, you come back in a week or so, and we fit the new porcelain veneers on."

At this, I snapped back into full listening mode. Did he say "file down your teeth"? That didn't sound good. Did he say "come back in a week"? Oh no no . . . I was going to be long gone, sleeping in my old room by then. I didn't quite know which one was more disturbing.

"Wait . . . what? Am I going to look like Dracula? Why would you file my teeth?" I said frantically. "And . . . what about Christmas? I can't wait around here for a week . . . that's, like, December twenty-second! That's my whole break!" I couldn't stop my voice from cracking, and I felt the tears coming on. Why did Attila have to ruin everything? I was saving Christmas! I wished I wasn't one of those people who cried in response to stress.

Dr. Tan put his arm around me reassuringly. "Well, we want the veneers to fit as closely as possible to your regular teeth, so we file the old ones down completely—we just shave the teeth right off. You don't need them anyway; porcelain is much better, and then you can never get cavities. We can have them done in maybe four or five days; that's faster than we ever do it, but for you . . ."

He seemed disturbed when I started to hyperventilate at the mention of "four or five days." Anxiety quickly gave way to anger as I thought of Attila, enjoying her . . . whatever she did at home. This was insane. New teeth? Over Christmas? Is this what they did to Hilary Duff? Now I had more sympathy for her. I read this interview where she said one of her front teeth fell out during a concert (because she's a singer now) and she had to get her teeth capped in Arkansas. So . . . they filed down her teeth first? The thought of little Hil Duff (who I had met once at a club) with tiny Dracula-like teeth sent me into a fit of giggles. Then I started to laugh for real. I was missing Christmas for vampire tooth filing, then Chiclet teeth?

"Are you OK?" said Dr. Tan apprehensively.

"I'm fine," I said, composing myself. I could tell I was starting to make him nervous, and I didn't want anyone in his office calling the tabloids to tell the world how weird I was.

"Go ahead . . . I'm ready." I sighed.

Dr. Tan gave me a few shots of Novocain to numb my mouth, and then he hit me with the laughing gas just to be on the safe side. Dust flew for what seemed like three hours as he "shaved" my teeth, getting them ready for the new veneers. After a while they started to make that burny smell, and even with the shots and the gas it was starting to hurt. I tried to say so, but with the suction thing in my mouth, it just came out "eeee huurrrrrs." Finally he seemed to understand, took a little break, and gave me a tranquilizer. At that point, I would have taken anything to get rid of the raw discomfort of the tooth shaving. Through the haze I looked at my watch, which said 9:00 P.M.

At midnight they woke me up and handed me a mirror so I could see the temporary teeth. They looked good, but I felt like I was holding up a mirror in order to look at someone else's face. The teeth I'd had since my grown-up teeth came in were *gone,* and in their place was a perfect set of straight, white replacement teeth. Would anyone in Bay City notice how different I looked? I felt like I needed an owner's manual for them—could I floss them? Could I still say the letter "S" without sounding like I had dentures? Would the show start getting letters about my teeth now? Did they get letters before? Why was it so important to do this now?

As I was leaving the office, the nurse handed me a small slip of paper. "What's this?" I said, stuffing it in my purse.

"Oh, you should read that; it's a list of foods you can't eat from now on," she said earnestly. "You don't want to break the new teeth!"

"You mean the temporary teeth, right?" I said. There was no way I was limiting my diet for the rest of my foreseeable future. The new teeth had to be stronger than that.

"Um, no . . . ," she said. "Once he puts the porcelain veneers on, you'll need to be careful with them from then on, or else they'll break and you'll have to come back."

My mind started to race. Foods I couldn't eat? Why was this not mentioned before? It was Christmas, for God's sake! I figured it was going to be some random list, like when my friend Karen got braces in the seventh grade, and her orthodontist gave her a list that said, "Don't eat popcorn balls, candy apples, or corn nuts," like Karen lived at the state fair.

But it wasn't. The list consisted of hard foods like nuts, chips, popcorn, hard candy, chicken, ribs, and celery. At the top of the list, I saw the word "carrots."

My eyes welled up with tears. When I was a little kid, I loved carrots so much, my dad started calling me Bunny Luv, after the girl rabbit on the outside of the carrot bag. In fact, "Bunny" was his nickname for me, and he kept calling me that, even when I was seventeen years old. Carrots were my favorite food . . . I think I consumed at least a bag of baby carrots every day on the set. If I gave up eating this, my staple food, I would have little else to eat.

"Is this a joke?" I said to the nurse. "I'm not giving up carrots."

"Oh, but you have to, carrots are the worst. You're for sure going to break your teeth if you keep eating them. You can eat strained carrots, like baby food, if you're really desperate, or a carrot muffin, but you are probably never going to be able to, like, bite into a carrot ever again." She said this all so calmly, she could hardly have been prepared for my reaction.

Despite my best efforts to the contrary, I burst into tears. Suddenly, I felt like one of my fondest memories of my dad had been stolen. Also, was she crazy? I hadn't eaten a muffin in five months.

After two more visits to Dr. Evil, Bunny Luv was gone, and in her place was a perfect-teeth-having replacement. Here's the thing—you really *can* tell the difference between your teeth and artificial teeth. I mean, once they're gone, you can totally remember what your old teeth used to look like, and it's a little bit sad. Yes, they looked great— perfect, straight, white movie star teeth. But this was how they'd look forever now . . . teeth never grow back, so they'll never look the way they did the last time my dad saw me. I wondered if you could hold a funeral for teeth. I wondered if it was the Percocet that was making me all philosophical. I wondered how quickly I could get to the airport.

I arrived at the Detroit airport at 10:30 P.M., exactly two days before Christmas, face swollen, jaws and teeth aching. Who knew your gums actually swell on the airplane?

IT WAS AFTER MIDNIGHT when we finally got home from the airport. My mom looked so tired, I almost offered to drive when we pulled over for gas. My youngest brother, Ian, and I settled back into our old friendly kidding and banter, but my brother Adam, who had just turned eighteen, was sulky and silent.

I felt a nostalgic pang when I walked into my old room, which Adam had turned into a music studio. The next fall he'd be going away too, leaving my mom and Ian in the house. I wondered if, when Ian was gone, she'd decide to move to L.A. with me, or live somewhere else. It was weird to have everyone in the same house again, and even weirder to think about not having that house at all anymore. I had started paying the mortgage regularly, but I wondered if she'd be one of those moms who decides that "the house is just too big" and moves into some condo. Part of me wanted her to keep the house, just so I'd have a place to come back to. I looked around the room . . . Adam had taken down most of my movie posters, replacing them with posters for the Killers, Panic at the Disco, and the Strokes. My stuff was still on the ceiling, though . . . I lay down on my old bed, staring up at posters of *Waiting for Guffman; sex, lies, and videotape;* and of course *Say Anything,* and thinking about high school, which seemed like a million years ago. Things seemed so much easier when I was an idealistic indie film chick.

Adam was not thrilled about me reclaiming my room. "Don't touch the iMac," he said, grunting as he lifted my suitcase onto the bed. "It's got Pro Tools on it, and I'm mixing our album. If you touch it, you might mess it up." His face looked more and more like my dad's, especially his eyes, and I wished he were nicer.

"What if I have to check my e-mail?" I said, tempted to mention that my job had *paid* for his fancy computer. "I don't think I can live without the Internet."

"Use the one in Ian's room . . . seriously, Amy, I'm going to know if you touch it. Why can't you sleep in the guest room?"

"Um, because I live here too, this is my old room, and I'm older than you?" I said, pushing the suitcase with my toe and looking up at him. "Now, go away so I can get some sleep." Adam's competitiveness with me had intensified since I'd been away and gotten my job on *Autumn Leaves.* Ian and I had actually become closer and e-mailed several times a day, but I only knew what was going on with Adam through secondhand reports. I knew he had applied to colleges and was waiting to hear. I knew he was hoping that his band would become the next Strokes before that so he wouldn't have to go. I knew that my mom was going to try to force him either way.

He rolled his eyes. He was taller than me and had the choppy faux-hawk hair I always saw on rocker kids in L.A. I almost told him that if he were nicer to me, I would convince our mother to let him come live with me when he graduated, but the look on his face was so snide and resentful, I decided to keep my mouth shut and let him be forced to go to college.

"Get out!" I shouted. "Why do you do this?"

He muttered something under his breath.

"What?" I said, standing up. "What did you say?"

"I said you're fake now, Amy. You went to L.A., you got the Hollywood car wash, and now you think you're better than everyone else. You look like you have fucking anorexia, you're blonde, and you totally sold out. You look like Barbie. You're on TV, which up until two years ago you didn't even watch . . . what happened to you?"

"Hollywood car wash?" I yelled. "What is that even? Is that a term you and your poser friends made up? Give me a break. You're not going to last five minutes in the real world, Adam. You have no idea what people are going to want from you if you ever get *your* big break." My jaw throbbed, and I felt like crying but wasn't going to give him the satisfaction. He loved to make fun of me for being the "crier" in the family.

Adam's face turned red and he opened his mouth to yell something else, but Ian's face appeared in the doorway. "Adam, oh my God . . . she just got here. Can you leave her alone?" he said, looking over at me plaintively. We'd had many e-mail discussions about Adam's attitude.

"Whatever," Adam said, turning and walking out. "I'll be shocked if she eats anything at Christmas dinner."

Ian sat down on my bed. "He's just jealous," he said. "You figured out the mysterious code for success, and he's wondering how you did it."

I laughed. Ian was the smartest of all of us—fifteen years old, and studying physics and calculus. He was going to be the one who ended up making our mom the proudest.

"We should totally watch something," he said, walking over to the wall that was lined with bookshelves full of DVDs. "Did you see *The Science of Sleep?* It's pretty deep—not as good as *Mindwalk,* but really engaging."

I was struck with the sudden urge to hug Ian and never let him go. "I need to sleep," I said. "But definitely tomorrow."

"OK," he said, walking toward the door. "Don't worry about Adam. Tomorrow I'm going to bulk-erase his hard drive."

I laughed, laying my head down on my pillow. "Ian, I love you." My head ached and I tried to go to sleep, but I couldn't get Adam's words out of my mind. Had I really sold out?

The next morning, the pain in my gums had subsided long enough for me to try eating by chewing with the back of my mouth. My mother had managed to hold off on the "you're too thin" comments so far, but I could tell she was concerned.

She turned around when I came into the kitchen. "Did you sleep well?" she said, hugging me. "Did Adam yell at you? I don't know what's going on with that boy. He's going through a phase. Now Ian is mad at him . . . I just want all of you to get along."

I laughed. For once, I didn't mind the family drama. It was good to think about something other than scripts, or calories, or who was doing what with whom in L.A. I noted with some surprise that I actually missed Michigan.

"Any good gossip?" she said, stirring the mashed potatoes. Though she'd casually enjoyed her weekly *People* magazine before *Autumn Leaves* started, now she was celebrity obsessed in a way that I found extremely amusing. "Are you seeing anyone yet? Is it true what the magazines say about your relationship with Matt Pierce? A reporter called here to get a quote from me, but I said 'no comment.' That was right, right? I mean, are you dating him?"

I rolled my eyes. "Mom!" I said, pouring coffee into a mug shaped like a tulip. I didn't really want to get into the subject of Matt, since I barely knew where we stood myself and since I had it on good authority that his character was about to be written off the show in favor of an "indie rock" guy so that the show's producers could start incorporating music into the show and selling CDs as product tie-in. I also neglected to mention that Vince had finally started hanging out with Perez Hilton, the most famous gossip blogger in the world, and probably knew enough underground Hollywood info to blow her mind.

Ian ran in behind me. "Amy, I'm glad you're up . . . I have discovered a way to make a smoothie out of carrots that retains the original flavor without tasting like baby food. This you are going to like . . . I have several versions in the fridge for you."

I sat down at the kitchen table. "Ian, you are the best brother ever," I said. "I need more coffee before I try a carrot smoothie, though."

After the initial blowup with Adam, things quickly settled back into about what they'd been before my dad died. We spent Christmas Eve day wrapping presents, watching *A Charlie Brown Christmas,* and making a very long popcorn string for the tree, and managed to stay ahead of the dull ache that we all felt whenever we were together— the pain of life without Dad. Sometimes it was fine, and sometimes it felt like the minute any of us mentioned him, whatever was keeping us upright would give way, and we'd all just dissolve into a heap of grief.

By that night, the pain in my teeth was gone, and I got my first drug-free night's sleep in months. Adam even stopped calling me Barbie after a few days, and we discovered the one thing we had in common—the fact that our mom didn't know that either of us smoked. Before long we were dragging Ian on impromptu trips to the mall, the grocery store, and Adam's friend's house, where his band rehearsed. "I'm glad you guys are getting along so well," said my mom as we walked out the door one afternoon. I punched Ian in the arm before he could tell her the real reason.

During the course of the week, I was thrilled to find that no one from my hometown seemed to give a crap that I was famous.

It was good to be home. The week passed by too quickly, and on the last night my mom and I were up late, sharing hot chocolate in the kitchen. I had to be back on set the next day, and I was already feeling sad about getting to spend so little time with them.

"Amy—are you OK?" she said. "I just want to make sure you're not taking on too much responsibility. You're still young, you know. Sometimes I wonder if we should all move out there so you'll have your family."

"I'm fine, Mom," I said. I had briefly entertained the idea of asking her to move to L.A. to be my manager, but the thought of us all living together was a little much. Still, we were all pretty close before I left, and I didn't want to lose that.

"Mom, how are you guys? I mean, is it weird still living here, doing the same stuff . . ."

"You mean without your father?"

"Yeah—I mean, I'm working and my life is totally different, and I still think about him all the time, so I can only imagine . . ."

She smiled, squeezing my hand. "Sometimes it's easy, and sometimes it's hard. I think about him all the time too, honey. Life is unpredictable, as we've learned."

I hugged her. "I miss you, Mom."

B Y THE TIME I got back from visiting my family, I was totally
conflicted about my Hollywood "transformation," as if I'd
been living among a tribe of African pygmy warriors and had
adopted all of their customs, then gone back to civilization and had to
deal with the local townspeople pointing out the war paint and nose
rings that had seemed so normal in my quest to fit in. Was I better
the old way?

On the one hand, it was true. I had been starved, my hair had been
bleached and straightened, and my face had been injected, de-acned,
and bronzed. My teeth had been shaved and capped, and I was eating less and smoking more than I ever had in my life. I was a rich and
successful Hollywood star, I was a Golden Globe nominee, and I had
a killer wardrobe, two stylists, and a personal trainer. But . . . wasn't I
still the same person inside? Wasn't I still a good daughter, paying off
medical bills and tuition, taking care of my family like my dad would
have wanted?

To compound the paranoia, with each successive step in the Star
transformation, I wondered a little more—wouldn't people who

TiVo'd the show start to notice that things were gradually different about me? Would I ever be able to go back to just being a normal person, or was I destined to end up one of those pinched, overly plastic-surgeried ladies that everyone talks about at parties?

I mentioned this to Michele on the first day back from break. She snorted derisively. "First of all, America expects us to look good. Secondly . . . everybody does it. Look at the people on *Friends*. Jennifer Aniston, season one, is, like, a totally different animal from Jennifer Aniston, the 'Brad and Jen' edition. That transformation took serious teamwork, and now she looks hot. I hope she cleaned up in that divorce. Can you imagine, a guy as hot as Brad Pitt living in freaking Africa? Good Lord. They don't even have indoor plumbing there, Star! I bet you can get AIDS just by skinning your knee there!"

She was an idiot, but she had a good point about Jennifer Aniston. You wouldn't catch a regular person with flaws on a show like *Friends*. One thing is for sure—there was no one who looked like they were from Bay City on TV, then or now. Even me.

A FEW WEEKS BEFORE the Golden Globes, word came from the network that since it was our first awards show, we could bring our families, after which I immediately got my mom and my brothers tickets, outfits, and seats in the family area of the auditorium. My mom and Ian were beyond excited, and even Adam seemed grateful to finally be coming to L.A., even if it was because I bought him a ticket.

"Who are you bringing?" I said excitedly to Michele during a cigarette break.

"Oh, I'm not." She sniffed. "My dad is busy, and my mom is"—she lowered her voice and looked around—"fat. I don't want her on the red carpet with me. I mean—can you imagine the photo captions? I don't want the tabloids doing a story about how I had to 'overcome my fat genes,' like they always do with Jessica Alba. I'm not even going to tell them they could have come," she said, casually going back to her *Variety*.

I laughed, then was immediately horrified at myself. I wanted to tell her to go to hell, that if I could have my dad back for one minute, even one second, I wouldn't care if he weighed five hundred pounds. It didn't register with her, though—she was so lost in her own narcissistic world, even having fat parents was out of the question. Besides, I didn't want to share too much personal information with her, since I never got the impression I was seeing the real Michele McCann behind the carefully constructed persona. She was like a master craftsman who had skillfully molded herself into a "success in show business" robot, from the perfectly sculpted body to the mind trained to be as aggressive and opportunistic as the plague. Not that she even had to try—she'd been in her father's shows since she was eight. Maybe being born into the business meant that you just lacked any sort of sympathetic or "real person" genes.

WITH SIX DAYS TO go until the Golden Globes, the awards show prep had taken on a life of its own. We'd just finalized the outfit (Zac Posen dress, Louboutin heels, Fred Leighton necklace and earrings), the hairstyle (messy half up-do), and the makeup (smoky eyes, pale lips, and medium-bronze fake tan) when Sondra's office called. "We're sending you to We Care Spa for the weekend," said Emily, her eager assistant. "Just a little insurance to make sure you look amazing in all your Golden Globes red carpet photos! You'll just go down there, detox, get massages, and relax. You'll come back glowing!"

"Sounds great," I said. "What should I bring?" I wasn't sure what she meant by "detox," but I didn't care. We'd been shooting marathon days, and I was in desperate need of a massage and some sleep.

"Oh, they'll take care of you," she said. "Let me know if you see

Gisele or anyone else there. That place is crawling with models and celebrities right before awards shows."

I was released from shooting uncharacteristically early that Friday night, and by midnight, I was in the back of a car going out toward Palm Springs. On the way there, I read the informational package that Emily had put together for me.

THE WE CARE PHILOSOPHY

At We Care we base our programs on the theory that most people are taking on an excess amount of toxins through today's diet which is composed of processed foods with many additives and preservatives. These toxins tend to be difficult to breakdown and build up in the colon where they have long lasting negative effects on one's health and contribute to disease. These effects include low energy, digestive problems, decreased mental alertness, fatigue and weight gain. Our approach at We Care is to cleanse the system (specifically the large intestines and colon) of these toxins which have accumulated over the years through use of a natural all liquid diet.

Liquid diet? Colon? Large intestine? All at once, I realized that this was a network-sponsored trip to celebrity fat camp, aimed at getting me to look better in my Golden Globes photos.

LIQUID DIET

The We Care liquid diet is rich in nutrients and offers many specific ingredients to address flushing various organs including the liver and kidneys which act as filtering systems for the body. As the body easily accepts the natural liquid diet, it allows the digestive system to utilize more energy in cleaning out the life long accumulated waste products and toxins. This process is accelerated through the use of colonics: a safe, effective measure for accelerating the emptying and cleaning of the colon and large intestine.

Some of the specific products used as part of the We Care natural liquid diet include Kyogreen, Spirulina, Wheat Grass, Barley, Acidophilus, freshly squeezed vegetable juice, lemon water, enzymes, liver and kidney teas and blood purifying tea.

I momentarily considered having the driver turn around, or at least having him stop at In-N-Out Burger before dropping me off. But because I had no way to escape from the car and we were already halfway there, and because I feared incurring the wrath of both Sondra and Attila if I attempted a prison break, I sat back, lit a cigarette, and tried to get my head around "detoxing" my body on a liquid diet for the entire weekend. My mind raced. Could you die from fasting? How hungry would I be by Monday? What was a "colonic," anyway? I bet Attila was sitting in the office laughing.

I arrived to find the We Care Spa very quiet and placid, not at all like the diet jail I'd been expecting. On the way to my suite, the only famous person I saw in the community area was not Gisele, but Declan McManus, a hot Scottish actor who had been appearing with some regularity in industry magazines and who I'd seen around town. He came up to me immediately, and my heart skipped a beat. Did he recognize me?

"You're Star, right?" he said, his Scottish accent sounding even sexier in person than it did in the movies. "Can't fit in your party clothes either, eh?" he said. "Fooking bollocks if you ask me—two thousand dollars to drink swamp juice and have people shite for you!"

I could barely make out what he was saying, but the whole detox thing sounded even more absurd when he said it. I couldn't tell if he was flirting—he was supposed to be engaged to a British actress, though they were seldom photographed together. Michele had once told me that they were staying together for the publicity because they both had movies opening—a strategy she seemed to really admire.

I laughed, trying to act cool and not starstruck. "Yeah," I said. "Tight dress. I'm focusing on the spa part and trying not to think about the liquid fiber diet and how hungry I'm going to be by the end of the weekend. Besides, what's a colonic?"

He told me, and I couldn't believe I was actually discussing poop in any way with a famous hot guy, though I decided if anyone needed "internal cleansing," it was probably him. I'd never seen him in a picture without a beer and a cigarette, no matter what time of day it was.

"I'm in the villa in the back," he said, winking. "Call me if you get lonely or hungry. I smuggled in a secret emergency stash of cigarettes, beer, and Hostess cupcakes. Fook healthy living!" He took my cell phone number and immediately sent me what would be the first of many flirty text messages over the next forty-eight hours.

By the next afternoon, I was grumpy, had a raging headache, and was in desperate need of a cigarette. Having just had my first colonic of the day, I felt a little violated and like I needed a shower. A colonic is probably not something I would have ever done willingly. In fact, it *is* a little like you're paying someone to take a crap for you. While she was pumping my insides, my "colonic technician" Ermina (who smelled strangely of coffee beans) made chatty conversation.

"Wow, you have a ton of buildup. Do you eat a lot of protein?" she said, calmly not acknowledging the fact that she had just inserted a tube into my (ahem) private pooping area.

"No, I eat a lot of nothing. Thanks for asking," I said, unable to disguise my discomfort and annoyance.

"What's going to happen on your show? Does Seth come back?" she said nonchalantly, and I laughed a little bit. It's true, there really is no escape from your fans.

Needless to say, I was in no mood to scoop the crap lady on upcoming plot points. I tried to stay as quiet as possible by pretending to doze off for the rest of the "procedure," but mostly I was just faking through an uncomfortable silence. Although I promised myself I would be one of those "totally down-to-earth" celebrities, I found that Sondra was right—I should really stop chatting with service people. I was only opening myself to stupid questions that I couldn't answer anyway and to everyone wanting to get their niece into the business.

Afterward, I had to admit that my system did feel "clean," though I was light-headed and dying for coffee. How did people fast for two or three weeks? I was going on twelve hours, and I felt like a truck ran over me. How was I going to be Golden Globes fabulous in four days?

With hunger gnawing at my stomach and my head throbbing, I skipped the liquid kelp lunch and went back to my room to lie down. Since there were "no TV or radio" and "minimal cell phone use" policies in effect, I was forced to send many e-mails to Vince, then attempt to get the tiny browser in my BlackBerry to work so I could at least keep up on the news. I was waiting for the *New York Times* website to load when I heard a tapping at the door.

It was Declan McManus, holding a six-pack of Diet Coke.

I'd thought he was kidding when he invited me to his villa, but as it turned out, he wasn't. "Where ya been, girlie?" he said, looking into my room. "What ya been eatin'?" He pulled a Hostess cupcake from behind his back. "Ye must be hungry by now, eh?"

I laughed. He smelled like cigarettes and beer and was covered in tattoos—not really my type, but still hot. It wasn't like I thought he was going to tell anyone; no one was supposed to know either of us was there anyway—the very definition of a lost weekend. I laughed to myself as I thought of how horrified Attila would be if I showed up to the Golden Globes on his arm. Declan McManus had a reputation as an international party guy, to say the least—definitely not "supportive of my brand equity." Still, they'd sent me there against my will, so why not have a little fun until Sunday?

After weighing the pros and cons, my stomach was growling so loud I agreed to accompany him back to his villa, where he claimed to have a huge stash of contraband food. I skipped the second day of fasting in favor of coffee, cigarettes, and Declan McManus.

Something must have worked. When I got back to the set on Monday, I was repeatedly complimented on my post-detox glow, and I'd actually lost two pounds.

TWO DAYS BEFORE THE Golden Globes, the cast attended a mandatory "Awards Show Etiquette" seminar put on by the marketing department. We were pleasantly surprised to find that Sondra, rather than doing the presentation herself as we'd been expecting, had hired Cindy Harrison, a comedian/former red carpet commentator from E! turned consultant whose specialty was keeping famous people out of the "Celebrity Oops!" section of magazines. It took me ten minutes to stop staring at her face, trying to discern what plastic surgery she'd had. Her face was truly a wonder of nature.

"I know some of you have done this a million times," she said, uncapping the lid on a dry-erase marker. "We're just going to do the basic overview, and then some of you are scheduled for one-on-one time. I've created Awards Show Boot Camp to basically be a fun way to keep you guys out of the tabloids." She laughed. "Even if you don't win, the night of the awards show can still be fun, if you follow certain guidelines."

I was so excited about the Golden Globes, I didn't know if I could actually retain anything, but she seemed funny, so I made an effort.

"OK," she said, writing FOOD in red marker on the dry-erase board. "As many of you are aware, the Golden Globe Awards are presented by the Hollywood Foreign Press Association, and the actual awards show is a formal dinner. I would not recommend eating during the ceremony, for several reasons. For one, the food is your standard rubber-chicken-type dinner, and we don't want the cameras to catch you making an "I don't like this food" face if they pan over to you while you're eating. Second, you run the risk of being photographed chewing on a big piece of steak or chicken, and that is never attractive, even for you, Mr. Handsome Golden Globe Nominee," she said, pointing at Greg, who laughed.

"Also, even though the dinner is usually served before the televised portion starts, you still don't want the camera to pan over to you and you've got a napkin bib on, cleaning off the last of the gravy on your plate with a roll. Not good! Also, ladies—please do not think you're going to be able to be nervous, eat, stare at George Clooney at the table next to yours, and manage to avoid getting A1 steak sauce on your fifty-thousand-dollar dress. Not gonna happen. Do yourself a favor and eat something before you put on your dress, so you can politely sip your sparkling water when the awards are going on.

"Any questions?" she said, pausing momentarily. She wrote MENTION DESIGNERS under FOOD and quickly moved on.

"Next, your stylists will tell you this, but while you're on the press line, try to remember to always mention the name of the wonderful individuals who designed your dress, shoes, jewelry, etc. Remember, you're wearing their styles for free, and this is the best advertisement they get all year. So, even if someone like Joan or Melissa Rivers or Isaac Mizrahi doesn't ask during your mini-interview, try to fit it in there anyway. Sentences can be started with 'Well, I'm wearing Ungaro,' or 'I'm wearing Prada,' et cetera. You can even throw in kicky expressions like 'I'm wearing (blank), so I'm just really comfortable tonight!'

"Anyone want to give this one a try?" she said, and Michele raised her hand.

"OK . . . I'm wearing Dolce and Gabbana, so I'm really comfortable tonight?" she said timidly. Michele was all about the calculated perfection, and I could tell she didn't want to screw up the press line at the Golden Globes, especially since this was the first time attending as part of a nominated show.

"Good try," said Cindy. "But everybody knows Dolce stuff is notorious for *not* being comfortable. I haven't seen your dress, but I'm going to guess it has a few straps and laces, am I right?" she said, and Michele laughed.

"Right," she said.

"So just say 'I'm wearing Dolce and Gabbana, so I'm having a great time tonight!' This is ambiguous yet positive, makes you sound knowledgeable about the designer, and easily leaves you open to talk about your shoes, jewelry, and what your life is like now that you're on a hit show."

The next thing she wrote was LIE, and we all laughed.

"For the record, I have personally coached hundreds of celebrities before, during, and after the red carpet, and one thing is always true: People spend a lot of time getting ready, and everyone, and I do mean everyone, says it took less time than it did. Now hear this: on the red carpet, you are perpetuating the image that Hollywood people just look that good when they roll out of bed in the morning, which of course I know you do! So, even if they needed a crane, a can of spackle, and a team of wild horses to get you into your girdle, you will *never* say you spent seven hours getting ready. That, my dears, would make you sound like you *need* a team of people in order to look this good, and that is bad for your image. Just duck and cover when a reporter asks you what time you started getting ready, and say something clever like 'I just spent the morning with my family, relaxing.'"

Next item on the list: WEIRD FACES.

"The red carpet is an opportunity for you to get great exposure, but beware: they take so many photos in such a short period of time, if you're not careful you're going to end up with a lot of goofy angles that can be used against you in the future in a 'Weird Faces' photo montage. Therefore, you must practice your good camera angle a hundred times every night in the mirror over the next few days. You know that little turn-around, peek-over-the-shoulder thing that Paris Hilton does? Definitely rehearsed. Practice your poses at home, people."

She opened up the pen again, this time writing AVOID LECTURES.

"Listen, I'm not going to lie—if we catch you making one of those 'smile with your full mouth' double-chin faces, you will get a post-awards-show lecture, probably from me. If you end up in the 'What Was She Thinking?' section of US Weekly, you will see me again. If you forget to say the name of the person who designed your dress, your stylist will give you a lecture. Generally speaking, you want to avoid these lectures. That's why you have me here now!"

She wrote a few more large words on the dry-erase board, stopping for further explanation and jokes after every one.

JEWELRY. "Regarding expensive jewelry: if jewelry exceeds the price your parents paid for their house, this guarantees that you will think of nothing other than the jewelry for the entire night, whether or not you're sitting next to Gwyneth Paltrow. However, it is likely if your jewelry costs that much, it will come with its own security guard, so try to let them worry about it for you. Believe me, they'll notice if it falls off."

THE BATHROOM. "Listen carefully—if in fact it did take a team of wild horses and a crane to get you into your dress, don't kid yourself and think you're going to sit around drinking wine all night. Because you know what? Those people aren't going to be able to help you when you're in the bathroom crying because you can't get your dress off (or back on). Also, even if you have a dress with a zipper down the side, when they call your name, you *never* want to not be there to accept it, then say 'I was in the bathroom,' even if you're Renée Zellweger. The American public does not want to think about its celebrities relieving themselves in a public restroom. You are America's royal family—remember that!"

GREAT! "When a reporter asks you if you're having a good time, you have only a few possible answers: 'Great! I'm so glad to be in the company of so many great actors!' or 'Great! I just saw Reese Witherspoon! I'm so excited to be here!' or 'Great! I feel so lucky to be included in this amazing evening, and I'm wearing Ungaro!' Anything that sounds like jealousy, intrigue, or rivalry will end up a sound bite on E! the next day, and a sound bite will get you a lecture."

"If you're singled out and ambushed by a reporter, just say something like 'This year has been a crazy roller coaster!' Then move on," said Sondra, who up until now had been quiet.

Cindy continued, writing CIVILIANS on the board. "If you have a boyfriend or girlfriend who is a civilian, don't bother bringing them on the red carpet with you. The more times a photographer says 'Can we just get your picture . . . alone?' the madder your significant other will be at you once you get inside." I made special note of this, since I was planning to bring Vince and my family. Matt would also be there; I was sure this would be the end of our affair.

Next up, SMOKING. "You must never, never, *never* smoke on the red carpet. If you're going to smoke, do it out on the balcony with Scarlett Johansson and that whole crowd, but definitely don't do it in front of a photographer, and *definitely* don't burn a hole in the dress. Valentino will not understand."

BY THE DAY OF the Golden Globes, I felt like my mind would explode from all the new information and the excitement. Shooting was even cancelled for the day. I woke up at 10:00 A.M., trying on my dress first thing in the morning to make sure it still fit (it did). After that brief moment of calm, Award Show Day Chaos kicked in.

My mom, who was staying in the suite next door, was the first to arrive, then Vince, then the hair and makeup people. Sondra had arranged for the cast to arrive in the same limo so we could all enter, walk the red carpet, and sit down as a group. "Create a unified front," she'd said as she gave us each our pickup time and bullet points. Mine was 3:30 P.M., which meant I had exactly four hours to get ready, eat, and hopefully not spill anything on the dress.

"Wow, honey, this is like getting ready for a wedding," said my mom, who was watching the flurry of activity from the couch as she ate a muffin from the brunch tray we'd ordered. Ian and Adam had flown in with her and were staying in her room, but then Adam refused to do anything with us, opting instead to take Ian to Magic Mountain on Golden Globes day. "When your dad and I got married, I swear I remember putting on the dress, then eight hours of whirlwind, then we looked at each other and said, 'Oh my God—we're married!'" she laughed.

After being girdled, plucked, sprayed, pinned, and taped by a team of "don't try this at home" professionals, I barely had time to eat before it was time to put on my dress and go downstairs for my pickup. "OK, how do I look?" I said, coming out into the living room to show off the results.

"You look like a princess," said my mom. "But . . . do you have a shawl? I think you're showing too much skin. And you're so thin . . . don't you want to cover up your arms?"

Vince and I laughed. "It's fine, Mom," I said. "This is how everyone in Hollywood looks now. OK, see you at the show!" I said, hugging her. "Wave to me on the red carpet!" With that I ran downstairs, the limo pulled up, and we were on the way.

When we actually got to the auditorium, all I could think was, *I hope I don't make a mistake, I hope my dress doesn't come off, I hope I don't end up on* E!'s 101 Biggest Celebrity Oops! "Have fun, but remember—nothing off-message!" said Sondra, smiling; then she steered us toward the first reporter. The press line and red carpet were much longer than I'd imagined, and bleachers filled with cheering people flanked the sidewalk. Though I'd been photographed before, the hundreds of cameras taking our pictures at once were blinding. Matt, whose character was in the last stages of being written off the show, was my "date," though we hadn't really talked in two weeks and I didn't want to introduce him to my family. He'd already gotten a job on another show. He put his arm around me and smiled, and I could tell his feelings were still hurt.

It was times like these when I really wished I liked him, because on the surface, he was perfect.

"Sit by me at the table," I said, and he smiled hopefully. Why did I keep doing this to myself?

Greg Forster, who had done this a million times before, did most of the talking on the red carpet. The show was a hit, and people were loving him. We followed the usher to our table, and Ross seemed to know or to have worked with everyone we passed. He worked the room, but not in a phony way. I was impressed.

The Golden Globes ceremony worked like a well-orchestrated dance. Five minutes of intro banter for each segment, then the award is given, then commercial break. No one is allowed to get up during the broadcast, so during the breaks, it seemed like everyone got up at once to smoke, talk to people on other shows, or go to the bathroom. If someone didn't make it back in time, a seat filler ran up to fill their space. I was fascinated by the whole thing, and a little starstruck at the same time. It all went by so fast—it seemed like one minute we were just sitting down, and then the waiters were serving the dinner (of which I took only the tiniest bites during commercial breaks, being so careful not to get any on my dress), then a musical guest was performing, then our category was up. I tried to take in every minute of it to remember in case I never got to experience this again.

Even though they made my mom and Vince sit at a table in the back with some of the other relatives (there are no cameras back there, I guess because the networks don't air footage of civilians), it was still a thrill to see her in a beautiful dress, makeup done, her face shining with pride. I hadn't seen her that happy since my dad died, and it gave me a secret joy to be able to make her smile. Granted, I was a little disappointed when I didn't win (the only award of the night for *Autumn Leaves* went to Ross for Best Supporting Actor), but I was beyond thrilled to be there in the first place, having conversations with real celebrities who actually watched our show.

Backstage, I noted with surprised amazement that the gift bag for presenters and nominees was so big, it actually came in a rolling suitcase—a medium-size monogrammed Louis Vuitton suitcase, to be exact, which I'd recently seen at Bloomingdale's for $2,000. I couldn't tell what was most exciting—sitting at a table next to George Clooney, being nominated for a Golden Globe, or the wealth of goodies that I knew was waiting for me in the Gift Bag when I got home.

10

TWO DAYS LATER, THE Gift Bag was still on my mind as Vince and I drove my family to the airport, then sped back to the hotel to crack open, catalog, and admire the sweet swag. Even though we'd been in L.A. for nine months, when it came to really expensive free stuff, we were both still in the honeymoon phase.

We ran immediately up to my room, where the Gift Bag was laying on the bed like that suitcase from *Pulp Fiction*. Vince unzipped it slowly. "I feel like I need special music for this," he said reverently. "Do you have to send thank-you notes?"

"I think the places get good press if I show up there," I said. "Sondra would probably be horrified if she knew how impressed we are right now."

He flipped open the cover of the suitcase. "Interesting," he said. "A lot of paper in here." He pulled out a monogrammed leather portfolio and opened it, taking a fancy piece of paper from the top of the stack and holding it up. "Gift certificate for an 'amazing Antarctic adventure package worth twenty-five thousand dollars. Includes kayaking, wilderness treks, and extreme camping,'" he read. "Oh my God—I can totally see you as Nanook of the North, in a cute little fur-lined parka!" He laughed. Neither of us were camping types, so the thought of us in snow boots, sleeping in a tent, or kayaking sent us into fits of convulsive laughter.

"Yeah, probably not going to use that anytime soon," I said. "No time, and besides, can you see me camping? I think not." I made a mental note to see if I could transfer the gift certificates, because the trip sounded like a great Christmas present for my aunt and uncle.

He pulled out another sheet of paper. "Mr. Handyman gift certificate for one day of free service?" he said, and we laughed again.

"Keep it for when I buy a house," I said, realizing that soon I might actually be able to buy a house. Good Lord.

"Gift certificate for spa treatments at Bliss?" he said. "One-thousand-dollar value."

"Throw that over here," I said. "I am calling about that one right now."

"OK, this is good. Swarovski crystal-encrusted bra and thong set. Sexy!" he said, holding them up. "You wear them or I will."

"Yes, I will wear that," I said. "Though I wonder how uncomfortable a crystal-encrusted thong is—ouch!"

He pulled out a gold box. "What about specially made gold M&M's with *Autumn Leaves* stamped on each individual M?"

"Are you kidding me?" I shouted. "Get out! How do they even do that?"

"I don't know, but there's also a box of truffles in here with your face painted on each one." He produced a gold box with a cellophane lid from the magic Louis Vuitton suitcase. Each one did, in fact, have a tiny picture of my face painted on it. They even got the teeth right.

"Oh, we're keeping those," I laughed. "We are totally getting drunk and eating my face." The pamphlet that came in the box with the individually painted truffles also advertised the fact that the company could paint *anything* on your truffle, including an ultrasound photo. "That is positively gory!" said Vince, laughing. "I'm going to eat your baby!"

After two hours, I was wearing the crystal-encrusted bra and a pair of brand-new cashmere pajamas, and Vince had wrapped himself in a vintage raw silk kimono and had a Frette cashmere, leather-trimmed blanket thrown jauntily around his shoulders. We'd been through everything in the Gift Bag and had separated each item into piles labeled REGIFT (for friends or family), USE (too fabulous to pass up), or KEEP FOR LATER (like the gift certificate for dog training and day care, if I ever came up for air and had time to get a dog). One of the beds was covered in wrapping paper and ribbon rubble, the piles, and empty boxes. We lay on the other bed, exhausted from laughter, excitement, and too many custom-made M&M's.

SADLY, BEING RICH AND famous does not exempt you from catching viruses. Two weeks after the Golden Globes, I woke up from a nap in my trailer freezing, teeth chattering and feeling dizzy.

I so should have gotten that flu shot.

Unfortunately, unless you're getting some kind of transplant, there's no calling in sick and halting the shooting schedule of an hour-long drama, even if you're the star and you feel like hell.

By 11:00 A.M., word had spread around the set that I was sick, a doctor had been called, and Juliet the second assistant director had been to my trailer twice to assure me that she was trying to rearrange the day's shooting schedule, but that they were definitely going to need me by 4:00—"Is that doable? Can I tell Mindy four o'clock?"

I tried to nod my head and say "I'll try," but even the thought of getting up made me tired again, so I just stared at her and groaned. I wanted my mom. I wanted Vince. I wished I had time for a boyfriend, just so he could come take care of me. I almost called Matt, then decided against it. I whimpered quietly, closed my burning eyes, and tried to sleep, so feverish I had lost all concept of time.

Sometime later (or maybe it was five minutes), a doctor came into my trailer. "Star—I hear you're sick," he said, and I could only slightly move my head in acknowledgment. "Headache?" he said, and I nodded. "Let's take your temperature." He put the thermometer in my ear, and even that was uncomfortable. "One-oh-three," he said, whistling as he breathed out. "I'm going to start you on an IV and give you a megadose of acetaminophen to see if we can't bring that fever down."

I recalled an article I read once about a girl who took too much acetaminophen and then needed a liver transplant, but I felt too sick to mention it. I just wanted to fall into the folding parts of my sofa bed and die; I think I would've allowed him to give me an IV filled with antifreeze if it would have made me feel better. Through my fevered delirium I began to wonder—was this the doctor who prescribed the seemingly endless supply of black pills that were keeping me thin? Was any of this really happening? On the bright side, for once I had absolutely no appetite.

Two hours later, I felt well enough to sit up and watch TV, and Vince had arrived with some chicken broth and crackers that I refused to eat. I still saw little chance of climbing down the stairs to my trailer, walking across the lot to the "main house" set, and shooting my scenes. I felt like I'd reached another dimension of illness and was so uncomfortable all I could do was writhe and whimper on my bed, the sheets of which were now soaked in sweat.

More time passed. Juliet poked her head in again. "Any better?" she said hopefully. I tried to think of ways to get her as close to me as possible, so I could breathe on her. "Mmmmmmhhhnnnnn," I said from beneath my pillows.

"We've been holding the scene for you . . . they even did a rewrite so you can shoot all of your scenes in bed, if that helps at all, but we need you to come over in the next fifteen minutes, or it's going to push the crew into overtime." When I didn't respond, she said sheepishly, "OK—they told me to do this if you didn't come to set." Momentary silence, then I heard her say, "Ms. Steinman? It's Juliet. I have Star here. Hold on."

I looked up deliriously at Juliet, who mouthed the words "I'm sorry." I felt the cell phone slide onto the pillow next to my face, and then I heard Attila's voice.

"Star, what's going on over there? I hear you're holding up shooting for the day. Money down the drain because of delays caused by the talent is unacceptable, Star. Do you hear me? Unacceptable."

I mumbled something incomprehensible about the fever and how I was delirious, and this made her yell even louder. "Star—are you listening to me? When Martin Sheen was making *Apocalypse Now,* he had a heart attack—a heart attack—and Coppola had him back on the set the next day. Did you have a heart attack, Star?"

"No," I said weakly. "Flu." She wasn't on speakerphone, but she was screaming so loud I could hear her just as clearly. "If you're not on the set in ten minutes, you are in breach of contract, and we are filing suit. Call a lawyer," she said. The phone flashed "Call Ended." I shut my eyes and saw spots.

Since I thought I might need a liver transplant after the megadose of acetaminophen and couldn't afford to be unemployed and without health insurance, I performed a small miracle, willing myself to get up, put on my costume, and walk to the set. Somehow, I remembered my lines and we shot all the scenes in two hours, after which the cast and crew gave me a standing ovation and Ross carried me back to my trailer.

Mercifully, the flu was mostly gone in twenty-four hours, so I was able to keep shooting the whole time.

Next time, I thought, *I might just have that heart attack.*

★ ★ ★

SIX WEEKS BEFORE WE wrapped shooting on season one, I was doing a "what it's like to work on a TV show" report in order to get school credit for my work on the show. Ellie Simon was developing a class on acting in Hollywood and using my success story as an example of the fact that even when you get really lucky and get your big break, there is still a lot of hard work involved. I was supposed to answer a series of questions to help convince the students that the life of a Hollywood actress wasn't all fun and games. During hiatus, I was going back to Michigan to talk to the class. I had put off filling out the questionnaire for too long, and now it was overdue.

What's your typical day like?

I took out a pen, attempting to answer the questions as clearly as possible—I had gotten so used to texting everything in abbreviated form, I'd almost forgotten how to write with a pen.

I'm called to the set in the morning, usually at nine or ten. I go to my trailer, have coffee, and read any memos or letters from the studio or the network.

I wondered if I should put what I really did: get to the set and mentally curse Juliet because she always calls everyone too early so she won't get in trouble; make a serious effort to pass by the craft services table laden with delicious breakfast items; smoke the first of many cigarettes; have coffee; and avoid phone calls from Attila until I could hear from the rumor mill of production assistants, cast members, and tech people whether it was a "red flag" or a "green flag" day. On a red-flag day, I just turn off the phone, because I know she's going to call and say something like "Star, we just got a letter from someone in Germany—they don't like the way you say the letter 'P'—can you work on that?" or, even worse, call me into her office for a "one-on-one" meeting, where she can really get out her claws. And, let's face it, even on a green-flag day, she wasn't much nicer. So really, I tried to avoid calls from the network altogether.

I laughed out loud. That would definitely never do. I continued writing:

I integrate revised script pages into the script I received the night before, try on my costumes for the day, and call the wardrobe department if they need to be adjusted.

Actually, most of what I did was wait. First, I waited for a production assistant to come tell me that it was time for me to go into hair and makeup, where I not only got my hair and makeup done, but also got updated on any gossip that might have broken (in the industry in general or on set) by Roxanne, the head makeup woman, who had by that time completely digested *The Hollywood Reporter,* the *New York Post,* and several other publications.

Then I study my script to learn my lines for the day until it's time to shoot my scenes.

Then I waited to be called to set. After the first six months of shooting, I didn't bother learning lines before scenes anymore, because with all the delays and hours it took to reset after each scene, combined with all the times we had to reshoot because Greg Forster was always either hungover or actually drunk, we'd end up shooting the scene so many times that not only did I not need to memorize the lines, but by the end of the day, I usually wished I could forget them.

Do you have a close relationship with the other cast members? Are you friends outside the show?

I avoided scribbling "Michele McCann, who plays my friend and next-door neighbor on the show, is a manipulative weasel who got her job through nepotism and can't act her way out of a paper bag" on the page, and wrote:

Autumn Leaves is a family show, and it's great because we're all so close, we're like a real family! When you spend fourteen to eighteen hours a day with people, you really get to know them well. I'm lucky to have such great people to work with every day!

I chuckled, commending myself on my perfection of marketing department rhetoric. Maybe a dysfunctional family at best.

Almost on a daily basis, Vince came to the set (we were not allowed to leave, lest all the elements actually fell into place by the time on the call sheet). Once he got there, we had lunch and discussed the gossip of the day—I brought what I'd learned from Roxanne, he brought news and updates from his other celebrity clients and straight from Perez, and we augmented that with what we'd pulled off the websites, including *The Superficial, Defamer, Just Jared, DListed,* and *Pink is the New Blog,* among others.

After he left, I'd e-mail, watch movies, and listen to music for a few hours, then usually it would be time to go to the set and shoot some scenes, then shoot some more scenes because Greg had only a short window when he could remember his continuity. Then I went over to Ross's trailer to run lines (scenes between us were where we tried to make up for lost time, since we only had to do them once or twice). I made phone calls to friends back at home, to my mom, or to see what gossip Vince had heard out and about. I listened to music while I surfed the Internet or read a book and waited to be called back to set for more scenes.

At around 4:00 each day, I'd start trying not to think about the sumptuous array of desserts (and, deadliest of all, the giant bag of

Famous Amos cookies) that adorned the craft services table, after which I'd take one of the black pills. I also spent a lot of time in the gym on set (a converted trailer); three days a week the network sent over a personal trainer to work on my "problem areas," and I sweated through ninety agonizing minutes of squat crunches, weight training, and trying to run on the treadmill while the trainer, a buff guy named Eddie, told me about how he was working on a screenplay, and could I maybe get it through to one of my contacts in the industry? Every time this happened, I tried to be cool, but I couldn't help but get annoyed. Wasn't everyone supposed to be responsible for their own career? Why did people always think I had all the answers?

What do you do to develop your craft?

I thought Sondra would probably kill me if I said "sit around with the other cast members, smoking cigarettes and gossiping," even in jest, so instead I wrote:

> *We have private acting coaches that come to the set, and occasionally, if we're not on a heavy shooting schedule, we'll attend an acting class with one of the numerous fine acting teachers available in the Los Angeles area.*

Not entirely untrue. We'd had an acting coach on the set a few times, just to get some of us through tough scenes. This man, Sid Stockwell, supposedly a famous acting teacher from the 1970s, reminded me a little of James Lipton from *Inside the Actors Studio.* He'd given me a few pointers about eye contact and the subtlety of hand gestures on camera, but mostly I'd just seen him chatting with the network executives and coaching the guest stars. He did seem to be very adept at schmoozing.

If you had to give a newcomer to the business one piece of advice, what would it be?

I laughed. I really had less than no idea what to tell people about how to get their big break. I wasn't really sure how I'd even gotten to where I was, and I suspected that if it were not for the divine hand of fate, I'd probably be taking my finals that very moment. I wrote:

Two words: hard work! Really, all parts of the process of becoming successful in show business require absolute dedication, patience, and a great work ethic.

This was actually true. Though I had lucked out in the "getting the part" portion of the process, I still worked hard at staying thin, doing well on the show, keeping myself in the magazines enough but not too much, and making sure Attila was happy. I knew I wouldn't be able to say all of this at the lecture, but I was the only twenty-year-old I knew with chronic insomnia and a family to support.

What's the one thing that is the most different about your life since you started working on the show?

This was a question I thought I could actually answer with some honesty and authority. When I first arrived in L.A., I noticed something very interesting—this was before the show became really popular, and I was still a nobody. In L.A., people look you in the eye for just a moment too long—they're trying to see if you're somebody before moving on with their day, letting the moment pass by, whatever. Maybe to see if you're anybody worth getting excited over or spending any energy on. I still couldn't determine whether it was just the tourists or everyone, but it's definitely a thing I hadn't observed in any other city. At first, I thought it was because everyone in L.A. looks like they might be someone famous. But once the show got popular and I started being in the magazines and stuff, I could definitely see the difference—I saw the glint of recognition in people's eyes, as it went from "Isn't that . . . ?" to "That is!" to "Should I say something/

ask for an autograph?" It's weird how people think they know you when they see you on TV every week.

This was happening all the time now, and I just tried to ignore it. Does it make you more valuable as a person if you pass the "recognition" test in L.A.? Once you have that glimmer of recognition from people, you start to expect it from everyone—to the point where if I went out and didn't get recognized, I felt a little bad about myself.

Also, since more and more people recognized me from the show, one of two things happened when I went out in public. For one, people came up and told me they liked my work. For some reason, this was always followed by the comment "Oh my gosh, you look so much smaller in person!" or they'd tell me they think I'm ugly or fat, and that they hate the show or my character, and how for some reason, they felt like they knew me, so they could be totally honest with me and tell me all of this in detail. Some, especially preteen girls, came up and told me really personal stuff, like how they hated themselves, had abusive boyfriends, or had eating disorders, and how I was so lucky to have such a fast metabolism. This just made me feel like a liar. Even though I was on TV, I thought, I was still just a regular person.

But maybe I wasn't anymore.

"DON'T GO. IF I have to, I will physically prevent you from leaving!"

Carrie Ann made a face, continuing to pack too much stuff into an exhausted-looking suitcase. She'd come to visit during a break in school, and Vince and I were determined to convince her to stay in L.A. with us. I was lying on the bed at the hotel, watching her pack and encouraging her to take some of the sample stuff that got sent over practically every day. "Take the Chloe jeans, Car—they sent six pairs."

She made a face. "Yeah, right—those would seriously never fit me. You are way taller than me, and besides, you're like a skeleton now."

I sighed. Somehow, you just can't understand it unless you're in it. I knew I was an impractically small size by her standards, but according to Hollywood, I was just on the heavy side of normal. I was tired of these comments, but it had been fun having the gang back together, and I was sorry to see her go. Vince had taken time off from being a fancy celebrity stylist to come over and regale us with scandalous tales of who had to be sewn into her dress, who was the biggest diva, and who was totally down-to-earth and nice to work with—a category I made him promise to include me in when he talked about me. Our favorite story involved a certain singer and her refusal to perform unless she was provided with a bucket of chicken wings. Somehow, even though I was a celebrity, I still liked hearing these bizarre stories. The only difference was that after having the celebrity experience first-hand, I could sort of sympathize with how you can become that way.

It starts with privilege—everything being handed to you on a silver platter. Anything you could ever want or need is available, immediately. Want a really specific latte? Done. Prefer only Swiss cheese in your sandwiches? No problem. People are overly accommodating to you when you're a celebrity—so much so that it makes you feel a little bad at first. Eventually, though, you come to expect it and are actually surprised when you want something and can't have it. After all, you're surrounded by people who never say no, so when you can't get whatever you want, it feels wrong. This is how a person can start out as a normal girl from Queens and end up Mariah Carey. It could happen to anyone; in fact, this might also be what happened to Michael Jackson's face.

She seemed annoyed. I poked her suitcase with my foot. "You're never going to get all that stuff in there. Have the front desk pack up a box and ship it to you. Or . . . you could just not leave at all. That's always an option. Stay here! Vince has room in his place, or you can just live here with me. I have two beds, and I'm almost done shooting season one—we can play for my whole hiatus!"

She stopped packing and looked up. "Yeah, that sounds really fun," she said flatly. "I'll stay here and be 'unidentified friend of Star Spencer' from now on." She sighed. "Amy, I've had fun seeing you guys, but honestly, I can't wait to get out of here and get on with my life. I mean, I'm graduating soon, then moving to New York—now is the time when we should be focusing on building our craft, you know? I mean, you're not going to live here forever, right?"

I didn't know what to say. Carrie Ann and I had always been able to talk about anything, but now I could feel the distance between us growing as she got more and more into her theater career. Besides, it kind of pissed me off that she was so blatantly rejecting my life in L.A. when she was the one who'd told me I had to be "willing to do anything" to make it. "It's not that bad, "I said, trying to lighten the mood. "You get used to the fake people after a while."

She looked up, "It's not even that—you totally don't even need to be talented to make it here. It's sick; it's all about who you know and how you look, and eventually the fakeness becomes reality. I wouldn't even respect myself if I made it out here." After she finished, she looked surprised. She covered her mouth, as if to keep any more words from coming out. There was a long silence, then she added weakly, "I wasn't talking about you."

Too late. I was mad. "You don't even know how hard I've had to work, Carrie Ann. You don't know the long nights, or the sacrifices, or the constantly watching every morsel I put in my mouth. Not to mention the talent it takes to learn a whole different kind of acting and carry a show. Are you kidding me with this?" She was packing faster, but I'd gotten up from the bed and was standing close to her face, yelling. We'd never had a fight before, and my heart was beating a mile a minute.

Her face turned red, and her eyes filled with tears. "Don't give me that crap—you fucking *fell* into your big break, and everybody knows it. I've been working every day since I was twelve years old to get my shot, and I'm going to New York, where they care about talent, to earn my success." She was yelling too, and I didn't think I'd ever seen her that mad. "Besides," she said through tears, "I signed you up for that audition—you didn't even want to go, remember? I was supposed to make it first. It's not fair!"

One silent moment passed, then another. "I'm going to miss my plane," she said. I wanted to tell her how fraudulent I felt when I first started, or how I'd just recently overcome feeling all the time like everything would go away in a heartbeat, and how I was never really sure what I could do to make my good fortune keep going. I wanted to tell her how hard it was to have all this responsibility at such a young age and to have people depending on you. Then I thought of my dad and how it's important to not be mad when you say good-bye. I didn't want her to go like this, but I didn't know what to say. I started to be the bigger person, to apologize for whatever I'd done.

But I couldn't. She'd insulted me, and I was too tired, too hungry, and too stressed out to take it from her. Instead I just said, "I'll call you a cab," and watched while she struggled to get her huge suitcase out the door. When she was gone, I attempted to block out the voices in my head, took an Ambien, and tried to sleep.

11

THE LAST WEEK OF shooting season one, the network finally made the announcement that the show was getting a full pickup for season two. As soon as the news broke, every cast member was on the phone, presumably with their respective agents. Within the hour, everyone was renegotiating their contracts.

Since it was my first show, I didn't know whether to do this or not. First of all, I still thought the $500,000 I was already getting paid was a lot of money, so when my castmates started talking about how they were "undervalued," it made me want to laugh. Still, I knew the network was making millions of dollars from the show, so I could sort of see their rationale. The mood on the set was alternately one of joy and righteous indignation, as the attitude of "they couldn't do it without me" spread throughout the cast.

Todd's office had been calling my cell phone every twenty minutes since the very moment the network announced the pickup. "Hi, this is Amber from Todd Whitley's office . . . Please return his call at your convenience . . . Hi, this is Amber from Todd Whitley's office, we've been calling you all day . . ."

During the day's second break in shooting, I finally called him back. "Todd, what's up?" I said, not wanting to let him make me into one of those greedy actors who go for the jugular. Definitely not my image of myself.

"Star Spencer, my favorite client, how are you not calling me back after the big announcement? Do you not know what this means? This is big big big! You are getting a big raise, baby!"

"Todd, my contract is for five years, and it says 'nonnegotiable' all over it. I thought I was only getting an 'incremental' raise . . . how much can that be? Why are you so excited?" I said.

"Oh, little Star Spencer . . . so naïve. This is why you have me. I'm an animal, baby. I kill for you. Hello! *House* took off, and Hugh Laurie gets over three hundred grand an episode! I'm in contract negotiations with your network since the announcement this morning, and I've already got them up to seventy thousand per. I can get them to go higher, but they have a few conditions they need met."

Seventy thousand an episode? I thought. *This is insane.* I did some quick math in my head. Over $1 million per year. That was before residuals, before bonuses, and before Todd the Animal told me the conditions. With $1 million, even for one year, I could make sure my family was taken care of forever, and make my own films. This was big. But . . . what were the conditions?

"What do they want, Todd? I'm already on the set every waking hour of the day, I never eat, and I have no life. Do they want to control my thoughts as well?"

Todd did not laugh. "They are exercising the appearance clause in your contract that says they can request that you undergo certain 'procedures' to 'update or maintain your look.'" I knew he was making the quotation marks in the air with his fingers, even though we were on the phone. "It's no big deal, Star . . . they can do it over the hiatus, and the network is going to pick up the tab for everything."

"Todd, what are you talking about?" I said, but I thought I knew what was coming.

"They want you to get plastic surgery, and they're prepared to pay you to get it. You should definitely do it—it will be good for your career, you'll look like a team player, and you'll get a huge bonus. If you say no, they're just going to try to say you're violating your contract and you won't get as big a raise, and they might even find a way to fire you. So . . . I'm going to say yes. Can I say yes to this?"

This information was at once repulsive and intriguing to me, and I paused for a long moment as I felt the blood rush to my cheeks. The concept of being forced to have plastic surgery was something out of a Ray Bradbury novel. Could they do that? Could I get fired for saying no to altering my body?

"What do they want me to have done?" I said finally.

"Just the basics—definitely lipo, some filler stuff in your face, a little off your nose. Trust me, I've seen them demand a lot worse," he said, chuckling.

My mind started to race. "Todd, I need to call you back," I said, snapping the phone shut. *Get your head on straight,* I thought.

I sat down, trying to sort the feelings out. Revulsion, for sure. *Requiring someone to get plastic surgery is so wrong!* screamed the rational side of me. Then a guilty twinge of excitement—*I could finally be thinner than Michele!* I sent Vince an emergency text message: *Come to the set right now . . . need to discuss something very important.*

I was sick to death of worrying about my weight and had been considering a secret visit to a plastic surgeon just to see if anything could be done about some fat on my butt and thighs that wouldn't seem to go away no matter how thin I got. I'd always hated the way I looked in jeans, even before I became a big TV star. Now I was being offered the chance to fix something I didn't like about myself anyway, for free, and they were going to pay me to do it. Somehow, it was too good to be true and a little disgusting all at once, like when your best friend makes a joke about your parents that you know is true, but you're too full of pride to laugh. Could I actually let them "fix" something on my body without feeling like they were somehow buying a piece of my soul? This was definitely not something I could run by my mother, as she was forever telling me that she thought I was too thin anyway.

What I needed was a rational opinion from someone who was actually in the industry. What I needed was Vince.

Millions of people get plastic surgery every year, right? I thought, pacing the floor of the trailer. *Why not?* I thought. *Isn't being young, thin, and gorgeous one of the job requirements? Wouldn't this take the pressure to always be dieting off me?*

Vince burst into my trailer in record time. "Where's the fire?" he yelled, kissing me on the cheek. "Is this about the contract negotiation? How much did they offer you? I'm *dying*! There's a rumor going around that Greg left the set with a fake migraine. Is it true?"

"Sit down . . . it is about that," I said. "You're never going to believe . . ." I trailed off. "They want me to have plastic surgery over the hiatus . . . they're going to pay for it and give me a bonus." I watched his face carefully for signs of revulsion. "Do you think if I do it, I've sold all the way out?" I said pleadingly. "Am I a media whore?"

More silence. I could tell he was carefully formulating his response, though for once I couldn't tell what that would be. Slowly, a smile crept onto his face. "Do you think they'll pay for me to get my back hair lasered?" he said, laughing.

I picked up a pillow from the couch and chucked it at his head. "I'm being serious!" I shouted. "Be serious! I guess I can fight them on it, not take the raise—"

"Oh my God," he said. "Why is this even a question? You have been complaining about that fat you can't lose since, like, the beginning of time. You hardly eat, and yet you're always stressed out about not being able to fit into the costumes. Now they want to pay probably the best plastic surgeon in Beverly Hills to *help* you with this problem, and you're worried about selling out? Are you kidding me with this? Who *cares* if you feel like they're buying you? You probably would have done it anyway!"

I let out a long breath. "Are you sure?" I said quietly. "Will you respect me? Do you think it's insane? Will I lose my edge?"

"You're going to look so hot!" he laughed. "You know you want to get it; just let the network think it was their idea. What's the big deal? You know, on older actresses they call it the forty-thousand-mile tune-up. One of my clients just had everything lifted—I mean *everything*, Aim." He threw the pillow back at me.

After swearing Vince to secrecy, I thought some more. I decided I felt better.

I called Todd back.

I said yes.

THREE DAYS AFTER THE new contract was signed (with a $150,000 bonus and free plastic surgery), I was accompanied to the office of a prominent Beverly Hills plastic surgeon by none other than Attila herself, who wanted to "oversee my transformation." I assured myself that it was still my choice and that I could always back out. Besides, with the bonus I could pay off the last of my dad's medical bills, *and* I wasn't going to have to worry about everything I ate. What could be better?

The face of the girl at the front desk lit up as she recognized me. "Oh my gosh—hi!" she said, realizing an instant later that she was supposed to be subtle. I prayed she wouldn't call the tabloids.

Immediately, she got up and rushed us back to an examination room. I changed into a paper gown, then there was a knock at the door, and the doctor entered, already chatting with Attila (with whom he'd previously worked in this capacity, I gathered). I caught the tail end of their conversation, which I discerned was a summary of all the times I wasn't able to fit into a size 0 since she'd known me. Charming.

"So anyway, she just needs a little off the butt, hips, and stomach, definitely some filler in the face, and her nose could use some shaping.

We also think her lips could be a little fuller. Also, she's only got about six weeks for the whole thing, beginning to end, so if you could do everything at once, that would be great."

The doctor had obviously heard this a million times before. "OK, let's take a look," he said, getting out a bright light and shining it at my face. He was short with a thin face, and his bright blue eyes peered at my skin. "Your skin is sun damaged—how old are you?"

I looked at Attila. I was supposed to be sixteen on the show, and the marketing department had been telling the press I was eighteen, so that's how old everyone thought I was. Even my IMDB listing had me as eighteen, though I really wasn't sure how it had gotten that way.

"She's twenty, Frank. That goes strictly under doctor-patient confidentiality, of course," she said, laughing.

"Well, for twenty you're wrinkling a little more than we might want. We'll take some of that lipo fat and use it to fill out your cheeks and lips, and some of those fine lines. That'll make a big difference." He said this all nonchalantly, while peering at me through a magnifying glass.

I wasn't sure, but I thought he was talking about taking fat from my ass and putting it in my face. Was I in the Twilight Zone? Was this an accepted practice? I made a mental note to tell this to Vince the very moment I got back, because this was something we thought was made up for *Sex and the City*.

I was considering the possible ramifications of having ass fat in my cheeks when he spoke again. "Now, as far as the lips go . . . the upper lip is a little thin, and we can definitely put some of the fat in there as a base, then follow up with regular injections of Restylane so that it looks the same for continuity. She shouldn't need a Gore-Tex lip implant yet. What size were you thinking?"

Before I could answer, I noticed that this question was addressed not to me, but to Attila—a woman from whom I had personally heard the words "mmmmm . . . butter."

"Not that big—we don't want her to be one of those hideous 'before and after' comparisons that *US Weekly* is doing these days. Just plump the lips a little bit—add some fullness, but don't go overboard, you know?" she said, pointing a sausage-like finger at my top lip. I nodded, resisting the urge to bite her finger like a rabid dog.

I ignored the fact that they were talking about me like I was not only grade-A steer, but also like I was not in the room. "I love Angelina Jolie," I said hopefully. "Can I have her lips?" Attila shot me the all-too-familiar "I wish I could put you on mute" look, and the doctor shook his head.

"Those lips would overpower your whole face. She can pull them off because she has angular features and high cheekbones. You don't have that. With those lips, you'd end up looking like Ronald McDonald," he said, chuckling.

I started to add something else, then Attila interrupted me again. "We're also thinking a little refinement on the nose, Frank. Nothing too drastic. Just flatten out that bump a little bit—the makeup artist wastes a lot of time shading it, and they're tired of having to shoot around it. The real work is going to be on that butt."

"OK—let's take a look." The doctor nodded his head, indicating that it was time for me to disrobe. I looked again at Attila, mentally willing her to leave the room. "Can you . . . I mean, can we have some privacy?" I said sheepishly.

She snorted. "Honey, it's not like I haven't seen every 'before' body in this business. Get over yourself." She did not budge.

I knew there would be hell to pay if I argued any more, so I gritted my teeth, dropped the paper gown, and waited through the agonizing silence as they surveyed my stomach, butt, and thighs, which were covered only by paper underwear. I could feel the last shreds of my dignity slipping away as the minutes crawled by. To exacerbate this heinous situation, the room was lit fluorescently, ensuring that I would certainly die from sheer embarrassment before ever getting to collect my $150,000 plastic surgery blood money. I went to my happy place in my mind, where I took the TV money and turned it into quality independent films.

With a serious expression, the doctor poked at the fat that protruded at the place where my hip and thigh meet. I remembered for a moment that at five foot seven and 117 pounds, I was skinny everywhere else in the world. I was in the middle of giving myself a mental pep talk when he finally broke the silence.

"You have a lot of fat for a skinny girl. I think you're going to get great result." He turned to Attila. "I think I can get six pounds out of her, easy. She's going to look amazing. We'll put her on the calendar for a month from now, get her in the hyperbaric chamber right after so she'll heal faster, and the show will go up at least ten points in the Nielsens, guaranteed."

It took me a minute, but slowly I realized that not only were they still talking about me like I wasn't there, now they were actually equating the size of my ass with the Nielsen ratings of the show. Could there really be a direct correlation? Was this study based in science?

"What will the downtime be?" said Mindy. "We need to start shooting again in July at the latest, and we can't have her looking puffy for four months like that Ashley Tisdale. Can you get Raj Kanodia in here to do her nose?"

"We have someone who's great—they do everything at once, and the bruising is minimal. Don't worry, Mindy. It's going to be fine." He smiled at her, then put his arm around me.

"Isn't this exciting? It's probably what you've always wanted—doesn't every girl want to get rid of her problem areas all at once? You are going to be so beautiful after this."

I tried to smile, to hide the sinking feeling I had inside.

"Sure—of course," I said, but when my smile faded I felt exactly like Michele McCann. I hoped he wouldn't make me look like her.

★ ★ ★

ONE WEEK LATER I was having a déjà vu experience as I walked through the UM quad toward the drama department. Having delayed the mandatory plastic surgery until after my trip back to Michigan to be the guest lecturer at Ellie Simon's "Acting in Hollywood" class, I walked through the campus with a weird sense of wonder. It hadn't even been that long since I'd left campus for the *Autumn Leaves* audition and never come back.

I looked around at all the students, who had been back from spring break for maybe a month. Most of them were scraggly and carried heavy backpacks, and I had a momentary pang of nostalgia as I realized I would never be one of them again. I vaguely remembered the feeling of getting back into classes after a break, stressing over papers and finals, and staying up too late obsessing over a thousand minidramas. It seemed like a lifetime ago.

I walked up the familiar creaky stairs to the drama department office. Ellie Simon and I were supposed to have coffee and go over the schedule beforehand. I remembered the twinge I used to get in my stomach when I approached that office. I laughed when I thought of how afraid I'd been of Shannon, the mean MFA student who worked there. Attila could eat Shannon for breakfast and still have room for bacon and eggs.

When I opened the door to the drama department, I drew in a sharp breath as I saw Shannon's familiar face. She looked up, and I saw a flash of recognition, then watched as she forced her face into a tense smile. "Hi . . . Star," she said slowly. "Nice to see you again. Ellie will be right out."

This was bizarre, I thought. I had sort of counted on the fact that even though I was famous and everyone else wanted to be my friend, Shannon would still refuse to treat me with any respect. While I could see it was just the fame and success that were keeping her from being a bitch to me, I was a little surprised that she would even play that game. For some reason, it made me feel horrible that she was still in the same place, doing the exact same job, while my life must seem to her like some Cinderella fantasy. I sort of wanted to help her—to see if I could get her a job on the show. I knew this would make it worse, though, so I just said, "Thanks," and took a seat in the ancient wooden chairs outside the office.

She looked like she wanted to cry, she was holding back so much vitriol. Ellie had probably told her to be nice to me, and she needed her job. I didn't want to hold this kind of power over her—I'd rather have just let her yell at me if it would make her feel better. This just felt artificial and gross.

"How have you been?" I said slowly. "How are things in the department?"

She looked up slowly. "Great—things are great. I'm graduating in June, and I just found out I got a summer gig in the Oregon Shakespeare Festival."

"Congratulations!" I said, and I actually meant it. I wanted to tell her that while she was doing Shakespeare, I was going to be having plastic surgery to stay "competitive in my field," but even thinking of sharing that information with her would violate my contract, so instead I said, "Wow, that's great!"

She snorted. "Yeah, I'm sure it seems big to you, after going to the Golden Globes and starring in a hit show," she said. I kept trying to see the old Shannon snark from the year before, but instead she just seemed sad.

I wanted to pull the curtain back on her impression of my life, just to make her feel better. In fact, I wanted to scream "I make a million dollars a season, mostly for waiting in my trailer! I have no idea how I even got here!" but instead I just tried to smile and said, "Believe me, I wish I could be doing some good theater over the summer"; then I waited through the rest of the thick silence that hung in the air. Did she hate me more, now that I was successful? Did all the students feel this way?

Ellie came out of her office, rescuing me from this infernally awful exchange. "Amy, welcome back! How are you?" she said, giving me a welcoming hug. Over her shoulder, I could see Shannon staring at her computer screen.

"I'm great," I said. "So glad to be back!"

Ellie laughed, squeezing my hand. She always had the power to make me feel better about things. "Let's go get some coffee."

Twenty minutes and three autographs later, we were sitting in the campus coffee shop and discussing the lecture. "Just give an overview of what you do, then let them ask questions. They all watch the show, and they're dying to know some insider dirt." She smiled. "Obviously, don't tell them anything that will get you in trouble, but, you know, just tell them what it's like to work with Greg Forster and Ross Wong, let them ask you how you prepare for your dramatic scenes, that kind of thing." She smiled. I wanted to cry from the sheer relief of being able to just let my guard down and be myself again. I realized what it was—Ellie Simon was real, and she wasn't hiding anything. No one is really "what you see is what you get" in L.A.—everyone is sort of like Shannon, with the forced smiles and niceties. Once you get to a certain level of celebrity, you lose all chance of having someone want to know you for who you are.

I laughed. "Will you move to L.A. and work with me?" I said. "I need a real person on my side. Seriously—is there anything special you want me to tell the students? I have no idea how I even got to where I am."

She smiled. "Don't underestimate yourself, my dear," she said. "You were in the right place at the right time with the right talent. I always knew you were going to go far."

I sighed. "Sometimes it's so amazing, like a dream, and then sometimes I get scared that it could all go away in an instant," I said.

She winked at me. "That's why you have to be smart, hang on for dear life, and take all the opportunities you can while you're on top."

It was a whole other out-of-body experience to be giving a lecture at my old university, in my old drama department, in front of some of my old friends. It was just like Ellie said—the students all watched the show, and they just wanted to know what it was like to work with the other actors, what we did all day, and that kind of stuff. I went over my typical day, told some amusing anecdotes about Greg and the rest of the cast, then opened it up for questions.

"Girl in the back?" I said, feeling like I was impersonating a college professor. Someone asked if I'd met George Clooney, just like I would have a year before. "No," I said, "but I did sit kind of near from him at the Golden Globe Awards. One of our frequent guest stars was there as well, and he tried to make me laugh all night by trying to poke George with a fork. The show organizers were not amused." Everyone laughed, and I felt like a million bucks. *Is this what stand-up comedy feels like?* I thought.

Another person raised her hand, and I called on her. "Amy, can you tell everyone what you did to get the part?" The girl's voice sounded familiar, and I thought I should find out who it was and say hi, but I was on a roll.

I tried to outline the audition process as briefly as possible, but the voice interrupted. "No," it said, "what, exactly, did you do . . . or should I say *who* did you do to get a part like that?" A twittering of laughter, then an uncomfortable silence. Finally, I could place the voice.

Rebecca.

Rebecca Hartford was the drama department's own version of Pamela Anderson, complete with raw ambition, marginal acting talent, and questionably large breasts. I'd totally forgotten about her being right before me at the very first audition.

"I . . . um . . . well, I seriously just read the part as best I could, and everything fell into place," I said, wanting to move on. "There's so many factors that go into casting, you really have no control over it. You could be an inch too short, or your hair could be the wrong color, and you're out. It's totally arbitrary." Having seen this happen first-hand over and over again with guest stars and other cast members, this was one thing I could say with authority.

"Right," said Rebecca's voice. "Are you really asking us to believe that you didn't get that part on the casting couch? Do you think we're that stupid? This is total bullshit." She laughed, picked up her purse, and walked out of the auditorium, and I felt like someone had slapped me in the face.

Ellie looked over, mouthing "sorry." "OK, that was a good example of the competitive nature of the business and the possible jealousy of your comrades," she said. "I'm sure Star has had that experience more times than she'd like to recount here for us today. Any other questions?" she said, downplaying the awkwardness. Someone else asked a question about hitting your mark, and then the lecture was over.

"That was weird," I said to Ellie as she walked me to the car. "Does she really think that? That's not what happened . . . I was just right for the part, you know? If I knew what I did right, I'd tell her, but . . . honestly, there's no way to bottle it or replicate it."

"She'll learn that eventually," she said softly. "You should feel thankful that you're learning these lessons so early in life." She smiled. "Or maybe she'll become a porn star." She laughed. "Don't tell anyone I said that. I'm supposed to be the impartial and wise Ellie Simon, but sometimes that girl drives me nuts. I can't wait for her to get out in the real world so someone can break it to her that she just can't act."

I laughed, taking a breath of the fresh spring air. Despite the Rebecca Hartford ambush, it was good to be back at UM.

12

EVEN AFTER TAKING TWO Ambien to sleep the night before the surgery, I was still haunted by dreams of going under anesthesia and never being able to wake up. Dr. Romano had assured me that it was completely safe to undergo multiple procedures at once, and I'd agreed, thinking I was probably only going to be brave enough to go under the knife one time. So, by the end of the day I'd have lipo, fat injections to my face and top lip, and a little off my nose. That's how they said it: "a little off the nose," like my face was turkey that you buy in a deli. I couldn't sleep, and I couldn't stop obsessing about a story I'd read where a woman had her legs amputated after a freak staph infection following a botched liposuction.

"Can that really happen?" I asked Vince in the car the next morning. I had a horror-movie-type "death by liposuction" scene playing in my head, and I couldn't quite turn it off. The questions wouldn't stop—*What's it going to feel like? Is it going to be horribly painful? What if I wake up in the middle of the surgery? What is Sondra going to tell the press if I die on the table? What if something goes wrong? Don't only socialites over fifty actually die from plastic surgery procedures? Am I going to end up drooling in some nursing home because I pushed it too far?*

I tried to make myself stop. I was young and healthy. I'd never had a medical problem. I wanted this stuff done anyway. It was going to be a piece of cake. But . . . what if it wasn't?

I'd already taken the big fat emergency Xanax that I saved for bumpy plane rides, and it started to hit me just as we got off at the Overland exit on the 10 freeway. By the time we turned two corners and arrived at the surgery center in Beverly Hills, I felt the warm rush of the drugs taking over, and I started to care a little less about the latest irreversible step in my "transformation."

It was just like the doctor said it would be: we entered through a back entrance so no one would see us and call the *Enquirer*. I could just see it now: "Star Spencer's Surgery Nightmare!" The nurse took us right into the exam room. I changed into the dreaded blue paper gown again and waited for the doctor.

"Are you nervous?" Dr. Romano said as he came in. "Do you need a hug?" He put his arm around me, and suddenly I wanted him to be my dad—in fact, I wanted to be a little kid again, hugging my dad when he came home from work. Before Hollywood, before college, before high school, before the big dreams. Before the plastic surgery.

He took out a big purple marker, just like on those plastic surgery TV shows, and started circling my fat. After he was done drawing on my hips, thighs, and abdomen, he moved on to my face. *My God,* I thought, *If* US Weekly *could see me now.* "We'll inject the fat here, here . . . and here," he narrated as he drew little purple dots on my face where the needles were going to go. I wanted to tell him that this was too much information, but I found the sound of his voice soothing, like he was reading me a plastic surgery bedtime story. "Once upon a time there was a girl from Bay City, Michigan, and a magic wizard with a tiny vacuum took the fat out of her behind and injected it into her face."

After he was done drawing on me, he left the room and then the nurse came in to take me to the OR, which (surprise) was attached to the exam room. *Last chance to bolt,* I thought, and I almost did it. Then I pulled myself together and climbed up on the table, and the anesthesiologist immediately poked me in the arm. I thought they were going to do the "count backwards from one hundred" thing, like in the movies, but after thirty seconds I felt sort of warm and funny, like I'd been in the Jacuzzi too long and fell over when I tried to get out. The room went kind of sideways, and literally the next thing I knew, they were trying to wake me up.

"Star? Star . . . can you hear me?" It sounded like the nurse was yelling from somewhere very far away.

The whole waking up from anesthesia thing is completely unnerving, like you're going through a long tunnel in a dream and you can never find the ending. Then your eyes are open, you're struggling to snap out of it, you're freezing, then you're asleep again. After a few hours of this, I was lucid enough to be moved to the "recovery center," which was like a fancy hospital room and hotel room combined. Of all the things I'd experienced since becoming a TV star, secret plastic surgery was definitely the most surreal.

The first twelve hours after the surgery were a complete blur. While I was under, they'd somehow put me into a very tight black spandex "garment" that extended from my ankles to right below my armpits and was held up by suspenders, with only a small hole designed to enable me to *never* take it off—not even to go to the bathroom. The purpose of the garment was to hold everything in place and compress the skin. I also had a splint covering my nose. By the time I really woke up enough to know what was going on, I felt like I was a wrestler who'd lost a match. The pain was unlike anything I'd ever felt before; every part of my body was throbbing and felt like it was on fire. I had to take the prescribed pain pills every three hours, and even then, I felt like screaming and I felt like parts of my body were dangerously close to falling off at any moment.

"How long until I look normal?" I said to Dr. Romano a few days later. The edge had come off the pain a little bit, but I was still afraid to look in the mirror.

He laughed. "Just relax—watch movies and read magazines. You're not going to look normal, kid; you're going to look amazing. Trust me on this. I've been doing this for twenty-five years." He checked my incisions and stitches and poked at the splint on my nose. "Did you know we got seven pounds of fat out of you?" he said, as if he was sharing information about his golf game or where he'd had dinner the night before. "I told you you had a lot of fat for a skinny girl." He laughed. "Don't worry—you're going to look great," he said. "Call me if you're worried or if you want me to come back."

TEN DAYS AFTER THE surgeries, the pain was at least manageable (though still ever-present), and I was well enough to start getting hyberbaric oxygen treatments; I could already see the difference in my thighs and butt. I showed up at the first appointment moving slowly and wearing dark glasses, praying that no paparazzi had followed me.

"Just take a deep breath . . . if you feel faint or like you're going to panic, let me know."

Mike, the nurse, was trying to tell me what to do while he locked me in a sealed chamber and pumped it full of oxygen. This was supposed to make my bruises go away faster, and the doctor wanted me to do it twice a day every day until season two shooting started, to ensure the bruising and swelling from the surgeries would be gone by then. If I could take the claustrophobia of the closed chamber, I'd be home free.

The initial "exam" had consisted of a doctor coming in and asking me a bunch of questions while trying to pretend he didn't watch my show. I could tell he was tempted to say something about me or the show as he ticked off items on his clipboard. Since I knew he recognized me, I actually felt a little braver, like I had to maintain my composure not just for me, but for him.

"Any history of blood clots in your family?" he said nonchalantly.

"No."

"Stroke?"

"No."

"Clotting disorders?"

Good Lord . . . what did the oxygen chamber *do,* anyway? I took a deep breath and thought of the big raise. I'd already let them operate on me. What was the big deal?

The chamber itself looked just like the one Michael Jackson supposedly used to sleep in. It was basically a big, see-through coffin. "Here's how it works," said Mike. "First, you get in and lay down, we lock and seal the chamber, and then we pump in pure oxygen for thirty minutes. Your ears might pop, and you might feel a little light-headed. I'll be out here the whole time to talk to you, and you have a TV here that you can watch. Are you ready?"

I could not get up and run out of the office, mainly because if I moved too fast, my legs felt like they were going to fall off. *How bad can it be?* I thought. *People do this every day, and you never hear about a "hyperbaric oxygen chamber death."*

"This is going to really help with that bruising and swelling. Just lay back and try to relax, and if you get scared at all, just let me know and we'll bring you out of it. We have to take you 'down' into it very slowly, because if we go too fast, you'll get the bends, like in scuba diving."

Yeah, that's not freaky at all, I thought. Seconds ticked by. My ears popped. "You're doing great!" said Mike, whose voice was now muffled by the hissing sound of oxygen filling the chamber. Was the tingling I was feeling in my toes a side effect of the "pure oxygen treatment," or all in my mind? Was this helping? Was I having a stroke?

Cynicism aside, after I relaxed about the whole "being locked in a sealed chamber" thing, the pure oxygen made me kind of sleepy, and I swear the bruises went away at twice their regular rate. After ten days of twice-daily hyperbaric sessions, I felt ridiculously good.

Well, not good enough to tell anyone in Bay City that I'd been frequenting a Michael Jackson–style oxygen chamber, but pretty great nonetheless. After two more weeks, the pain was finally 90 percent gone, and I could pull on my pants again without wincing and jog without feeling like the sides of my legs were going to fall off. My black eyes had gone away, my nose looked more sculpted, my lips were returning to a normal-looking size, and when I looked in the mirror, I looked like myself again, only better.

In fact, I looked amazing. Hollywood amazing.

SEASON
TWO

13

WHEN WE ARRIVED ON set in July to start shooting season two, it was like the first day back to school when you're a kid. Everyone was rested and relaxed, and even people who hadn't gotten along that well in season one seemed happy to see each other. We also had new sets, a new cast member (Sharon Hikida, who had been hired to play the role of Ross's character's sister), and we were all basking in the glow of our newly renegotiated contracts and raises.

For the first few hours, I was incredibly self-conscious about my new look. Would anyone notice my amazingly small ass? I certainly noticed it when I got dressed every day—it was incredible! Would they say I looked like a freak? Since it was generally regarded as uncouth to say anything about people's "work," I thought I could probably only count on Michele's reaction as a measure of how it really looked.

After the table read, she walked over to me slowly, like one of those gunslingers in the Old West. "Hi . . . ," she said cagily, making no effort to disguise the fact that she was checking me out. "How was your break?"

"Great!" I said, trying to feel out the vibe. "I went back to Michigan to see my friends, gave a lecture at my old school, then came back here and just sat by the pool. It was awesome."

"Well, you look . . . great," she said slowly, almost testily. "Really. What's your secret?"

I laughed. "Clean living, of course!" I said. There was no way I was telling her anything. I suspected she had the tabloids on speed dial as the *Autumn Leaves* inside source, trying to leak some information that would get me fired.

"Well, whatever you're doing is totally working," she said glumly. That's when it hit me. I actually looked *better* than her now, and it was killing her. Without meaning to, I had finally gotten the upper hand on Michele McCann.

"Nice to see you too," I said, smiling and turning to go back to my trailer.

This time, I really meant it. The victory was thrilling. Who knew crushing a person could feel so good?

"HERE'S A GOOD ONE. 'Dear Star, I think you are so beautiful. I have a problem. I went to jail for drugs and lost my job, and I think if you wrote a letter to the warden, I could get out early. I just thought because I feel a real connection with you, you might be able to really help me.'"

My new assistant, Olivia Garcia, had created a file with all of the weirdest fan letters sent over from Todd at International Artists Unlimited, and we'd started reading the highlights over lunch in my trailer every day. Even though I was Hollywood fabulous and had had the plastic surgery, initially I had still objected to the whole concept of having an assistant. "No way," I'd said to Todd. "She's older than me, and I'm going to feel totally weird having someone clean up after me. That is wrong. I'm not the 'hired help' type."

"Get over it, Star Spencer," said Todd. "I am tired of not being able to get you on the phone. I am sending Olivia over, and you will love her."

I'd kept insisting that I was fine getting my own groceries and buying my own stamps, but with the show frequently shooting late into the night, I finally relented. Not only was Olivia funny and cool, like one of my friends from Michigan, but she had a really no-nonsense attitude about the whole assistant thing. Most of the time, she just picked up stuff for me while I was at work, and then on my days off we went shopping and went to lunch.

Olivia was almost done with law school and on her way to an internship at International Artists Unlimited, and she'd been doing the assistant thing for three years. Her stories over lunch were becoming the highlight of my week, ranging from weird celebrity shopping lists to mental breakdowns to three-A.M. calls to "bring over a single slice of Jarlsberg cheese," and everything in between. Immediately, I promised that I would never become that person and made Olivia swear to let me know if I was doing anything that would cause her to tell a story about me later.

Because she had more experience with this sort of thing than I did, Olivia quickly took over the management of the celebrity fan mail project. Mostly this just involved sorting, filing, and sending back signed photos of me (or the cast) to those who asked. Weird mail was separated into several piles. There was the "How Dare You" pile, where people ranted about everything from how much they hated my outfits to how I should be ashamed of myself for "fraternizing with the gays" to how I was too fat, or too thin, or too blonde, or my nose was too big (no longer a problem), or they didn't like my elbows. The "Funny But Not Dangerous" mail was separated out into a file and enjoyed over lunch, along with Olivia's famous celebrity nightmare stories. The really mean, crazy, or threatening ones went back to the agency for routing to the police or F.B.I.

One Sunday, we drove with Vince out to Shutters in Santa Monica for brunch and stories. As soon as we sat down, Olivia launched into a doozy involving a famous actress invited to be the guest speaker at a wedding. "To start, she'd just had a lip implant, and it hadn't 'settled' yet, so the reading she was asked to give ended up sounding like she had a speech impediment. I had to go with her and drive her, because she was still taking the maximum dose of painkillers from the surgery and couldn't even back out of her own driveway. No one said anything, but by the reception, everyone was talking about what must be wrong with her. She made me bring a change of clothes for her—I always kept a big box of extra clothes in her car in case she wanted to appear somewhere else or change her look in the middle of the day. For the wedding, she was wearing this really conservative, Jackie O–style pink Chanel suit, and for once her boobs were actually covered. However, by the reception, she was sick of this look, and we went to the hotel where the reception was being held so she could change. She was so high that she couldn't decide on an outfit, so she had me take the whole box of clothes into the women's lounge so she could pick for herself. Then she realized she'd left her makeup in the car, so she sent me outside for it. When I got back, there were clothes all over the lounge, and she was gone."

She took a sip of her coffee and paused for effect, leaving Vince and me on pins and needles. "What was she wearing?" said Vince. "A leather bikini?" These were Vince's own personal version of scary campfire stories.

"How much do I want her to just be naked at the reception when you find her?" I said. The best parts of Olivia's stories were the endings.

"Better," she said. "My white spandex running pants that I'd put in her car for the gym. Black G-string, tie-on halter dress that barely covered her huge fake boobs, and knee-high purple furry Ugg boots." She paused while we laughed, then finally said, "The father of the bride actually came to ask me if I would cover her up with a coat, because he didn't want her to appear in any of the pictures for the album."

Between Vince and Olivia, they could probably have made a million dollars just from blackmail or stories sold to the tabloids. Thankfully, they were both too honorable to do it, so everyone's secrets were safe.

I THOUGHT BY SEASON two that I had seen everything, but every time I got that feeling, something happened that proved me totally wrong.

Jamie Powell had been cast as a "bad girl who comes to town" for a five-episode run, and she started a couple of weeks into season two. Up close she looked at least thirty, but she was playing a bad seventeen-year-old on the show.

From the amount of food that Jamie consumed at the craft services table, I surmised that she either had a fast metabolism, a raging case of bulimia, or a costly drug habit.

After shooting scenes with her and chatting in between takes for a few days, I learned it was a combination of drugs and an eating disorder that she was oddly proud of. "You should try it," she said with impunity. "People say throwing up is bad for you, but it feels good, and if you keep it to once a day or so, it doesn't even hurt you." Aside from this skewed notion of reality regarding food, she seemed like a pretty nice person, and I was eager for new people to talk to when Olivia and Vince weren't around. Also, everyone knew that Jamie used to be the girlfriend of one of the Red Hot Chili Peppers, and I wanted some crazy behind-the-scenes stories about Anthony and Flea.

One Thursday night she came into my trailer at the end of a shoot, just as Olivia and I were discussing plans for the weekend. We were in the middle of discussing a shopping excursion to the outlet stores in Cabazon when Jamie flung open the door and barged in. "I like you," she said, plunking herself down on my couch. "Let's go do something fun." As usual, she did not acknowledge Olivia, who rolled her eyes. Jamie had a nasty habit of completely ignoring anyone who couldn't help her career.

Jamie Powell was the kind of girl who never would have given me the time of day in high school, or even in the drama department, for that matter. With luminous blue eyes, shiny blonde hair, and a body so effortlessly perfect it hurt me to even look at her, she fit easily into the "Malibu world" of *Autumn Leaves*—so much so that she sometimes made me feel like an outsider on the show even though she was just a guest star. She looked like the kind of girl who would be your friend one minute, then talk an outrageous amount of shit about you when you turned your back. I actually sort of wanted to see Jamie and Michele together in a cage match, just to see who would be more vicious. I preferred the company of Vince and Olivia Garcia, superassistant. Perhaps because she was bound by a confidentiality agreement, I felt comfortable telling Olivia stuff I would never have told anyone other than close friends and family. Certainly not Michele, and probably not Jamie Powell.

"I can't . . . I have to learn lines for tomorrow," I said, shooting Olivia a look. I was curious as to what a girl like Jamie did when she left work, but I also was a little scared of her. Where did she live? Who did she hang out with? Who did she know?

Jamie chimed in again. "Are you kidding me? You are *not* going home, Star Spencer. You are fabulous, and fabulous girls go out at night, to eat and dance and be with cool people. Let's go."

My curiosity got the best of me, and before I knew it, we were speeding up Melrose in Jamie's silver BMW M3 convertible. Olivia had begged off for the night, claiming that she had to study, even though I know that she, too, was curious about Jamie. "Isn't my car great?" she said. "It goes totally fast. I get pulled over all the time, but I never get tickets," she said, giggling. "I love the LAPD."

I'd only known Jamie for three weeks, but she had already told me about the "totally harrowing" time she had when she got her boobs done and scooped me on lots of other well-known people's plastic surgery. "Totally worth it, though—my career has improved so much since my procedure. What have you had done?"

"Oh, nothing . . . just diet a lot," I said. According to everyone on my team, celebrities were never supposed to share plastic surgery information. For all I knew, Jamie could call US *Weekly* and be "sources close to Star Spencer." I liked her, but I couldn't risk it. "What's it like to have fake boobs?" I said, diverting her attention. "I've been thinking of having that done. Does it feel weird forever, or do you get used to it?" *Considering* plastic surgery was much easier to deny, and I thought maybe it would get her off the subject of stuff I'd actually had done.

"You totally should—you would look hot!" she said, reaching over and pinching my leg. I couldn't tell if she was high or just weird. "I would be all over you!" she yelled, then commenced with a series of high-pitched barks, like she was a Pekingese in heat. Then, out of the blue, she leaned over and licked my cheek. Her tongue was warm, and the lick left a snail-like trail of saliva on my face. I wanted to wipe it off, but I didn't want to offend her, so I tried to subtly let it dry without thinking about just how weird that was.

"You are sexy!" she yelled, resuming the barking, which became a low howl. She managed to keep driving despite this apparent break from reality, and we pulled up to a stoplight. I put my head down to avoid making embarrassing eye contact with the people in the car next to us, to avoid being recognized driving down Melrose with a barking blonde girl, and to avoid the very real possibility that I might be licked again.

I never knew what to do when people acted this unpredictable and weird. Like, did I just laugh, did I bark along with her, or did I just ignore it? Plus, Vince always teased me that I was a terrible judge of character and so naïve that I was always the last one to catch on to things. Most of the time I just tried to play along and hoped that the weird stuff would pass. Mercifully, she turned her attention back to driving, and soon we pulled up to a tall white apartment building. "You have to come in and see my place!" she squealed. "I'm going to change, and then we'll go out, OK?"

I looked at my watch. 7:42 P.M. I really, really wished I had just gone back to the hotel to learn lines. I didn't want to go into Barking Girl's apartment, I didn't want to wait for her, and I didn't want to have dinner at 9:00 when I had to be on set at 8:00 the next morning.

"That's OK—I'm pretty tired actually. I'm just going to call a cab and go back," I said, but she was dragging me by the hand up the stairs to her apartment. "Just come up and wait . . . I'll be ready in, like, two minutes and we'll go around the corner to the Spanish Kitchen for margaritas. Come on! Don't be a poop!" she yelled, and resumed barking.

I resisted the urge to break her grip and run down the stairs. "OK—ten minutes, and then I am leaving without you," I said, watching her pull out keys and open her front door. I was glad to see that even though she seemed to live on another planet in her mind, she had the wherewithal to manage practical, everyday things like paying her rent and finding her keys. She had a driver's license and a guest-starring role on a hit TV show, so she must have been doing something right. Something inside me wanted to know what made weird people tick and how they functioned in the universe.

While she was changing in the other room, I checked out her apartment. Nice enough furniture—green Pottery Barn–looking couch, geometric rug, black coffee table and entertainment center, plasma-screen TV. Small desk area with normal-looking bills, headshots, and a bulletin board with some photos of friends tacked up on it. Maybe the barking was just for effect.

"What do you think?" she said, and I turned around as she came out of the bedroom wearing a tight black skirt and nothing else. Her large, tanned breasts stood straight out, and she was rubbing her nose and sniffing. "Aren't they great? Dr. T. did an amazing job. Touch them! I want you to." She walked slowly over to me, and all at once I felt like the stupidest person in the world. "I like you," she said softly, and leaned in to kiss me. Her lips were soft and touched mine for the briefest second before I pulled away.

"Jamie . . . I can't . . . I don't . . . I'm not . . . ," I stammered.

She looked crushed. "Don't be silly," she said. "Everybody does it. Just touch them. Don't you think I'm pretty?" One tear, then another rolled down her perfect cheeks.

"I . . . Jamie . . . let's just go eat," I said, sighing. I was exhausted, and I wanted no part of the barking, or the boobs, or the crying. I should have been used to crazy Hollywood people by then, but somehow I always forgot where I was and expected people to act normal, then suddenly they went all barky and tried to get me to touch their fake boobs. "Come on . . . what's Anthony Kiedis like?" I said, trying to draw her out of her obvious funk. "Can't we just be friends?" I said.

Despite her obvious mental imbalance, barking Jamie's story line was extended, and she was promoted to special guest star on the show.

TIME WAS FLYING. WE were almost to the winter break of season two, the show was a huge hit, and Todd decided I needed my own publicist. "I'm setting up lunch with you and Arden Stone from RMG," he said one Friday. "You need more exposure—trust me. Best five thousand a month you'll ever spend. The offers are going to come rolling in. You're going to be huge! Bigger than Mischa Barton, out walking around in her pajamas. Arden is a force of nature. She'll get you *Vanity Fair, InStyle,* even Oprah if you need it."

The frugal Midwesterner in me balked at the sound of five thousand dollars a month, but I had really been wanting to get into *InStyle* magazine, and my loathing for Sondra was up there right underneath my hatred of her boss. Sondra was obsessed with getting us into *TV Guide* as a whole cast, handling the backlash from the show's themes, and making sure we didn't embarrass ourselves or the show in public. Since I knew I could use a better advocate, I decided to at least meet Arden to see what she had to offer.

Arden Stone was in her midforties, tall, beautiful, and forceful in a "Samantha from *Sex and the City*" kind of way. As soon as we sat down for our Todd-arranged lunch at Koi, I knew she was in a whole different universe from Sondra.

"Honey, you should be much bigger right now—it's about time we started working together. Where's your *Vanity Fair* cover? Who tips off the paparazzi for you when you travel so the big executives know you're a busy girl? That network publicist—is it Sondra Mitchell? We worked together years ago—she's fine for the whole cast, but she's not going to grow your career. We need to strike while the iron is hot with you. You should be *everywhere* right now! My God, you can't even pass a newsstand without seeing Scarlett Johansson on the cover of six magazines. Even Britney Spears is still on magazine covers, and she's not even promoting anything! She was pregnant for a hundred years, then *bald,* then crazy, Star. Come on!"

Arden knew everyone at Koi—in fact, Arden knew everyone everywhere. "You are carrying a major hit show with your character's name in the title. Honey, that is huge! *Ugly Betty* huge! We need to show your network that you're a hot commodity and that if they don't treat you well, they're going to lose you. Now—first things first. We should start with the magazine placements right away. Do you know how to knit? I'll have some stuff sent over, and then we can start getting you mentioned in the publications when they do 'stars who knit' stories. You know—Julia Roberts, Kate Hudson, Liv Tyler—they all do it. Knitting is the new yoga."

I laughed, thinking back to a few years before, when my mom had bought me some knitting stuff and tried to teach me. "It will relax you," she'd said with a well-meaning smile. Four hours, a twisted knot of multicolored yarn, and some frustrated tears later, I had put the stuff in the closet, claiming that it made me more stressed-out to learn knitting than I had been before.

"I can't knit," I said to Arden. "Apparently I am missing the knitting gene."

She laughed. "That's fine—we'll just say you do, and you can learn later if you want to. Or we'll think of something else for you. How do you feel about fashion shows?"

HYDE IS A PRETTY small club, and when someone really famous is there, you always hear about it in the magazines. Arden had decided I needed to do the "see and be seen" thing at least twice a week, and this plan was just fine with Vince. The thing is, when you're on a show that shoots five days a week (sometimes six), you don't have a lot of energy to go out. That's why it's the movie people (and Paris Hilton) that you always hear about being out every single night. The rest of us have jobs. On Saturday nights, however, I usually made an exception, and we went out to Hyde, LAX, or whatever other club was hot.

"What about that guy?" Vince pointed to a model. He always tried to make a game out of it for me, like maybe at least one of us could find a cute guy. We huddled in a booth, sipping martinis.

"Gay," I shouted over the DJ. "How do you not know that? Everyone knows." Vince had been trying to find me a replacement guy since I'd finally ended things with Matt once and for all on Arden's recommendation. Our breakup had been coming for a long time, especially since he was already off his new show and mostly just auditioning for commercials. He really couldn't take being with someone more successful than he was.

Not that Hollywood is easy on a relationship anyway—even for former costars. Every time I even looked at another celebrity, in Hyde or anywhere else, photos would come out and then everyone would assume we were either dating or at least friends, and then I would have to be on the phone with Matt, reassuring him that I wouldn't date someone more successful than him. Before I was famous, I used to wonder how all the stars knew each other. Now, I realized that all the recognizable people just had a familiarity because we shared the same life: no privacy, lots of secrecy, and insecure significant others who just didn't understand.

The club was packed, and we moved toward the semioutdoor patio area to smoke. Brody Jenner walked by and checked me out. "What about him?" I said absentmindedly, just to mess with Vince. He took the job of maintaining my public image very seriously.

"No, no, no," said Vince, stepping in front of me. "One photo with him, and there's a big story about how the bad boy brought you over to the dark side." He lit a cigarette and took a drag. "We need you with cute people—Blake Lively—from—*Gossip Girl*—type people."

"Those girls live in New York, unfortunately," I yelled, bumping my hip against his. "Let's just go dance." We moved out to the center of the room, and for a second, I forgot who was famous, who was a nobody, and who was still waiting outside to get in.

ARDEN'S AGGRESSIVE STRATEGIES FOR getting me "seen" sometimes bordered on the absurd. At eight A.M. the next Saturday morning, I stood in an unknown person's living room as a fluffy white Persian made its way toward the couch, stepping nonchalantly over my feet. For the day, at least, this was my home. "Arden, do I have a cat?" I asked half-jokingly. Soon the photographer would be there, and I was walking around, trying to get my bearings in a house where I had supposedly been living for a year, laughing to myself at the shameful artifice of it all.

Actually, I am deathly allergic to cats, and as soon as this one touched me, the journalist was going to know that this whole thing was fake, because my eyes were going to swell up, and I was not going to be able to breathe. Arden laughed, scooping up the cat with one hand while she pressed a perfectly manicured finger to her lips with the other, shushing me. She would have nothing ruin her perfectly orchestrated photo shoot.

"Here's a Claritin," she whispered. "Don't let the writer hear you say this isn't your place."

"Get this cat out of here!" she yelled to a PA. "Put it someplace where it can't get out. Or, better yet . . . take a shot of it in the guest room. That will make the place look more homey."

In an attempt to make me seem "more accessible and relatable" as a big TV star, Arden had booked me a shoot and interview for a magazine feature called "Young Stars at Home." This was by far the most bizarre idea she'd had so far, considering the fact that I still lived at the hotel, and even then I was hardly home enough to sleep, much less decorate a whole place like that and hang out in the living room eating biscotti. But for that day at least, I lived in a three-bedroom bungalow-style home in Beverly Hills. She'd even gotten some "family and friends"–type photos from me that she'd strategically placed around the house to make it look like it was mine. By noon, I was being photographed sitting on my plush suede couch, pretending to read a book.

The weirdest thing about this, to me, was that the purpose of a shoot like this is to show you the private lives of stars, and yet even *that* was manufactured. Even the "interview" I gave after the photo shoot was just a series of talking points invented by Arden and her team. In fact, right before the actual interview began, I was once again in the bathroom, trying to learn more about myself. The journalist couldn't just read the bullet points and write the article about me; the words had to actually come out of my mouth. How I found the house, where I got all the stuff I decorated with—"This one I got in Tahiti; I love vacationing there . . . so relaxing!" "This is where I make enchiladas for my friends!"

The only small victory for me of this photo shoot was that originally, I was supposed to actually be *cooking* something in the kitchen when the writer got there, so I could serve her lunch. Apparently Arden had read a similar *InStyle* interview with Jessica Alba and thought this would be a good way for me to go. I had actually laughed at this suggestion, then refused. "You have to cook," said Arden. "It will look so great!"

"You don't understand," I said. "I know less than nothing about how to cook . . . in fact, if I try to cook, I might actually injure myself, and that would make me look even worse. No way."

Arden had an advance copy of the article sent over to me as soon as it was ready. It looked great, but I just couldn't shake the feeling that while the whole thing was beautiful on the outside, inside it was empty and hollow as the rented house. That was sort of the way I was starting to feel.

RIGHT BEFORE THE WINTER break in shooting for season two (before I got so famous I couldn't pee in a public restroom anymore), Vince and I were having brunch at Toast in West Hollywood. Actually, I was picking at a salad I hoped didn't have too much cheese in it and trying not to think about the basket of bread sitting on the table, and Vince was eating a delicious chicken frittata thing called Power Protein. Toast on Saturday was our ritual, before we hit the Melrose Trading Post at Fairfax high school, then Buffalo Exchange. Vince had a bunch of celebrity clients now (besides me), and he was always trying to create new and exciting looks for them by mixing vintage stuff with the clothes the designers sent over. His apartment was filled to the brim with designer clothes—hanging up, spilling off furniture, even in the kitchen. You never knew what you might find at Vince's place, or even in his car. Vince was like the Felix the Cat of L.A. celebrity fashion.

Sitting outside at Toast, we liked to play the "see and be seen" game, to watch who was out walking around and see who was most popular in Hollywood that day (by watching to see who attracted the most paparazzi). On this particular day, I was beating Mary-Kate Olsen for the number of photographers crowded around. A group of youngish-looking girls were frantically whispering and staring at us. Eventually, one of them broke away from the cute girl herd and came over to our table. I figured she was going to ask for an autograph, and I winked at Vince.

She walked up slowly. She was thin and blonde, and she was wearing tiny, low-waisted jeans. She looked like one of those "I can eat whatever I want and not gain weight" types. "Star Spencer!" she said. "You're on *Autumn Leaves.*"

"Yes," I said. "Do you want an autograph?"

"No, I . . ." Her voice trailed off. "I'm Sara McClellan. I had the part of Autumn before you." She looked down. I studied her more closely. In fact, she did seem to be the exact size of the tiny costumes that had given me so much angst during the pilot.

"Wow . . . I . . . I'm so sorry," I said haltingly. But actually, I wasn't sorry. If something hadn't been wrong with this girl, if fate hadn't intervened to take away her big break, I would never have gotten mine. Now I just wanted her to go away. "What are you doing now?" I asked, just to make conversation. I was really not in the mood to hear this girl's sob story.

"Oh, I'm still in school, actually—I *was* really bummed about losing the part and I cursed you every time I saw you on a billboard for a while, but I'm still auditioning all the time, and I just started my third year at UCLA. That's just the business. I've been doing this since I was ten, so I'm used to it. My friends and I love the show now . . . you're really good." She smiled. She actually seemed cool, like someone I'd be friends with.

"Um . . . thanks," I said, and stopped to take a good look at her.

She was beautiful and young, and she was out to brunch with her friends. She looked well rested and happy. She didn't have the money, the fame, and everything that went with it. Then again, I thought, she was allowed to eat, and to have pimples, and to just be herself. Suddenly, I felt like telling her that she could have the part back and that I wanted my old life back. But I didn't. I couldn't. Instead I just smiled.j

"Why did they fire you?" blurted Vince before I could shush him. "I mean, did you not get along with Greg? Did you look bad on camera? Come on—tell us."

She looked around like she was in the CIA and on a covert operation. Then she leaned forward and said in a hushed voice, "Don't tell anyone, but there was this insane producer, Mindy something, who got me fired because she didn't like my hairline. My hairline! She called a plastic surgeon, and when he told her the 'hairline revision' surgery wouldn't heal in time to start shooting season one, I was gone. My agent was furious and made them pay the contract anyway. I mean, that is just psycho." She looked at me. "Good thing you don't have a widow's peak."

I sighed. A widow's peak would have been the least of my worries.

MY CELEBRITY LIFE WAS going along pretty normally when suddenly, almost without my having to do anything, I had a famous boyfriend. It started with lunch at the Ivy, arranged by Arden.

I pushed the grilled chicken salad around on my plate, praying I didn't already have spinach stuck in my teeth. I. Was. On. A. Date. With. Brad Rockwell. Star of the most famous action movie series of all time, *Blood Vengeance*. Even in my former life as an indie film snob, I still knew who he was. I could hardly believe it myself—even with the show, the famous friends, and the money, I still never thought I would actually *know* someone as famous as Brad, much less be out on a pseudo-date with him. Sometimes the stuff that happened in my life surprised even me.

Apparently, this kind of fix-up is not uncommon in Hollywood. At first, Arden claimed that it was just for the photo op of the two of us out together, but then a couple of times she said, "You two would make such a great couple!" hopefully. I later found out that she was friends with his publicist and that they'd been trying to construct a "power couple" for months. I found the whole thing a little weird, but I agreed to go to the lunch, mostly because my brothers would have killed me if I didn't at least meet the guy and get some good stories for them.

"So . . . how did you get started in the business?" I said, trying to make normal-person conversation. The fact is, I had never considered that he might be a real person—what did he talk to people about? Did he read the newspaper? When the question came out, though, I realized I sounded like a magazine interviewer. Why didn't I know more about him? He was only one of the most famous movie stars in the world. My brother Ian had actually dressed up as his *Blood Vengeance* character for Halloween a few years before. *He's going to leave,* I thought. *He thinks I'm quirky.* I was momentarily ashamed to realize that I really did care what he thought of me.

I tried to remind myself: *I'm on a hit show. I'm famous too . . . besides, I don't even like this guy's movies.* Still, I kept having that feeling that I was floating outside my body, watching myself in a dream where I was a fabulous Hollywood actress, going on a date with a fabulous Hollywood movie star. To be honest, it was a little like going on a date with Santa Claus or the Easter Bunny.

Brad looked at me with his amazing blue eyes. "You're cute," he said, taking my hand in his. What was going on? When I arrived at the restaurant I thought this whole thing was a killer photo op. Now, though, I wasn't so sure.

"My management team heard about your show, and they wanted me to meet you to maybe work on some movie projects. Would you want that?"

"I'm—I mean, sure," I said, still feeling totally surreal. The UM me would never have even considered taking a stupid part in an action film, but I was actually curious to see how far this was going to go. "I mean, the hiatus isn't for a while, but I'm supposed to start reading scripts soon, I guess."

He smiled. "We have a few projects in mind. I'll have my managers call your agent to set something up, OK?"

"OK," I said, continuing to push my salad around. Once I got past being shell-shocked from eating with a person that famous, he actually turned out to be pretty nice. After lunch, he asked if I wanted to go for a ride on his motorcycle sometime, and took my number. It was all surprisingly nonchalant.

By the time I got back to the hotel, photos from the lunch had appeared on the gossip sites, and I had six voice mails from Vince, who was already in my suite when I opened the door.

"Omigod!" he screamed. "Brad Rockwell is H-O-T hot! What were you guys talking about for two hours?"

"Oh, it's nothing—just work stuff," I said. Arden had told me to be as discreet as possible about the Brad Rockwell fix-up, so I tried to downplay it as much as possible.

"Really? Is that why he's on JustJared.com holding your hand? How could you not tell me about this date?"

"Vince, I can't tell you everything—"

"Since when? You will continue to tell me everything, minute by minute, or I will get Perez to draw cocaine on your nose in pictures." He laughed. "Kidding, of course. But don't stop telling me things, Aim. I am your nearest and dearest out here."

"I'll keep that in mind."

TWO DAYS LATER, I got a call from Todd.

"Come into the office," he said. "I've got a really interesting offer for you." Since I was already working eighteen hours a day on the show, I couldn't imagine what other offer I had time to consider, but if there was money involved, Todd would find a way. I think if he could've cloned me and sent the clone out on appearances, he would definitely have done it.

Todd was dancing excitedly around his office holding a large manila envelope when I got there. "It's a standard work-for-hire contract from Brad Rockwell's office. Basically, Brad's nominated for a Golden Globe, a SAG Award, and an Oscar this year, and his people want him to have a new romance to start right before the awards season. His company will hire you to play the role of Brad's girlfriend for no less than one year," Todd said, not even fazed. "It's got the standard benefits—use of his jets, rooms in his mansion, and an unlimited expense account, plus bonuses for awards shows and other public appearances. It also has you on a tiered payout schedule—one year is $250,000 cash, more for engagement, marriage, a baby, etc."

"Todd, is this a joke?" I said, incredulous. "Seriously . . . are you kidding? We had lunch. He was really hot. We talked about our cars. Now I'm his girlfriend?"

"This is not a joke, Star Spencer. This is going to make your career," he said in a loud whisper. "I haven't seen an offer this good since . . . well, I can't say, but she's an Academy Award winner, she gets better looking every year, and *her* contract was the best career move she ever made."

Something Vince had told me in my Hollywood crash course rang a bell. "Oh my God!" I shouted. "I know this! Is it—"

"Don't even say it," he said. "I couldn't tell you even if you were right, and I don't need her lawyers coming after me. I was an assistant at CAA when that deal came through, and I wasn't even supposed to know about it. I just photocopied the original contract." He looked around as if someone might be listening, right there in his office.

This was by far the weirdest thing I had ever heard. "I mean— does he want to go out with me? Why can't I just go out with him? Wait—why does Brad Rockwell need to hire a girlfriend?" I wondered if he had some deep, dark secret, like he was once a woman or had a disfiguring disease that had left him without a penis.

Todd looked up at me over the contract. "Hello? Brad Rockwell is an international movie star. He's a workaholic. He's committed to four films this year and he travels nonstop. He doesn't have time to put into a relationship. This is what his company does around awards season. Maybe you'll like each other, and it will grow into something more. Maybe you'll make a few appearances together and go your separate ways. It's really not that big a deal."

I stared at him, still confused. "Really? This is how things work? I mean—does he even like me?"

"Not that it matters, but he thinks you're adorable. He loves your show. He had his manager Jon send over the contract right after your lunch. Listen . . . you're not even going to have to see him that much—between your shooting schedule and his, plus whatever film you're doing over this year's hiatus, you'd be lucky if you actually spent a weekend with him every couple of months. It's mostly just for awards shows, appearances, and candid photo ops to generate media. Plus, you can see other people just make sure that no one sees you, especially not photographers. You should definitely take it, but, Star . . . this is really important. You cannot tell anyone about this contract, ever. Not your best friend, not your mother, not your brothers, not your assistant. Nobody. Ever. I am totally serious."

I stared at him for a moment. "But—does this mean we're in a relationship? Why can't I just date him without a contract?"

He made a face. "Brad Rockwell can't just date anymore. He's not even like a real person—he's an empire. To even have a second conversation with them, you have to sign a nondisclosure agreement."

"OK," I said. "So—how does it work? I mean, do I get a paycheck?" I was more curious than anything. I was at one level of celebrity, but I was always interested in how the next levels worked.

"Basically, for the next year or so, if you want to hook up with someone else, go ahead—you just have to be in the closet about it. You can't let the paparazzi see you in public with anyone else, and you need to make sure you're seen with Brad enough to make everyone think you're a couple. Sometimes people in contracts like this have affairs with each other, just because it's easier and no one can tell. Do you want me to fix you up with some guys who are in contracts right now? I've got one client who just married an older TV star as part of a contract, but he's open to the down-low. You know what I mean?"

"That's OK, thanks." The truth was, I had no problem meeting guys just to hook up with, even when I was just out with Vince in West Hollywood. The fact that I never wanted any of them to call me or actually hang out with me and watch a movie was a totally different story. I still didn't seem to be able to let myself feel something for a guy.

"I have to think about it—I mean, what if I fall in love or something?" I didn't want to tell Todd, but this was probably unlikely. Vince had convinced me to visit his therapist about this very issue after I didn't fall in love with Matt Pierce, and she said I created "emotional distance" in order to protect myself. This seemed to be a reason *for* getting into the contract—if I was emotionally distant anyway, what was the harm in being in a fake relationship? At least this way, I knew I wouldn't get hurt.

"I'll think about it," I said.

"OK, but don't let this pass by. This is a win-win—money for you, good publicity for the show, *and* good for your career. You would be a *fool* to pass this up, Star Spencer! This will put you on the map and increase your brand recognition from mere TV star to international commodity."

I stared at him blankly.

"Let me know tomorrow, OK?"

"OK," I said, already on the way out of his office.

"I'm calling you tomorrow!" he yelled.

★　★　★

I WAS SAD THAT I couldn't even run this situation by Vince, but if I was going to go through with it, there would be a big chunk of my life that I couldn't share with him anymore. Aside from the initial moral weirdness, I was really leaning toward saying yes. I was still hooking up with guys and not wanting to commit, and this was going to make that a lot easier. If I took the contract, I'd have the best excuse in the world—I was already in a "relationship." Plus, I figured a few public appearances wouldn't kill me in exchange for $250,000. With that kind of money, I was well on my way to making sure my entire family was set for life.

I hated to admit it, but I did get a secret thrill just considering the fact that I might get to make out with Brad Rockwell. He was so charismatic, I felt like I was being drawn into his orbit by tractor beam. How do you say no to dating a big movie star, no matter what the circumstances?

You don't. And so, two days later, despite a slight feeling of "this is a bad idea," I had signed the contract and was touring Brad Rockwell's mansion.

"What do you do with all this space?" I said, calling out from a bathroom with a huge fountain in the middle. "This place is amazing!"

After his private chef made bone-in filet mignon and lobster for me, Brad took me on a tour. I was straining myself trying not to act overly impressed, but I really was. A few years before, I had been a college student in Michigan, and now here I was, in the home of a man who made $50 million per film.

I had a million questions as the tour went on. This was bizarre. Did I live there now? Did I have to have sex with Brad? Or . . . did I *get* to have sex with him? Was that totally weird to wonder? I'd been too chicken to ask Todd or any of the members of Brad's team that I'd met. Now we were alone, and I was dying of curiosity. Sadly, though, the one thing that had been made abundantly clear was that no matter what dirty secret I found out, I was never going to be able to tell a soul.

For all his wealth and incredible success, Brad was quiet and shy in private, and he seemed distant, like he was putting a big smile on an ocean of sadness. I felt an odd kinship with him over this. Did everyone feel this way about their Hollywood life? He shrugged. "The house is mostly just an investment—I've got another one in the Hills where I never even go. I have to put the movie money somewhere, you know . . ." His voice trailed off, and I pictured him as a little boy. Was this what he'd wanted to be when he grew up?

"What kind of stuff do you do at night?" I said. This was the weirdest second date I had ever been on, for sure. Without cameras or other people around, Brad was the complete opposite of his exuberant public persona—like a withdrawn, depressed teenager. Had this mopey man actually hired me to act like his girlfriend for a year? This was better than the weirdest David Lynch plot. I was sad that I couldn't tell anyone the details of the contract. Vince would have died.

He sighed. "Watch movies in the screening room, or I learn lines if I'm shooting or looping something in town. Depending on what I'm shooting, when it's coming out, or what I'm promoting, I'm pretty much always traveling, so when I'm here, I try to just chill out. Sometimes I go out—we'll go out, you know? Anywhere you want. Mr. Chow, Dolce, Skybar, Morton's—whatever. Just let my office know, and they'll set it up."

I nodded. "What kinds of films do you like?" I said, hoping against hope that he was a secret indie film fan.

"I never tell anyone this," he said, "but . . . I love Westerns. And, of course, anything with fast cars and gadgets."

I smiled, making a mental note to tell my brother Adam that he and Brad Rockwell had the exact same taste in films. Then I remembered that I hadn't heard from Adam in at least three months even though we were supposedly getting along now, and I got a little depressed. Maybe my new relationship would bring him around. I knew he was a huge Brad Rockwell fan.

I followed Brad down the hall, past an enclosed indoor atrium filled with what looked like a small rain forest. "This will be yours," he said, opening a dark wood door. "Stay whenever you want . . . it probably says 'twice a week' in the agreement, and you can start that in a couple of months once we start being seen together more. Just make sure your car is parked outside in the driveway, where the photographers can see it. The chef can cook anything, you have your own screening room, and the butler can get you whatever you need, like clothes or whatever. Just have your assistant give him a list." He waited for me to say something. I just nodded.

There was a distinct lack of chemistry between us. He stopped, turning around to face me. I could see his perfect muscles through his white cotton button-down shirt. Even his feet were tan, and he looked so good in his Versace jeans, I thought I might pass out. This was the moment . . .

He reached down, and I waited for the movie star kiss. He pulled me close and I could feel his strong arms around me.

"Thanks," he said, giving me a positively parental kiss on the forehead. "You're a good friend. Don't worry—we'll have a great time this year. Have you ever been to Mexico?"

With that, he turned and walked away, going into one of the rooms at the end of the hall and closing the door. I thought I heard voices coming from inside, but it could have been the TV. He didn't invite me in. I was left standing at the end of the hall, baffled. *What's going on here?* I thought. *Is it me? Does he think I'm fat? Why the contract if he doesn't even find me attractive?* I didn't want to *have* to have sex with him, but now I was a little offended.

I decided to wait a little while before I moved any of my stuff into his place.

THE NEXT WEEKEND, MY confusion was compounded as Brad and I engaged in an epic makeout session at Morton's, after a steak dinner and a few martinis. "Is this OK?" he whispered. "I really like you." He seemed a little drunk and like a totally different person. I didn't even know where to start trying to figure him out.

Part of me was thrilled beyond belief. I knew how it looked to the rest of the world. *He does like me,* I thought as I hugged him, running my fingers through his beautiful blond-streaked hair. His lips were full and soft, and he kept his arm around me the whole night, like he never wanted to let me go. I felt great—I had made the right choice. This contract was the best of both worlds.

He held my hand on the way out of the restaurant, past the waiting line of photographers who had gathered outside in anticipation of our exit. As he helped me into the back of the waiting Land Rover, I felt like a princess.

As soon as we were in the car, though, he dropped my hand. "Good work," he said, smiling. "You're a really good actress."

And just like that, I turned back into a pumpkin.

Luckily, Vince was doing costumes for a film and was on location in New Orleans, so I could dodge his questions over text and e-mail rather than in person. My official line was supposed to be "I'm dating Brad. We met at a business meeting, and we've been inseparable ever since," and that's what I was sticking to, even with my closest friends.

MY SECOND GOLDEN GLOBE Awards was worlds away from my first. For one, my mom had the flu and could not come out. For the other, at this Golden Globes I was debuting in my new role as one half of the celebrity couple now known as "RockStar." Now, the regular award show craziness and chaos was compounded by the fact that I had new lines to remember—the "I'm dating Brad" script.

This year, I arrived on the red carpet not with my cast, but on the arm of Brad Rockwell. I was nominated again for *Autumn Leaves,* and he was nominated for a serious role in a period piece. We were the golden couple of the Golden Globes.

Brad leaned forward, whispering softly in my ear. "Act like I said something funny," he said, and I laughed. He kissed me on the cheek, and the photographers went wild. We were momentarily blinded by flashbulbs and people yelling, "Brad, Star . . . over here, over here!" I felt dizzy and overwhelmed by the spectacle of it all, and I wanted to sit down, but Brad had his arm around my waist, anchoring me to reality. He was used to celebrity of this magnitude. He leaned in again to whisper what I'm sure looked like sweet nothings in my ear. "It's OK—you're doing great. Ten more minutes on the red carpet, and then we sit down." I wondered if he ever fantasized about walking the red carpet with someone he really loved. I wondered who he really loved. Truth is, I saw Brad so rarely, I knew almost nothing about him. Because we were photographed together every time we went out, though, it looked like we were together all the time. I always felt a little sad and alone, even though I was part of this amazing power couple.

A team consisting of Arden; Brad's publicist, Liz; and several assistants from their respective offices shepherded us down the runway, stopping us to chat with interviewers from the major networks. "Stick to the script," Brad whispered in my ear. "I'll do most of the talking." I remembered the red carpet lecture from the year before and how long ago that seemed.

When we got to the interviewer from E!, she asked what we did to get ready. "The usual," said Brad. "We slept late, ordered breakfast in bed, chilled out by the pool until it was time to go." I nodded and smiled, wondering if that's how he had spent the morning before his manager picked me up in the limo.

"Are you nervous?" the interviewer asked me.

"No, not at all—not with Brad by my side. This is just a fantastic night, and he's an amazing person." We proceeded down the red carpet line, repeating the same sound bites until it was time to go and pose for still photography. Brad leaned in again. "Good job," he whispered.

Our outfits were color-coordinated—gold Prada sheath for me, Armani tux with gold cummerbund and tie for him. Instead of being nervous and observing every little thing that happened at the Globes this time, I was more self-conscious about how many people were staring at us and coming over to our table to say hi during commercial breaks. I didn't have time to even take a bite of the dinner, and by the end of the night I was exhausted from trying to keep everything straight in my head. I hated to admit it, but Todd was right—this fake relationship was already doing wonders for my career. Producers, directors, and movie stars were talking to me, and Todd had already started getting calls from people wanting me to be in their films. I was on the map in a big way.

Once again, I did not win the Golden Globe, though Greg Forster finally received his Best Actor award for the show, and Ross collected another Best Supporting Actor award. Brad won Best Actor in a Drama. In his acceptance speech, he dedicated the award "to new love," and they cut to me.

It's too bad I didn't win the Golden Globe. I was a much better actress than anyone realized.

MAYBE BECAUSE THE REST of my life was so full of intrigue, waiting on the set to shoot my scenes was becoming unbearably boring. I needed Olivia around most of the time to entertain me, since I was tired of watching movies, listening to music, and trying not to answer any personal questions about my relationship with Brad. How do you keep your personal life a secret from the people you're closest to? I felt like a traitor every time my mom asked how things were going or wanted to know some details. I addressed this problem by hanging out with Olivia, who was very entertaining and didn't ask too many questions.

"Boob job." Olivia turned to a photo of a popular blonde actress. "There is no way you have tits that big when you have the body of a twelve-year-old Asian boy." She pointed to a photo. "And how does anyone not know her nose is fake? She looks like a different person now."

My new favorite thing to do with Olivia during downtime on the set was to look through *US Weekly* and speculate about who'd had what plastic surgery. Our "speculation sessions" made the long hours of waiting on set very entertaining; Olivia was so good at this she could even identify which doctor had done which procedure. The fact that I'd had a little (though definitely not as much as some of the other girls) just made the game more fun; it was as if I was now in some secret club, the entrance price of which was being surgically enhanced.

Technically, I was supposed to be learning my lines, but with a new writer on staff we'd been inundated with constant rewrites and script changes, so I was relying on my skills of fast memorization to get me through. Besides, I was 99 percent sure they wouldn't fire me. *Autumn Leaves* had finally cracked the top ten, and I was expecting a huge raise when season three negotiations got under way, otherwise I was considering the migraine trick.

She flipped to the next page. "Collagen lips, for sure. Botox, and a slight brow lift. Surprising for someone so young, but not unheard of. She's also had a lot of laser hair removal. She looks so different from her first movie ten years ago! She had, like, baby fat and a mustache in her first movie, and now she's flawless. All I'm saying is some quality money and time went into creating that girl, and someone hasn't gotten their investment back yet. They just need to put her in a movie that grosses over $100 million, and they'll be able to recoup their initial outlay of cash."

She folded the magazine back, making a giant red circle around the face of an aging film star who I was always saying looked too amazing to be real.

"The key is, if you end up saying 'Wow, she looks like she doesn't even age,' or if they still look like themselves, only a tiny bit older, then you know they have a good plastic surgeon. She, for instance, started early, and she just gets better looking every year. Did you know she's forty-eight years old? The bad ones all go to the same doctors, and they all look the same—huge lip implants, those hideous cat eyes, and the face that keeps growing vertically because of the chin implants, cheek implants, and face-lifts. I once worked for a former superstar who couldn't even close her eyes, she'd had so many face-lifts."

"Really? No—seriously. Really?" Some of these stories had to be made up, but I had a sick, Discovery-channel fascination with hearing them. Once she started, I could never tear myself away.

She put her hand on her heart. "I swear to you, there was a time in her life that she could seriously, barely close her eyes. It's totally plausible. It happened to Kenny Rogers too, you know."

This was much more fun than learning lines.

WHAT ABOUT THIS ONE? It's a *Scream*—style fun teen horror feature that's being released in time for Thanksgiving break. You'd be great in that."

Todd was reading to me from a list of potential projects for the hiatus during our weekly check-in meeting. Since I'd spent the first hiatus getting "made over," he and Arden both thought it was a good idea if I did a big-budget film to raise my exposure and capitalize on my newfound RockStar fame. Todd had been receiving numerous scripts for projects people wanted to cast me in. Most of them fell into one of two categories: *Bring It On*—type teen pop comedies, or summer blockbusters. All of them wanted to pay me obscene amounts of money, just for the huge box office numbers they were assured if I appeared at their premiere with Brad Rockwell on my arm. This time, I was sticking to my guns. After doing what had essentially become a nighttime soap for two seasons, I was tired of the show and looking forward to my indie film debut.

I sighed. "Todd, where's my *Boys Don't Cry*? I want to do something challenging, something indie. I'm sick of the soap and bubble gum," I said, putting my boot up on his desk. "What about an off-broadway play?" I knew this would drive him nuts.

"Bite your tongue," he said. "Now is the time in your career when you should strike while the iron is hot. I can get one of these guys up to half a mil, for sure. You should definitely go with a big studio for your first film. It will establish you as a bankable star. Trust me on this. Your IMDB STARmeter rating went up from number four seventy-six to number thirty-five *overnight* after the Golden Globes and your new relationship. You are hot, baby! You need to cash in!"

"No way," I said. "I'm definitely doing an indie film. What about that script Josh Stein gave me?" I said. "Did you read it? It's really good, and it's shooting in New York."

Even though Josh had been unceremoniously replaced by the network after they shot the pilot of *Autumn Leaves,* he and I had kept in touch. The previous week, I'd been having coffee with him when he took a script out of his bag. "I think you should read this, My company is developing it, and the lead would be a great role for you," he said.

He slid a script across the table, and I picked it up. The cover page said, "*Blue Gray* by Daniel Roberts."

"OK, I'll read it and get right back to you," I said. "Todd's going to be pissed, though—he wants me to do the *Scream* movie for the big money." I laughed. Josh looked at me seriously for a moment. "Amy, if there's one thing I've learned in this business, it's that you have to do things that fill your heart, whenever you can. I can't tell you what to do, but you definitely won't be sorry. Dan is great—very creative. And I even have a place where you can stay in New York to help with the budget." I was glad we'd kept up our friendship after he left the show; I'd told him many times about my indie film aspirations, and I was thankful he was keeping me on track.

He was right, of course—*Blue Gray* was an amazing true story about an artist who loses her mind and disappears in New York right after she starts becoming known on the 1970s art scene. I'd read and loved it, and given it to Todd the next day, hoping that he'd stop bugging me about the summer blockbuster list.

"Don't need to read it," said Todd. "Art house crap. They have less than a million to make that film, so you're going to end up sleeping on your friend's couch the whole summer and shooting in some abandoned building. Also, they haven't even called me with an offer, which means they are going to try to pay you scale. No way, Star Spencer. No way! No scale for you!"

I didn't know how to break it to Todd that I'd already pretty much decided to do *Blue Gray* and that I actually had a meeting set up with the writer/director the next day to discuss logistics. Todd hated being out of the loop, since he thought he had his finger on the pulse of the whole industry.

He inched the stack of scripts toward me with his finger. "Just don't decide yet, OK? If you stick to marketing to the Disney tween market, you can easily do a whole series of straight-to-DVDs, like the Olsen twins did; *then* you can do the indie film thing. You need to be thinking 'money' right now. What does fucking *Josh Stein* know about building your name into a franchise? Nothing—that's what. He's the guy who was fired from *Autumn Leaves,* OK? You need to read the other scripts before you make this decision."

It was already too late. The minute I read *Blue Gray,* I knew I was going to New York. That is, if the director would have me.

EVEN WITH MY STARMETER rating at an all-time high, breaking into the indie film world was turning out to be harder than I thought. The day after my Todd meeting, I met Dan Roberts, writer and director of *Blue Gray,* at Le Dome for lunch. Apparently, it wasn't up to *me* to say I wanted to do the film—*he* wanted to suss *me* out to see whether I was too "teen pop" for his precious script.

I wanted to meet him just to see if he was as arrogant as this request made him sound. Who did he think he was? Did he not know who *I* was? Did he not know I was turning down half a million and pissing off my agent just because of my undying love for indie films? From what Josh had told me, Dan was desperate to do the project but still wanted final say in casting. Who was this guy, anyway? I thought for sure he was going to be some granola type in his midfifties who'd just gotten lucky with a good script.

And so when he arrived at the meeting, I didn't expect him to be twenty-six years old, and I didn't expect him to be from my neighboring Midwestern state of Wisconsin. Also, I didn't expect him to be disarmingly attractive.

With a plaid shirt, dark curly hair, and piercing blue eyes, Dan was the exact kind of guy I would've had a huge crush on back in college. By the time I sat down, I was already a little in love with him before I remembered that I was, in fact, supposed to be Brad Rockwell's girlfriend, at least for seven more months.

Over lunch, Dan told me the story of how he wrote the screenplay during film school at NYU, then pushed it through the system—a sad tale of waiting tables, eating ramen, and almost giving up hope a few times while dragging his script to every agent and production company in L.A. and New York. As he told me the story, I secretly wondered if I would've had the staying power to withstand that kind of rejection.

Finally, he'd gotten his screenplay to the right people at Josh's office, who came on board to produce, on one condition—that I play the role of schizophrenic artist Marie Couret. Dan had almost walked away from the deal but had finally agreed to meet me for lunch, to "see what I was about." I had to admire the nerve of a totally unknown writer and director standing up for his project like that.

"So . . . did you really tell Josh you thought I was too 'teen pop' to play Marie Couret?" I said as we sat down to lunch. "That is cold. You don't even know me." I smiled.

He laughed. "What can I say . . . your show is huge, you're so famous, and I suppose it would be good box office just from people showing up to see if you can really act, but this story means the world to me, and if I'm only going to get one chance to tell it, I have to do it right."

"Why is this story so important?" I asked, genuinely curious. "Couret's work isn't even in the mainstream." I'd done my homework, and I could tell Dan was impressed.

"I need an actress who can handle this role because this film could put her work into the mainstream. She died in an institution before her work could gain recognition." He paused, looking me straight in the eye. "It's important, because Marie Couret was my aunt," he said softly. Now I was impressed. We talked for three hours, and I learned that not only did we have the exact same taste in films, but we had both gone to Michigan, both lived in the fine arts dorms, and both had grandparents who lived in Milwaukee. The next day, we signed the contract and announced that I was attached to *Blue Gray*.

Todd was madder than I'd ever seen him. But finally, I felt like my life had purpose and like I was making decisions for myself.

15

"I GUESS YOU DID THE right thing, if you're going for a serious film career when the show ends. Look at that girl who plays the nurse on ER—Linda Cardellini. She did *Brokeback Mountain* for no money during her hiatus, and now she's poised for a really meaty lead in something once that show finally ends. Though, I mean, you can't get any good recognition in the film industry unless you play a retard or a psycho, or get really ugly," Michele said, filing her nails. "I can respect that. I'm doing the *I Know What You Did Last Summer* prequel—I just couldn't pass up the big paycheck right now. I'm doing the 'one for me, one for them' thing, you know? Plus, I just don't know if I'm ready to get ugly for my career right now."

I nodded, taking a drag of my Camel Light, having come to regard Michele's philosophical musings on her career as white noise. Actually, if not for Josh and the good script, I might also be doing the typical teen horror flick. Instead, I seemed to have lucked into an amazing project. I was so sick of the show, I couldn't wait for the hiatus to start. I wondered—if *Blue Gray* was "one for me," then what was the "one for them" I'd have to do next hiatus? I couldn't worry about that, though, because I was too excited about my summer in New York.

Two weeks before shooting wrapped on season two, the set had that "school's almost out" feeling, so much so that there was no way I was learning lines, even though the season finale was a special double episode that had my character graduating from high school and my two dads adopting a baby from China.

I'd recently told a magazine interviewer that Brad and I liked "staying home and watching movies" and that we had "really become homebodies," and actually, that was half-true. Since my contract precluded going out to clubs and hooking up with guys (because then people would know we weren't really a couple), I spent a lot of time at home or in my suite at the hotel, which I still kept for when I needed to get away from Brad's. In reality, Brad was usually shooting films on location (something he'd seemed to do nonstop ever since we met), or vacationing at his place in Mexico, always when I happened to be working or at an inconvenient time for me to get away. We ended up seeing each other and making a public appearance about once a month, unless Brad had a movie coming out, in which case we did the red carpet and a few PDAs to get the tabloids talking, and then he left again. All in all, not a very labor-intensive job, and it left me with a lot of after-hours free time, during which I couldn't really go out for fear of being spotted and starting the rumors flying.

"AIM—NOT THAT OUTFIT AGAIN! You have a hundred thousand dollars' worth of clothes in your closet, and yet this is the fourth day in a row you're insisting on this black sweater and jeans combo. What is going on with you?"

Vince was right. It wasn't like I was becoming some manic-depressive or a homeless person or something . . . in fact, quite the opposite. I was very aware that I should never go out in public wearing

the same thing twice, so when I was hanging out inside or on the set, I wore the same thing every single day, just for the sake of familiarity and comfort (and perhaps to defy the system by being a slob in private).

I now had so much choice that I craved the routine of having some kind of uniform to put on every day, so I did. The more outrageously expensive clothing piled up in my suite at the hotel, in my trailer, and at Brad's, the more I was compelled to wear roughly the same outfit—Chip & Pepper, Rock & Republic, or Seven jeans; white T-shirt, black Chanel cardigan; black Gucci boots; and black Fendi bag. There is just something about having to change clothes multiple times per day for work, and again when you go out at night to appearances or awards shows, that makes you frightfully unimaginative when it comes to dressing yourself. The actual amount of time I ended up wearing my favorite outfit always ended up being so small, I figured that over a month's time, it would just equal out to be a whole day in the life of a regular person.

"Actually, you're so wrong . . . this is like the ninth day in a row of the same outfit," I said, sighing. "But it's just BCD, so I never wear it for long anyway. I just don't like having to think about what I'm going to wear when I'm not out, OK?"

"BCD" was a new term we'd made up to describe things that were "behind closed doors." This applied to everything from clothes to hookups to drug habits, and it described a Hollywood world to which the general public has no access. For instance, if the majority of the world thinks a certain Hollywood actor is a macho action hero hunk type, but everybody in Hollywood knows that he's actually a screaming queen who enjoys getting blow jobs from young boys in gyms, that's BCD information. Hollywood insiders are really good at keeping BCD secrets. I even had a few of my own now—the thing with Brad being the biggest one, and my being a repeat offender with the same outfit, but also how I saw Jessica Alba in a Rite Aid without her makeup. Did I call the *Enquirer*? Did I take a photo with my camera

phone? No, I did not. Would I have done that two years ago? Yes, I would have. The difference was that now I was bound by the "BCD Code of Honor," whereby celebrities never rat each other out. That means whether I saw a famous actress doing coke in the bathroom of Cipriani in New York or a well-known movie star kissing his boy-friend at a Golden Globes after-party, I kept it to myself.

"You have to be careful—if you go out carrying that Fendi once more, *US Weekly* is going to do one of those 'I Love My Bag!' photo spreads of you carrying it at the airport, on Robertson, coming out of Crustacean, leaving the studio, etc., etc. Then you're never going to close that Coach deal." Vince grabbed my beloved bag and ran onto the balcony of the suite, threatening to throw it over.

He was, of course, speaking of the endorsement deal offered to me by Coach just the week before. Todd had called excitedly: "Star Spencer, guess who is trying to crack the youth market and wants you as their new face?"

"I don't know—Louis Vuitton?" I'd said. I hated it when Todd made me guess.

"No—they're doing the same thing, but they've got Scarlett Jo-hansson. Coach is trying to compete with them, so they're trying to sign you, my sweet little potato! This is going to totally make up for you betraying me with your crunchy granola hippie film."

I laughed. Todd had fallen into my TV deal in the first place and even made money off my "relationship" with Brad, so I didn't feel too bad. "Coach is sending over bags, shoes, and other stuff for you to use, so you can get a feel for their products," he continued. "This deal is going to be huge. Seven figures huge!"

Todd had been sniffing around for an endorsement deal for weeks, since my STARmeter rating had been on the rise. "Mischa Barton has Keds . . . the *American Idol* girls have Candie's . . . Cover Girl has the *America's Next Top Model* contestants and Queen Latifah . . . we have to get you on this bandwagon, baby! Endorsements are the next big thing for you!"

I thought of an *E! True Hollywood Story* I'd seen recently about the "death of the supermodel," where they discussed how the celebrity endorsement was killing the world of modeling. Was I contributing to the extinction of the supermodel now? If I signed the Coach deal, would I actually be cheating some waifish model wannabe out of a day's wages? Sometimes it amazed me how much stuff I got for free. Not unlike the craft services table dilemma of too much free food and the inability to eat it, I found that the more money I made, the less I had to pay for. Since my rent and food were mostly covered by the network as part of my deal, I had only to pay for gas, cigarettes, and sometimes a meal out here and there, if I wasn't at a business-meeting-type meal (usually paid for by the instigator) or recognized in a restaurant (usually paid by the restaurant for the free publicity of just having me there). I sometimes wondered if this was how Paris Hilton stayed so rich. A few years before, when I'd had no money and needed to get stuff for free, I couldn't. Now I could pay, but I didn't have to. In fact, the more popular the show got, all I had to do was mention a product or an item of clothing, and the next day there was a box in my trailer.

I mentioned to Arden that I'd been regifting stuff I received at awards shows and other appearances, and she laughed. "Honey, everybody does that—my clients always give me stuff like those gift certificates for massages and facials that are in the gift bags at the Oscars. I haven't paid for a visit to Burke Williams in seven years. That practice is strictly Behind Closed Doors, though. The advertisers and sponsors hate it when they realize you gave your great aunt something that they hoped they'd see on you. Hate it! Nothing worse than some big star's never-photographed great aunt Hazel talking into a fabulous Swarovski crystal-encrusted Razr phone. The worst!"

I was glad to hear that my BCD term was catching on, at least Behind Closed Doors. I was less thrilled to learn that one of the stipulations of the proposed Coach deal was that I had to banish my beloved Fendi to permanent BCD status, never again to be carried in public.

Apparently, being "the face" of a brand extends not only to advertisements but to anytime you're in public and might be photographed. Since this was pretty much every time I went anywhere, anytime, for anything, this meant I had to send the favorite Fendi to my mom and forget about it.

As I packed it up, I made a note to myself not to sign any more exclusive deals, lest I be forced to give up my last shred of freedom—my black jeans and sweater—or be told what underwear to wear.

EVERY TIME I WENT back to the hotel to relax, see some friends hanging out by the bar, or just get away from the cavernously lonely inside of the Brad Rockwell mansion, where I was contractually obligated to sleep "at least three times per week," I always ended up regretting it. Case in point: on a night when I (of course) had to be on set early the next day, the people in the suite above mine were having an all-night party that apparently involved clog dancing, or maybe dragging around dead bodies, from the sound of the thumping.

Exasperated, I flung aside the pillow I had been hiding my head under and picked up the phone to the front desk.

"Hello, can you ask the people upstairs from me to stop stomping? I'm trying to sleep."

I rolled over and looked at the clock. The blocky numbers of the digital display flashed two A.M. which was exactly six hours from when I had to be on set. While I was a big enough celebrity to live there, I wasn't Lindsay Lohan big, or they'd have moved me to the penthouse suite.

The phone rang in the room upstairs, then the stomping got even louder. My luck, it was probably Vince Vaughn and Owen Wilson with some indie film starlet, or maybe the singer from Maroon 5 with one of his latest conquests. I lay back on my bed, readjusting my earplugs as random thoughts appeared in my head. Why did I keep living in this celebrity dorm? I could have my own wing of Brad's mansion. Oh—right—then I'd have zero chance of having sex ever again. At least this way I could hook up anonymously with cute boys in the bar, take them back to my suite, and then swear them to secrecy. This was very Charlie Sheen of me, but it seemed to be working so far. I was more than halfway through my RockStar contract, and I hadn't been caught yet.

I pulled the pillow over my head, trying to go to my quiet place in my mind.

Pound pound pound.

The insomnia problem had sort of crept up on me after my dad died and was nothing new. It wasn't like one minute I was one of those "I sleep like a log" types, then the next I was wide awake at three A.M. More like when I was a kid I couldn't go to sleep when something big was going to happen the next day, like the first day of school, a trip to Disney World, or a big test. Then it just grew from there, and before I knew it, I had a whole world of sleeplessness, complete with ear plugs, a sleep mask that made me look a little like a sleep astronaut, sleeping pills of all varieties, and quiet activities that could be performed in the company of others without waking them up while I lay awake in the darkness.

It didn't take much to wake up the insomnia demon. Lately, one caffeinated beverage after three P.M., and I was pretty much guaranteed a bad night's sleep. I was dozing off again when I heard a peal of laughter coming from the hallway. "You guys, don't be rude . . . I was on *Baywatch!*" screamed a drunken voice. Exasperated, I got up and looked out the peephole to see a blonde head go by. Hotel rumors had her retiring from the industry, picking up a wealthy sugar daddy, and hanging out by the pool all day. My money was on her having a secret life as a porn star.

Finally, *Baywatch* Girl and her crew were gone, so I turned the light back off and got back into bed. The noise upstairs continued, but I was powerless to do anything. Because of RockStar, no one was really supposed to know I was there, so I couldn't go up and tell them to be quiet. Arden would probably say it was bad for my image not to be at Brad's, and one of the partygoers was likely to e-mail Perez the minute I left or show up on some website with a "celebrity sighting" report. I was lonely at the hotel, but I was even lonelier at Brad's.

Maybe Hilary Swank was in the room next door or Kirsten Dunst had an early call, because finally security heard from someone who outranked me and sent someone to stop the insanity. The hotel was as reflective of the Hollywood food chain as the city itself; even when you're sleeping, it's all about who you know.

I was asleep for what seemed like four minutes when the phone rang with my wakeup call. As I was leaving, I picked up the phone, dialed *519, and let it ring until one of the stompers from the night before picked up. "Good morning," I said cheerfully, before slamming down the phone.

THE FOLLOWING WEEK, I was once again at the hotel, home from the set for ten minutes, when the phone rang. "You have a package at the desk," said the concierge. "It's from your mother."

How did they know everything? "OK, bring it up," I said. *It must be the photos I asked her to send. Maybe I should order a drink to prepare myself for this,* I thought.

Since *Blue Gray* followed Marie Couret's life from when she was a kid to when she disappeared, as part of pre-production Dan and Josh had asked me to contribute real photographs of my childhood for the photo montage at the beginning of the film. I said I'd ask my mom to send some, then promptly put it in the back of my mind under "things I don't want to do" when it occurred to me that my dad was in most of my family photos, and that I hadn't looked at any of those photos since he died, that I didn't know if my mom had either, and that I didn't want to upset her by making her go through a bunch of our family albums to pull them out. Thus, I had put off the choosing of the family photos until the very last day before the deadline. Now the box was here, and I was going to have to face it.

First, I called in emotional reinforcements. Vince arrived in record time, speeding over from his apartment. The box was still sitting on the bed when he arrived.

"I am pouring you a drink," he said, reaching into the fridge for the vodka and Red Bull. "Then we'll get down to business." I felt better already. There was no reason why he couldn't do this for me, right? He could just show me the ones he thought would be right for the film. I didn't even have to look. But the minute he dumped out the box, one of the photos fluttered over and landed on my foot, catching my eye. It was a photo of me on my dad's shoulders when I was about five. Hot tears leapt to my eyes as I picked it up. For some reason, I remembered that day so well—the smell of the air, the feeling of my hand in my dad's. The pain of missing him made me feel like someone was stabbing me in the heart.

"Ugghhh . . . I can't do this," I said. "Can't they just Photoshop something?" I didn't want to think about it. Even with the serious subject matter of *Autumn Leaves,* I felt like I'd put my personal experience in a box in my mind, and I didn't know if I wanted to get it out again. It just hurt too much. *If I let myself go all the way over this cliff,* I thought, *I might never come back.*

"It's OK . . . you're doing great," he said. "It's almost over." He pulled out a family photo from Thanksgiving when I was nine. As usual I refused to smile, was making a crazy face, and had my arm around Adam's neck. I held up the photo and remembered the whole day like it was yesterday, and I vehemently wished I could travel back in time and do it all again. I didn't know it then, but at that moment there were almost exactly eight years left in my dad's life. Would I have been less of a brat, eaten more of my turkey, enjoyed his company more if I'd known the clock was ticking? My eyes filled with tears, and I shook my head.

"Not that one," I said, wiping my eyes. "They need some of me alone as a little kid, or at least something where they can cut out the other people. It's supposed to be a photo montage of the artist growing up."

Finally, we found one of me as an awkward eleven-year-old, smiling a big grin into the camera after getting a "Perfect A+" sticker from the dentist. Dad had picked me up from school early to take me to my appointment, then we went to lunch, just he and I. Right before he'd taken the photo he'd said "Smile, Bunny Luv!" and I'd made a big smiley face. I ran my tongue over my now capped teeth.

"Use this one," I said, handing it to Vince, who put it in an envelope. "At least I can pretend I am still the same person." I wondered—if my teeth were different, and my hair was different, and my body was different, would my father still recognize me if he saw me today? Seeing all the old photos was making me wish I could go back to a simpler time, before I was a hot Hollywood property.

"Don't get like that," Vince said, shuffling through another pile of photos. "Everyone has parts of their job they don't like. At least you don't have to go to some office every day and be an investment banker. Now *that* would be tragic."

"Ugh!" I snorted. "Can this be over? It's really bumming me out." Suddenly I remembered why I never wanted to do any of my mom's scrapbooking projects when I went home for Christmas. I always hated the flood of memories that rushed back so easily.

"Here, I found some more," he said, pulling out a smaller envelope containing a series of embarrassing school photos. "This one is nice . . . is this a perm? Good choice."

I laughed. "Fine, use those," I said. "Send them to the production company, and let's go. It's not like I'm even that person anymore anyway."

* ★ ★ ★

"THERE'S A RUMOR GOING around again that Teddy's is closing . . . some scandal over mistreatment of civilians. Like, who cares
if you mistreat a nobody anyway? We have to get you in there before
they shut their doors altogether—what about the one of the private
concerts. It would look great for you if *US Weekly* saw you there and
included you in the 'Scene and Heard' column."

Arden and I were discussing my schedule of appearances (both
casual and official) over dinner and Corzo Collins at Dominick's. I
still loved ordering a big plate of spaghetti, even though I had almost
no appetite and could only eat one or two bites before I felt full and
totally sick. After six months of working with her I had to admit it:
Arden was a PR and marketing genius. Sure, she was ruthless and cal-
culating and I would never have wanted to be on her bad side, but her
brutal honesty about the Hollywood scene was amusing, and since I'd
been working with her, I had been in so many magazines that I was a
little sick of seeing my own face.

"Isn't that Friday night?" I said, taking a tentative bite of a crunchy
bread stick. "We never get done shooting until, like, three A.M. on Fri-
days, but if I'm still awake, I'll try to go by."

She looked up from her BlackBerry. "Don't go if you're going to
look tired in the pictures. We don't want to give them a reason to
run a 'Star Spencer is dying!' headline, which they will do if you appear somewhere looking thin and slightly less than perfect. Let us
learn from Natasha Lyonne, shall we? Now . . . let's talk about New
York."

Arden was also less than thrilled about my choice of film project
over the hiatus. I was so excited about New York I couldn't have
cared less, though I did agree to keep my image in the press as much
as possible while I was there. She was also not happy that I still hadn't
hired a manager, despite her repeated suggestions and meeting fix-

ups. It wasn't that I wasn't career motivated; it seemed like everything I did was career focused, from the time I woke up in the morning to the time I went to sleep at night. It was partially the money—I really did object to the concept of giving another 15 to 20 percent of my earnings to another person. Mostly, it was the fact that with Attila, Sondra, Arden, and Brad's whole team, I just didn't want anyone else weighing in on every decision I made in my life. I knew I probably needed more career guidance, but I just didn't think I could take another cook in the kitchen, so to speak.

She pulled out a piece of paper. "Here are some places you should be seen in New York, while you're on breaks from shooting. I'm not going to be there twenty-four/seven to make you go out to do your 'see and be seen,' so make sure you make an effort. You know how you get." She laughed.

She definitely had me figured out. Without her to force me into fashionable clothes and makeup, I was practically guaranteed to go back to my borrowed apartment and watch TiVo'd reruns of *Project Runway* on breaks from shooting the film. She'd threatened to assign me a "representative" from the New York office of RMG, but I'd declined, since I'd never shot a real film before and didn't want someone pressuring me to go out and do things all the time. Besides, I *was* supposed to be on hiatus.

"At least you're not shooting in Arkansas," she said with a laugh. "Do you know how hard it is to get the paparazzi to travel? I've been in this business a long time, and let me tell you, nobody would even cross over to New Jersey to get shots of Zach Braff and Natalie Portman shooting *Garden State.* They could have been lost forever in Newark and never heard from again for the lack of press they got when they were shooting.

"OK," she said. "I had my assistant make this for you." She pulled out a typewritten list with NEW YORK in large block letters at the top. After each item on the list, she paused to elaborate.

"First thing on the list is Soho," she said, leaning forward to make a note on the paper. "There are usually photographers at the corner of Houston and Mercer, waiting for celebrities to come out of the Marc Jacobs store. Go in there on a Saturday and buy something, just so *People* can show you out and about."

"OK," I said. I had no problem going shopping. "Do I take the subway?"

She laughed. "I am going to pretend you didn't say that. I have one word for you: taxi!" She pointed to the next item on the list.

"Also in Soho, do the see and be seen at Butter, definitely. Ashley Olsen doesn't hang out there anymore since she and Scott Sartiano broke up, but they'll comp your whole evening just to keep the restaurant in the media.

"Oh, finally, in Soho, I'll set up an interview for you at the Mercer Hotel—everybody stays there. It'll be great for them to get a shot of you leaving."

She pulled out a map of Manhattan and set it on the table, pointing to the right side. "Here's the Upper East Side—you know? From *Gossip Girl?* There's a restaurant up there called Elaine's—George Clooney goes there when he's in New York, but if you see him there, I do not want to read a Page Six rumor that you were 'at his table for half an hour canoodling' or that you two were 'getting very cozy.' That will not fly with Brad's people. Just go there, get the steak and the martini, and get out. Wave at George if you must, and say hi to the bartender for me. His name is Charlie.

"There are some good movies premiering in Manhattan this summer, but whatever you do, don't go with a man, even if it's a male friend. Even if he's gay. Show up alone, or you will end up with a call from the Brad Rockwell camp."

I nodded. I'd already gotten this lecture from Todd and from Brad's manager, Jon, who let me know that they were not thrilled with this arrangement because they didn't want a two-month-long gap in our appearances together, but that they would make it work and Brad might try to show up in NYC for some photo ops. Todd said this meant I was on "thin ice" in the contract, but for once, I didn't care.

She pointed at the upper left-hand corner of the map. "Magnolia Bakery is a must," she said, smiling. "This one I included because I know how much you love your sweets. Don't go nuts, but I swear they put crack in their cupcakes. They are like nothing else you've ever experienced, and there's always someone like Gwyneth Paltrow or Jennifer Connelly down there."

She took a sip of red wine, leaning forward. "There are just a few things you must avoid while you're there—off the record, of course. Listen, I do not want to see a photograph of you waiting in line to see the Empire State Building," she said earnestly. "That is something that civilians do. If you feel that you cannot live without seeing the view (which is spectacular, I must say), let me know and I'll set it up for after-hours viewing. This includes the Statue of Liberty, Coney Island, or one of those red double-decker buses. And Star—seriously, I know you're obsessed, but even if they're still doing the *Sex and the City* tour, don't take it. I will tell you where everything is, if you're curious, and you can go there in a cab."

I stifled a laugh. I *so* would have taken that tour.

"Please do not hang out with your less-than-attractive costars," she said, her expression growing serious. "I mean, I don't know what the film is about, and good for you if there's a five-hundred-pound blind guy in it or something, but don't lead him through the West Village, eating ice cream from a Mr. Softee truck. That will make you look bad." I pulled out a napkin and a pen. There was no way I was going to remember all of this stuff.

"If you want to go see a Broadway show, let me know—we have to be careful, though, because we don't want the press to pick up the story that you're thinking of doing a play. That will piss off your network and make them think you want to leave (though you might be able to work that to your advantage when it's time to renegotiate your deal). Also, don't go to anything Ben Brantley gave a bad review to—you don't want to be Rosie O'Donnell, flogging that tragic Boy George musical. Know what I mean? Since you're doing the indie thing anyway, stick to off-Broadway stuff that's got good buzz. You'll probably see Ethan Hawke in the audience.

"Food: If you're getting a little too thin and you notice the press is running a lot of 'scary skinny' stories about you, New York is a great place for street food photo ops. Just go to Central Park, buy a hot dog or a pretzel, make sure the photographer gets a photo of you taking a bite, then toss it. This throws them off the scent and makes the public think you're eating. Avoid the shawarma guy at the corner of Thirty-third and Third, though. A friend of mine got sick there once."

I folded up the list and put it in my purse.

"OK, now that we've done New York, let's talk about L.A. Fashion Week, which is coming up before you leave. We need to get you in the front row at a few good shows so you can appear in the fashion wrap-ups in the magazines." She pulled another sheet of paper out of her leather portfolio. "Did you hear about that request for you to model black underwear for Frederick's of Hollywood? I heard Sondra was *livid*." She laughed. "Coach probably wouldn't want you to sully your image either. I just thought it was funny. Why would anyone want a girl who plays a seventeen-year-old on TV to do a lingerie show? It just doesn't seem like a good fit to me. Sondra probably ripped them a new one." She paused to order another drink.

"Anyway," she said, "I have your estimated shooting schedule from the show for next week, and I've got you appearing in the front row of all the shows that correspond with your breaks."

"Can I bring Vince?" I said. "He's my fashion brain."

"Has Vince been cleared by Brad's people?" she said. "They're not going to want you to appear with a guy unless the press knows he's gay."

I laughed a little inside at the fact that I was having a conversation that made me sound suspiciously like I was in the CIA.

"Yes," I said. "He's been cleared."

BRAD AND I HAD been "dating" for four months at the beginning of my season two hiatus. We both had a few weeks off at the same time before I was leaving for New York to start shooting, so his people suggested we go away to Costa Rica for ten days to stay at Villa de los Amigos, a famous beach resort.

Part of me was excited. I had to admit it sounded amazing to be able to sleep in, lay by a beach all day, and drink umbrella drinks. Another part of me was terrified. What was I going to talk to Brad Rockwell about, all alone for ten days? I had a hard time getting a whole sentence out of him when we hung out at his place or had dinner with just the two of us. I always felt stupid, like I was trying too hard or like he thought everything I said was weird. Even though Brad was older than me, he and his friends spent most of their free time getting stoned, playing video games, or watching Jackie Chan movies. I never felt like I fit in, and I never, ever knew the right thing to say.

Sure enough, I felt like I'd used up all of my conversation starters by the second night of the trip. My face ached from smiling for the multiple paparazzi that had followed us down there and were capturing every moment of our "love fest," which had consisted mostly of us lying on the beach next to the $15,000-a-night villa. We did spend a few moments cuddling and frolicking in the water, but once we were inside, it was business as usual, and I'd run out of ideas. In fact, it seemed the only thing we had to talk about was our respective crazy work schedules—the thing that usually kept us apart.

I was drinking an umbrella drink and watching *Say Anything* in my room when I heard Brad call out from the screening room. "Star, come in here—you have to see this!" My heart soared, and I instantly kicked myself. Why did I care if he liked me? He didn't even know who Hal Hartley was. He wasn't my type, and he didn't have to love me. Still, being around him made me feel so lonely sometimes that I wanted to crawl out of my skin. When he actually initiated conversation, I felt like crying from relief. Something to break the silence! I walked into the screening room to find him drinking a beer and watching the latest cut of the about-to-be-released *Blood Revenge 4*.

"This is awesome . . . you have to see this," he said, beckoning me into a seat. "I actually jumped down the side of this mountain and fell five hundred feet. This Swedish guy who is famous for skiing these crazy sheer drops plays the villain. This guy is insane!" He paused the film on a particularly scary-looking shot of him chasing the movie's criminal down a mountain, both of them on snowboards. "The snow is so powdery there—it feels like falling into baby powder," he said, and I nodded. I'd never been skiing, but I was grateful for the conversation. We watched the rest of the cut and I offered my comments on the story, which Brad actually seemed to find helpful. "You're good at this stuff," he said, smiling. "You should write, or be a producer or something—then you'd have a say over the story line, and you get a share of the profits. You have to start thinking big!"

I smiled. Maybe Brad was deeper than I thought. Somehow, in the midst of our crazy fake relationship, it felt like we were becoming friends. I almost asked him if he wanted to watch *Say Anything* with me, but then I changed my mind, deciding to quit while I was ahead.

I wished him good night, went up the stairs to my room, and turned the movie back on, dozing off right around the "one hundred songs about Joe" scene. I woke up again to turn it off right at my favorite part, where John Cusack is standing outside of Ione Skye's house with the boom box. I don't know whether it was the umbrella drinks or finally having had a good conversation with Brad, but before

I knew it I was sitting on the floor crying. I'd thought I was doing the right thing accepting this Brad deal, but the loneliness was so bad I could barely breathe. Why did I sign the deal in the first place?

I thought of calling my mom, but it was late and I didn't want her to worry. Besides, what would I tell her? As far as she was concerned, I was dating Brad and things were going great. Why would I be upset? I'd been dodging Vince's questions about my relationship with Brad for months. I couldn't wake up Brad—what would I say, "I'm lonely and I want out of the deal"? It seemed absurd. Todd said people did stuff like this all the time.

My soft, choking sobs seemed to echo throughout the cavernous halls of the villa. Why was I so upset? I thought I could do the "just friends" thing with him, but the loneliness was crushing me whenever we were together. This wasn't worth $250,000, but now there was no way out.

I got up, wandering down the stairs of the villa to the private beach. The night was black, and it was dead quiet except for the sound of the crashing waves. I sat down on the sand, staring out at the ocean. Maybe I was overreacting. Technically, I could date whoever I wanted—I just couldn't go out in public with them, explain why not, or tell them anything about Brad and me.

Maybe I wasn't overreacting.

Somehow, this had made starting a relationship seem kind of pointless, so most of this was my own fault. I listened to the waves, watching the tide go in and out and thinking about my dad, wondering what he would say.

After wearing myself out, I lay down in one of the cabanas, finally falling asleep to the crashing sound of the waves, counting the minutes until *Blue Gray* started shooting. *It's almost over,* I told myself. *I just have to get through this trip, and then I'm free.*

★　★　★

AFTER WE GOT BACK from Costa Rica though, I got an e-mail from Todd on my BlackBerry. "Come to my office," it said. "Re: Brad Rockwell promotion."

"Brad's camp thinks you're doing a great job," he said. "They want you to think about getting engaged before you leave for New York for the summer." He took a sip of coffee. He did not laugh. Todd never laughed when we talked about money.

"Engaged at twenty?" I said, incredulous. "Doesn't that seem . . . young?" "Young" seemed like a better word than "fake" at that point. In an attempt to avoid the obvious fact that my pretend boyfriend was never in town and didn't even seem to like me that much when he was, I offered the "I'm too young" defense when Todd informed me that Brad's camp had offered me a "promotion." *This thing was fun while it lasted,* I thought, *but enough is enough, especially after my meltdown.* I wasn't marrying this guy just for money and publicity. My mom had only one daughter, and if I ran off and got married without telling her, she'd be heartbroken, especially since I could never explain that it wasn't real.

"You don't have to really go through with it," he said. "I think it's a good idea. Look—Jessica Alba was engaged at twenty, and Jessica Simpson at twenty-one. You have no idea how much press you can get out of a broken engagement, especially if it's nasty. I mean, first there's the rumors, then the actual event, then the fallout, then who you're dating on the rebound. I'm telling you, that's six months' worth of *Life & Style* and *US Weekly* covers, guaranteed. Nick and Jessica are still milking their breakup, and they were a real couple, Star Spencer. Come *on*! They're even offering to let you pick your own ring!" He pounded his desk vehemently.

"Stop pushing me!" I snapped. I stared out the window at the city of Los Angeles sprawling below. I thought of all the little girls in the world, dying to come to Hollywood, become famous, and marry a movie star, and I got even sadder. I gathered myself up to give Todd a piece of my mind. I started to tell him he was crazy, that arranged

dating was one thing but engagement quite another, and that my
mother would kill me if she read in the *Enquirer* that her only daughter was engaged. I started to tell him about the lonely nights at the
mansion, the awkward lack of conversation, and my absolute lack of
chemistry with America's favorite action hero. I started to tell him
that I wanted someone to want to marry me for real and that acting
like part of an in-love couple was just about the loneliest thing I'd
ever done in my life.

Then Todd did something unprecedented, even for him. He took
his headset off, walked over to the window, and put his arm around
me. Then he started talking to me like I was a real person.

It was even more shocking than the prospect of a fake engagement.

Todd was being sensitive.

"Listen," he said quietly. "I know that things aren't how you
thought and that it's not all fun and games being in a relationship
that's just for the benefit of the public . . . but think of it this way: it's
a lot more money and exposure, and you're basically in the same contract anyway. Nothing will change at all—just ride out your contract,
buy your mom a bigger house, and keep the ring when it's all over.
No one will be the wiser. Besides, I checked Brad's schedule, and he's
going to be in Montreal shooting *Avenger* for most of the summer anyway; you'll probably only have to see him once or twice. This is free
money and publicity—you'd be crazy to turn it down. I know what you
want is to have a good career in independent films after you're done
with the show, and I think this is really the way to do it. The more
exposure we get you now, the more the world is going to be open for
you once you're done with *Autumn Leaves*. You're never going to have
to worry about money, or auditions, or anything like that. After this,
no one in your family will ever have to work again. After this, you can
write your own ticket. You could start your own production company.
Amy—I'm being serious. This is the chance of a lifetime."

I started to object, but he was actually making sense. If what I wanted was a career that didn't depend on the show, I needed enough money and power on my own to be able to call my own shots. And, I thought, if I had the opportunity to take care of my family for life, I should take it.

"OK," I said, wiping my eyes. "I'll do it." I tried to put the creepiness of the situation out of my mind.

After the engagement was announced, my IMDB STARmeter ranking went up to 19.

16

THE DAY BEFORE I was supposed to leave for New York, I got an e-mail from Vince marked URGENT. He'd been busy working eighteen hours a day with clients and going out with Perez, and I'd just been busy, so we hadn't seen each other in a week or so.

I'M LEAVING FOR CARRIE ANN'S GRADUATION THE DAY AFTER TOMORROW. WHAT FLIGHT ARE YOU TAKING? WE SHOULD GO TOGETHER.

I read the e-mail twice, and then it started to come back to me in a rush of details. Graduation? Graduation! How had I completely forgotten my friend's imminent graduation from the college that I had attended with her just two years before? Was my life really so hectic that I had lost track of an entire year?

I flipped open my calendar. Tickets, reservations . . . crap crap crap! If I booked everything right then, stayed up all night packing, and left the next day, I could still make it to the graduation ceremony, then to New York by the time shooting started on *Blue Gray*. Why hadn't I remembered this? What was wrong with me? This was only going to be the most important day of her life ... Vince remembered, why didn't I? Was I becoming a terrible person? Carrie Ann and I were still in touch, though not as often as I would've liked. I should have remembered.

I dialed Vince's number.

"Hey, it's me," I said into his voice mail. "I ... I'm going to the graduation—we should talk before we go, so we're not late for Carrie Ann's big day." I didn't have the guts to say I'd almost forgotten, and if not for his e-mail, I would have gone straight to New York. He didn't know, but that message had probably saved my friendship with Carrie Ann, since if I'd forgotten her graduation, I was pretty sure she never would have talked to me again.

The next morning, Vince and I were on a flight to Detroit. We had just enough time to get a rental car, change, and get flowers before the graduation ceremony started. Aside from a few autograph-seeking freshmen, the people at UM were surprisingly cool about my being there. I knew the paparazzi wouldn't follow me all the way to Ann Arbor, but crowds of people were sometimes a problem. What I was most concerned about was stealing Carrie Ann's thunder. She was receiving the Outstanding Senior Award and was graduating summa cum laude.

As it turned out, her news was even bigger than me that day. Carrie Ann had already started living her Broadway dream, keeping in touch with everyone she'd met during the previous two summers. During spring break that year, she'd been to New York to finalize her apartment and had gone on auditions for Broadway shows. As Dr. Simon called her name, he also announced that the next day Carrie Ann would be leaving for New York to join the cast of *Phantom*. A cheer went up through the crowd, and Carrie Ann took a little bow as she accepted her diploma. Vince and I wiped away tears. "Now we're all living our dreams," he said, squeezing my hand.

I had to agree.

"So . . . why didn't you tell us?" Vince said to Carrie Ann as we sipped champagne at the drama department reception.

"It all happened so fast . . . it just didn't seem real," she said, looking over at me sheepishly. "I still feel a little like it could all go away at any minute."

I hugged her. "I totally understand," I said. "Don't worry—it's not going to go away. You earned your success through being talented and dedicated, and no one can take that from you. Remember that, OK?"

She laughed, wiping away tears. "I guess I just had to see for myself, right?" she said. "I'm really sorry, Aim. I didn't get it."

"It's OK," I said. "I'm just glad we're back. Now . . . what flight are you on to New York? Did you know we're going to be neighbors for a few months?"

Dr. Simon came over. "Girls, let me get a picture of our two biggest successes," she said, pulling out her camera.

"This is definitely going in my *Biography* story," whispered Carrie Ann as we posed for the photo. "Did you know that Danny DeVito and Michael Douglas were roommates in New York before they got famous?"

I laughed. "I did not know that," I said.

THE NEXT DAY, A cab dropped me off in front of Josh's friend's apartment at Thirty-first and Madison.

As soon as I said "Apartment five-H," the doorman raised his eyebrows. An older, handsome Latino man with bushy eyebrows and a freshly pressed suit with BORRERO embroidered on the coat, he looked like he'd turned a lot of people away from this apartment. "You sure?" he said. "Nobody's up there . . ."

"I know," I said. "It's . . . a friend of a friend's place. I'm using it for eight weeks while I shoot a film here. The producer . . . Josh Stein's office faxed over the paperwork, and the super confirmed that there would be a key waiting for me when I got here."

He riffled through several pieces of paper behind the front desk. Was he the only person in America who didn't watch my show? How did he not know me? Had he never heard of RockStar? "Oh, OK . . . Star Spencer? Right . . . here you go," he said, handing me two keys attached to a round silver key chain. "Take the elevator to five, and make the left. I'm Miguel; call down on the intercom if you need anything. We don't let anybody into that apartment without authorization."

"Whose apartment is this, anyway, Madonna's?" I said, joking. Most likely it was just some investment banker/producer friend of Josh's.

Miguel winked. "You don't know? It's your friend's friend!" He laughed. "You'll see."

I shrugged, took the keys, and lugged my Louis Vuitton duffel bag over to the elevator. "I'll get the rest," called Miguel down the hall, loading my stuff into a rolling silver cart. I pressed "5" on the elevator panel, made the left, and put the key in the door.

So, having seen lots of movies where the heroine lives in a shoebox-size apartment in New York City, and having looked at Carrie Ann's online photo albums and seen the tiny places where she had stayed during the last two summers, I was in no way prepared for either the size or the opulence of Josh's friend's apartment. A spiral staircase cut through the ceiling of the first floor, leading to God only knew where. The kitchen, to the left, was spotless, outfitted with brand-new, expensive-looking brushed-steel appliances and granite countertops. "Oh my God," I said out loud to no one in particular. I walked into the living room, which contained immaculate furniture upholstered in burgundy and white stripes. Did no one live in this apartment? Above a huge fireplace, one soft light was turned on—the light beneath a lovely painting that I thought I recognized as a

Picasso from a freshman year art history class. Good Lord. I thought about my suite at the hotel, strewn with clothes, makeup, scripts, and DVDs. *Someday, when I have a break and can pull myself together,* I thought, *perhaps I will be able to decorate an apartment like this.*

"This is crazy," I said, walking through the cavernous apartment. The living room had an enormous baby grand piano with a single black and white photo in a frame on top of it. Maybe this was the mysterious owner of 5H. Now I was dying of curiosity. I tried to turn on the light on the piano without smudging it with my fingers. When I did, I found that this black and white photo was of a man holding a little girl on a merry-go-round. Upon closer inspection, I determined that the man in the photograph was not just a man. The man in the photograph, in fact, was rock star Pete Wilde, of one of my favorite bands, the Cassandras. Then it hit me. I. Was. Standing. In. Pete Wilde's. Apartment.

My first impulse was to run upstairs to what seemed to be the master bedroom, to look for the leather pants and eyeliner. Did that make me a geek? I thought back to the vintage Cassandras album that Vince had found for me on eBay the Christmas before and let out a silent scream. Pete Wilde's apartment!

Pete Wilde's gigantic outdoor patio had an up-close view of the Empire State Building; I promptly went out, lit a cigarette, called Vince, and screamed out loud about Pete Wilde's apartment. When that was done, I dialed Josh's number. "Amy!" he said, picking up on the first ring. "Did you get there? When do you start shooting? Do you like the apartment?" He sounded very amused with himself.

"How do you not tell me that your 'friend' is Pete Wilde?" I said, incredulous. "I'm staying at Pete Wilde's apartment? Where is Pete Wilde?" I think I knew that Pete Wilde and his latest wife, a Russian supermodel, lived in New York City—but there? Were they going to come home and find me there?

He laughed. "I know him through friends. I think he's on tour. Actually, it's a place he never uses, but he's owned it for a long time,

and he keeps his art collection there. More of a real estate investment. I use it when I'm in New York too. Don't worry about it. You'll be fine."

"Josh, oh my God—this place is too nice. I can't eat Peanut M&M's on Pete Wilde's Mies van der Rohe furniture! There is a Picasso on the wall and a signed photograph of Muhammad Ali hanging in the hallway."

He laughed. "Have fun," he said. "See you in June. If you see Pete, tell him I said hi."

"Oh my God—Josh! This is too much. Thank you!"

Finally—things were starting to look up. I had a great apartment, a cool job on an indie film, and an entire summer off not only from the show, but from appearances with Brad. And the best part—I was actually sleeping. Who'd have thought I'd have to go all the way to New York to get a good night's sleep?

AFTER TWO WEEKS OF shooting in New York, I was finally getting comfortable in the city. From Pete Wilde's apartment, I could find east, west, the subway, and the Magnolia Bakery. I was sleeping nine hours a night and felt like I had a grip on my sanity again. I was in love with the city.

"Amy, I can't believe you haven't spent more time here," said Allen Shepherd, who played Marie's art teacher/lover. He was on hiatus from *Law & Order: SVU* and also cared about indie films, so he'd signed on to *Blue Gray*. His show was one of my favorites for bouts of late-night sleeplessness, though I had refrained from telling him how much I loved him on *L&O* the moment I met him, so as not to break the "I'm a big celebrity" mystique, but finally the veneer had caved, I fessed up, and he'd started calling me Amy like all my friends. During days off, Allen was my unofficial New York tour guide. Since the press knew we were shooting *Blue Gray* and his wife and kids were always with us, they seemed to be uninterested in creating scandal for t

moment, so we could roam without fear of cheating reports
back to Brad's camp. Besides, it was fun to have a friend who w
another popular show and understood the schedule.

Since shooting had been limited mostly to Soho, I felt like I h
that area covered. Allen had taken me to Chinatown for dim sum, to
the top of the Empire State Building (after-hours, of course), and to
some of the great museums on the Upper East Side. "You're not at all
what I thought," he'd said on the second day of shooting. "They make
you out to be this famous diva princess, like—"

"I know, don't say it," I interrupted. "You have no idea how much
of my life is made up by other people." Finally, a person who actually understood my pain, who had his own network problems and
was unlikely to rat me out. Allen confided that he was contractually
obligated to wear a hair replacement system whenever he was out
in public. "They glue it on once a month with silicone," he laughed,
leaning forward so I could examine the top of his head. "As if there
are no photos of me from ten years ago, when I was bald. I went along
with it for the salary bump, but I have to admit—during the summer,
I wish I could take it off. It kind of itches."

I studied his head, trying to detect the place where the mesh
netting stopped and his scalp started. "Impressive," I said. "Want to
see my fake teeth?" My liposuction scars had faded, or I would have
shown him those too. "Sometimes my hair breaks off from being dyed
so much—I wonder what would happen if *I* went bald?" I laughed.

I felt like wilted lettuce in the heat of the New York summer, but
I was more satisfied and happy than in the past two and a half years
combined. I didn't even mind the fatigue, the heat exhaustion, or the
lack of trailers and craft services. It was possible that Dan's whole
budget for *Blue Gray* was equal to the budget for one episode of *Autumn
Leaves*, so I had learned to drastically scale back my needs—all the way
back to not complaining about using an abandoned building as our
primary set.

Four days into shooting, in fact, I felt something brush against my leg and looked down to see a rat scurry by, then down into a hole in the floor. Unintentionally, I let out a scream so loud and so long, when I was done everyone was laughing. "It's OK," said Dan. "I think you scared him off." If not for his easygoing nature, we might have all been complaining by then. But Dan's commitment to the film was so deep that he had us all pulling for his success, and nothing could quell our enthusiasm—not even rats, garbage, and fifteen-hour days in the New York heat.

Somehow, possibly because of Dan's determination, this film was coming together despite the odds. Shooting it had already been one of the greatest experiences of my life. Every day, I wished that *this*, instead of the show, were my real job. Sadly, my scenes with Allen were almost over, and he was moving on to Mississippi to shoot another indie film. Already I felt like a New Yorker. I never wanted to leave.

"You should guest on my show," said Allen, munching a slice of pizza. "You could be the guest star who has a breakdown—did you ever notice that if you see a famous person's name in the *Law & Order* credits, they always have a breakdown by the end of the show?" He laughed.

"Oh my God!" I shouted. "I thought it was just me who noticed that. And why does the victim always have to have glass shards in their anus? Is that some kind of *SVU* rule?"

"Oh!" he shouted. "Hey, without the shards, we'd just be regular *Law & Order*, right?" He leaned in. "OK, now I have a question for you. Is it true that they have to powder Greg Forster's face between takes because his gin blossoms show through? I worked with that guy on a TV movie, and I swear I got drunk just from being in scenes with him."

I laughed. "Is that even possible?"

Dan walked up. "Hey, we're about ready to shoot your scene," he said, and despite myself, I smiled. My contract didn't say anything about not being friends with my director, right?

★ ★ ★

IT WAS DARK WHEN the production van picked me up at 4:30 A.M., but it had already begun to get hot on the streets of New York. Half the cast and a very groggy-looking Dan had already been picked up, and we rode together in silence. We were shooting the big "Marie disappears" scene that morning, and Dan's vision was to have me walking aimlessly up Fifth Avenue, just as the sun was rising over the Empire State Building. Apparently, that was the last time Marie was ever seen before she was discovered ten years later in a Rhode Island mental institution. This was the final time the character would be seen in the film. While researching the screenplay, Dan had interviewed a witness who saw her turn toward the west at the Empire State and walk down Thirty-fourth Street. That morning, we were going to try to capture that moment in a scene that would be set to a Red House Painters song.

It was dark in the car, but I could see that Dan was upset. It couldn't be easy for him to be shooting these scenes about his aunt's life. I knew I would've had a hard time shooting anything to do with my dad's death without becoming horribly depressed. I leaned over and put my hand on his. "Are you OK?" I said, and he smiled. Why didn't I feel this comfortable with Brad?

I'd told Dan about my dad's death almost immediately after meeting him. It wasn't like this was a fact I shared openly with everyone—some of the cast of my show still didn't know. Maybe it was the fact that he obviously felt the loss of his aunt the way I did that of my dad. Maybe it was his warmth and how close he was to the script. Maybe I just felt like I could be myself. In just a few weeks of shooting, Dan already knew more about me than I'd told Brad the whole time we'd been "dating" or most of my cast mates in two whole seasons of shooting the show. I was sort of glad we were almost done with the film, because I was really starting to have feelings for Dan, and I knew that was definitely not part of my RockStar contract.

I wondered if this was as big a deal for Dan as it was for me, but I didn't dare ask him.

Once the crew started setting up for the shot, Dan shook his head as if to clear it, then wrapped a blanket around me to shield me from the cold air leaking into the side of the van.

"So, you know this is the day—she's starting to disconnect from reality, she's wandering down Thirty-fourth Street, and then she disappears. I know you can do this, Amy. We have to get it all in one shot before the sun comes up."

I nodded. "I get it—any specific shots you want? Looking straight into the camera or anything like that?"

"Yeah—I mean, this is when she's feeling the most lost, so I just need to get that from your face, you know? You are really good at conveying emotion with just your eyes."

"Thanks," I said. "We'll get it in one shot. Don't worry."

He squeezed my hand and leaned in so close that for a moment I was sure he was going to kiss me.

"Thanks. I knew I could count on you. OK—let's go."

I caught my breath, and we went out in the street. Wearing a torn camisole and with my hair dirty and messy, I was really feeling the part of a crazy person who'd lost her way. In fact, this was how I felt inside on nights when I had really bad insomnia—like nothing was going to be OK ever again, and like I might just fade away.

Once Dan called action, I slowly walked a jagged path down Thirty-fourth Street, thinking about the times late at night when I miss my dad so much and I feel so hopeless. Honestly, sometimes I wished I could just disappear like Marie did; it seemed like life would be so much easier if I could just go back to the way things were before.

"Cut!" Dan ran up to me and put the blanket around me again while the crew set up for the over-the-shoulder shot. As he hugged me, I thought I felt his chest shaking a little.

"Thank you," he whispered. "You got it."

I hugged him back, and he swung me around. For a moment, it was like no one else existed on the streets of New York.

"I wish my dad could see me," I said, my eyes filling with tears. Whenever I felt happy or proud of something, my mind always went right back to him, making every good experience bittersweet.

"He can," Dan said. "Both of them can. They're proud of us."

THE DAY AFTER *BLUE Gray* wrapped, I was sleeping in when there was a knock on the door of my apartment. Crap! Would I never sleep again? I opened the door to find Dan standing in the hallway, looking impossibly awake and cute for nine A.M. He had a Dunkin' Donuts bag under his arm and was smiling his amazing smile.

"Um . . . can I help you? How did you get past Miguel?" I said playfully. I couldn't believe he was actually on my doorstep.

"Yes, I thought that since you'd be leaving tomorrow and we are no longer working together, I would take this opportunity to hang out with you."

My heart skipped a beat. "At nine A.M.?" I said. "Wow, you are ambitious." I wondered how much trouble I would get in with Brad's camp if someone saw me in public with Dan. *He's the director of my movie,* I rationalized. *The press doesn't know the exact day we wrapped. What can it hurt?* I thought. *I'll probably never see him again anyway. We're going for a walk. What's the big deal? We're just friends!*

He grinned. "Listen, it's our last day in New York, and I wanted to hang out with you as long as possible, but I figured six A.M. was out of the question, so I waited until nine. Get dressed! I have many surprises in store."

I wondered if he'd figured out the "arrangement" I had with Brad. Dan seemed to really like me for me and didn't care at all how famous I was, how the show was doing, or who I knew. When I was around him I could just be myself—my real self, like when I hung out with Vince and Carrie Ann back in Michigan. I was really going to miss him when I went back to L.A.

There was no time for a shower, makeup, or anything resembling fashion, so I brushed my teeth, put on sunglasses, and we were off. I was walking on a cloud as we passed the barking dogs in Madison Square Park, turned, and walked west on Twenty-third.

"Where are you taking me? What if someone sees us? Do you want to be 'Mr. Unidentified' in *US Weekly* next week? You are going to get me in trouble," I said.

He punched me softly in the arm and laughed. "That is three questions in one, Miss Amy—the answers are: 'it's a surprise, no one cares, and I don't care, in that order. You are my friend, and I like hanging out with you and we are going to do that now, OK?"

Somehow, I didn't care either.

We made our way down into the subway station. After an impossibly long ride on the F train (patience—not my strong suit), we got out and walked along a creaky boardwalk. It was like we'd taken the subway to 1950. The place smelled like beach, mixed with the scent of suntan lotion and hot dogs, and the air was filled with the sounds of delighted kids on summer break.

"Welcome to Coney Island," he said, smiling. "Surprise!"

It looked like an amusement park that was frozen in time—there was even a really old roller coaster, a freak show, and a shooting gallery with real shotguns. "Feeling brave?" he asked as we approached the Cyclone. "In 1927, this was the tallest roller coaster in the United States. It's probably still got all the original equipment. Amy Spencer, are you man enough for the Cyclone?" he said, laughing.

I was amused to note that we had to wait in line for the Cyclone, even though it had been more than two years since I'd had to wait in line anywhere, for anything. Coney Island, apparently, hadn't gotten word that I was a big big star! It felt kind of good.

My heart leapt to my throat. My dad and I loved roller coasters. In fact, I had always prided myself on my tolerance for scary roller-coaster rides. My dad and I had ridden every roller coaster in Disney World, Mall of America, and Six Flags. I looked up at the very tall and creaky-looking Cyclone. This was my big chance to show Dan I wasn't one of those breakable Hollywood types.

"I'm game if you are," I said.

Up close, it was even more imposing. If the Cyclone really *was* one of the first roller coasters built in the U.S., it seemed possible that the same freaky fat guy who was ushering people onto the ride had been running it since day one. In fact, when the wind blew, I swore I could see the whole monstrous structure swaying and creaking in the breeze. My mind briefly shifted into "Attila paranoia" mode—how mad would she be if she knew I was there? Was there some clause in my show contract that prevented me from doing dangerous things? I was, after all, not even allowed to cut my hair or eat a cracker without getting permission from the powers that be. "*Autumn Leaves* Actress Maimed in Freak Roller Coaster Accident," screamed the headline in my mind, and I had visions of Attila threatening to sue me for getting hurt. I was supposed to be packing to go home, and instead I was on a pseudo-date with a guy who wasn't my fiancé, riding a dangerous-looking roller coaster. How irresponsible of me! *But,* I reminded my-self, *I just turned twenty-one. Sometimes you get to be stupid when you're twenty-one years old.*

With great effort, I pushed Attila out of my mind. "Let's go!" I said, pulling Dan into the seats. The man running the ride, who wore a stained plaid shirt and a nametag that said STEVIE, laughed as he pulled the handle. When he smiled at us, I noticed he was missing most of his teeth.

This roller coaster exceeded anything else I'd ever been on in my life, including the stand-up roller coaster that leaves you dangling upside down and the one where they put you in a big chair, take you up to the top of a tower, and just drop you. In fact, at the top of the Cyclone, I looked down and couldn't even see any tracks below us. *Oh my God,* I thought, *I am going to die on this ride with a man I hardly know.*

Maybe it was the fact that I was very thin and overcaffeinated. All I knew was that the Cyclone was, by far, the scariest roller coaster I had ever encountered in the history of my life. I hung on to Dan for dear life, screaming bloody murder into his shoulder. It was at once fun, terrifying, and otherworldly, just like the rest of the day. Totally unshaken, Dan was my rock, my beacon of calm. He laughed and screamed right along with me and never looked scared.

Somehow, Dan had found the one place in New York with no photographers, no Attila, and no pressure. With no one watching, I found it was OK to be hungry without getting nervous, and Dan encouraged me to eat whatever I wanted. We had hot dogs at Nathan's, shared cotton candy, and drank cold beer from plastic cups. With the setting sun pink in the sky, we sat on the pier, our legs dangling over the side and barely touching the water.

I didn't want the day to be over—in fact, I wanted to cry like a three-year-old at the prospect of going home, back to my life, back to work, back to my RockStar business arrangement. "This was amazing," I said, resting my head on his shoulder. "This was a great day. Thank you."

I shouldn't have let him put his arm around me. This was my perfect moment. Nothing in my life had ever compared to this feeling. This was real, and solid, and amazing, and I never wanted to let it go.

Suddenly I heard a clicking noise behind us. We turned around just in time to see a photographer, who had captured the whole thing.

My heart started to pound. "I . . . um . . . we have to get out of here," I said, jumping up off the dock. I wanted to grab Dan's hand, but I knew that would just make it worse. The crowd of photographers seemed to be growing by the moment, and some of them started yelling.

"Is this your new boyfriend, Star?" they shouted. "Does Brad know? Are you and Brad still together?"

"We're just friends," I shouted. "Everything's fine. I'll be back in L.A. with Brad this week." By now we were running. Finally, we made it inside—the freak show, of all places, where they wouldn't let the paparazzi come in.

"What is that?" Dan said, looking out the window at the huge crowd that had now formed outside.

"That is my life," I said, starting to hyperventilate. It would only be a few minutes before I started getting e-mails, texts, and calls about my "date" with Dan. I kicked myself for even going in the first place; I'd let it go too far, and now I'd probably never be able to see him again.

"Dan, I'm sorry," I said, surveying the various exits of the building. By then I'd dialed the number for the car service Arden had given me, and I was looking for something to cover my head with as I ran out to meet the car. Dan looked at me like I was crazy.

"For what? You didn't do anything. They can't hunt you like you're an animal. You still have rights."

"No—you don't understand. This is bad. I have to go. Just don't say anything to anyone about me, OK?"

. He looked confused. "OK."

I grabbed my stuff and ran out the back entrance, into the waiting car.

Right then, I got the feeling that the real roller-coaster ride was just about to begin.

SEASON
THREE

A S IF THE POSSIBILITY of Brad's people killing me for being
photographed with an "unauthorized" guy wasn't enough,
I also got it from the Network for the negative publicity.
Almost immediately upon my return to L.A., I was brought in for a
sit-down with Attila to discuss the "Coney Island problem." I'd barely
shut the door and sat down before she started yelling and pounding
the desk with her flabby fist.

"There is no way, no possible way you can be seen with a civilian
at this point in your career!" she yelled. "Are you fucking kidding me
with this? You have Brad Rockwell and the lead in an award-winning
TV show, and this is what you do? You really must be an idiot!"

She was so mad, I could see a tiny blue vein starting to protrude
from the side of her head, and it reminded me of a chapter I read in
bio class once on overweight people, high blood pressure, and strokes.
I supposed there was no chance she would succumb to one of those
at that moment, but a girl could dream. Somehow she'd heard about
the photos of Dan and me, and she'd been plotting my death for the
entire time it had taken me to fly back from New York. Either of-

ficially or on her own, Attila had been keeping tabs on me for Brad's office, and now she didn't even care if I knew. This was bad on so many levels.

She continued, her voice rising to a pitch I was pretty sure only dogs could hear. "Your team has created one of the greatest Hollywood power couples of all time, and you are throwing it all away on a guy with a hot dog stand?" She gasped for breath. "You . . . are . . . such an idiot!"

"Actually, his name is Dan Roberts, he's the director of my movie, and he took me to Coney Island for hot dogs," I said. "Don't worry about it. Brad's manager Jon called me and told me they paid off the photographer. He was pissed, but it's already taken care of." I tried to sound nonchalant. In fact, I'd gotten the bitching-out of a lifetime from Jon, who had even threatened to sue me if I ever saw Dan again, but I didn't want her to know that.

"Why are you still talking?" she said. "I don't care who he is or what he does. You are never seeing that nobody ever again. Is that clear?"

I took a deep breath. "It's really OK," I said. "I've got it covered. Brad and I . . ." My voice trailed off as I remembered the meetings, the contract, and Todd's warning about lawsuits and confidentiality. She didn't know about the contract, and I wasn't allowed to tell her. This thing was bigger than all of us and extended further than she could ever realize. It killed me not to be able to take Dan's phone calls or e-mails or even tell him why I couldn't see him again. I'd found the perfect guy, and now I had to act like I didn't like him. I knew Brad's people weren't even going to let me do press for *Blue Gray* when it came out, and I knew this meant the film wouldn't get distribution.

Sweat dripped from the top of her pudgy upper lip. "You have no idea what you have, and you're just throwing it all away. Well, I'm not going to let you drag the show down with you. You're going to pull it together." I visualized the blood clot making its way up into her brain, but no luck, she was still standing.

She slammed her hand down on the desk. "Listen to me, little girl. You will keep being the girlfriend of Brad Rockwell for as long as is humanly possible, or I'll send you back to Podunk, Michigan, to work in some fucking fried chicken house, then I'll call the *Enquirer* and give them the address so they can do a 'Where are they now?' cover on you. You will never be able to show your face anywhere ever again. You won't even be able to get a job on that fucking *Flavor of Love.* Is that clear?"

I laughed to myself about how nervous she used to make me. Now I just sat there calmly as she screamed. For some reason, her rampages were having less of an effect on me. Finally she dismissed me, and I figured this wouldn't be the last I heard of this issue. Now there was just the matter of getting Dan out of my mind for the next few months.

THERE WAS STILL A week to go before we started shooting season three, so Attila sent me back to Dr. Romano again for some more "routine maintenance." This time, he suggested a chemical peel to get rid of the sun damage from New York. "It's going to hurt a lot," he said, "but this is the best way to get a good result in the shortest period of time. You'll really need to stay out of the sun, and of course out of the public, until the peeling stops. Then your skin is going to be as smooth as a baby's bottom on camera. Trust me."

When a doctor says "It's going to hurt a lot," you know it can't be good. I accepted the "light IV sedation" he offered.

A physician's assistant came in, putting a headband over my hair. She was a short Asian girl with flawless skin, sparkling brown eyes, and absolutely no wrinkles. "This is the best!" she squeaked. "I had it a month ago, and it made a *huge* difference!" The IV sedation was starting to kick in, so even though I was thinking *Your skin looks great,* I couldn't quite form the words, so I just nodded. "OK, have fun!" said Melissa. "The doctor will be right back."

I was dozing off when Dr. Romano came in. "Are you ready?" he said. Again, I could only nod. He started to wipe some liquid from a bottle onto my face with gauze pads. When the burning started, I felt a little like my face was on fire, and I managed to say, "You're burning my face." Even though I wasn't stressed out about it, my face was *killing* me.

"It's OK," he said. "You're doing great. It's almost over."

I could feel my face burning and sizzling as the acid ate off the top layer of skin. How the hell was this going to heal in only a week? Surprisingly, when I looked in the mirror it just looked a tiny bit pink, like I'd been in a windstorm or out in the cold for too long.

"Wow, I thought it would look worse," I said.

He laughed. "Just wait. In two days your face is going to look like a leather handbag. Then it's going to peel off."

I could not wait.

THREE DAYS LATER I looked like Freddy Krueger and was hiding out in my suite. Luckily, that was the day I got the advance copy of the *Vanity Fair* cover I'd shot in New York, so Vince was on hand to read and celebrate with me, even though he insisted on shrieking like a little girl every time he looked me full in the face. He and I hadn't been hanging out as much anymore, but I could still always call him for comic relief.

He read the article aloud while we smoked Camel Lights and drank vodka and Red Bulls. Even I had to admit that Arden had outdone herself this time, setting me up with the reporter she knew had the biggest crush on me and would write the most flattering article.

Star Spencer saunters into the lobby of the Mercer Hotel like she's living in another era. Her alabaster skin glows as she slides into the leather banquette in the back, her sparkling green eyes revealing a hint of something left unsaid. If this were the Enlightenment, she would certainly be George Sand in a salon in Paris.

Vince looked up. "Amy—my God. What did you do to this man? You mesmerized him!" He fell back into his chair, laughing. "Good God—this is better fiction than Tori Spelling's *E! True Hollywood Story.*"

"Oh, that's just the beginning, baby," I said, mixing another drink. "Wait till you get to the part with the cheeseburger."

Vince flipped frantically through the glossy pages, skipping over four shots of me in all my airbrushed glory. Arden thought it would be good not only for my career in general, but for the show as a whole for me to do a cover while I was in New York. "To expand your market share to women age twenty-eight to thirty-five," she'd explained.

With the grace of a dancer, Star folds her impossibly lithesome legs up under her delicate chin, which she rests for a moment on her red-nailed hand. Defying logic, she orders a cheeseburger, fries, and a Coke. "Extra cheese," she says with a smile.

"*Who is this reporter?*" said Vince. "Did you drug him to get him to print these outrageous lies?"

"Notice how I never actually *consume* the cheeseburger during the course of the interview," I said testily. Actually, the waiter had brought it and set it down in front of me, but since we were going to start shooting season three soon, I was back on food restriction, so I'd had to do the old-school "take one bite then push the rest around" anorexic trick. I did keep wondering, though, what the reporter would have written if I'd just grabbed the cheeseburger and started eating like my life depended on it. Which, I guess you might say, it did. "Read more," I said, poking at my scabby face with my fingernail.

Vince looked up at me, shrieked again, then continued to scan.

"That's actually a really good picture of you—they shaved, like, half an inch off your chin," he said, tearing it out. "This one's going in the air-brush wall of fame. You look a little like Hilary Duff here." I scowled at him, and he started again.

Since being plucked from her dreary Midwestern existence and catapulting to fame as Autumn on Autumn Leaves, Star Spencer has quickly captured America's heart and assumed her rightful place on the throne as America's Sweetheart, a title previously held by such luminaries as Julia Roberts, Sandra Bullock, and Reese Witherspoon.

Vince wiped away a pseudo-tear. "Our little Star is all growed up," he said. "We so proud of her back on the farm." He lit another cigarette.

I looked over his shoulder at the magazine. "Damn . . . they cut the part about my uncle Jerry's emus," I said, flipping to the next page. "I thought that story was funny."

THE NEXT DAY, MY cell phone buzzed in my pocket. I took it out and saw Ross's number. He'd been on a trip to Europe, and so I hadn't seen him since I'd been back.

"Ross!" I said excitedly. "How are you? Are you back? My trip to New York was so great . . . the movie was amazing . . . I can't wait to see you!"

"Amy, did you have your season three meeting yet?" he said, sounding uncharacteristically downbeat.

"No . . . why? Is everything all right? What's going on?"

Ross sighed. "I just had my meeting. Let's just keep this between us . . . They gave my character cancer, and he dies in the middle of this season."

My heart started to pound.

"What are you talking about?" I said. "What does that even mean? They can't do that . . . you've been in the cast since the pilot. We're a family! They wouldn't . . . what? Why?"

"They didn't say. They're killing off Peter, and I'm off the show after the first five episodes, except in occasional dream flashback scenes with you and Michael."

My head was spinning. Ross was one of my only links to sanity on the set, and without him, I might just go over the edge. Besides, I'd come to love him like a father or big brother, and I didn't even want to think about doing the show without him. Not to mention the fact that I really didn't want to relive my father's death yet again for the purposes of television.

"They can't do this!" I shouted. "We can't do this show without you. This is totally wrong. Do you want me to do something? What can I do? I can threaten to quit if you want!" I was serious.

While I was trying to think of favors I could call in or RockStar clout that I could use, Ross laughed softly. "That's just the business, darlin'. I'm sad that it's over, but there will be another show. I've already got my agent looking around for pilots, since I'll be done in December."

We hadn't even started shooting season three yet, and already I was dreading going back to work. I felt like I was losing yet another member of my family, and once again, I didn't know who to blame. The thought of being on the set without Ross was heartbreaking. How could they just kill off a major character who had been in every episode since the pilot and won two Golden Globes and an Emmy for the role? It just didn't seem right.

"FIND YOUR MENTAL STAIRCASE," said the man in my trailer. I stifled a laugh.

Two weeks into shooting season three, the stress of the plotline was already getting to me. I was going days without sleeping, and it was starting to show. I shut my eyes, determined that hypnosis was going to be the key to solving the insomnia situation.

"Jesus Christ," said Attila the last time she'd seen me. "It looks like someone hit you in the face. What is wrong with you? Can't the makeup department cover up those eye bags?"

"I know," I'd said. "I can't sleep . . . insomnia. It just takes one thing—"

"Well, now we're getting letters about it: 'Why does Autumn look so tired all the time? What's wrong with Autumn?' You've got to do something about this. Get some sleep, or figure out a way to look like you got some. I'll send over a hypnotist."

And so they made me sit in my trailer in between scenes with a white guy named Saresh who wore a flowing white skirt, trying to visualize myself climbing down a beautiful white staircase, one step at a time.

"OK, just try to relax. I'm going to count back from ten."

I wanted it to work. In fact, I would have given anything to completely give over to sleep, blissfully unencumbered by the constant hunger and stress that had been keeping me awake. More than anything, I would've loved to just take a deep breath, fall back into my bed, and succumb to the pressing fatigue and exhaustion that had made me a walking zombie for weeks. I reminded myself that this was the job that 99.9 percent of the world would die for, and all I wanted to do was sleep it away. I felt my heart skip a beat and tried to push the heavy thoughts out of my mind.

I tried to picture how this was going to work when I was lying in my bed at the hotel or at Brad's place, haunted by the fact that I had to shoot yet another day of scenes in a hospital. The show was getting to me, I couldn't stop thinking about Dan, and all I wanted was a good night's sleep and a banana split. Even though I'd guaranteed Brad's people that Dan and I were just friends, they didn't want me talking to him, and seeing him again was out of the question. Since I couldn't explain any of this to him, I had to just watch as his calls and e-mails came less and less frequently until finally there were none.

Needless to say, I could not picture the staircase.

THREE MORE DAYS (AND still no sleep) later, I sat on a lounge chair on the roof of the hotel at 3:30 A.M., smoking cigarettes and shivering in my favorite sweater. The Santa Ana wind blew in circles around the city, and I could almost feel the seasons changing. More and more often I sat up there and watched the cars going by, wondering where people were going and if somehow, some way, I could just get into one of them and leave my life forever.

With Brad shooting an action-adventure movie in Japan, I was off of RockStar duty temporarily, though his manager Jon had been calling me frequently to see if I was minding my manners in his absence. "Are you OK? Do you need anything? Let us know if you're going out with anyone, just so we know, OK?" Jon also did not sleep, had a Rolodex in his brain, and had three thousand numbers programmed in his cell phone. He liked it better when I stayed at the mansion— that way he could keep an eye on me. Since I'd been back from New York, though, I felt like going over there less and less.

"When does Brad get back?" I asked absentmindedly.

Silence. So unlike Jon.

"Um . . . Brad's shooting schedule got held up—he'll be back next week. Is there something you want to talk to me about instead? Are you OK?" Jon was sweet, but he was business, and I never got the "warm fuzzy" vibe from him.

Vince had been off with a new guy lately, and I hadn't seen him in weeks or met his new boyfriend, both of which were very unlike us. I'd pretty much been going to the studio to shoot my (very depressing) scenes for the show, going back to the hotel, and trying unsuccessfully to sleep. On days when I was not called, I took one of Brad's assistants and his black American Express to Lisa Kline or Barneys, though they'd been sending over so much stuff I was hardly hurting for clothes. Mostly, I just felt lonely. Since season three had started, I'd had this gnawing homesick feeling growing in my stomach, like I was going to disappear into nothingness. Despite the outward appearance that my life was perfect, I felt more and more out of place.

I got out my cell phone, scrolled down, and dialed Carrie Ann's new number in New York. Voice mail. Of course—she got home from the show at two A.M., probably went right to sleep. Next, Vince. Voice mail, as usual. I was seriously considering waking up my mom in Bay City, just to hear a friendly voice. I'd promised Olivia I would never call her in the middle of the night. I wondered what Dan was doing. I lit another cigarette and fought the urge to jump off the roof. That would be a great headline. Would it even matter? Really, I wanted to run outside into the street, to see a familiar person—anything that would reconnect me with the world.

What do you do when you have everything but still feel like nothing?

That's it, I thought. No matter what he was doing, Vince wouldn't care that it was late. He would hug me and make Jabba the Hutt jokes about Attila. He would make me hot chocolate and play my favorite Miles Davis CDs. We would watch *Say Anything* for the millionth time. Maybe at Vince's, I would be able to sleep. This was a good plan.

I quickly went back to my room, grabbed my stuff, and ran downstairs, already cheered. Vince was the answer to my loneliness.

There was hardly any traffic on the surface streets, so I cruised right down Laurel, past the Coffee Bean where I always saw Perez, and parked on the corner, relieved to finally be going someplace that felt like home. I marched triumphantly up the stairs and down the familiar corridor to Vince's place, apartment 2F. No lights . . . that's OK. This was still a good plan.

After some persistent knocking, both at the door and the window, I figured I'd just use my key to let myself in, like I had in the past. Since moving to West Hollywood, Vince had been quite the party boy—sometimes he came home from the clubs and would regale me with his exploits. He never brought guys home, though, because the apartment was so packed with clothes. Just as I found the key and put it in the lock, I heard voices from inside the apartment.

"Darling!" I whispered playfully. "Didn't you hear me knocking? Let me in . . . I can't sleep, and I miss you."

The door didn't budge. "Vince, are you holding the door closed? Is something wrong with you?" Now I was worried. "Seriously—I'm standing in the dark, it's late, and I'm worried. Let me in or I'm calling 911." I leaned on the door even harder, trying to force it open. Was he passed out against the door? Was someone in there killing him? What was going on? I started to panic.

Suddenly the door opened, and I fell into the apartment, spilling the entire contents of my bag all over the hardwood floor. As I picked up my stuff, I look up to see Vince with a strange look on his face. "Oh my God—is something wrong?" I said, picking up my stuff. "I just wanted to see you . . . you never called me back . . ."

Just then I had a strange realization. From where Vince was standing, it couldn't have been him holding the door closed. All at once I was thinking, *Vince never has guys over, I'd better go,* and *I wonder who it is.*

Vince was speechless; he looked like a dog that'd been caught on the Thanksgiving table eating the turkey. His mouth kept making this little "O," like he was obviously trying to think of something to say but was frozen. "Aim . . . I . . ." He trailed off, looking plaintively behind the door. Slowly, the door closed, and I turned around to see a half-naked Brad Rockwell emerge from the shadows.

"Brad . . . what are you . . . ," I started, but I couldn't finish. My mind was racing. Jon said Brad was still shooting, but instead, he was in my best friend's apartment with no shirt on. Brad had never tried to make a move on me in private, and we were supposed to be engaged. Brad only wanted to kiss me when we were in public.

Brad was Vince's new boyfriend.

"This is covered under our confidentiality agreement," Brad muttered, buttoning his shirt. "Don't mention this again, or you'll be hearing from my lawyer." He pushed past me and walked quickly out of the apartment. "See you later," he said to Vince over his shoulder. Vince looked crushed.

"AIM—YOU'RE PALE," VINCE SAID, grabbing my arm. I felt dizzy and stood there for a second, completely overwhelmed. I didn't even know where to put this new information in my mind. Of course, I never thought Brad was in love with me . . . but Vince? How did they even know each other? This was totally wrong. I sank back to the floor in the middle of my stuff and cried for a good twenty minutes in Vince's living room as I thought of all the awkward conversation I'd tried to make, all the times I'd felt deathly alone with Brad, the countless warning signs I'd tried to ignore. Was there something about Vince that suddenly made Brad into a warm and compassionate person? It seemed so unfair . . . it was as if I'd been jilted by both of them, and to top it off now I felt seedy and used, like my personal and business worlds were colliding. Vince was my only solace in the world, and he was supposed to be separate from this whole stupid thing.

"Why would you do this to me?" I wailed. "I need you. You're not even supposed to know about this . . ."

"Aim . . . I'm so sorry. It didn't start out this way—I didn't mean for this to happen. He made the first move—I can't believe I'm saying this . . . Amy, I love him."

Now I was mad. "Vince—he's supposed to be my fiancé, and furthermore, he's Brad Rockwell . . . a big straight movie star. You're not in love, and even if you are, you're not going to be a couple. This is insane. You have to stop this, or you're going to get hurt. Besides, you're *mine*." Tears streamed down my face, and I could barely talk from all the sobbing. "You don't know how lonely this whole thing has been, and now you—"

"But Brad told me you guys had an open relationship and that you were about to break up anyway. I thought you were just doing that 'emotional distance' thing you always do. I didn't even think you liked him that much, or that it was a big deal."

"It's a big deal to me, OK? You and I used to tell each other everything."

He snorted. "You stopped telling me everything a long time ago," he said, looking hurt. "You shut me out right after you and Brad got together. In fact, I wouldn't even be with him now if I hadn't gone to his house looking for you."

The look on my face must have conveyed how hurt I was, because he finally dropped his defensiveness and started crying too.

"Aim . . . he loves me," he said over and over. "I kept trying to tell him it was crazy, but he said he doesn't care. He comes over here all the time, without his entourage, and we just sit and talk for hours."

Part of me really wanted to ask him what they talked about, but I was still reeling. "Vince . . . he's supposed to be marrying *me*. He's sneaking around behind your back *and* mine. Who knows who else he's dating? He doesn't bring anyone here because no one knows he likes guys. Can you imagine what would happen if his fans found out? The studios? Oh my God, Vince . . . his career would be over. *Blood Revenge Four* starring an out gay man? No way. The studio would pull out for sure. Look—I'm his fiancée, and even I don't know about this part of his life . . . don't you find this strange?" I never in a million years envisioned a scenario where my personal and professional lives would intersect in this way, and I was too scared and ashamed to break down and tell him everything.

"Aim, he said he had a plan, and I trust him—that's good enough for me. Are you mad because he's not in love with you? He said you guys had an understanding and that I wasn't supposed to ask you about it . . . oh my God—do you love him? Am I a horrible person?"

I wondered how much Brad had told him, and I was afraid to fill in the blanks. Suddenly, I wanted to be far away from him. Vince was abandoning me. I felt the too-familiar feeling of grief start to rise up and tighten my chest, and my eyes filled with tears.

I gathered up my stuff. "I should go back . . . I have a nine A.M. call, and they're already pissed about my eye bags. I need to get some sleep." I rushed past him out the door and started down the stairs.

"Amy . . . don't leave like this." Vince ran down the stairs after me, following me all the way to my car. The combination of shock and exhaustion had combined to make me feel like I was going to pass out, and my heart was racing. I longed to be back in my bed.

"I just need to get my head around this," I said, speeding off. "I'll call you later."

I had never felt more alone.

"OK, ONE MORE SUN salutation."

Desperate for human companionship after the Brad/Vince situation exploded, I did the unthinkable.

I let Olivia take me to yoga class.

And so, instead of being asleep on Sunday morning like a sane person, I was lying on a mat at Santa Monica Yoga, gathering my strength before I attempted the yoga sun salutation that would surely kill me while secretly plotting the death of my assistant, whom I had joined for what turned out to be ninety minutes of pure torturous hell.

"Just try it," Olivia said. "It's relaxing, and it will help your insomnia. Besides, paparazzi love to photograph celebrities coming out of yoga class. They'll put the photo on the 'Stars—They're Just Like Us!' page!" she'd said jokingly. She knew I hated this kind of stuff, but occasionally she'd work with Arden to set up a photo op that wasn't totally loathsome to me.

Finally I'd relented. Olivia was one of my best friends now, and she'd been trying to get me to go to yoga with her forever. Now, with the "Peter has cancer" plotline heating up and many emotional days on the set, I found that I often felt like one big raw nerve. I sort of wanted his character to die already, just so I didn't have to shoot any more scenes in hospitals or where I was crying. But then there would be the funeral scene, which, frankly, I was not looking forward to either. Even with another big raise and a new trailer, season three was already turning out to be more challenging than any of the others, and many of us had started showing up late to set. Olivia suggested yoga as a way to get my mind off the depressing vibe.

Now, with my upper arms burning and my head spinning, I was seriously regretting that decision. A girl in front of me was twisting herself into a pretzel, looking back at me occasionally as if issuing some kind of yoga challenge. "Take that!" her perfectly arched back seemed to say.

I extended my legs as far apart as I thought they would go, and the yoga teacher came over and repositioned them to go even farther, after which I fell over.

"Olivia, I want to go," I whispered frantically. "Everyone is better than me."

She smiled. "Find your center," she whispered back, giggling. "Be the tree."

Pretzel girl looked back at us and scowled. "Shhhh," she hissed.

I collapsed onto the mat. If there were photographers outside, they were going to love the sight of me with rubbery legs, covered in sweat and unable to stand up straight. After ninety minutes of yoga that was supposed to be "introductory," I was longing for a nice game of tennis or the long walks around campus that Carrie Ann and I used to count as cardio. Whatever the case, I liked yoga, but not enough to go all Gwyneth Paltrow or Christy Turlington.

In Hollywood, even stuff that's supposed to be relaxing is stressful.

★　★　★

MY PHONE HAD BEEN showing "15 voice mail messages" for two days, and finally I had stopped being mad at Vince long enough to pick them up. I knew it was probably him leaving the messages, but I just didn't have the energy to sort the whole thing out. Shooting season three was wearing me down to a nub, and I had made a tentative plan to avoid everyone in my bizarre gay love triangle for at least two months. It all seemed so unbelievable—did I really just find out that my best friend was having an affair with my fake fiancé? Wasn't this the stuff of daytime talk shows? I mean, I knew we had an arrangement and that we weren't in love or anything, but it kind of hurt to find out that Brad had this whole secret life that I knew nothing about.

My voice mail clicked in: *"Hey, Amy, it's Mom—I don't know if you're still coming here next week to visit, and I was trying to make some plans."*

Note to self: call Mom back.

"Star, it's Jo with your call time for tomorrow—I'll send you a text."

Delete.

"Aim, it's Vince . . . I have some stuff I want to say."

I sighed and dialed Vince's number. He picked up on the second ring, sounding paranoid.

"Hello?" he whispered. In spite of myself, I laughed. What was he hyperbolizing now?

"Hi," I said. "It's me. What's up?"

Long pause. Was he being coy?

"Vince? Are you still there?"

"Yes—Aim, I need to come over there. I'm a little freaked out right now."

"Where are you?"

A long silence, then: "I'm in Santa Barbara. Hiding . . . sort of. Some weird stuff has been happening."

Two hours later, he met me at the restaurant in the hotel, insisting that we had to be outside. "Oh my God," I said, annoyed already. "Are you in the CIA now?"

"I know, I'm sorry—it's just . . . after that night when you saw Brad and me together, I haven't heard from him or you, and I keep getting these hang-up phone calls from 'Unknown Number.'"

"Well," I said, trying to be the voice of reason. "Brad left for Toronto a few days ago, so maybe he's just busy. It's not me calling; you know my number."

"Aim, I know—but it's weird for me not to talk to him for this long. We are usually on the phone, like, every two hours."

Was he trying to rub in the fact that my fake fiancé liked him more than me? He grabbed my arm and pulled me close to him. "There's something else," he said. "Two days after you saw us, I found a dead pigeon on my car—its neck was broken." A cold chill ran down my spine. "There was a note tied around the bird's neck—it said 'Squawk and die.'"

"Are you making this up?" I said, but I could see that he wasn't. "Who would do that?"

Vince was pale and trembling. "I don't know," he said. "Do you think they mean about Brad? I can't get him on his cell phone, I'm totally panicked, and I can't sleep. Aim—his people must know where I live. There's been a black car parked outside my house practically since you left. I couldn't take it anymore, so I went to Santa Barbara. Why would he do this? Everything is really opening up for gay actors now. I thought he was going to come out. I mean . . . I really did."

I smacked him in the arm. "Why don't we start with 'Amy, I'm sorry I stole your fiancé,'" I said, only half-kidding.

He looked a little shocked. "What are you talking about? He said you guys weren't that into each other. I thought you wouldn't care."

"Wouldn't care? Vince, did you ever wonder why I couldn't tell you anything about Brad and me? I mean, didn't you think he might have been lying? What about hurting my feelings?"

"What feelings? You're like an emotional robot when it comes to people. You still haven't even liked a guy since your dad died. You're going to have to let someone in eventually, Amy . . ."

"I did, OK? I did let someone in. But I can't . . ."

I wanted to tell him about Dan, and how he really got me, and how I thought I might love him. I wanted to tell him about the contract, about how Brad and I had never even slept in the same bed, how Brad's "team" would never let him come out in a million years, how he wouldn't be a bankable movie star if he was openly gay. Then I thought of the dead bird and figured that was the least of my worries if I told Vince the truth. According to Todd, no one broke the movie star confidentiality agreement. "Basically," he'd said, "you play out your contract's time, then you're still bound by the terms for the rest of your life. Like, you can't go writing a book in ten years about your life with Brad, and you can never give an interview about what really happened while you were dating."

I shuddered. Vince didn't have a contract, and he actually had feelings for Brad. Should I warn him? I decided against it, figuring the more he knew, the more trouble he could get himself in. "Listen," I said. "Just drop it. Maybe he decided he wasn't ready, or he needs some time, you know? Maybe he'll call when he's done shooting. Don't wait around for him, though." I tried not to make it sound too urgent, because I didn't want to scare him, but I hoped he'd somehow get the message and drop the whole thing since I couldn't go into too much detail. He must have known the engagement was still on, because a RockStar breakup would have been front-page news on PerezHilton.com as well as all the tabloids. "You can stay here until everything blows over," I said, and he looked relieved.

He nodded and sighed. "I'm thinking of moving to Santa Monica," he said. "Away from all the Hollywood drama."

"Good idea," I said. "Stay away from movie stars, OK?"

I knew Brad would never talk to him again.

I MADE IT THROUGH one more week of long days shooting season three before I began to seriously explore ways to get out of my *Autumn*

Leaves contract. With my unhappiness at a peak, I hired Barry Schoen-feld, a private attorney, to advise me on the possibility of leaving the show.

"No, no . . . I just don't think it's possible," said Barry, sliding the contract across the table back to me. "Why would you want to leave a hit show, anyway? You've only been in the business a few years. Why would you want out already?"

I laid my head on his desk exhaustedly. The glass top felt cool against my cheek, and for a moment I thought I might just be able to go to sleep. "Barry, I've played the exact same character for two and a half seasons. Every week, it's the same plot. I can't do movies or other shows because I'm working eighteen hours a day there, and my producer doesn't want me to wreck my 'image.' I just want to know how soon I can get away from it . . . get on with my career. Plus, this plotline we're shooting is seriously driving me to the brink of a nervous breakdown." I knew it sounded weird to be complaining, but I didn't care anymore. "What can I do?" I said. "Do you think a *Playboy* shoot would work?" Somehow, I knew this was a moot point too, as nudity would probably violate my RockStar contract, which was still in place, even though I hadn't seen Brad since that night at Vince's apartment. He'd left for Canada to shoot a Western, and I hadn't heard from him since. Still, his manager Jon had sent me a harsh e-mail informing me that all the terms of the deal were still in place, which was right about when I got the tension headache that was still squeezing my head like a steel band.

Barry ran his hand over his greasy, bald head. "Yeah, cry me a river. You're young, beautiful, and rich, and you're trapped in everyone's dream job." He sighed. "This is not the first time I've heard this, sweetheart, but I'm sorry—they're never going to let you out of a hit show with your character's name in the title. You're the lead—do you know how much retooling it would take to put the focus of the show on someone else? Look what happened to *The O.C.* after Mischa Barton left, and she wasn't even the lead!"

I could feel my frustration growing. Why did I think he was going to understand this problem? "Barry, I need you to tell me my options. I don't want to do the next two seasons. I want out of this contract. I am totally serious here."

He looked me in the eye. "I'm being serious too, Star. They've got you for at least the next two and a half years. Short of killing someone or robbing a bank, there is nothing you could do to make them let you out of this contract."

The pressure began to build up in my head again, and I rubbed my temples and took a deep breath to keep from crying. I carried a heavy feeling of dread with me almost all the time; I felt like an animal trapped in a cage.

"OK, thanks for your time," I said, fighting through the pounding behind my eyes. If he couldn't help me, I was just going to have to hope for a miracle.

"OH MY GOD . . . AMY, SPEED up . . . that guy is following too close."

At 7:30 P.M. on a Thursday night, Vince and I were in my convertible Mercedes (an engagement gift from Brad), speeding along the winding curves of Sunset Boulevard in an attempt to avoid traffic on the way to Gladstone's in Malibu. I hadn't slept in so long that I felt like I might black out, I was freezing even though it was seventy-five degrees, and I was struck by the overwhelming urge to just lay somewhere and be quiet. Now I regretted having committed to the long drive. I wanted to pull over and let him take the wheel, but there was nowhere to stop; I was trying to decide what might be more dangerous, driving down the precarious divided road or pulling over to switch. Sunset has no shoulder, it was dark, and he was right—there was a car driving so close, I was being blinded by its headlights in my rearview mirror. To further add to my anxiety, Vince kept getting up and turning around in his seat, yelling *"Get off our ass! Are you crazy?"* I was really afraid he might fall out of the car.

I needed to get some sleep soon or I was going to go over the edge, and I was intermittently feeling dizzy, hot, and cold. The air whipping by felt like knives cutting my face. *Can you go through menopause at twenty-one?* I thought. That's the thing with sleep—you only get a certain number of good days without it, and then you're just a walking zombie. Still, when Vince called to say he wanted to go to Gladstone's for some oysters, I went to pick him up after work instead of going back to the hotel to lie down. Work had been stressful—many script changes, retakes, and twelve long hours of shooting. The cancer plotline was still dragging on, and Attila had visited the set that day. Whenever I tried to eat in front of her, I caught her staring at me disapprovingly, my throat started to close up, and I couldn't swallow. Also, the numerous pills I took every day were starting to make me a little shaky all the time.

We got past a really curvy area, almost over the 405 freeway into Brentwood. I looked to the left, thinking maybe I could get on the freeway to at least make the guy stop following me. No luck—even the on ramp was bumper to bumper, and I was in the wrong lane to merge.

We were almost to Bel Air when Close Follower pulled up beside us. I breathed a momentary sigh of relief, which turned immediately back into panic as I realized that not only did the car contain two paparazzi, but that one of them actually had a video camera. We were all still going fifty on a winding road at night, the wind was whipping my hair around my face, and it was starting to rain.

"*Slow down!*" screamed Vince, maybe at me and maybe at the photographers. "*Are you insane?!!*"

The driver, a fat, balding white guy with a stained brown shirt, laughed and threw his cigarette out the window. His friend with the video camera, a smaller, filthy-looking guy in a plaid shirt, never took the camera off us. "Hey—smile for the camera!" he yelled, punching his friend in the arm. "Get closer to them," he shouted, hanging out of the side of his car.

Fat Guy veered even closer to our lane, and my heart was pounding as I sped up to get away from them. "Who's your friend?" screamed Little Guy as Fat Guy hit the gas and pulled ahead of us, slamming on his brakes. The dizziness was increasing, and I felt like I was falling over. The faster we drove, the harder my heart beat, and I was having trouble catching my breath. I needed to get off the road, right away.

"Vince, call 911!" I screamed. "Tell them we need help." He grabbed the phone and dialed as I tried to speed up even more to lose the photographers. The more adrenaline went through my system, the more I felt like I was going to lose control, making me crash the car. *Keep it together,* I said to myself over and over again. *Concentrate on the road.* The middle divider was going faster and faster, until it was the only thing keeping me conscious. Vince hunkered down in the bottom of the seat so he could hear the phone.

"Hello . . . we're being chased by photographers, and we need help," said Vince frantically. "It's Star Spencer in the car . . . we're on Sunset near the Palisades . . . the photographers are swerving and have almost hit us twice . . ."

Fat Guy's car veered precariously close to ours, and I swerved to avoid them. Vince looked up at me in fear, then went back to the call.

"What do you mean, what do I want you to do?" he yelled. "Send someone to arrest them. They're putting our lives in danger." He threw the phone down in disgust. He turned to me. "Just pull over . . . the side of the road is better than this. I'll drive."

But I couldn't pull over. Fat Guy was driving like he was a Formula One racer, matching me turn for turn. When I slowed down, he slowed down, and when I sped up to try to lose them, he was right on my tail. Since he was in the right lane, it was impossible for me to get past him to pull off to the shoulder. I felt like I was driving fast and leaning to the right at the same time. Everything started to spin.

Finally, we approached the top of the hill and the left turn on

Temescal right before it starts down the hill toward the Pacific Coast Highway. If I could just keep myself conscious until we got through the light, everything would be fine. This was my chance to pull over and wait for the police to arrive, and I knew for a fact there was a gas station just after the light and a little ways down the hill. The light was green at the intersection, and I gunned it, trying to get us through the light and down the hill. Surely the photographers' beat-up Toyota was no match for the Mercedes 500 series in this capacity.

We were almost to the light when Fat Guy decided he was going for it—he was going to try to make the left, only it wasn't a double left turn lane, it was a single. In what seemed like slow motion, I saw him speed toward our lane, trying to catch up with us. I was still looking at his face when the sedan crashed into the back of my car, turning us the wrong way toward traffic and landing us in the intersection. Next, we were hit from the other side by a car that had pushed through the yellow light and just made it.

The next five seconds felt like three hours. First, I very clearly saw the words "I am having a car accident" in my mind, and for a moment everything became perfectly clear, like the surface of a lake. I observed that I finally didn't feel exhausted anymore, everything had stopped spinning, and in fact, I was kind of relieved. Then the questions started. How did I get here? What was happening? Was I dead? Was that me screaming? Was this a dream?

And just as quickly, the sound of crunching glass and metal, screeching tires, and screams filled the air. Then silence.

IT TOOK A MOMENT or so for all of us to realize we were OK. Fat Guy and Little Guy's car was undriveable, and all of my airbags had deployed. Vince had a gash over his eye, and blood had begun to pour down the side of his head. No broken bones, and, from what I could see, no concussions.

Little Guy got out of the car, still holding the camera. "Hey, Eddie—check it out! We're the first on the scene for the Star Spencer car crash! This footage is going to be worth a million bucks."

Suddenly, my mind was flooded. The pressure, the lack of sleep, the cancer plotline, the hunger. I looked up at the face of Fat Photographer, who had gotten out of his car and come over to ours. He was unhurt and was leaning in close to my face. He smelled like stale beer and too many cigarettes. "Anything to say, girlie?" he laughed. "You're not a very good driver. Where's your fiancé?"

And that was it. I didn't care anymore. I didn't care about the money, or the fame, or the show. All I wanted was to kill this guy, who embodied every frustration I'd had in the past three years. He was Sondra, and Attila, and jealous people, and all the food I couldn't eat. He was lack of sleep and bad press. He was Brad Rockwell and Todd Whitley, who wouldn't even look twice at me if I wasn't a somebody. He was everything, and I wanted to kill him.

I jumped out of the car, forgetting we were still in the middle of the intersection; ran up to Fat Guy; and punched him in the face as hard as I could. "Is this what you want?" I screamed, sobbing so hard I could hardly get the words out. "What do you want, some fucking scandal? I hope you die. I hope everyone you love dies. You prey on people, you filthy parasite. You animal. You created me, and now you're destroying me. Is this a game to you?"

I didn't hear the sound of the police sirens in the background. Rage had filled my mind and my body, and I just wanted to tear this guy limb from limb. I kept hitting him in the face and arms, and he kept laughing. "Are you getting this, Jim? Little fancy girl has lost her shit, and she's trying to kick my ass! This is fucking great! Don't stop rolling!"

Over his shoulder, I saw his camera sitting in the front seat of his car, telephoto lens sticking out. If I couldn't kill him, I thought, maybe I could destroy his livelihood. Still screaming, I ran over to the car, picked up the camera, and smashed it to the ground. "Is this what you love?" I screamed. "Were you going to kill me to get your story? Fuck you, you worthless piece of shit. I hope you die!" I stomped the camera with my boot. "Is this what you want? Crawl on the ground and get it! You'll do anything for a picture, right?"

He knocked me out of the way to get to his camera, and I tried hitting him again. Just then, the police arrived and restrained both of us. "What's going on here?" said one of the officers.

"I got the whole thing on film," said the Little Guy. "She assaulted my partner and destroyed his property. We were just involved in a regular car accident, and then she went nuts. Maybe you should test her blood alcohol level, officers."

"They were chasing us all the way from Hollywood," said Vince. "We called 911, and no one came. These guys wouldn't let us off to the side, and then they crashed into us." The police officer was still holding on to my arm as I tried to swing at the photographer. "They tried to kill us," I said.

Then I felt it. It started out as a hot black feeling around my eyes, and then it seemed like I was melting. I was passing out. Just before I hit the ground, I heard myself saying, "Don't call my mom . . . she'll worry."

TWO MINUTES LATER, I woke up, as if from a nightmare. I was already in the ambulance, and it felt like we were going downhill. I tried to reassure myself that I was alive, that everything was fine, but for some reason, I couldn't calm down. I felt hot, then broke out into a cold sweat, started gasping for air, and wanted to run away, or to crawl out of my skin. My heart was beating too fast. It felt like every system in my body was shutting down at once, and I was trying to get away from the failure. I started to scream, then to cry, then to scream again. I was twitching uncontrollably. And, over and over again, I was thinking, *Get ahold of yourself . . . you've lost control, but you can get it back . . . come on . . . you can do it . . .* But I couldn't. I tried to focus, and the next wave of adrenaline transported me back over the edge into nightmare land. I looked around—where was Vince? I tried to focus on the cop and the paramedic who were riding with me, but I kept blacking out.

I screamed again, but it was like a scream inside a dream, where your mouth is open and you can hear someone far away making the noise. The scream lasted for what seemed like a long time. I tried to lie back, tried to take deep breaths to slow my heart down. I was freezing and so uncomfortable I couldn't even lie back without writhing around. Every time I closed my eyes, I could see the inside of my skull. This in turn was so scary that it made me freak out even more. The paramedic kept trying to tell me to calm down, only he didn't understand—I couldn't calm down, I was just observing what was happening from the outside, like him. *If I could stop it I would,* I thought, *but I'm just along for the ride.* The scariest part of this episode was that intermittently, I felt totally normal, like I'd just woken up from some bad dream where something was wrong with me. That lasted for a moment or two, and then I was slammed back into the worst terror of my life, times ten. Slowly, I realized that I felt a crushing pain in my chest. What was happening? Was I having a heart attack? I looked up into the face of the paramedic. "This isn't me," I whispered. "Something's wrong."

"You're OK . . . just calm down. You were in an accident," he said. "You probably broke some ribs. Keep the oxygen mask on."

Now time was coming in segments. I was lying in the emergency room, and someone was yelling, "Star, what did you take?" It actually was a little like the show *ER.* I kept wanting to snap out of it, only I was still in it. I wanted to say "I didn't overdose . . . some fat photographer crashed into my car," but I couldn't. In fact, I couldn't breathe at all.

That's the last thing I remember; then I passed out again.

★ ★ ★

"OH MY GOD . . . WHAT DAY is it? I have to be on set!"

The first thing I noticed when I finally woke up was that the room was filled with people. I felt like I was in a drug-induced haze. I could tell I was in the hospital, but from the amount of people present, the timing didn't make sense. Carrie Ann had to have come from New York—that would take at least six hours. My mom—how did she get a flight from Michigan? *How did all these people get here so fast?* I thought.

"You're awake!" My mom's face unfurled itself from desperate worry to relief. "We were worried."

"I told them not to call you," I said weakly. Slowly I began to notice that my whole body hurt. "What's going on?"

"You were dehydrated, and you had a fever, and you had a car accident," she said softly. "And, Amy," she said with tears in her eyes, "you weighed ninety-nine pounds. Why did you do this to yourself? Are you on drugs? Do you have an eating disorder?"

"I wanted to take care of you guys," I gulped. "It was so much money, and we had the bills, and dad would've wanted me to take care of you, but I was so hungry, and stressed out, and I couldn't take it anymore." I looked up at her. "I'm sorry . . . I didn't mean to hit that guy. I was so tired . . ."

She leaned over, taking me into her arms and hugging me like she was afraid she'd break me. She stroked my hair. "I had no idea you were under so much pressure."

All at once, I felt like I was seven years old, when I'd have a bad dream, go into my parents' room, and they'd hug me until I felt better. I felt one tear slowly make its way down my face, then another. "I missed you," I whispered. "I miss Dad." Then I was crying for real. "I tried to be strong, but I'm so scared—everything could just go away, just like that, with no warning." The tears washed over me like a warm river. I just didn't care anymore. Finally, I let it go.

My mom cried too and hugged me. "You're going to be OK," she said. "Everything's going to be fine."

★ ★ ★

WHEN THERE WERE NO more tears left, I slept for real, for twelve hours. It wasn't just sleep, either—it was the little-kid sleep, where it takes you away and nothing can get to you. When I woke up, my mom and Vince explained more about what happened to me. The combination of stress, lack of food, lack of sleep, and diet pills had resulted in fever, dehydration, and tachycardia. In other words, while my idle always ran a little high, I had redlined my engine and burned it out. My body was so overworked, I needed to rest and recover.

Just hearing all this made me tired.

I went back to sleep again for another four hours. When I woke up, I was antsy. "Can I have the remote?" I said groggily.

Vince shot my mom a look. "I don't think you want to watch TV right now, Aim."

I went back to sleep again. This time, I dreamed about a car chase, a fat photographer, and me screaming. Then I woke up, realizing that it wasn't a dream. "How long have I been here? Did we crash?" I said to Vince. He hadn't shaved or changed clothes. *That must mean I'm really sick,* I thought.

"Sweetie, you have a concussion," he said softly. "We can talk about this when you're better."

A few hours later, when I could finally keep my eyes open for more than two minutes at a time, my mom came in. Standing behind her was a handsome Indian man. They both smiled. "Amy, this is Dr. Shah from cardiology, and he wants to talk to you. Do you feel up to it?"

Great. First I crashed, then I hit a guy, then I freaked out, and now a cardiologist wanted to talk to me. Did I also have a heart defect, like my dad? "Did I have a heart attack?" I said, bracing myself.

"No," said the doctor, and I exhaled. He was holding a manila folder, which I assumed was my chart, "Have you ever heard of clenbuterol?"

"No," I said. This was not Behind Closed Doors. I really didn't know what he was talking about.

"It's a drug that's commonly used to treat asthma in horses, and some people in the industry have been using it as a tool for weight loss. We found high levels of it in your blood."

My mom chimed in. "Amy, you need to be honest with the doctor so he knows how to help you. Why have you been taking this drug, honey? What's going on?"

Without thinking, I blurted out, "The black pills!" stopping myself before I also said "given to me by Mindy Steinman, executive producer of *Autumn Leaves*."

"Black pills?" said Dr. Shah. "Do you have any more? Can I see them? Where did you get them?"

"In my purse," I said weakly. I didn't know what was going to happen, but I knew that no good could come from ratting out Attila. I had visions of a horse's head in my bed. "Someone on the set gave them to me," I said. "I don't remember who—they said they were appetite suppressants and that they were totally safe." There was no way I was turning state's evidence in the war on drugs in Hollywood.

"You're not in trouble . . . we just want to know what kind of clen it is, so we can tell if it's caused permanent damage to your heart. You're actually lucky you didn't have a heart attack or a stroke taking that stuff. We need to do some more tests and to test the pills you have, to see what we're dealing with."

Now I was listening. "What?" I squeaked. Did Attila really give me a potentially lethal drug to make me thin enough for her Nielsen ratings to go up when she knew heart problems ran in my family? What the hell?

Luckily, the clenbuterol I'd been taking was "clean" (though still illegal and banned by the FDA). After a battery of frightening tests and about a gallon of blood drawn, I was informed that the drug had not caused permanent damage, but that I needed to rest, in bed, for at least two months in order to allow my heart time to repair itself. "No working," said Dr. Shah, and he offered to write me a doctor's note. Pieces of Attila's phone call flashed through my head: "Martin Sheen . . . *Apocalypse Now* . . . heart attack . . . back on the set the next day." If she hadn't had me written off the show by now, this would probably do it. Through the fear and weakness, I felt a glimmer of happiness.

IT DIDN'T TAKE LONG for them to fill me in. The footage of me beating up the photographer had been running nonstop the whole time I'd been in the hospital. The tabloids had been having a field day. No one wanted to hear my side of the story. People love to see celebrities go nuts, even when they don't know the circumstances. I never believed it until it happened to me. Footage of me unraveling was now the most downloaded clip of all time, flying back and forth in cyberspace. A techno song had been made, the backbeat thumping over me screaming, "I hope you die! You filthy parasite!" Spoofs had been made, *Saturday Night Live* was developing a sketch, and the incident had been mentioned on late-night talk shows around the world. There was no escaping it. The only thing to do was wait it out.

The official line from Sondra and the show was "dehydration," which is what they always say when a celebrity goes into the hospital for anything drug related. Shooting was on hold until the studio and the network decided what to do about my "health problems." Todd was in emergency phone-call mode and had basically set up camp in my hospital room. The police were investigating Vince and me, and Fat Guy and Little Guy were not only pressing charges for assault and for destruction of property, but were also filing a civil suit against me. I felt a little like I should be resting, but I had a strong sense of dread, like this was something from which I could not come back.

After another nine-hour "nap," I awoke to find my room crowded with people. Mindy Steinman, two assistants, and several other serious-looking people in suits were there, as well as Todd, Arden, my mom, Vince, Dr. Shah, and two nurses.

"Wha . . . ," I said weakly. Had something else happened? I looked at my mom. "Can you . . . I mean, can you get them out of here?" I watched as everyone but Todd and my mom filed out.

Todd spoke first. "Star, the network has to make a decision on what to do. They're willing to work with us to spin the incident, as long as you take full responsibility for your drug problem and the accident and agree to go into rehab for the next two months." He leaned forward. "You don't really have to go to rehab, of course . . . we can get you a condo or something where you can just rest. But they have to issue a statement ASAP."

I rubbed my eyes and looked over at my mom. "Todd, Mindy gave me the pills. I'm not a drug addict—I have a heart problem caused by a drug that she gave me." The unfairness of it all gripped me like a vise. She could give me poisonous drugs, then blame it on me when I got sick? There was a special place in hell for her.

Maybe it was the newfound clarity from sleeping so much, but the answer seemed crystal clear to me. Doing what other people thought I should do had almost gotten me killed.

"Tell them I'm not going to rehab. They did this, and people should know."

Todd rubbed his hand over his face. "Star, they're going to fire you from the show and enforce the NDA you sign as part of your contract. If you go into rehab, we can file a disability claim and possibly get you back on as a guest star. It's going to work better for everyone. What's the difference? You're never going to be able to tell anyone about this anyway. Just take the rehab, then get back in the game. I'm going to say yes to this. Can I say yes to this?"

"Todd, you're fired," I blurted out. I was surprised at how good actually saying the words felt. "Get out."

Todd's eyes widened, and then he packed his briefcase up and left. "No one is going to touch you after this," he said casually as he packed up his briefcase and started to walk out the door.

"Hey, Todd," I called after him. "My name is Amy. *Amy!*"

I heard him laughing as he walked down the hall. "OK—Amy, you are fucked," he called out.

"Don't worry about it," my mom said. "We're just fine, Amy. You don't have to do this anymore if you don't want to." She squeezed my hand. "I'm proud of you."

I'd been out of the hospital for exactly two days when I got a letter messengered to the hotel. Inside it was a single sheet of paper from the law firm representing the network.

September 15
Dear Ms. Spencer,
Please be advised that, as of today, your contract with the network has been terminated, on grounds of violation of statute 76.011. If you have further questions, please feel free to have your attorney contact us.

Very truly yours,
Martin Franklin
ATTORNEY AT LAW

It turned out that "statute 76.011" was the often cited but almost never invoked "morality clause," where the network contends that the actor can no longer fulfill the function of playing the role because they haven't held up sufficient morals in their personal life. In other words, because of the "incident," viewers would not be able to picture me as wholesome, naïve Autumn anymore. The show would go on without me.

Because I could no longer do any public appearances or events with Brad, the terms of my RockStar contract were also null and void.

The next day, the headlines read "RockStar Splits, Star Cracks Up!"

19

S NOW STARTED TO FALL early in Bay City that winter; by mid-November we were assured a white Christmas.

Around ten a.m., I was awakened by the soft sound of my mom knocking at my bedroom door. "Amy, are you awake?" she whispered. "Someone is here to see you."

I'd probably slept more in the seven weeks since leaving Hollywood than in all of my previous twenty-one years combined. Something about the darkened windows of my childhood home, the silence, or maybe the mandatory bed rest had immediately taken the pressure off, and I felt like I could finally just relax and drift away. With Carrie Ann in New York, Vince still in L.A., and my high school friends off doing their respective careers, I couldn't imagine who would be dropping by for a visit on a Tuesday morning at ten. The show would be in the middle of a marathon session of shooting in order to get new episodes in the can that explained Autumn's decision to go back to the Midwest for college and refocused the show on her little sister, Jessie. Besides, Attila had probably issued a decree that they weren't allowed to talk to me anyway.

"I'll be right down," I said, slowly pulling the covers off and stepping out of bed.

I pulled on my jeans and black Chanel cardigan. After I got fired from the show, the network had taken away my suite. My mom had packed up everything I'd accumulated at the hotel and shipped it back to our house (along with me, of course). Even after almost two months of unpacking and sorting, trying to make sense of the last few years of my life, my room was still two feet deep in expensive designer clothes, purses, and shoes, as well as old books, scripts, and my DVD collection. For once, my mom had not been giving me a hard time about cleaning my room.

I surveyed myself in the full-length mirror on the wall. My eye bags were gone. In fact, daily walks had left me looking positively healthy. Though still a size 2, I looked a little less like a skeleton, and my collarbone no longer stuck out at the alarming angle it did before. My golden blonde hair was showing an inch of sandy-brown roots and sat in a scraggly bun piled on top of my head. Surprisingly, I just didn't care. Weeks of bed rest and watching DVDs had healed my heart, and I'd passed my last cardiologist checkup with flying colors. Soon I would have a clean bill of health, and I'd have to figure out what to do with the rest of my life. Go back to college? Try Hollywood again? Move to Fiji? I had been sitting up in my room writing in a journal and pondering these questions for weeks. Did I even have any leverage in Hollywood that I could use, or had I blown it all? I almost didn't want to know.

At first, the press was relentless. I stopped reading the magazines almost immediately, especially when I saw the incredibly stupid headlines and theories. "Star Breakdown!" they screamed in the largest font possible. "Broken Engagement Pushes Her Over the Edge!" "Little Girl Lost!" All with pictures from the crash and from my nights out in L.A. I remembered when Vince used to sit in my dorm room at UM, devouring the weekly magazines and speculating on the real stories behind the tabloid headlines, and now I knew firsthand that most of them were fake. Luckily, no paparazzi had followed me back to Bay City; Arden was right—once you were gone from Los Angeles, it was like you didn't exist. I'd even been out to get pizza with some of my old friends from high school, and we just sat and ate like old times, with no one staring or talking about me.

I brushed my teeth and put on a little bit of makeup. Maybe my high school boyfriend was back from being on tour with his punk band and had decided we belonged together. If I'd learned anything, it's that you just never know what (or who) is around the next corner, and it's always good to be prepared.

As I walked down the familiar stairs, I constructed numerous scenarios in my mind. I was still trying to guess as I turned the corner into the living room. "Mom . . . who is it . . . ?"

I stopped, frozen in my tracks, as I saw Dan Roberts sitting on my living room couch.

If Dan could have gotten better looking since Coney Island, that had happened. Flecks of snow were caught in his curly brown hair, and his green eyes lit up when he saw me. He swept me up into his arms for a hug.

He started talking fast. Was he nervous? "I'm so glad you're OK . . . I'm sorry to just show up, but your voice mail was full, so I called your old agent Todd a thousand times, and finally he gave me Vince's number, then I bugged him until finally he relented and gave me your mom's address. I had to see you, to see if you were OK and to tell you the good news. Are you OK?"

I laughed out loud. "What's the good news—the network didn't put a hit out on me?" I said. I was so happy to see him, he didn't even need good news.

Dan was serious. "Amy, *Blue Gray* got into Sundance, and there's good critical buzz. We actually might win."

"Oh my God!" I shouted.

"Mom, we're going to go out for a while," I called over my shoulder, grabbing a set of car keys from the peg beside the front door. "Come on," I said to Dan. "There's something I want to show you."

"Take your coat, honey! I don't want you getting chilled," Mom called from the kitchen.

THOUGHTS FLEW THROUGH MY mind as we drove down the quiet snowy roads. I didn't know if I should tell Dan about the "emotional distance," or the fact that after a few years, the first feelings I'd had were for him. I'd spent so long not caring about what guys thought that it felt weird to be concerned. Would I scare him away? Would he think I was weird and needy? Then again, if he didn't feel something for me, why would he have come all the way to Bay City?

It was kind of nice to be nervous about this stuff again, actually. It was good to know I still had feelings.

We pulled up to the cemetery just as it was getting dark, and I took Dan's hand as we walked down the familiar path.

I took a deep breath. "I wanted to show you something that no one else has seen, so you'd know what you mean to me," I said. "You know—in case I don't see you again."

We stopped in front of the gravestone, where my mom had put fresh flowers that weekend even though it was eight degrees outside.

He smiled. "I knew you'd come around, Spencer. I didn't think it would take a freak show and a car crash, but I had a feeling I'd see you again."

"Good," I said. "Because I want to tell you about my dad. He really would have liked you."

His eyes were bright. "I am honored," he said. "And I think my aunt would have felt the same way about you."

Then he kissed me, and it was perfect.

★ ★ ★

THE MOMENT WE STEPPED off the plane in Park City, I felt everyone's eyes on me. Park City is packed with Hollywood types for the whole week of Sundance, but there's always one person who gets photographed more than the rest. Right then, that person was me. People really wanted to see if all the rumors were true, if I'd really gone nuts, if I was on drugs, and if I could really act. One drop of insecurity here, one ill-timed Mariah Carey–inspired striptease, and I was doomed. Luckily, I felt healthier and saner than I had in years.

"You look amazing," whispered Vince, squeezing my arm. He had always been able to know exactly what I needed to hear. Dan took my hand, and my stomach flip-flopped a little. We'd been together ever since he came to my mom's house in Bay City—going back and forth to L.A., doing press for *Blue Gray,* and texting and calling nonstop whenever we weren't together. I finally had the guy I'd always wanted, and there was no chance I was letting him get away again. My heart felt like it had been mended, not just physically, but emotionally too, like I could finally feel again, and what I felt was love.

Carrie Ann had taken a three-day weekend from her show (the first time ever) and was flying in from New York to meet us. We headed back to the airport later in the afternoon to pick her up in time for the screening. We were all trying to act as normal as possible despite the thousands of questioning eyes staring at me everywhere we went. I wanted to get a big megaphone, stand on a mountain, and yell "Hey, I'm not crazy—I got squashed by the Hollywood machine, but now I'm back!" Instead I went snowboarding, saw films, and waited for the screenings of *Blue Gray.* With no agent and no publicist, I could say whatever I wanted, and yet I was surprisingly silent. Besides, who would have believed me?

The first screening of *Blue Gray* was packed with people, presumably wanting to get a glimpse of how crazy I was. Dan led a Q&A session with the cast first, and I could tell the press was dying to ask about the accident. Like the dedicated director and gentleman that he was, Dan deftly avoided all questions that didn't relate to the film. Most of the reporters looked pissed as Dan ignored them for the whole Q&A and then signaled for the film to begin.

Dan held my hand through the whole screening. It felt so good to see a record of my time in New York, our hard work, and the great summer before everything went so crazy. I was more certain than ever that this was what I really wanted to do with my life.

As soon as the lights went up, the audience gave us a five-minute-long standing ovation. Ryan Seacrest came up afterward and hugged me. "Welcome back!" he said with a smile. "We'll have to get you on the show right away!"

The day after the screening, Vince, Dan, Carrie Ann, and I were on Main Street coming out of brunch at Morning Ray when I spotted her.

Attila had come to Sundance.

Flanked by two new interns with fresh faces and hope in their eyes on her right and a low-level producer-looking guy on her left, she was barking instructions in her usual militaristic style—head down, not looking at them. "Do you think you can manage that, Samantha?" she snarled to one of the assistants. She looked up as she almost ran into us. I watched for a second as she gathered up her game face, with Vince poking me in the side the whole time. None of us moved, so they either had to step off the curb to get by or talk to us. Her eyes seemed even beadier than usual, and even though it was twenty-four degrees outside, she was sweating.

"Star! Oh my God!" she fairly shouted, drawing attention from some of the onlookers and photographers. She probably thought she would never see me again after she'd had me fired from the show. If anybody found out she was the cause of my downfall, she would probably be fired herself.

"Star, I was just telling John here how great I thought your film was. Great! You were just . . . fantastic." She put a chubby hand to her mouth in a gesture of fake emotion. "I felt like my little girl was all grown up!"

For a moment, I didn't know what to say. I'd played this reunion a million times over in my head, and somehow it always involved a good head stomping or karate-chopping her in half like a giant melon. Watching her have to kiss my ass in public, though, was nearly as good. Now I just wanted to see her squirm.

"Thanks, Mindy," I gushed sarcastically in return. "What was your favorite part?" I knew she hadn't seen it. I definitely would have sensed her evil aura in the audience.

She was quick with the duck and cover. "I just . . . you are so great! Star, I need to have you come into the office so we can talk to you about the independent film division we're opening up. I'm spearheading it. It's going to be a great opportunity for you!"

I stared blankly at her. Two months before, I was persona non grata, never up to her standards, and now she wanted to work with me again? I wanted to tear off her head and spit in her neck. She was the embodiment of everything I hated about the business—as if every fake smile and disloyal word had been boiled down to form her pale, puffy, squinty-eyed face. I took a deep breath.

"Thanks, Mindy . . . actually, I just ran into Mitch Greenwald, and I'm having lunch with him next week. His network does indie films too now—did you know? I'm pitching him one about an insane network executive who tortures everyone around her, including giving them illegal drugs. It's going to be really big."

She squinted, trying to read my face to see if I was serious. I saw her assistants trying not to smile. Mitch, who'd been in the audience of *Blue Gray* and had led the standing ovation, was a development executive at a big rival network and used to be Mindy's boss. I actually *was* having lunch with him the following week. I had been bluffing about the pitch, but it was just enough for Mindy to know that the balance of power had shifted and that she could never push me around again.

Vince, Dan, Carrie Ann, and I quickly walked past them, leaving Mindy, her assistants, and her producer friend in our wake. "That was awesome," Dan said.

I felt free.

A COUPLE OF WEEKS after Sundance, Dan and I were having lunch with Vince at Polly's Pies in Los Feliz. Since the success of *Blue Gray,* we had been in meetings nonstop. Everyone in Hollywood seemed to have forgotten about the accident, the video, the supposed breakdown, the whole thing.

I'd been staying with Dan since returning to L.A. With him, I never felt like I had to pretend to be something I wasn't. This was maybe the only thing that had allowed me to come back and not fall back into the Hollywood mindset.

Brad Rockwell never spoke to me again. Right after the accident, Jon leaked the Coney Island photos to the press, and the breakup was the scandal of the year. Brad referred to me publicly as "the one who broke my heart," though I liked to think of him as "the one who broke my contract." Of course, I could never tell this to another living soul without risking something worse than a dead bird in my car. Unfortunately for Vince, Brad never spoke to him either, stayed in the closet, and got a new blonde fiancée. I kept the money, the ring, and the Mercedes, which I got fixed.

Since I was a "viable commodity" again due to the success of *Blue Gray,* every agency in town was now looking for me. I'd been attempting to assemble a team of people to help with my "relaunch." Problem was, I was having a hard time finding anyone who didn't make my skin crawl. Arden, who promised to be on her best behavior and not give me grief about my weight, was allowed back on the team. I still had no agent, though; I kept avoiding Todd because—well, because he was Todd. Finally, everything was up to me.

I had never been happier.

Dan, Vince, and I were in the back of Polly's finishing lunch when I heard a familiar voice. "Amy? Oh my God!"

Olivia Garcia walked up to stand next to our table. "How are you? You look really great."

"Dan, this is Olivia," I said, and he shook her hand.

"I've heard a lot about you," he said, smiling. "Sit down."

Vince moved our stuff over to give her room. Dan said he felt like he knew her already from all of my stories, and he knew I still regarded her as one of the only people I could trust.

While I was gone, Olivia had finished law school, completed her William Morris internship, and had become an agent in the same office as Todd. "I was going to call you for a meeting," she said, "but I didn't want it to be weird. I wanted to respect your privacy and give you your space." She paused as tears came to her eyes. "I'm so glad to see you. It was awful what happened. I want you to know that I never told anyone any stories about you."

I looked at Dan. "Olivia, I want you to represent me."

She broke into a huge smile. "I would love that!" she said. "You are officially my first big celebrity client. Todd's going to be so pissed!"

We sat and talked strategy for the rest of the afternoon. After a while, the waitress came over to see if we wanted anything else. Olivia looked at me quizzically, and I remembered that the last time I saw her, I was on the five-hundred-calorie-a-day Hollywood starvation diet.

I winked at her, then looked up at the waitress.

"I'll have the key lime pie."

ACKNOWLEDGMENTS

FIRST AND FOREMOST, I would like to thank my wonderful husband, Stephan, who encouraged me to keep going even when I was beyond done, gave amazing feedback, stopped what he was doing to brainstorm with me, and read every draft of a book that isn't even in a genre he reads. That is love!

This book would not be where it is without the dedicated and wonderful readers who took a chance, liked it, and told their friends. Thank you to everyone who sent me a MySpace message about how you took the day off to finish the book, or how it made you laugh when you were sad, or how you stayed up past your bedtime to find out what happened in season three.

Thank you to Brent Stinski for coming up with Media Predict and Project Publish, to Touchstone Fireside for choosing it as the winner, and to Amanda Patten for working with me to make it even better. Thanks to David Dunton, who deserves a "World's Greatest Agent" mug if he doesn't have one already.

And finally, thanks to my mom, who is not with us anymore, but who we think of every day.